# BRAVOS FOR THE BISHOP'S HEIR
Volume I of *The Histories of King Kelson*

"A RICH FEAST OF MEDIEVAL CHIVALRY, ROMANCE AND MAGIC—THE BOOK THAT ALL KATHERINE KURTZ'S FANS HAVE BEEN AWAITING."

**Marion Zimmer Bradley**

"...at her best Kurtz's love of history lets her do things with her characters and their world that no nonhistorian could hope to do."

*Chicago Sun-Times*

"Kurtz has created a fascinating idealization of the Middle Ages and infused it with a kind of magic one can truly believe in."

*Fantasy Review*

"AN INCREDIBLE HISTORICAL TAPESTRY OF A WORLD THAT NEVER WAS AND OF IMMENSELY VITAL PEOPLE WHO OUGHT TO BE!"

**Anne McCaffrey**

By Katherine Kurtz
*Published by Ballantine Books:*

**THE LEGENDS OF CAMBER OF CULDI**

CAMBER OF CULDI
SAINT CAMBER
CAMBER THE HERETIC

**THE CHRONICLES OF THE DERYNI**

DERYNI RISING
DERYNI CHECKMATE
HIGH DERYNI

**THE HISTORIES OF KING KELSON**

Volume I: THE BISHOP'S HEIR
Volume II: THE KING'S JUSTICE
Volume III: THE QUEST FOR SAINT CAMBER

THE DERYNI ARCHIVES

LAMMAS NIGHT

# THE KING'S JUSTICE

## VOLUME II OF
## THE HISTORIES OF KING KELSON

## KATHERINE KURTZ

A Del Rey Book
BALLANTINE BOOKS • NEW YORK

A Del Rey Book
Published by Ballantine Books

Library of Congress Catalog Card Number: 85-6198

ISBN 0-345-33196-6

Map by Shelley Shapiro

Manufactured in the United States of America

First Hardcover Edition: November 1985
First Mass Market Edition: August 1986

Cover Art by Darrell K. Sweet

For
Cameron Alexander MacMillan
What a Neat Kid!

# CONTENTS

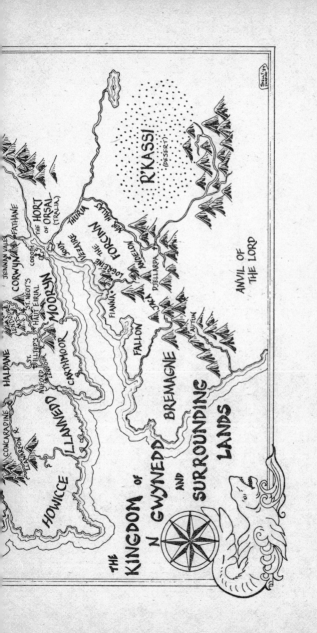

THE
KINGDOM of
N GWYNEDD
AND
SURROUNDING
LANDS

# PROLOGUE

*And the king shall do according to his will.*
                                        —Daniel 11:30

"I tell you, he isn't *going* to change his mind," the Deryni Bishop Arilan said, slapping the ivory table with both palms for emphasis as his gaze swept the three men and three women seated with him in the vaulted chamber. "Not only will he not change—he refuses to even *discuss* it."

"But, he *must* discuss it!" Laran ap Pardyce, wizened and frail-looking in his black scholar's robes, was clearly appalled. "No Haldane king has *ever* done this before. Surely you've warned him what might happen."

In the wan, purpled light filtering through the room's great octagonal dome, Arilan leaned his head against the high back of his chair and breathed a forbearing sigh, praying for patience.

"I have—repeatedly."

"And?" the woman to his left asked.

"And if I continue to press the point, he may cease to confide in me at all." He turned his head to look at her wearily. "You may not think that likely, Kyri, but it could yet come to that. God knows, he certainly doesn't trust us as a group."

The group was the Camberian Council, of course; and the subject of their discussion was the seventeen-year-old King of Gwynedd: Kelson Cinhil Rhys Anthony Haldane, now more than three years on his murdered father's throne.

Nor had the last three years been easy, for Council, king, or kingdom. Any boy-king might have fostered uneasiness among those designated to advise him—and despite the fact that few outside the room even knew of its existence, the Camberian Council considered itself so designated for the House of Haldane. But Kelson, unlike most sovereigns come prematurely to their thrones, had fallen heir to magic: the puissant and forbidden Deryni bloodline of his mother, Queen Jehana, her heritage unknown even to herself before she was forced to use it at his coronation, and the equally powerful Haldane potential for the assumption of magical abilities from King Brion, his father.

In anyone but Kelson, the combination might have been deadly, for Deryni were almost universally feared through-out Gwynedd, and hated by many. Before the Haldane Restoration two centuries before, Gwynedd had lain under De-ryni domination for generations, Deryni sorcery enforcing the will of a despotic line that had not hesitated to advance Deryni fortunes over human in whatever way was most expedient. So had Deryni magic come to be despised as well as feared; and few knew or remembered any longer that De-ryni as well as humans had fought to overthrow the Deryni tyrants, or that a discredited Deryni saint, besides giving his name to the Council that met in this secret chamber, had first triggered the magic of the Haldane kings.

Kelson knew, of course. And like generations of Haldanes before him, he had managed to represent that magic as an aspect of his divine right as king, walking a narrow balance between impotence, if he did not use his powers, and heresy, if he did—for much might be overlooked in the protection of people and Crown. Such a ploy was vital camouflage in a land where many humans still sought retribution for the years of Deryni persecution, and where any extraordinary power not demonstrably come of divine favor was regarded with fearful, often deadly, interest by a hostile and jealous Church.

Nor had the Church's suspicion of magic arisen only with the coming of the Deryni. Extraordinary or seemingly mi-raculous occurrences outside the limits defined by Scripture had always fallen under the wary scrutiny of those whose function it was to guard the purity of the faith; and irre-sponsible use of magic, either by or in the service of the new overlords, only tended to reinforce the belief that magic was very likely evil. As reaction set in after their overthrow, ecclesiastical restrictions followed close on civil reprisals, and the Deryni themselves came to be regarded as evil, even though there had been Healers and holy men among them. The Church's hostility toward the Deryni as a race continued to the present, even though civil restrictions had begun to abate in the last two decades. Outside the Council, not a dozen persons knew Bishop Denis Arilan's true identity as Deryni—and he was one of only two Deryni priests he knew.

Nor was that other Deryni priest free of controversy, though his Deryni blood was almost as well kept a secret outside the Council as Arilan's. Father Duncan McLain, recently become Duke of Cassan, Earl of Kierney, and also a bishop, was Deryni only on his mother's side—a half-breed, in the eyes of the Council—but they held him at least partially responsible for the king's continued reluctance to accept Council guidance.

For Kelson had been assisted to power, both civil and magical, not by the Council, with its emphasis on "proper" training and formal recognitions, but by Duncan and his equally half-breed cousin Alaric Morgan, the powerful but grudgingly respected Deryni Duke of Corwyn, both of whose mastery of their powers had come largely from chance and their own hard work.

So might Kelson also have been counted—half-breed and, therefore, outside the pale of Council protection—were it not for his father's Haldane blood, and the addition that made to his already powerful Deryni heritage. It was the former that concerned the Council today, as rebellion grew in one of Gwynedd's western provinces and her king prepared to designate his uncle as his heir before going on campaign to quell it, having yet no heir of his own body.

"Well, he does no service to Prince Nigel if he *does* succeed in what he plans," old Vivienne said, shaking her grey head in disapproval. "Once Nigel has tasted even a part of the Haldane potential, he may not be eager to give it up."

"He will *have* to give it up, once Kelson has a son," Arilan said.

"And if he refuses, or he cannot?" asked Barrett de Laney, from Arilan's right, senior member of the Council and Coadjutor with the older woman seated across from him. "I know you believe Nigel's scruples to be as pure as your own, Denis—and indeed, they may be. But suppose Kelson can't reverse the process. Will *you* be able to reverse it, if he cannot?"

"I, personally? Of course not. But Nigel—"

Across the table, Tiercel de Claron yawned indolently and slouched a little deeper in his chair.

"Oh, we needn't worry on *that* account," he said, his voice edged with sarcasm. "If Denis can't undo it, and Kelson can't, I'm sure *someone* will find a way simply to eliminate our good Prince Nigel. That's what will have to happen, you know," he added, looking up, at several mutters of indignation. "After all, we can't have more than *one* Haldane holding the power at once, now, can we?"

"Tiercel, you're not going to start *that* old argument again, are you?" Barrett asked.

"Why not? Tell me what earthly harm it would do if more than one Haldane *could* hold the Haldane power at a time. We don't know that it can be done, but what if it could?"

As Tiercel leaned his head heavily on one hand and began tracing a slow, spiraling pattern on the inlaid table, Vivienne, the second Coadjutor, turned her grey head majestically toward their youngest member.

"I'm sorry if we bore you, Tiercel," she said sharply. "Tell me, is it your deliberate intention to stir up dissent, or have you simply forgotten to think? You know that the very notion is forbidden, even if it were possible."

Tiercel stiffened, and his hand ceased its idle movement, but he did not look up as Vivienne continued.

"And as for Nigel, if circumstances demand it, Nigel *will* be eliminated. The terms and conditions of the Haldane inheritance were set down two centuries ago by our blessed patron. In all that time, they have not been broken. There were reasons for that, which I cannot expect you to understand."

Tiercel finally looked up at her last comment, his expression eliciting more than one raised eyebrow and indrawn breath. For though it was not unusual for the pair to spar at one another, older generation against new, Vivienne's caustic retort struck perilously close to Tiercel's chiefest insecurity: that, having less than half the years of nearly every other member of the Council, his experience, of necessity, must be somewhat less extensive—for he was only a few years older than the king himself. In *fact*, his theoretical knowledge was matched by few of them; but that reality did not always enable him to ignore what he perceived as attacks on his personal worth. As genuine anger glinted in Tiercel's almond-colored eyes, cold and dangerous, the physician Laran laid a warning hand on Vivienne's arm.

"Enough, Vivienne. Tiercel, both of you, stop it!" he murmured, automatically glancing across at Barrett, even though the man had been blind for half a century.

*Barrett, do something,* he sent mentally.

Barrett was already raising the ivory wand of his office in a ritual gesture of warning, his emerald gaze locked sightlessly on Tiercel's face.

"Tiercel, let it be," he commanded. "If we quarrel, we accomplish nothing. Every effort will be made to spare Nigel."

Tiercel snorted and crossed his arms across his chest, though he did not speak.

"We must not forget Kelson's part in this, either," Barrett continued. "In sharing his authority with his uncle, he but answers his duty as he sees it—which is to leave his present heir with the ability to carry on, should he fall in battle. Surely you would not have Kelson abrogate his responsibility by failing to make the proper provisions?"

Only barely subdued, Tiercel shook his head, apparently still not trusting himself to speak.

"And you, Vivienne." Barrett turned his attention to the other. "You need not be so deliberately cold about Nigel's fate. It is a solemn duty he accepts when he submits to the power that will be laid upon him. Our duty is no less solemn, should we be called upon to exercise it."

"He does not bear the blood," Vivienne murmured, low and petulant.

"Oh, Vivienne . . ."

From across the table, between Barrett and Tiercel, faintly mocking laughter floated like the chime of precious crystal: Sofiana, the one among their number who had not yet spoken, the most recent but by no means the youngest or even the most junior member of the Camberian Council.

More than twenty years before, when even younger than Tiercel, Sofiana of Andelon had served the Council brilliantly, resigning only on the death of her father without male heir. Now Sovereign Princess of Andelon for more than a decade, her children grown or nearly so, she had returned at the Council's behest the previous summer to fill the seat of Thorne Hagen—threatened with suspension if he did not resign, for his connivance with Wencit of Torenth and Rhydon of Eastmarch in the Gwynedd-Torenth War. A second vacancy, more directly caused by the war, remained unfilled: the seat of Stefan Coram, Vivienne's predecessor as Coadjutor, who, unknown even to the Council at the time, had chosen to play a doubly dangerous game of deception that eventually cost him his life—though it spared Kelson his crown.

Sofiana's record, and her lack of involvement with the intrigue and internal bickering that had marred the Council's deliberations increasingly since Kelson's accession, made her uniquely qualified for the position she now filled. She had also brought a breath of fresh insight and rare humor into the formerly stodgy assembly.

"What does that mean anymore, to be 'of the blood?'" she asked quietly, leaning her pointed chin on the back of one slender hand, lively black eyes turned on Vivienne in droll curiosity. "After two centuries of persecution, perhaps there are very few among our race who can truthfully attest to *pure* Deryni lineage, even to the time of Camber."

Flame-haired Kyri, the youngest of the three women, raised her chin toward Sofiana in exception, her resentment at the newcomer's more exotic beauty only thinly veiled.

"*I* can so attest," she said haughtily. "And for two centuries before *that*. Nonetheless, have we not always held that the proof of the blood is in the doing?"

"I will grant you that," Sofiana conceded. "However, by that definition, Brion himself was Deryni."

"That's preposterous—"

"And Nigel, like Brion, carries the Haldane blood—which may be just as powerful, in its way, as the purest Deryni— whatever *that* is. So perhaps Nigel is Deryni. And Warin de Grey. He can heal, after all," she added.

The ripple of their objection began to appear in outraged eyes, on parted lips, but she stayed them with a gesture of her free hand without even lifting her head from its resting place, coolly regal and assured in her desert robes of silver-shot purple.

"Be at ease, my friends. I am the first to concede that we are not talking about healing at this juncture, though I know that is of abiding interest to our esteemed senior Coadjutor and the faithful Laran.'' She smiled indulgently at both Barrett and Laran.

"We are concerned here with the Haldane potential. What is it that makes this particular family susceptible to having Deryni-like powers placed upon them? For that matter, Wencit of Torenth, for all his villainy, apparently discovered a way to place similar powers upon supposed humans—witness Bran Coris. The late Duke Lionel and his brother Mahael also seem to have received this benison. Perhaps what is called the Haldane potential in Gwynedd, then, occurs elsewhere as well, and is actually a lesser degree of *Deryniness*—or a greater one.''

"A greater one?" asked a surprised Tiercel.

"It is possible. I say 'greater' because the Haldane power comes upon the recipient full-blown, fully accessible, even if not fully understood. In some respects, at least, that is surely superior to having to *learn* how to use one's powers—which is what most 'pure' Deryni have had to do, from time immemorial.''

Arilan, though more inclined to Sofiana's reasoning than to anyone else's, stopped his impatient turning of his bishop's ring and furrowed his brow.

"Take care, Sofiana, or soon you will be asking us to believe that everyone is Deryni.''

Sofiana smiled and leaned back in her chair, silvery earrings chiming melodically as she shook her head.

"Never that, my friend, though it would certainly solve many problems—and doubtless create other worse ones,'' she added, at Vivienne's look of horror. "Consider, too, that the Haldane potential could be just such an obscure facet of our Deryniness as Morgan and McLain's 'rogue' healing talent, both gifts requiring special training and handling, and both sometimes arising spontaneously.''

Arilan whistled low under his breath, and Laran glanced at Barrett in astonishment as the others buzzed among themselves. Privately, Arilan himself had examined that very possibility more than once, and felt certain he was not alone in that, but no one had ever dared to voice it in full Council. Laran, as a physician, and Barrett, whose sight might conceivably be restored if the healing gifts could be re-leashed, also would have given the subject ample consideration, Arilan felt sure.

"But, that, too, is a topic for another day," Sofiana went on. "Our immediate concern, if I understand correctly, is that Kelson is about to act against our better judgment. Short of our physical intervention, however, I fear there is little we can do to prevent it, in this particular instance."

"I believe you'll receive no argument on that point," Barrett said. "But your choice of words suggests some future remedy."

"If we are bold enough to take it—yes. If, as we seem to agree, there is no question that Kelson is to be regarded as 'of the blood,' as Vivienne so quaintly put it, then I suggest that we have the means totally within our power to control him—and have had it for several years, in fact. Bring him into the Council."

She ignored their gasps as she raised a hand toward the high-backed chair standing empty between Tiercel and Vivienne.

"Bring him into the Council and bind him by the same oaths that bind the rest of us. Or are you afraid of him?"

"Of course not!" Vivienne said indignantly.

"He is strong enough," Sofiana countered. "He is mature far beyond his years."

"He is untrained."

"Then, let us take his training upon ourselves, and make sure he receives proper supervision."

"He lacks other qualities."

"Such as?"

"Do not push me, Sofiana, I warn you!"

"What qualities does he lack?" Sofiana persisted. "I am willing to be persuaded that he is not, indeed, ready, but you must give me a specific reason."

"Very well." Vivienne lifted her head in defiance. "He is not yet sufficiently ruthless."

"He is not yet sufficiently ruthless," Sofiana repeated. "I see. Then, would you rather have Morgan or McLain?"

"Are you mad?" Laran gasped, the first one bold enough to intervene in the exchange.

"It's absolutely out of the question!" Kyri said, with an emphatic shake of her fiery mane.

"Then, elect some other Deryni willing to accept the responsibility," Sofiana replied. "We operate at less than our full potential, with our number incomplete. How long must Stefan Coram's seat sit vacant?"

"Better vacant than filled by one unready to wield its power," Vivienne snapped.

Arilan watched and listened in some amusement as reaction continued to run its course around the table: Vivienne and Kyri continuing to challenge Sofiana over the very notion; Laran deeply disturbed; Tiercel excited but thoughtful, not saying anything for once; only Barrett unreadable, sitting still and solitary in his own mind between Arilan and Sofiana.

Nor was bringing Kelson into the Council a bad idea—someday. In the beginning, though the Council quickly agreed to acknowledge the king as full Deryni, no one even tried to argue that he was skilled or experienced enough. But in the three years since truly securing his throne, Kelson had learned many a hard lesson of kingship and of manhood. Arilan was in a unique position to report to them on that. In fact, it was Arilan who had first broached the subject of Kelson's candidacy; Arilan who had continued to pursue the notion, albeit far more gently than Sofiana's efforts of late; Arilan who, alone of all the seven of them, had ongoing contact with the king and knew, better than any, just how hard and disciplined—and powerful—the king was becoming. No Haldane king had ever sat on the Council before; but no Haldane had ever displayed Kelson's abilities, either.

"I think we've talked around this subject long enough," Arilan finally said, when most of the outrage had died down. "Even if we were disposed to admit the king today—and you all know my feeling on *that* matter—that is not the time, with war imminent and a disputed ritual of magic in the offing for tonight. Nor do I think anyone is seriously arguing that Morgan or Duncan are viable candidates at this time."

"Well, thank heaven for *that*," Vivienne muttered.

"Don't worry, Vivienne," Arilan replied. "I am the first to agree that both of them are still very much unknown quantities. Besides—" he allowed himself a bitter grimace, "—they still haven't forgiven me for our apparent abandonment of them, once Kelson's throne was secure."

"Are you saying they mistrust you, then?" Tiercel asked.

Arilan waggled one hand in a yes-and-no gesture.

"'Mistrust' is perhaps too strong a term," he allowed. "Let us simply say they're cautious where I'm concerned—and who can blame them? They resent the fact that I won't talk about the Council—and of course, I can't tell them why I won't."

"Three years ago, you brought them here without permission," Barrett said stiffly. "They already know too much about us."

Arilan inclined his head. "I accept responsibility for that—though I still maintain I did the right thing, under the circumstances. I've observed the Council's restrictions scrupulously since then, however."

"And see that you continue to do so," Vivienne muttered.

"Let us not stray from the subject again," Barrett said quietly. "This is an old, old argument. Let us return to tonight. Denis, if you cannot prevent it, can you at least control it?"

Arilan allowed himself a curt nod. "To the point that any trained practitioner can control the course of the outward ritual—certainly. I can make sure that we're properly warded, that the forms proper to any serious working of high magic are observed. But what happens on the inner levels is and remains in Kelson's control."

"What of Richenda?" Laran asked. "Will she be able to assist you? Kelson trusts her, I believe."

"He does." Arilan shifted his attention to Sofiana. "And we now know that Richenda is possessed of both power and training we had not guessed before, don't we, Sofiana?"

Sofiana gave a noncommittal shrug.

"Do not blame me for that, Denis. Had anyone asked at the time, I could have told you."

"But she's your niece," Kyri said. "You knew she was formally trained, yet you let her marry a half-breed."

"Oh, Kyri, I did not *let* her do *anything*! Richenda is a grown woman, and Deryni, fully capable of making her own decisions. And as for being my niece—" she shrugged again, shifting to a more whimsical mood, "—I'm afraid I hardly know her. My sister and her husband decided that Richenda should marry outside our traditions and faith, when they chose her first husband. I did not agree, but I respected their decision. I saw little of the girl after she became Countess of Marley."

"But, to marry Morgan—"

Sofiana's dark eyes flashed ebon fire. "Are you trying to make me condemn him?" she retorted. "I will not. Because he has made Richenda happy and has taken my sister's grandson as his own child, and has given her a daughter as well, I cannot be but kindly disposed toward him—and curious, make no mistake. And though I have *heard* that his powers are formidable, if largely untrained, I have *met* him only once. Needless to say, he was both on his guard and on his best behavior.''

"Ah, then, you do not trust Morgan either," Vivienne said.

"How does one define trust?" Sofiana countered. "I trust him to be a proper husband and father to my kin; I trust my niece's *sincerity* when she tells me of his honor in all that he has done since *she* has known him. Beyond that, all else is hearsay. How could I trust him in the way that I trust all of you? We of the Council may often disagree, but we *all* have bared our souls to one another in our oath-takings. *That* is trust.''

Laran raised a silvered eyebrow. "Do you trust Kelson, then?" he asked. "Or you, Denis? Has the king bared his soul to you?''

"In the sense that Sofiana has just reminded us?" Arilan smiled. "Hardly that. He has come to me for confession on occasion, when Duncan McLain was not available, but that is another matter entirely. I *believe*, however, that his ultimate goals are the same as our own.''

"And what of Nigel?" Tiercel asked impatiently. "In case anyone has forgotten, Kelson is going to attempt to pass on a part of his power tonight.''

"Aye, we've not forgotten," Arilan agreed. "And I know where your argument is headed, Tiercel. Fortunately, the notion that more than one Haldane might hold that full power at a time has not occurred to our headstrong young renegades. But if all of you would like something else to worry about, consider this: Kelson has decided to have young Dhugal MacArdry present tonight. Now, *there's* a one for you. I don't know where he got it, but he's at least part Deryni as well; and just because he didn't know that until a few months ago doesn't mean he hasn't been learning since then from Kelson, Morgan, and Duncan.''

Kyri made an expression of distaste, and Vivienne muttered something about "another half-breed.''

"And then there's Jehana," Arilan went on, ignoring both women. "When she returns to court. . . .''

All of them grew apprehensive at that, for the queen mother was of the same bloodline that had produced one Lewys ap Norfal—a Deryni of enormous ability and training who had defied the authority of the Council nearly a century before. Though Jehana knew nothing of that, and had spent a lifetime denying her Deryni blood, yet she had been able to flex long-unused potentials at Kelson's coronation with sufficient strength to give serious pause to a highly trained sorceress who sought her son's life.

Nor had she yet reconciled that act with her conscience, even after nearly three years in the seclusion of a cloister. Her imminent return to court presented but another unknown factor, for Jehana was still quite hostile to Deryni.

"She will have to be watched closely," Barrett said.

Arilan nodded and sat back wearily in his chair, covering his eyes with his hand.

"I know that," he whispered.

"And the king," Vivienne joined in. "He must not be allowed to get the notion in his head that Nigel might keep his powers, once Kelson begets an heir of his own."

"I know *all* of that," Arilan replied.

But as the Council shifted its deliberations to other matters, Bishop Denis Arilan remained very much aware of the task laid upon him. He alone, of all the seven, must move regularly among the chaotic blending of uncertainties and try to maintain some sort of equilibrium.

# CHAPTER ONE

*With arrows and with bow shall one come
thither.*

—Isaiah 7:24

"Kelson," Alaric Morgan said, as he and his king looked
down on the bustling yard at Rhemuth Castle, "you're becoming a hard, cruel man." He ignored Kelson's startled
stare and continued blithely. "Half the ladies of this kingdom
and several other realms are pining for you, yet you hardly
give them a second glance."

Across the sunlit courtyard, bright as finches in their
spring silks and satins and sarcenets, nearly a score of young
females ranging in age from twelve to thirty chattered and
postured among themselves along an overlooking balcony—
ostensibly come to observe and applaud the men honing martial skills in the yard below, but equally to see and be seen
by Gwynedd's handsome and eligible young king. Admiring
glances aplenty there were for others of the keen young men
drilling with sword and lance and bow, for practicality recognized that the chance of any single one of them winning
the king's favor was slim, but their wishful glances always
darted back to him, nonetheless.

Self-consciously, Kelson spared them not only the glance
Morgan had accused him of begrudging, but a strained smile
and a nod of acknowledgment, eliciting excited twitterings
and preening among his admirers. He gave Morgan a sour
grimace as he turned back to his own survey of the yard,
raising one leather-clad knee so that he could half sit on the
wide stone balustrade of the landing.

1

"They're not pining; they're after a crown," he said in a low voice.

"Aye, most certainly," Morgan agreed. "And eventually you're going to have to give it to one of them. Or if not one of these, then someone else like them. Kelson, I know you're tired of hearing this, but you *are* going to have to marry."

"I *did* marry," Kelson muttered, pretending avid interest in a quarterstaff bout between two of Duke Ewan's squires. "My bride didn't live long enough to have the crown placed on her head." He folded his arms over the somber black he wore. "I'm not ready to marry again, Alaric. Not until I've brought her murderers to justice."

Morgan compressed his lips in a thin, hard line and recalled one such bringing to justice: the defiant Llewell of Meara standing with his back to the executioner on a bleak morning in February, wrists bound behind him, chin lifted proudly heavenward in stubborn assertion that his act had been justified. The Mearan prince had declined to make any statement after his sentence was pronounced, disdaining either assistance or the solace of a blindfold as he knelt on the snow-scoured scaffold. Only in that timeless instant before the headsman's sword rendered final justice did his eyes dart to Kelson's—accusing and defiant to the last.

"Why did he look at me that way?" the shaken king had whispered plaintively to Morgan, as soon as they were out of public view. "*I* didn't kill her. He committed sacrilegious murder in front of several hundred witnesses—his own sister, for God's sake! There was no question of his guilt. No other verdict was possible."

Nor did ultimate guilt rest on Llewell alone. Equal responsibility must be shared by his parents, the pretender Caitrin and her traitor husband Sicard, now leading Meara in open rebellion against their lawful sovereign. Where Kelson's great-grandfather had sought to unite the two lands peacefully by marriage with the eldest daughter of the last Mearan prince—a settlement never recognized by a large portion of the Mearan nobility, who held another daughter to be the rightful heiress—Kelson had attempted to reassert that union through marriage with a captive daughter of the current rival line: the fifteen-year-old princess Sidana.

Granted, Sidana had two brothers who might have disputed that succession. But Llewell, the younger, was already in custody by then, and the eventual neutralization of Caitrin, Sicard, and the remaining brother would have left Sidana sole heiress of the cadet house. Her and Kelson's children could have claimed unquestionable right to both crowns, finally resolving the century-long dispute over the legitimate succession.

But Kelson had not reckoned on the vehemence of Llewell's hatred for anything Haldane—or dreamed that the Mearan prince would slay his own sister on her wedding day rather than see her married to Meara's mortal enemy.

Thus, of necessity, had Kelson's marital solution to the Mearan question become a martial one—the campaign for which all Gwynedd now prepared. Llewell's father and his remaining brother, Prince Ithel, were said to be raising an army in the Mearan heartland west of Gwynedd even now—and deriving dangerous support from Edmund Loris, former Archbishop of Valoret and Kelson's bitter enemy, who lent religious zeal and anti-Deryni fanaticism to the already explosive Mearan situation. And Loris, as once before, had lured a number of other bishops to his side, making of the coming conflict a religious as well as a civil question.

Sighing, Morgan hooked his thumbs in his swordbelt and let his gaze wander back to the yard below, idly fixing on an archery match in progress between Prince Nigel's three sons and young Dhugal MacArdry, the new Earl of Transha, since that seemed to have captured Kelson's attention in preference to the watching ladies. Both Dhugal and Conall, the eldest of Nigel's brood, were giving an impressive exhibition of marksmanship this morning, Dhugal's the more remarkable, in Morgan's eyes, because he shot left-handed—"corrie-fisted," as they called it in the borders.

That Dhugal had managed to retain this idiosyncrasy was a source of recurrent amazement to Morgan—not because Dhugal was skilled, for Morgan had met skilled left-handers before, but because the young Earl of Transha had received a major part of his early schooling here in Rhemuth, some of it under Brion himself. And Brion, despite Morgan's repeated objections to the contrary, had held that left-handed swordsmen and lancers wreaked havoc with conventional drills and training formations—which was true, as far as it went, but neglected to acknowledge that warriors in an actual combat situation, if accustomed to fighting only other right-handed opponents, often found themselves at a distinct disadvantage when faced with a left-handed enemy, whose moves were all backward from what was familiar and, therefore, predictable to some degree.

Brion had finally agreed that training should extend to both hands, in case injury forced shifting weapons in midbattle, but maintained until his death that left-handedness was to be strongly discouraged in his future knights. The trend persisted, even more than three years after Brion's death. Far across the yard, Morgan could see Baron Jodrell putting some of the current crop of squires through a drill with sword and shield—none of the lads unfashionably corrie-fisted.

Not so Dhugal, of course. Though fostered to court as a page when only seven, even younger than most boys of his rank and station, he had been recalled to the borders before he was twelve, serving out his apprenticeship in an environment where survival, not style, was important. And survival demanded a far different fighting style than what Dhugal had learned at court. Border conditions dictated fast, highly mobile strike forces, lightly mounted and armored—not the more ponderous greathorses and armor of the lowland knight. Nor did anyone care which hand the future Chief of Clan MacArdry favored, as long as the job got done, whether meting out the justice of the sword with the patrols that policed the borders against reivers and cattle thieves, or practicing the skills of a battle surgeon afterward.

None of that made shooting a bow left-handed look anything less than awkward to Morgan, however, accustomed to more conventional shooting stance. And as he shook his head and glanced again at Kelson, who was still gazing raptly at the archers, he knew it was not Dhugal's unorthodox shooting that was troubling the king, either. Nor was it their earlier discussion of the necessity for remarriage, though that was sure to bring a rise, even under the best of conditions, whenever the subject was broached.

No, today's preoccupation had to do with what Kelson was—Deryni as well as king—and the necessity, this very night, to make Deryni confirmation of the man who would succeed him on the throne of Gwynedd, should Kelson not return from the Mearan campaign. For failing an heir of Kelson's body, which he did not yet have, the crown and the Haldane legacy of magic would pass to Prince Nigel, Kelson's uncle and brother of the dead King Brion.

Brion. After more than three years, the emptiness of the former king's loss no longer ached in Morgan's chest in quite the way it once had, but the uncompromising loyalty once visited on the father now lay upon the royal son—this slender, grey-eyed youth, only now verging on true manhood, who prepared to face yet another test that should have been reserved for one of greater years and experience.

At least the physical shell better matched the test. The boy-king who had been was gone forever. Intensive weapons training for the coming campaign had stretched and hardened boyish muscles to more manly proportions, and a winter's growth spurt had given him another handspan of height, in addition to chiseling the rounded facial planes of youth to sharper angles. He now stood nearly shoulder-to-shoulder with Morgan, and had recently been obliged to employ a razor several times a week to maintain the clean-shaven appearance that he, like Morgan, preferred.

But where Morgan still wore his fair hair cropped short for ease of care in the field, as most fighting men chose to do, Kelson had allowed his to grow during the past two years of relative peace—"like any common borderer," as Dhugal had laughingly noted, when first reunited with the king the previous fall. For bordermen traditionally wore their hair pulled back in a braid at the nape of the neck and tied with the colors of their clan; no one remembered why.

Unexpectedly, however, the whim of a few seasons of peace soon became a political asset, for it had enabled Kelson to sleek his black hair into a neat border braid like those sported by Dhugal and his kinsmen, underlining his own border connections with Dhugal as well as the clan and thereby binding his border allies more firmly to his support. Only after it had served its political purpose did Kelson discover that the affectation was also both comfortable and practical, working as well under a helm or mail as the bowl-shaped cut or the Roman style that most seasoned warriors favored.

Since then, many of the younger men and boys had begun to adopt the king's border braid as their hair grew long enough, though lowland purists and those of a more conservative persuasion still considered short locks to be the mark of genteel civilization. Conall was one such purist, and wore his hair accordingly, though both his younger brothers boasted stubby border braids tied with ribbons of Haldane scarlet—somewhat less consequential than Dhugal's coppery braid, to be sure, but meant as fervent compliment, both to their royal cousin the king and to his dashing foster brother, who took the time to coach them at archery, and did not laugh when their arrows went wide of the mark.

A patter of applause and girlish laughter from across the yard shifted Morgan's focus back to Dhugal himself, who had just placed an arrow very near the center of the target. The young border lord lowered his bow and leaned on it like a staff as he glanced at Conall, watching in silence as his royal opponent carefully drew and let fly, placing his shot directly beside Dhugal's—though no nearer the center.

"He's quite good, isn't he?" Kelson breathed, gesturing with his chin toward his eldest cousin.

As Conall's brothers, thirteen and eight, moved forward to take their turns, Dhugal giving the younger boys helpful pointers, Conall stepped back from the line and glared sourly at his chief rival.

"Aye, he's skilled enough," Morgan agreed. "Perhaps one day he'll learn to compete gracefully as well. I wonder where he gets his temper. Certainly not from Nigel."

Kelson smiled and shook his head, glancing instinctively across the yard where his uncle, Conall's father, was working with a pair of pages under his tutelage—lads too young to go along on the coming campaign. While an old, retired battle stallion plodded a patient circle in the mud, one youngster straddling its broad back behind the massive war saddle while a second attempted to stand and balance on the moving animal's back, Nigel walked alongside and barked instructions. Jatham, Kelson's own squire, led the horse.

"Watch it . . ." Kelson murmured to himself, as Nigel's pupil teetered and started to tumble headfirst into the hoof-churned mud—only to have Nigel snatch him in midair by his belt and a handful of tunic and boost him back into position.

They could not hear what Nigel said to the lad, though his words brought an immediate flush of scarlet to the downy cheeks. Almost at once, the boy found his balance and was standing up, erect if shaky, but moving more and more confidently with the gait of the horse. Lent new bravery by his companion calling encouragement from behind him, he even began to grin as Nigel nodded approval and started slowly backing toward the center of the circle the old stallion trod.

"God, I'm glad I've got Nigel," Kelson whispered, echoing Morgan's own appreciation of Gwynedd's Iron Duke. "I suppose kings have always had to ride off to battle not

knowing how their heirs will handle things if they don't return, but at least with Nigel after me, Gwynedd will be in
good hands.''

Morgan glanced at him sharply. "No prescience of im-
pending doom, I hope?"

"No, it isn't that."

Morgan raised an eyebrow at the note of distraction in the
royal answer, but he said nothing, only noting how the king
had begun twisting at a gold ring on the little finger of his
left hand. Briefly it had been Kelson's bridal token to the
Mearan princess who now slept eternally in the vaults below
Rhemuth Cathedral; the ring had a tiny Haldane lion etched
on a facet pared from along the top of the band, the eyes set
with miniscule rubies. He had worn the ring constantly since
the day of her burial. Likewise, when court protocol did not
dictate otherwise, he had taken to wearing black. He was so
attired today, not even a circlet adorning his royal head.

Nor did Morgan know how much the outward symbols of
mourning reflected the true extent of the king's grief. Kelson
*said* that both gestures were but visible reminders of the vow
he had made to bring the Mearan rebels to justice, but Morgan wondered whether the significance might run deeper—
though he would not have dreamed of prying. Faced with a
marriage of state to a girl who had been bred to hate his very
name, Kelson had let himself retreat to the more comforting
fantasy that he was falling in love with Sidana, and she with
him. By the time they recited their vows before the high altar,
he had nearly convinced himself that it was true—or at least
that he eventually could have *caused* it to be true.

Her violent death, then, before the fantasy could be tested
in the reality of a consummated marriage, had left the young
king foundering in a sea of unresolved adolescent passions
and shattered ideals. Playing the grieving and aggrieved widower gave him time to sort things out before circumstances
forced him once more into the matrimonial sea. Both he and
Morgan knew that he *would* have to marry again, however,
and fairly soon. And as before, he would always have to
place dynastic considerations firmly before considerations
of the heart.

"Well, it's natural to be a little nervous about tonight,"
Morgan said, guessing apprehension rather than grief to be
behind today's mood. "Don't worry. Nigel will do fine.
You've been preparing him all winter for this."

"I know."

"And *you'll* do fine," Morgan continued, covering that aspect as well. "Why, I'll wager that no Haldane king since Cinhil himself has had so many Deryni to help him designate his magical heir. Your father certainly didn't. All he had was me."

"What do you mean, *all*?" Kelson snorted, though the protest was a little too quick to be quite as casual as he tried to pretend. "Why, I'd rather have you standing at my back than any other man I can think of—no matter *what* I was about to do. And as far as magic is concerned—"

Morgan quirked him a quick, lopsided smile and chuckled aloud, knowing he had guessed correctly.

"As far as magic is concerned, you might do better with just about *any* trained Deryni at your back," he said lightly. "Even Duncan and I don't have a full set of training between us."

"Maybe not, but maybe formal training isn't that important. Besides, Richenda's trained. And Arilan."

"Arilan." Morgan sighed and managed not to look as uneasy as he felt. "You're aware that he'll tell the Council every detail, aren't you?"

"Perhaps. Perhaps not."

"Kelson, you *know* he will. Despite his apparent loyalty to you, he has oaths of far longer standing with the Council—and far more binding. Even *I* know that."

"Well, they'll have to find out sometime, I suppose," Kelson murmured. "Besides, they've got access to records we'll need if we're ever to restore Saint Camber to his place of honor."

"So you'll compromise our security."

"No, I'll encourage further dialogue among fellow Deryni." Kelson smiled. "Did you know that old Laran ap Pardyce has begun to use our library, for example? His scholar's mind couldn't *stand* not knowing what we had. And as a physician, he's fascinated that you and Duncan can heal—though he won't admit that to very many people."

"And just how do you know that?"

"Oh, I've met him there, once or twice."

Before Morgan could respond to that new piece of information, a raucous whoop from Rory and Payne, Kelson's younger Haldane cousins, drew their attention back to the archery match, where Dhugal had just put his last arrow squarely into the center of the target.

To a patter of appreciative applause from the watching ladies, Conall moved forward to take his last shot—though there was little chance he could even come close to Dhugal's, much less beat it. Nor did he.

"Well, that's that," Kelson said, as Conall's arrow thumped home a full handspan from Dhugal's—respectable enough shooting, but clearly not in Dhugal's class.

The ladies again applauded—for a prince was nearly as good a catch as a king—but Conall all but slammed down his bow, though he did manage a stiff little bow of acknowledgment before stalking off sullenly toward the stables. Kelson glanced wistfully at Morgan as a subdued Rory and Payne trailed along with Dhugal to retrieve the arrows from the target.

"Well, well, well," he said, sliding to his feet off the stone balustrade, "that was nearly *far* more exciting than anyone would have wished. Let's go congratulate the winner, shall we? I don't know how, but he even managed to keep Conall from losing his temper."

"Which is an achievement in itself, aside from the brilliant shooting," Morgan replied, as they headed down the stair and into the yard. "Perhaps one may venture to hope that Conall is learning."

"Aye. Perhaps the presence of the ladies helped a little."

They were waiting at the firing line when Dhugal returned, Rory and Payne carrying the arrows in adoring attendance. After the boys had made their duty to Kelson, Payne chattering excitedly about Dhugal's victory, the young border lord sent them on their way and gave his foster brother his own casual yet respectful salute. In public, at least, he was always careful to give Kelson the deference their ranks required.

"Well shot, Dhugal," Kelson said, smiling. "And a well-managed victory."

Dhugal inclined his head and returned the smile, golden-amber eyes meeting Haldane grey, exactly aware what Kelson meant.

"Thank you, Sire."

Though still not as tall as Kelson, he, too, had shot up over the winter—to the dismay of the castle armorers, who must even now rush to complete the season's second alteration of his steel and leather brigandine, before he left on campaign on the morrow. He wore new boots and supple new leather britches of the same russet hue as his border braid, but the linen tunic was old, and pulled across the chest, the sleeve not bound with an armguard for archery hitting well above the wristbone. He had laid aside his plaid in the noonday sun, but no one would have mistaken his rank.

No sword hung from the gilded earl's belt circling his narrow waist, but he wore a border dirk at his left hip, with a water-pale amethyst set in the hilt. The three eagle feathers of a border chief bristled from behind a MacArdry badge on his leather border bonnet.

Dhugal grinned as he dropped his arrows into a standing quiver, large, square front teeth flashing bright-white beneath the sparse, silky smudge of mustache that, at sixteen, was all the facial hair he could yet produce.

"Care to shoot a round, Sire?" he asked impishly. "We missed you just now."

Smiling benignly, Kelson picked up Conall's discarded bow and tested its pull, then nocked an arrow to string and casually drew.

"Conall didn't miss me," he said, letting fly and holding as he watched the arrow thump precisely into the center of the target. "And Conall hasn't yet learned the graceful art of losing."

He ignored the flurry of applause and the sighs of appreciation from the watching ladies as he lowered the bow and took another arrow from the wistful Dhugal, laying the shaft across bow and string and carefully fitting nock to string again.

"I see," Dhugal said, not resentful, but curious. "So *I* get the job of humbling Conall."

Almost lethargically, Kelson raised the bow and began to draw again, closing his eyes and turning his face slightly away from the target as he locked into full-draw.

"At least it was an honest competition," he said softly, releasing his second arrow after the final word.

Eyes still closed, he held the position as the arrow made its flight, lowering the bow to look at Dhugal only when the arrow had thumped home precisely beside the first, the two shafts touching all along their length, the fletching on the two arrows indistinguishable from one another. The ladies applauded even more enthusiastically, and Kelson half-turned briefly to glance up at them and incline his head slightly in graceful acknowledgment as Dhugal gaped.

"I'm afraid I must confess to taking what Conall could consider an unfair advantage on that one," the king admitted with a droll smile and a wink in Dhugal's direction. "Being Deryni does have its more mundane advantages."

He shifted his attention to Morgan. "And you will note, Alaric, that I am not totally insensitive to the interest of the ladies at my court," he went on. "I am simply cultivating an aloofness in keeping with my eligible status—though I must confess that it seems somehow to have taken on some of the mystery that you yourself used to generate when you were in your darkling phase—and still do, I suspect, known Deryni sorcerer that you are. Perhaps it comes from wearing black."

Any determination on Morgan's part to maintain decorum disintegrated into delighted laughter at that, for Morgan's own former penchant for black attire was well known and of only recent abandonment—and affected, in the past, for reasons very similar to those Kelson had just cited. Nowadays, he wore black for practicality, or because nothing else was handy—which was precisely why he had donned it this morning: serviceable black leathers over mail, for a predawn ride. The coincidence made Kelson's comment a singularly suitable retribution for Morgan's earlier jesting.

"Perhaps you ought to go ahead and try a shot," Kelson suggested, suddenly aware that the bewildered Dhugal was still puzzling over the implications of Deryni advantages. "Show Dhugal how we Deryni do it."

"You mean—"

Dhugal broke off in astonishment as Morgan merely raised an eyebrow and took up a bow, casually fitting an arrow to the string. He could not come to full draw with the shorter shaft the younger men used, but nonetheless his shot slammed squarely into the angle formed by Kelson's first two, even though he deliberately averted his eyes before locking on the target. Nor did he look up as he nocked and drew again, his second shot completing the square formed by the four shafts.

"*Bloody hell!*" Dhugal whispered, as sighs of awe and more timid applause issued from the ladies' gallery.

Morgan laid down his bow and favored his admiring audience with a courtly acknowledgment of his own before herding the two younger men along with him toward the target with vague shooing motions. Dhugal tried hard not to goggle.

"How did you do that?" he breathed. "*No one* can shoot like that! You really *did* use magic, didn't you?"

Morgan shrugged noncommittally.

"Simple enough, when one knows how," he said, keeping his outward demeanor casual and offhand. "Fortunately, our feminine admirers aren't aware how unusual that kind of shooting is. Nor, I suspect, should we titillate them very often with performances like this. Right now, they are probably only reflecting that Conall and his brothers are rather poor shots by comparison with the three of us. Conall, on the other hand, might have guessed the truth—and been furious."

"*I'll* say," Dhugal murmured. "He's insufferable enough when he doesn't win."

Kelson reached the target first, and began carefully pulling the telltale arrows and handing them to Morgan.

"And now you know another reason I declined to compete," he said. "It would have taken unfair advantage. When you've learned how to enhance a skill as Alaric and I have done, it's a great temptation to use what you've learned. *Your* skill, on the other hand, comes from genuine talent with the bow—and can become better yet, once you learn how to use your powers more broadly."

"You mean, *I* could do that?"

"Certainly. With practice, of course."

As they started back toward the line, Conall and a squire burst from the distant stableyard on fractious bay coursers and clattered across the cobblestones toward them, the squire, at least, giving flying salute to the king as they shot past. Conall pretended not to have noticed any of them. The two had to draw aside at the great portcullis gate to let a returning patrol enter the yard, but they were gone as soon as they could squeeze their mounts past the last tartan-clad riders.

"Ah, look who's back," Morgan said, spotting his cousin Duncan among the men bringing up the rear.

Bishop Duncan McLain, Duke of Cassan and Earl of Kierney, looked hardly even ducal, much less episcopal, as he urged his grey forward alongside the ordered ranks of men. Besides a mist-pale plume in his cap, only a shoulder plaid of green, black, and white set off his drab brown riding leathers. He grinned and raised a gloved hand in greeting as he spotted king and company by the archery butts; however, he jogged his mount smartly in their direction instead of continuing on toward the stables with his men. A smiling Dhugal caught the horse's bridle as Duncan reined in, gentling the animal with a word and a deft touch of hands to velvety nose.

"Good morning, Sire," Duncan said to Kelson with a nod, swinging a leg and his sword casually over the high pommel of his saddle and springing lightly to the ground on the off side. "Dhugal. Alaric. What's got into young Conall? One would have thought he was pursued by demons."

"Only the demons of jealousy." Kelson snorted, resting both balled fists on his narrow hips. "Dhugal outshot him, fair and square."

"*Did* you, then? Well done, son!"

All three of them echoed his grin at that, for calling Dhugal "son" in that context was one of the few ways that Bishop Duncan McLain could publicly acknowledge that Dhugal MacArdry really *was* his son—for Duncan's heartbreakingly brief marriage to Dhugal's mother, though consummated long before Duncan entered holy orders, had been irregular in the extreme, so irregular that its existence could no longer be proven except by magic, so irregular that neither father nor son had learned of their relationship until a few short months before, though they had known one another as priest and royal page for many years. The secret was still shared only by the four of them and Morgan's wife, Richenda, though Duncan was quite willing to acknowledge his son if Dhugal wanted it.

But both had agreed that the timing was not yet right for that. Public disclosure just now would only brand Dhugal a bastard, undermining his right to the leadership of Clan MacArdry and his rank as earl, as well as weakening Duncan's credibility as a Prince of the Church. It would also cloud the succession to Duncan's Cassan and Kierney lands—a factor in the coming Mearan conflict, since Prince Ithel held some claim to the titles if Duncan eventually died without issue, as bishops normally were expected to do.

A less immediate but far more dangerous result, in the final reckoning, was the possibility that Dhugal would eventually be branded a Deryni, once Duncan's Deryni status became a confirmed fact rather than the present whispered rumor. And of the several Deryni at court, Dhugal was the least well-equipped to deal with that accusation.

Never having suspected this aspect of his heritage any more than he had his true paternity, Dhugal had never learned to use his magical birthright while he was growing up; indeed, had been hampered at first by rigid shields that were only finally breached by Duncan himself, and still remained resistant to all but the most cautious and delicate probes of any other Deryni. Even Arilan had tried—though before Dhugal's kinship with Duncan was discovered.

"It was a good contest," Morgan said, enjoying the interplay between father and son. "Dhugal, however, was not aware that one might improve one's performance with the application of certain—ah—'alternate' skills, was he, Kelson?"

"We wouldn't dare use them with Conall," Kelson agreed. "He already rides off in a snit when he loses."

Duncan laughed and pulled off his leather riding cap, ruffling a gloved hand through short brown hair. In preparation for the coming campaign, with its need for long hours spent under arming cap, mail, and helm, he had grown out his clerical tonsure save for a small, token circle right at the crown, no larger than a silver penny. The rest of his hair was barbered in the same martial-style that Morgan favored, in marked contrast to Dhugal and Kelson's border braids.

"Oh, I think Conall has a paramour somewhere in the city," he said with a droll smile quite out of keeping with his clerical rank. "Perhaps that's where he was in such a hurry to go, when he nearly rode me down just now. I've noticed that he isn't too attentive to most of the ladies at court—and he nearly always comes back with a silly smile on his face. Perhaps our king should take his example?"

Kelson knew Duncan was only jesting, but he still was faintly annoyed as Dhugal elbowed him in the ribs, flashing his bright-white grin, and Morgan raised an eyebrow in an amused expression of silent approbation.

"*Must* we keep harping on that same tired theme?" he said a little sharply, taking an arrow from Morgan and pretending to sight along it critically. "How was your patrol, Duncan? Are your men fit?"

Duncan's smile vanished immediately, his blue eyes gone coolly serious as he put on his cap again, once more the restrained and efficient soldier-priest.

"Aye, fit enough, my prince. However, I fear we did come upon something I think will not please you overmuch. The queen's party is less than an hour from the city gates."

"Oh, no!"

"They must have made better time from Saint Giles' than we expected. I left eight of my men for escort."

"*Damn!*"

The expletive was barely whispered, but suddenly Kelson snapped his arrow across one knee and dashed the broken halves to the ground in a brief fit of temper.

"But, you knew she was coming," Dhugal ventured, clearly taken aback.

"Aye. But not today. She could have waited another day or two—at least until after tonight."

Morgan found himself wondering whether Jehana could possibly know what they planned, and said as much to the king, but Kelson only shook his head and sighed heavily, once more in control.

"No, I'm sure it's just poor timing." He sighed again. "I suppose there's nothing to do but greet her and hope she's changed—though I doubt that. Alaric, you'd better make yourself scarce until I find out whether she still wants your blood. She wouldn't dare *do* anything, but there's no sense asking for trouble."

"I shall become invisible, my prince," Morgan said quietly. "Also, we may need to start later tonight than we'd planned," Kelson went on, gaining confidence as he took charge again. "Duncan, could you please inform Bishop Arilan?"

"Of course, Sire."

Kelson sighed yet again.

"Very well, then. I suppose I'd better go and tell Uncle Nigel she's on her way. I am not looking forward to this."

# CHAPTER TWO

*Shall I give my firstborn for my transgressions,
the fruit of my body for the sin of my soul?*

—Micah 6:7

The enclosed horse-chair carrying the mother of the King of Gwynedd swayed and lurched as the lead horse minced around a muddy pothole. Inside, behind thick woolen curtains that filtered the spring sunshine to a safe, anonymous twilight, Jehana of Gwynedd clung to the wooden frame on either side and prayed for a better road.

She loathed travelling by horse-chair; it made her stomach queasy. But three years without so much as setting toe to stirrup, combined with the austerities she had practiced as a part of her religious discipline, had left her quite unfit to make the journey from Saint Giles' to Rhemuth in any other way. The pale, well-kept hands clinging to the chair's polished wood were painfully thin; the golden marriage ring given her by her dead husband would have slid from her finger with the slightest movement, were it not for the white silk cord securing it to her fragile wrist.

Her high-necked gown was also white, like the cord: the color of a postulant's habit, though the fabric was nubby silk rather than the simple homespun wool the sisters wore, and her mantle was lined with miniver. The rich auburn hair that had been her pride and Brion's joy was concealed beneath a wimple of white silk that also hid the grey beginning to thread the auburn at temples and crown. Her face thus kindly framed, the hollows of cheeks and brow gave an impression of ascetic beauty rather than gauntness, though a pinched look about the eyes betrayed the beauty's source as internal torment, not contentment.

Only the color of her eyes remained as it had been: the smoky green of shaded summer forests, rich as the darkling emeralds Brion had loved to see her wear. She was just thirty-six.

Hard male voices jarred Jehana abruptly from contemplation, and then the sound of many riders approaching. As her horse-chair lurched to a halt, she drew in breath sharply and prayed that Kelson was not among them, cautiously parting the curtains on her left until she could peer apprehensively ahead. All she could see at first was the hind end of Sir Delrae's brawny bay, its thick tail twisted up in a neat mud-knot, and a similar view of Father Ambros' white mule.

Then, as Delrae urged his mount forward to challenge the newcomers, Jehana caught a glimpse of leather and tartan-clad riders beyond him, in green and black and white, too many to count. She remembered seeing the pattern before, but she could not recall the particular clan.

She watched Delrae confer with one of the officers of the troop for several minutes—he was senior of the four Bremagni knights her brother had sent to serve as her escort. Then Delrae gave way and allowed several of the men to fall in with his own command. As the rest of the troop rode off, and Jehana started to let the curtain fall back into place, Father Ambros kneed his mule between her and the view ahead and leaned down to reassure her.

"We've been given a guard of honor, my lady," he said softly, with the smile that would melt the heart of an angel. "That was the Duke of Cassan's patrol. He's left men to see us safely to Rhemuth."

The Duke of Cassan. With both Jared and Kevin McLain dead, that would be Duncan McLain—*Father* McLain, Kelson's confessor of many years—and distant cousin to the Deryni Alaric Morgan. That Duncan was also Deryni had come as a complete shock to Jehana—though she never would have dreamed of betraying that knowledge to anyone not already aware of the fact. God would exact His vengeance upon Duncan McLain for daring to accept priestly ordination in defiance of the Church's prohibition against Deryni entering priestly Orders—though how He had countenanced Duncan's elevation to the episcopate was beyond her understanding.

"Yes, of course. Thank you, Father," she murmured.

She was not certain, as she hastily let the curtain fall, whether she had succeeded in keeping the panic out of her eyes or not, though she thought her voice had not betrayed her. Still, Ambros was a canny judge of character, for all that he was nearly young enough to be her son.

But thought of her son was not to be countenanced any more than that of McLain—and Morgan. Time enough, later on, to worry about *them*. Clasping folded hands fervently to her lips, she closed her eyes briefly and breathed yet another prayer for courage—then grabbed at the sides of the chair for balance as her procession lurched into motion again.

Reunion with her Deryni son was not the only reason Jehana was dreading the return to Rhemuth. Resumption of the very public life expected of a queen at court would not be easy, if only because she had grown unaccustomed to seeing anyone other than the sisters of Saint Giles'. Though she had taken no formal religious vows during the three years of her seclusion, she had lived and moved with the heartbeat of the community, performing all the Offices and praying for expiation of the terrible taint of Deryni evil she knew she carried in her soul, seeking release from the torment that her self-knowledge carried. Taught from childhood by family and Church that Deryni were evil, she had not yet reconciled the religious and moral dilemmas raised by the discovery that she, too, was of the race she had long believed accursed. Her spiritual mentors at Saint Giles' had assured her repeatedly that her sin was forgivable—if sin it was to use one's every resource to protect one's child from certain death at the hands of an evil adversary—but early indoctrination continued to warn a still-childlike Jehana that she had sinned.

The outward vehemence of her denial had lessened a little during her sojourn at Saint Giles'—for so long as she kept her seclusion, she had been able to insulate herself almost totally from contact with or even mention of other Deryni—but the dread rekindled and burned ever brighter as she drew closer and closer to Rhemuth and her Deryni son. Only for Kelson's sake had she left the abbey even now, anguished by the continuing toll his Deryniness seemed to take in human lives. Not even his young bride had been safe.

And that was why, ultimately, Jehana had finally chosen to leave the cloistered sanctuary of Saint Giles'; for Kelson, now nearly six months a widower, would need to take another wife soon to secure the succession. Jehana had no idea what the field of likely candidates might be like—only a notion that the right royal bride, chosen according to the standards Jehana espoused, might mitigate the negative aspects of Kelson's Deryni blood. Only thus might there be a chance to turn Kelson aside from the path he seemed to have chosen, to lure him away from the evil influences of the other Deryni at court and bring him back to salvation.

The horses' shod hooves began to strike more solid footing, picking up the pace as the way became smoother, and Jehana parted the curtains just far enough to glance outside again. Ahead, between the straight figures of Sir Delrae and a tartan-wrapped Cassani officer, she could just see the familiar walls of Rhemuth Castle shimmering silvery and pristine in the spring sunshine, bold against a sky pebbled with tiny white clouds.

*White sheep*, she thought fiercely to herself, fighting down a lump threatening to rise in her throat. *White sheep on a blue hill.* . . .

But the childhood image, intended to divert the double pangs of fear and joy at homecoming, did not have the hoped-for effect. Far from the meager comfort she had found at Saint Giles', she could feel the old emotions welling up— the terror for her soul, for Kelson's soul, threatening the composure she knew she must regain before she dared face those who would be waiting.

And in the yard at Rhemuth Castle, on the landing of the stair that led to the great hall, Kelson, too, was experiencing no small amount of trepidation at what the coming reunion would bring. Only his Uncle Nigel, Archbishop Cardiel, and Nigel's two younger sons waited with him for the queen's arrival. He had thought not to overwhelm her with too many people at first.

"It's been so long," Kelson whispered to his uncle, standing at his left elbow. "What do you think she'll be like?"

Nigel's smile conveyed a reasonable composure as he glanced aside at his royal nephew, but Kelson knew that he, too, had misgivings about his sister-in-law's return.

"She'll be somewhat changed," the royal duke allowed softly. "Hopefully, the changes will be for the better. God knows, she'll see *you've* changed."

"Not all *that* much, have I?" Kelson asked, surprised.

Nigel shrugged. "What do *you* think, Kelson? You've become a man in her absence—the magic all aside. You've fought a war, you've killed—you've had to make some very difficult decisions that *I* certainly wouldn't have wanted to make."

"I'm told it comes with the job," Kelson murmured, managing a brief, wry grin.

"Aye, but some men do a better job than others," Nigel returned. "You're one of them. Even now, on the eve of another war, you've kept your personal anger in check when most men of far more experience and years would have let vengeance run wild. I don't know that *I* could have kept from killing Llewell right there in the cathedral, if I'd just had my bride butchered before my eyes."

Kelson half-turned away and began furiously twisting the ring on his little finger.

"If I'd really been in control, she wouldn't have been killed in the first place."

"Are we going to have to go over *that* again?" Nigel replied. "That's past. It's regrettable—but continuing to reproach yourself won't change things. You can't do everything exactly right. You *can* make a difference for the future, however."

"Yes, and my dear, superstition-blinded mother will help things enormously!"

"She's only your mother, for God's sake, Kelson. *You* haven't done anything you need to be ashamed of. If she wants to keep flagellating herself with guilt, that's between her and her God. Don't ask me to hand *you* a whip to do the same thing."

Kelson snorted and started to cross his arms skeptically across his chest, then glanced at the gatehouse, his eyes caught by movement in the shadowed passageway. As the first of the Cassani escort trotted through the opening, he stood a little straighter and tugged nervously at the bottom of his tunic.

"Sweet *Jesu*, here she comes," he whispered.

Two pairs of Duncan's elite lancers rode at the head of the modest procession following, blue and silver silk pennons fluttering gaily from the tips of gleaming metal lances, McLain tartan bright on shoulders and saddles, horses jigging and prancing as they sighted the gate to the stableyard.

Behind rode Sir Alan Sommerfield, the seasoned McLain captain, beside a stylish-looking younger knight bearing the black ship and crimson crescent of the Bremagni kings on his white surcoat. Two horse-chairs followed close behind, the first carried by a pair of pale matched greys and escorted by a young cleric on a white mule. Behind the second horse-chair followed three more Bremagni knights and another four Cassani lancers.

"Come, Sire," murmured Archbishop Cardiel, touching the king's elbow to lead him down the steps. "She'll be in the first chair. We should be there when she alights."

"Why isn't she riding?" Kelson whispered to Nigel, as they followed Cardiel and the cousins down. "You don't think she's ill, do you?"

"It's a long journey," Nigel returned. "Perhaps this was easier for her."

The queen's horse-chair reached the bottom of the steps at about the same time the king and his party did, the priest and the two captains dismounting immediately to attend the chair's occupant as the other knights lined up to either side in salute. As the Bremagni captain drew back the heavy curtains and opened the tiny half-door, the priest offered his hand inside with a bow. Then Jehana was emerging, all white and *in* white and looking even paler for the blaze of her eyes in her pinched, wan face.

"*Mother*," Kelson breathed, reaching out to her and seizing her in a fierce embrace when she would have knelt to him on the dusty ground beside her chair. As he held her to his chest, a hand taller than last time they had met, he could feel her heart pounding beneath her silken robes—and was shocked to realize how little there was of her to embrace.

She must have sensed his surprise, for it was she who broke the embrace first, to back off a step and bob in formal curtsey, subject to king. Then she was moving on to Cardiel, bending to kiss his ring in homage, bringing forward the priest and a youngish-looking nun who had emerged from the second horse-chair.

"I beg leave to present my chaplain, Father Ambros," she said softly, not meeting Kelson's eyes, "and Sister Cecile, my companion. Sir Delrae commands my guard. I have no other household anymore," she finished lamely. "I did not wish to presume upon the King's Grace."

"'Tis no presumption, Mother," Kelson said softly. "Until I take another bride, you are still queen and mistress of this castle. And you must have a household befitting your rank. Aunt Meraude will assist you to choose new ladies-in-waiting. I pray you to take as many as you need."

"Your offer is most generous, Sire, but I have found my needs to be far less in these past three years than one might believe. Sister Cecile shall continue to attend me—and if a place might be made at court for my chaplain, my Lord Archbishop?"

Cardiel bowed. "I shall see that Father Ambros is housed in my own palace, my lady," he murmured. "In fact, if you have no further need of him for the rest of the afternoon, I shall take him now to begin meeting some of our brethren."

"Thank you, Excellency," she breathed. "Father Ambros, I shall not require your services until morning Mass."

"As you wish, my lady."

"And now, Sire," Jehana went on, "if we may be shown to our quarters? Sister and I are very weary from our journey."

"Certainly, Mother." He cocked his head hopefully. "May I tell the court that you will join us at table tonight?"

"Thank you, no, Sire. I fear I am not yet ready for so public an appearance. I would be grateful if my knights could be afforded that courtesy, however. They have served me most loyally."

Kelson inclined his head coolly, not surprised that she had declined his invitation. "Sir Delrae and his fellows are most welcome at our table, Mother. Gentlemen, our royal cousin, Prince Rory, will conduct you to lodgings befitting your rank. And now, if I may," he went on, returning his attention to Jehana, "I'll take you to your rooms."

"Thank you, Sire, but I prefer that Nigel escort me, if you do not mind."

Kelson minded, but he was not about to make a further fool of himself in front of so many witnesses, albeit that almost all of them knew what had raised the frosty barrier between Jehana and himself. As an apologetic Nigel set his hand under the queen's elbow and led her up the stairs, Sister Cecile following meekly behind, Kelson watched them go. Young Payne stood by him, even after Rory had taken away the knights and Cardiel had drawn the young priest Ambros in the direction of the episcopal palace.

"She must be really mad at you, Kelson," Payne whispered after a moment, glancing shyly at his silent cousin as his father and aunt disappeared through the great hall door.

Snorting, Kelson laid an arm around Payne's shoulder and shook his head sadly.

"I'm afraid she is, Payne. I'm afraid she is."

"He seems so grown," Jehana murmured, as soon as she and Nigel were out of Kelson's earshot. "I had no idea he would be so tall."

Nigel glanced at her in surprise, but waited until they had passed a bowing knot of courtiers before answering.

"You've been away for three years, Jehana," he said softly. "Children do grow, whether their parents are there to see it or not. Wait until you see Conall—and I wonder that you even recognized Rory and Payne."

"I would have known them," Jehana replied, as they passed out of the great hall and headed down a long corridor leading to the residence wing. "They bear the Haldane stamp. No one could ever mistake a child of yours or Brion's."

"Perhaps not. But I might never have recognized *you* in a crowd. Jehana, what have you done to yourself?"

"I don't know what you're talking about," she murmured, averting her eyes and thrusting thin hands briskly into her sleeve openings as she walked a little faster.

"Oh, yes, you do. You look like you've been in a dungeon rather than a cloister. How much weight have you lost?"

"Fasting is good for the soul," she replied, lifting her chin defiantly. "But I wouldn't expect you to understand that, knowing the company you keep."

Seizing her elbow, Nigel stopped in the middle of the corridor and spun her to face him.

"And just what is that supposed to mean?"

"Well, aren't they still at court?"

"Aren't *who* still at court?"

"You know: Morgan and McLain, and God knows what others."

His expression was so shocked that she could almost believe the thought had not occurred to him before that very moment. Coolly Jehana drew her arm out of his grasp and moved a few steps in the direction they had been headed, gesturing for the silent Cecile to draw nearer.

"If you'll show us where we're to go, we should like to rest now," she said quietly.

To her surprise and relief, Nigel did not pursue their discussion. Instead he led her to her old apartments close by the walled garden. She had been expecting lesser accommodations. At Nigel's knock, a serving girl opened the door and stood aside with a shy, deferential curtsey, but Nigel did not come in. As the door closed behind Jehana and her silent companion, the queen had just a glimpse of the solar beyond the little reception room, and a dozen or so strange pairs of eyes lifted curiously from various stitchery projects. Then Meraude, Nigel's wife, was darting toward her with outstretched arms, tears of joy streaming down her rosy cheeks.

"Jehana! Praise God, you're back at last! Poor thing, you must be exhausted!"

Jehana could feel the taut swell of Meraude's belly against her as they embraced—with child again, after so long!—and she pushed down a brief pang of envy that she herself had been able to bear no more children after Kelson. But on second thought, perhaps that was for the best, lest the taint of her blood be passed on to even further generations.

In fact, she was not sure she even approved of Meraude having another child—though the chance of it eventually assuming Kelson's dread heritage was so remote as to be almost nonexistent. If, for some reason, Kelson should not produce an heir of his own, the line would pass through Nigel and Conall—or possibly through young Rory or Payne, if Conall's line should fail. The baby Meraude now carried beneath her heart would never wear the Haldane crown, or know the curse of the Haldane taint.

"Meraude, Meraude, I *have* missed you," she said softly, searching the other woman's brown eyes as they drew apart to look at one another. "And you're with child again, at last. You and Nigel must be *so* pleased."

"How could we not be?" Meraude countered, grinning merrily. "Nigel hopes for a little girl this time, and I confess the thought pleases me as well, after three boys. We'll know in another month or so. But you, Jehana—how thin you've become! Are you well?"

"As well as I may be," she answered, turning slightly to motion her companion forward. "This is Sister Cecile. She came with me from Saint Giles'. Sister, this is the Duchess

Meraude, Prince Nigel's wife. May she wait in the solar with
the other ladies while we speak for a moment?"

"Of course. Sister, you are most welcome to Rhemuth,"
Meraude said, inclining her head to acknowledge the nun's
bow. "Please be at ease with my ladies. We shall join you
in a few moments."

As Cecile passed on into the solar, Meraude glanced back
at Jehana and drew her into the sunshine of a nearby win-
dowseat.

"So. What is it that cannot wait until you've rested?" she
asked, easing her back with one hand as she sank down on
a tapestry cushion.

Jehana did not sit; only stood in a pool of sunlight and
clasped her thin hands nervously, her eyes searching Meraude's for some sign of sympathy.

"Are you safe, Meraude?" she whispered.

"Safe?"

"Have Morgan and McLain corrupted your husband as
they did mine?"

"Jehana—"

"It's important to his very soul, Meraude!" Jehana went
on, sinking down urgently beside her sister-in-law, eyes
never leaving Meraude's face. "You must keep him from the
Deryni taint. Kelson is already in grave danger, but it isn't
too late for Nigel—and maybe not for Kelson, either. That's
why I've come back."

"To—save Kelson?" Meraude said cautiously.

But Jehana went right on, taking Meraude's response for
an invitation to say more.

"He must marry again, Meraude—and soon. He needs an
heir of his own. And I feel certain that the right bride could
overcome the evil in him. Just as you keep Nigel safe from
harm, so Kelson's queen must bring him back to a life of
righteousness. It's his only hope, Meraude. Say you'll help
me."

Wistfully Meraude returned Jehana's eager smile, letting
the queen take her hand.

"Well, there are certainly potential royal brides aplenty,"
she said noncommittally, "though I suspect Kelson himself
will have something to say about a choice. In any case, I
doubt he means to make a commitment until after the campaign." Her smile brightened hopefully. "But would you like
to meet a few of them? Several of my ladies are quite eligible.

In any case, you'll probably want to appoint a few ladies-in-waiting of your own. Come and I'll introduce them.''

Jehana lost track of the names after the first few presentations, but the prospect of involving herself actively in her son's choice of a new wife even brought a little color to her cheeks. Many of the ladies were quite young, and eminently suitable.

She was in growing good spirit until Meraude brought her to a beautiful young woman stitching at a tapestry frame near one of the windows. The woman's gown was the deep blue of mountain lakes, her heavy, flame-gold hair caught in a net of gold and pearls at the back of her head and circled across the forehead by a narrow golden fillet.

"This is the Duchess Richenda," Meraude said, as the woman rose to dip in a respectful curtsey.

Jehana's heart leaped into her throat, her entire body stiffening in shock.

"Duchess—Richenda?" she managed to whisper. "Have I not heard your name before?"

The woman straightened to meet Jehana's eyes with the bluest gaze she had ever seen, deferential but direct, even sympathetic.

"It may well be that you have, Majesty," she said in a low voice. "My late husband sat on King Brion's council. He was the Earl of Marley."

"The Earl of Marley," Jehana repeated tonelessly. "But Meraude said—"

"My young son Brendan is Earl of Marley now, Majesty," Richenda said. "My present husband is the Duke of Corwyn."

*Corwyn!* Jehana let the name register on a mind suddenly gone numb with dread. *Sweet Jesu, she is Morgan's wife! She married a Deryni!*

"I—see," she managed to whisper aloud.

But she could hardly see as she turned to move on with Meraude, stumbling stiff and half-blind through the rest of the introductions until she could call Sister Cecile to her side and seek the refuge of the little oratory adjoining her sleeping chamber. Prayer brought her some semblance of serenity, but she could not banish the feeling of dull despair that the wife of a Deryni should be so firmly entrenched in the royal household.

# CHAPTER THREE

*For they have begotten strange children.*
                                          —Hosea 5:7

The strain generated by Jehana's arrival set the tone for the rest of Kelson's afternoon. Nor was his mood improved by the circumstances dictated for that evening. Already tense about the ritual set for later that night, he could not even escape for a few hours of much needed solitude and relaxation over supper, for even though Jehana had declined his invitation to dine with the court, he felt obligated to sup with her in private. To help keep the affair on more neutral ground, however, he asked Nigel and Meraude to host it, and had the meal sent to their quarters. That arrangement would also prevent Nigel from dwelling overmuch on what was to come. Half spitefully, he deputized Morgan and Richenda to preside at table in the great hall in his absence, since Morgan himself was at least partially responsible for Jehana's attitude. Duncan and Dhugal could more than handle what few arrangements had to be made.

And so, he sat that evening with his mother, Nigel, and Meraude in his uncle's supper chamber and tried to make pleasant small talk while he longed to be almost anywhere else. The chamber was stuffy—or perhaps it was only him—and he toyed distractedly with Sidana's ring while his mother's conversation meandered over half a dozen old themes. Almost all of them returned ultimately to her hatred and fear of Deryni.

27

"So when the news reached me at Saint Giles'," Jehana went on, "I could hardly believe my ears. Continuing to keep Alaric Morgan around you is perilous enough; but to receive his wife, whose first husband was a traitor and apparently Deryni as well—"

"Bran Coris wasn't Deryni, Mother," Kelson said peevishly, suddenly concerned for the direction this conversation could take if he were not careful.

"But they say he stood by Wencit of Torenth in a magical circle—"

"And Bishop Arilan stood by *me*. Does that make *him* Deryni?" Kelson countered boldly.

"Bishop Arilan? Certainly not! But—"

"Of course it doesn't." Which was not precisely a lie, but it was sufficiently misleading to redirect any suspicions Jehana might have had about Arilan. "I asked his and Father Duncan's presence—and Morgan's—because the trial permitted four persons on either side. It was Wencit and I who were contending. We chose whom we willed to give us company and courage, but the power, if it had come to the Duel Arcane, would have come from Wencit and myself."

"According to whose authority?" Jehana challenged. "Those strangers who came on white horses? I heard about them, Kelson. Who were they? They were Deryni, weren't they?"

Kelson lowered his eyes. "I may not speak of them."

"Then, they *were* Deryni," she whispered. She turned a pinched, desperate face toward her dead husband's brother. "Nigel, you were there. What saw you? Who were they? Are there so many of them that they may walk unrecognized among us with impunity?"

Nigel, of course, knew little more than Jehana in that regard, for he had not been privy to the intentions of the Camberian Council—only their actual intervention. But his uneasy dissembling was sufficient to lead Jehana back to the old, relatively safe topic of Morgan, whose Deryni proclivities were a secret to no one. As Jehana launched into yet another variation on the old fears, Kelson let his thoughts turn to a delicious contemplation of the Deryni at court that Jehana did *not* know about.

She had not yet made the connection about Richenda, of course—though she had skirted uncomfortably close. And it obviously had not occurred to her to question Arilan. The knowledge that a Deryni had risen through the ecclesiastical ranks unbeknownst and attained the rank of bishop would shake her faith to the core; surely such a deception could only be the work of the Devil, an attempt to destroy the Faith from within. Of course, Duncan had managed a similar rise— but few outside episcopal ranks were certain that he was Deryni, and much could be blamed on his Deryni cousin Morgan.

Dhugal, of course, was an entirely different matter. Outside Kelson's immediate circle of close confidants—Morgan, Richenda, Duncan, and Dhugal himself—only Nigel and Arilan even knew that Dhugal was Deryni, much less that he was Duncan's son; and even Nigel and Arilan did not know the latter. One must assume that the Camberian Council also knew at least what Arilan knew—and that they fretted over Dhugal and the mystery of his powers the same way they fretted over Morgan and Duncan—but other than those few, Kelson doubted anyone even suspected.

He took a deep draught of the light, nutty ale Nigel had provided with supper—wine might have blunted their senses for the ritual still to come—and hid a smile behind his cup as he nodded and made noncommittal grunts in response to his mother's continuing monologue.

That Dhugal was Deryni, and Duncan's son, still amazed and delighted him. The revelation had even eased some of the awful, heart-numbing shock of Sidana's murder, that terrible Twelfth Night but a few months past. Letting the dull buzz of his mother's voice carry him back, he set himself to savor the memory—able, from this distance, to let even the echo of his grief lap at his emotions as he anticipated the joy to follow.

He had been sitting hunched in a bath before the fireplace in his bedchamber, trying to let the warm water ease the chill that seemed to penetrate to his very soul. He had long since washed Sidana's blood from his hands, but a part of him still kept going numbly through the motions, as if further ablution could somehow wash her blood from his soul as well.

He was vaguely aware of others moving about quietly in the room—Morgan, Duncan, Dhugal—and felt their compassion as a warm, comforting presence intended to ease his pain; but he was too tight-coiled in his own hurt and guilt and outrage to let their caring penetrate very deeply. He still did not know whether he had truly loved Sidana, but ultimate responsibility for her death remained squarely upon him in any case, even though another hand had wielded the dagger.

She had been under his protection, and he had failed her. Her marriage ring glinted bright and accusing as his hands continued their vague movement underneath the water. He had slipped it on his little finger as he held her lifeless body in his arms, crouched there in the blood-spattered sanctuary that so short a time before had been witness to their marriage.

"I think you've been in there long enough, my prince," Morgan said quietly, suddenly appearing out of the shadows from behind him with a thick, thirsty towel. "Come dry yourself. Duncan's making you a warm posset to help you sleep."

As he obeyed, dully standing to let Morgan wrap him in the towel, he became aware of small sounds in the room: the crackle of the fire, metal clinking against pottery at the small table where Duncan worked by candlelight, his own shallow breathing. Stepping damply onto thick Kheldish carpet, he allowed himself to be guided to a deep, engulfing chair nearer the hearth. When he had settled, Duncan put a warm cup in his hand and sat down on a stool; Dhugal had already taken a similar seat within reach of Kelson's knee. Morgan remained standing, his back to the fire, one arm resting along the carved stone of the mantel, the firelight limning his golden hair from behind so that he seemed to be haloed.

"Drink what Duncan's given you," his mentor said softly, jutting his chin toward the cup. "It will help to blunt some of the pain."

He was aware, as he drained the cup obediently, that the three of them were exchanging a curious set of glances, but he sensed nothing but concern for him in their manner—certainly no reason for alarm. The posset was laced with strong wine, and almost too hot. It was not until Kelson handed the cup back empty that he could detect the faintly tangy aftertaste of something Duncan had given him before—the expected sedative. Dhugal coughed, looking almost nervous as Duncan set the cup aside, and Morgan laced his fingers together, one elbow still resting casually on the mantel.

"Dhugal and Duncan have something to tell you," Morgan said softly, the grey eyes dark with compassion. "I wish you could have learned it under happier circumstances, but perhaps it will help to ease your sorrow now. I think you will not be displeased."

Curious despite his grief, Kelson turned his gaze on Duncan, who had laid his hand on Dhugal's shoulder. The sedative was already blurring his ability to make his eyes focus, but his thinking was still reasonably clear and would remain so for several minutes, he knew.

"Dhugal and I made a marvelous discovery before we left for the cathedral this morning," Duncan said, smiling as Dhugal glanced at him and grinned. "It has to do with the cloak clasp he's wearing. I believe you've admired it at various times?"

For the first time Kelson noticed that although Dhugal had changed from border tartans to funereal black, he still wore the fist-sized lion-headed brooch that he said had been his mother's.

"What about it?" he asked, glancing back at Duncan.

Duncan's grin abruptly matched Dhugal's. "Well, it's a McLain badge—see the closed eyes?—the McLain sleeping lion. My father had it made for me. I gave it to my wife on our wedding night."

"Your wife . . . ?" Kelson murmured, stunned.

"To Dhugal's mother, as it turned out," Duncan went on happily. "You see, Dhugal is my son."

Even now, Kelson remembered few further details of that evening, though later explorations of the happy news brought him a joy that did, indeed, ease a little of the shock of Sidana's death. But as he flashed on the somber days of her lying-in-state and funeral, and his visits since then to the simple tomb in the crypt where she slept with other of Gwynedd's former kings and queens, he was jarred back to the present by her name on his mother's lips.

". . . cannot grieve forever over this Sidana," she was saying. "You hardly knew the girl. You have a duty to take another bride. That's why I've come back from the convent: to help you find one. A suitable wife can help to expiate the curse I've placed upon you."

"And what, pray tell, was not 'suitable' about the bride *I* chose?" Kelson said irritably, setting his cup aside with a hollow clunk. "Even by your standards, Mother, Sidana was 'suitable' in every respect: princess of a noble house whose union with our own might have forged a lasting peace; young and beautiful; almost certainly able to provide healthy heirs.

"Nor was she either Deryni or in sympathy with Deryni. And her own brother killed her, with a solid, reliable, un-Deryni knife!"

"You know that isn't what I meant—" Jehana began.

"No, don't lecture me about 'suitable' brides, Mother," Kelson went on. "I was prepared to do my dynastic duty, and chose my bride for all the 'right' reasons. You must pardon me if I do not seem overeager to leap into the matrimonial sea again, quite so quickly!"

Jehana shook her head, lips compressed in a thin line. "Not now, of course, Kelson. But soon—"

"Not *too* soon, Mother. In case you've forgotten, I have a war to fight this summer—one of the little legacies of my brief foray into matrimony. And as if the Mearan rebellion were not already far enough advanced, her family now blame me for Sidana's death as well as Llewell's. The dispute over Mearan sovereignty has taken on the added dimension of a blood feud, despite the fact that it was Llewell who killed Sidana—not I—and that Llewell was executed for his crime of murder, not because I particularly wanted him dead."

"You would have to have done away with him eventually, in any case," Jehana said coldly. "So long as he lived, he would have remained a threat. Any issue of his body—"

"Mother . . ."

Pushing himself away from the table with an exasperated sigh and a scraping of heavy chair legs against stone, Kelson stood and glanced at Nigel and Meraude, who had remained notably silent throughout this last exchange.

"Fortunately, the subject of Llewell's issue has been rendered academic," Kelson said patiently, catching Nigel's eye in signal that it was time to make their escape. "Nor have I any wish to discuss the matter further this evening. The commanders of my northern army leave for Cassan tomorrow morning, and there are matters Nigel and I must discuss before then. Uncle, would you please make your apologies to the ladies? We still have work ahead of us before we sleep."

He could only admire Nigel's coolness as the older man rose to take his leave. Though he knew Nigel trusted him and his Deryni colleagues implicitly, and they him, he must have harbored some apprehension about the "work" still ahead of them, if only for the fact that he was the object of that work and did not know what would be done to him.

Still, he showed no glimmer of anything but relaxed duty as he pulled a cloak around his shoulders and advised Meraude not to wait up.

"You know how long Kelson's staff meetings sometimes last, darling," he told her. "We could be half the night. You and the little one need your rest."

Meraude smiled and laid one hand on her swollen abdomen as her husband followed Kelson out, glancing aside at Jehana wistfully when the door had closed behind them. Jehana looked a bit taken aback, as if she could not quite believe how Kelson had managed his escape.

"He's become quite the young man while you were away, hasn't he?" Meraude said.

Jehana lowered her gaze. "I hardly recognize him," she whispered. "He's so stern and warlike—and grown-up."

"Children do that," Meraude answered gently. "I'm having to face the same realization about Conall. And Rory comes of age in the fall as well—though fourteen-year-olds still have a little time for being boys yet."

"Mine didn't," Jehana murmured.

"True. But Kelson was already a king by the time he turned fourteen. For Rory to face a similar circumstance would require tragedy indeed. No, Rory is my little boy for yet a while longer—and Payne, of course. And soon there'll be the new baby for loving. But I *do* hope this one will be a girl."

Jehana grimaced. "A girl, to become a pawn one day for a royal marriage?"

"A girl, to marry where her heart dictates, if God wills it," Meraude replied. "With three older brothers to carry on the line, I see little reason to force her into any marriage she would not want. Or perhaps she will prefer marriage with the Church. I gather that would not displease you."

Jehana smiled bitterly, tracing a fingertip through a small spill of ale on the table before her. "Would that my marriage had been with the Church, and saved the passing of the taint I carry within me," she murmured.

"And what of Kelson, if you had?" Meraude countered. "Aside from the fact that Kelson would not have been Kelson, given another mother, where would he have been without your inheritance and protection when he had to face Charissa?"

"He might have died," Jehana conceded. "But at least he would have been human, his soul unsullied by the Deryni curse I placed upon him by bearing him."

Shaking her head, Meraude pushed herself heavily back from the table. "You won't let go of it, will you? You're Deryni, Jehana. Nothing you can do will change that. But perhaps it doesn't *have* to be a curse. Surely it's possible *some* good might come of it."

"I fear you listen far too much to my son," Jehana said sadly. "It *is* a curse, Meraude. It is a canker that festers within me—and here at my son's court. Nor may I rest until I find a way to exorcise it."

Exorcism of a far different sort than Jehana had in mind was underway in another part of the castle, performed by a man who bore the very taint Jehana feared. Murmuring ritual words of purification, Bishop Duncan McLain slowly paced the circumference of the tiny Saint Camber chapel adjoining his study, methodically sprinkling the chamber with water from a silver aspergillum. Incense already hung lightly on the air. From the doorway leading back into the study, Dhugal watched and made the responses, eyes following his father's every move with reverence and respect. They had finished nearly all the other preparations necessary before the rest arrived. The censing and asperging of the chapel was the final touch, done as much to center and steady the two participants as to cleanse a room long sanctified by its sacred use.

"*Asperges me, Domine, hyssopo, et mundabor: lavabis me, et super nivem dealbabor.*"

"Amen."

"*Pax huic domui.*"

"*Et omnibus habitantibus in ea.*"

Peace be to this house. . . .

And to all who dwell in it. . . .

When they had done, and Duncan had put aside that paraphernalia of his office, father and son returned to the study, Duncan drawing into place the curtain that normally covered the door. Dhugal lingered a moment, eyeing the curtain with still-awed speculation as Duncan took a seat at the round table set before the room's fireplace. One candle burned at the center of that table, giving the only illumination save for the firelight. After a moment, Dhugal came and joined his father, though he still continued to glance at the curtained doorway from time to time.

"The chapel retains quite an impression of power, doesn't it?" Duncan said, smiling at Dhugal's startled glance in his direction. "I'm not surprised you'd notice. Saint Camber does seem to make his influence felt. And if you'd had the experiences Alaric and I have had, the difference between this chapel and most others would be even more apparent. Our good Deryni saint can be a very powerful intercessor."

Dhugal shifted a little uneasily. "Do you—really think he intervenes in earthly affairs? Does any saint?"

"Well, it's difficult ever to be certain, of course," Duncan replied. "Alaric and I know that a few of the things we'd ascribed to Saint Camber right after Kelson was crowned seem to have been done by—" He lowered his eyes. "By someone else," he finished. "I'm sorry, but I'm not permitted to say whom, even to you. It was a former member of the Camberian Council, but they've asked that we never mention names."

"I don't mean to pry," Dhugal protested.

Duncan smiled. "I know you don't, son. In any case, some of the things we'd ascribed to Camber weren't done by anyone we know of—so maybe he did intervene. Whenever I spend any time in that chapel, I begin to believe he did."

Dhugal glanced at the curtain again, then back at Duncan. "Kelson told me that's where you and Morgan did the ritual that invested him with power. Is that why we're doing Nigel's there?"

"In part," Duncan admitted. "However, it's also appropriate that we invoke Camber's special patronage, since it's said he was the first to give Deryni magic to any Haldane, more than two hundred years ago. And until his name is vindicated, as I'm certain it will be, one day, this may well be the only chapel in Gwynedd that's consecrated to him."

"Oh." Dhugal thought about that for a moment. Then: "Did—Kelson's father also receive his power in there?"

"I don't think so. Alaric had to do with that one—not I—several years before Kelson was born. He was even younger than you. As I understand it—"

A knock at the door cut off further retelling of that story, and Duncan rose to admit Morgan and Richenda.

"If Kelson weren't my king, I'd be tempted to box his royal ears for making me sit in for him at table tonight,"

Morgan said, as he and Richenda shed their hooded cloaks in the warm room. "Do you have any idea how boring it was, having to play at being the gracious host while I knew you and Dhugal were already here, making preparations? And why is it so hot in here?"

"Because," said Richenda, loosening the throat of his tunic, "the windows are closed and you've let yourself get in a dither." She glanced at Duncan. "I suspect it will be warmer still in the chapel, with as many bodies as we're going to have generating heat. Is there *any* ventilation in there?"

Duncan smiled and shook his head as he seated her at the table.

"Very little, I'm afraid. We'll just have to cope as best we can."

A second knock at the door heralded the arrival of Arilan, immediately bringing a greater degree of formality to the gathering. He glanced half disapprovingly at Dhugal as he swept past all of them to inspect the preparations in the chapel, calling Duncan to join him for several minutes.

When the two bishops rejoined the others now waiting expectantly around the table, Arilan automatically assumed the role of senior, gesturing briskly for them to be seated as he took his seat. He did not seem to notice that Morgan and Richenda had neatly interposed themselves to either side of him, thus shielding him from close proximity to either Duncan or Dhugal. Later on, Arilan would be too busy to notice any hint of the true relationship between father and son, but for now, it had been agreed that they would take no chances.

"Naturally, it will be Kelson's part to direct matters when we actually begin," Arilan said quietly. "However, until he and our—ah—subject actually arrive, I believe a period of meditation would not be amiss for any of us. A great deal of this will be new to young Dhugal, so I suggest we join hands around the table before we begin centering. The physical link will help to balance out the disparities in our levels of experience."

An expected hint of condescension was in his tone, but even Dhugal sensed Arilan meant well. Without demur they joined hands and obeyed, gazing through the candleflame for focus at first, then gradually dropping, one by one, into deeper rapport; breathing more slowly, eyes closing, even

Dhugal easing at last into calm, floating receptivity, passive
yet alert, waiting for king and kin. . . .

And in the castle, the king led their intended subject into
a darkened apartment that had been his own as prince. It
was Dhugal's now. The door was not locked, but even if it
had been, that would not have stopped a Deryni of any training whatsoever.

Drawing Nigel into the gloom and closing the door behind
him, Kelson paused just a moment to conjure handfire. The
faintly crimson ball of light cupped in his left palm revealed
a tight-jawed and apprehensive-looking Nigel, now that there
was no need to maintain the facade of casual competence he
had worn all through supper. Concerned, Kelson motioned
Nigel farther into the room, away from the door, pausing
before the darkened fireplace to turn and glance at his father's brother with apparent casualness of his own, though
his next words came of a far from casual concern for the
response he would receive.

"You don't want to back out, do you? Because even if
you did, at this late date, I couldn't let you."

Nigel managed a shaky grin and a chuckle. "Kelson, I
outweigh you by half. What would you do? Knock me out
and carry me to—where *is* it that we're going, by the way?"

"You'll see," Kelson replied. "And I'm sure you know
that I hadn't in mind to use any physical force."

"I hadn't thought you would." Nigel took a deep breath.
"I *am* nervous, though. You don't begrudge me that, do
you?"

Kelson moved a step closer, relieved, and shook his head.
"Of course not. I can ease a little of that for the time being,
though, if you'd like."

"Do it, then," Nigel whispered. "But I want to be back
in complete control before it's time for—the other."

"You can depend on it," Kelson said, raising his right
hand to touch Nigel's forehead as he locked the grey eyes
with his own. "Close your eyes and take a deep breath. . . ."

With a little shudder, Nigel obeyed.

"Now hold it for a count of five—and let it out. Feel the
apprehension drain away as you empty your lungs, until
you've reached a level of lower tension that you can handle.
Have another breath if you need to." He dropped his hand

as Nigel breathed in deeply again. "Now let it out and look at me."

As Nigel exhaled with a whoosh, his eyes fluttered open and he blinked.

"Better?" Kelson asked.

Nigel nodded bewilderedly. "A little dizzy—as if I'd had a glass of heavy wine on an empty-stomach."

"That will pass," Kelson said, turning away and pacing off a few precise steps to the left of the fireplace. "Now I'm going to show you something I first learned from Morgan. After tonight, you'll be able to do it, too. Are you watching?"

"Yes."

He could feel Nigel standing at his right shoulder, far steadier than he had been, and sensed that at least a part of his uncle's new calm had come as much from his own strength of character and trust as from anything Kelson had done. That was reassuring, for Kelson himself was not without his own apprehensions about the work ahead, though for different reasons than Nigel.

Lifting the handfire still cupped in his left hand, he raised his right hand as well to trace a smooth, intricate pattern in the air with his forefinger. A psychic triggering went along with the physical act, but Nigel would receive that along with the rest of the night's accomplishments.

"I—don't think I caught that," Nigel whispered, gasping as a section of the wall swung back to reveal a dark stairwell.

Kelson smiled and stepped into the opening, turning to beckon Nigel to follow.

"Don't worry. You'll remember if there's need. Many of the Haldane powers operate that way." As he started down the shadowy stairs, Nigel had to scramble to keep up.

"In fact," Kelson went on, "I'm going to try to give you a few limited abilities tonight, even though we're primarily just setting your potential. Some of mine started coming through in Father's lifetime, so I don't see that there's any conflict. We'd better be quiet now, though. We'll be passing close to some occupied parts of the castle, and I shouldn't want anyone to think they're hearing ghosts in the walls."

Nigel snorted at that, but they traversed the rest of the passage in red-lit silence, halting finally before an apparently blank wall. There Kelson quenched his handfire and peered for a long time through a peephole set at eye level. Then a narrow section of the wall was swinging back silently and a lighter patch of courtyard lay before them in the starlight.

The passage closed silently behind them as they emerged. Ahead, the silhouette of Saint Hilary's-Within-the-Walls loomed black against the dark night sky, the darkness broken by the occasional glint of starlight on shadowed glass. Kelson made no attempt to conceal their passage as he led Nigel briskly across the yard. Not until they had almost reached the top of the steps leading to a western door did Nigel see why.

"All's well, Sire," said Sean Lord Derry, stepping from the shadow of a column to give casual salute. "The others are already inside."

Kelson nodded. "You've posted adequate guards around the yard?"

"Lord Dhugal's own borderers, Sire." Derry's grin flashed in the darkness. "They have very precise orders."

"Thank you. I'm certain they have." Without further ado, he drew Nigel through the postern door and into the narthex.

The inside of Saint Hilary's had changed little since Kelson had come here the night before his coronation, he the subject that night, and Morgan the escort. It seemed, perhaps, a little brighter. To either side of the high altar, in what would have been the transepts of a larger church, racks of votive candles glowed sapphire and crimson before secondary altars to the Blessed Virgin and the church's patron, Saint Hilary. In the sanctuary itself, the expected Presence lamp burned above the tabernacle set behind the altar, where the Reserved Sacrament kept a place of honor. Nothing moved besides the captive flames dancing behind bright glass, but foreboding washed over Kelson like a wave—Nigel's as much as his own, Kelson suddenly realized.

Time to set things into proper balance and get on with it. Further delay would only make it more difficult for both of them.

"We'll pray for a moment before we join the others," he said softly, leading Nigel resolutely down the side aisle to a pew near the front, where he and his uncle knelt side by side.

When Kelson had finished, and composed himself to face the others, he reached out with his mind and released the slight control he had been holding on Nigel. As he raised his head, Nigel looked up with a start.

"I'm going to leave you to meditate for a few more minutes on your own," Kelson said. "When you're ready, you can join us in Duncan's study. We'll know when you've come to the door."

Nigel swallowed and managed a weak smile. "You've let me go, haven't you?"

Kelson nodded.

"You're sure I'll come?"

"Quite sure."

# CHAPTER FOUR

*This is the faithful and prudent steward, whom
the master will set over his household.*

—Luke 12:42

As the door closed behind Kelson, Nigel let out a slow, apprehensive sigh and slumped back on his heels, letting his back take support from the edge of the seat behind him. In a few minutes, he must also walk through that door.

He had hoped never to have to face what would presently be required of him—not out of any fear for his own safety or comfort, but for what tonight's work implied. To take upon himself the potential for the ancient Haldane power was to acknowledge, in a far more concrete way than hitherto, the possibility that he himself might one day be king. *That* was what frightened him.

For he had never sought or even idly wished for the crown. Until Brion's death, he had lived his life in the pleasant limbo of a much-loved younger son—close to the crown, unshakably loyal to it, whether worn by father, elder brother, or brother's son, but confident and relieved that he himself should never wear it. That was for his nephew's heirs, in the fullness of time; and Nigel was content with that.

And yet, if Kelson should perish before an heir could be engendered, then the crown *must* pass to Nigel or *his* heirs. That was a grim possibility Nigel had known from the moment Brion died—and something he prayed fervently would never come to pass. But if it did, then Nigel must be prepared to take up the mantle of his royal duty; must stand ready to sacrifice his own wishes for the good of the land. He felt himself a far from worthy vessel, but he must be ready to meet the test, if it was demanded of him. Tonight was the first step toward that readiness.

Still reluctant, then, but resigned, and with a weight of far more than years resting on his shoulders, he rose and dared to approach the high altar, lifting his eyes to the Christus gazing down at him even as he sank to one knee at the foot of the altar steps. He did not often feel the need for a physical expression of his religious feeling. Like Brion, he preferred to witness for his faith through the example of an upright life, rather than spend overmuch time on his knees, in a building that took the place of belief for many folk. Tonight, however, had its special demands, and seemed to demand more formal observance.

A little awkwardly, then, he bowed his head and framed his thoughts in far more formal petition than was usually his wont, entreating the Anointed One for strength to endure, should he be called one day to his own anointing as Gwynedd's king, but praying also that such fate should never come to him. He asked as well for courage to face the more immediate ordeal—but he would suffer that gladly if it might permit the greater cup of kingship to pass.

Whatever was given him, he knew that in the end he could only offer all he had, and pray that it would be enough. He would serve his king as he had always served, with faith, loyalty, and love, and he would either live or perish according to God's will. When he rose to join those who awaited him, turning inward now to draw his strength, his steps were steady and his head was clear.

He heard no sound as he passed through the doorway where Kelson had gone. A short corridor lay beyond, and as he closed the door behind him, another door opened ahead and to the left. Duncan inclined his head in silent greeting and stood aside to let him pass, both reassuring and vaguely alien in his episcopal purple.

The room Nigel entered was strange to him as well, of fair size, but lit only dimly by the light of a low fire immediately to the right and a single candle on the table before it. Weapons lay on the table: several daggers, a narrow stiletto Nigel thought he remembered seeing in Morgan's hand from time to time, and a sword in a scabbard set with cairngorms that was definitely Morgan's. Dhugal stood behind the table, his own sheathed sword cradled in the crook of one arm, the baldric wound loosely around the scabbard. There was no sign of Kelson or any of the others he had been expecting to see.

"I'll relieve you of your cloak first of all," Duncan said, already reaching for the garment as Nigel unsnapped the clasp and let it fall away from his shoulders. "I'll also ask you to leave your weapons here. The others are in a small chapel through that door," the bishop went on, nodding past Dhugal with his chin, "but only Kelson's sword is permitted inside."

He draped the cloak over a chair that already held several others as Nigel began obediently unbuckling his swordbelt, and caught the weight of the weapon as the belt came free. He coiled the white leather around the scabbard and laid it on the table with the others as Nigel produced a sheathed dagger from the small of his back and a stiletto from a narrow sheath in the side of his boot.

"Any more?" Duncan asked, with a faint grin. "You and Alaric are two of a kind when it comes to sharp, pointed things. Incidentally, I suggest you take off any outer layers you think you can spare; the rest of us have already done so. It's going to be a little close in there, with so many people."

Managing a snort of appreciation at the attempt to lighten the mood, Nigel removed a belt of metal placques set low on his hips, ducked out of the heavy, linked collar of his princely rank, then began unbuttoning a long, wine-colored overtunic with running lions intertwined around hem and cuffs. Now he noticed that Dhugal had already stripped to shirt and trews and boots, though Duncan's concession to undress appeared to be an open collar and the omission of his cincture.

"Why do I get the distinct impression that it's going to be more than 'close' in there?" he said. "I thought you Deryni could do something about such things."

"We can," Duncan returned. "But it would take energy we'll need for other things tonight. Besides, *you're* not Deryni."

"I take your point. I don't suppose you considered a different chapel?"

"Not for tonight's work," came the reply. "We'll be working under the protection of Saint Camber. I trust that doesn't surprise you?"

"Surprise me? Hardly. I can't say it reassures me, but it doesn't surprise me."

He knew he was talking to cover his persistent nervousness—and that Duncan knew it. Impatient with himself, he tugged loose three more buttons—enough to let the tunic fall around his feet—and stepped out of the pool of wine-dark wool. He would be well rid of it if it was going to be as warm as Duncan hinted. Beneath it he wore close-fitting britches of burgundy wool, midcalf boots dyed to match, and a full-sleeved shirt of fine linen. He untied the laces at the throat as he bent to pick up his discarded tunic, making a calming little ritual of folding the garment and laying it neatly atop his cloak before looking back at Duncan again, aware that he could delay no longer.

"I suppose I'm ready, then," he said.

Duncan lowered his eyes, obviously aware of what Nigel was feeling.

"You can have a few more minutes, if you'd like." He glanced to his right, where Dhugal had taken up a guard post beside the chapel door. "There's a prie-dieu there in the corner. You're welcome to use it."

Deep in the shadows, Nigel could see two red votive lights burning before a small ivory crucifix, the vague outline of a kneeler before them, but he shook his head.

"I'm as ready as I'll ever be, Duncan," he murmured. "You know I've never been much on ceremony."

"Come, then," Duncan said with a smile, taking him by the elbow and leading him toward the door Dhugal guarded. "As you know, you're going to have to bear with *some* ceremony tonight, but we've tried to keep things reasonably informal. It could be worse."

"It could?"

"Of course." Duncan gave him a reassuring smile. "You're an adult, coming into this of your own free will, able to give us your conscious cooperation. If you were a child, things would be totally out of your hands."

Nigel snorted at that, wondering whether it had *ever* really been in his hands—then flashed for an instant on the sudden realization that one day it might be Conall or Rory or Payne approaching the ordeal he himself now must face. The thought chilled him—it should be *Kelson's* son walking toward the door he now approached with Duncan; not himself or his own sons—but all of that was academic in the immediate reckoning. For now, there was no turning back.

Nigel had to duck a little as he followed Duncan past the curtain Dhugal held aside. The chamber beyond was dim and close—half the size of the room they had just left, and almost crowded even before they entered. Arilan and Morgan stood against the walls to left and right, Richenda, all in white, immediately to his right against the back wall, but it was Kelson who caught and arrested his attention immediately.

His nephew—no, *the king*—the king stood with his back to them in the precise center of the room, raven head flung back and hands hanging easily at his sides. He was more than human or Deryni in that moment of Nigel's first beholding, sacred kingship lying upon his shoulders as puissant and apparent as any physical mantle he had worn since his coronation day—though he, like Morgan and Nigel himself, had stripped to the basics of shirt and britches and boots, putting aside all weapons or other tangible insigniae of his rank.

The object of his attention appeared to be a very ornate crucifix of ebony suspended above an altar set hard against the eastern wall—or perhaps it was the wall itself that held his gaze, painted all around the altar and above it like the midnight sky, spangled with bright-gilt stars that caught the light from six honey-colored tapers. The stars shimmered through the heat rising from the candles, and the air tickled at Nigel's nostrils with the faint aroma of beeswax and incense.

"Come stand beside me, Uncle," Kelson said softly, turning slightly to beckon with his right hand, quicksilver eyes drawing him even if the gesture had not.

Without hesitation Nigel obeyed, taking the proffered hand and bobbing briefly to one knee to press it to his forehead in homage before straightening at his sovereign's side. Duncan passed to Kelson's other side and approached the altar—but a few steps in the confines of this tiny chamber— and Nigel dared a glance at Morgan, back pressed against the southern wall and arms folded across his chest, almost close enough to touch. As their eyes met, Morgan inclined his head slightly in a nod meant to be reassuring, then turned his gaze deliberately toward the altar, where Arilan had joined Duncan in the preparation of a thurible. Dutifully Nigel turned his attention that way as well.

They would ward the chamber first; he knew that. He even knew a little about warding. He had seen Morgan ward a circle once, long ago, when Morgan helped Brion assume his full Haldane powers before the battle with the Marluk. Nigel had been nineteen, Brion twenty-five, Morgan not yet fourteen.

Many years later, there had been another warding as well: in a tent at Llyndruth Meadows, the night before the final confrontation between Kelson and Wencit of Torenth. He had seen only the beginnings of that warding; that was the night he had learned that Arilan was Deryni. He remembered little else besides black and white cubes and Arilan's hand touching his forehead—and Kelson's eyes boring into his until he thought his very soul must be sucked out of his body.

Since then, he had learned not to fight or fear that kind of mental touch. Something akin to that would happen again tonight, but he put that knowledge from his mind for the moment and set his attention on the two bishops. Arilan was beginning: censing the altar and the East and then moving to his right toward the space between Nigel and Morgan.

They would cast a triple circle first. As they trod the circle, they would invoke the protection of the four great Archangels who guarded the Quarters and ruled the elements. Duncan was already aspersing the East with holy water, preparing to follow Arilan in the second circle. Morgan would cast the third with a sword.

The South was Nigel's especial favorite, however: first of the Quarters to be saluted after the East, where Morgan still stood and Arilan now paused to bow—for the South was the realm of Saint Michael, familiar to Nigel as the patron of warriors long before he learned the Prince of Heaven's other, more esoteric attributes.

To Saint Michael had Nigel pledged a special devotion those many years before, as he kept his knight's vigil before receiving the accolade from his brother. God willing, perhaps his son would conceive a like devotion. Before another year was out—if they all lived that long—Conall, Kelson, and Dhugal would keep their own knights' vigil, and receive the knightly accolade from *his* hand. He suspected that Kelson and Dhugal would reserve their special devotion to Saint Camber—which was certainly fitting—but he knew they reverenced Michael as well. He was surprised to realize that he did not know his own sons' feelings on the matter.

That realization so occupied him for the next few seconds that he was not aware when Morgan moved from South to altar—only that Morgan was suddenly there, drawing the fine-wrought scabbard from Kelson's sword—Brion's sword, his father's sword! Spellbound, he watched Morgan raise the blade in reverent salute to the East, candlelight flashing down the polished steel and taking on a life of its own—remembering another Morgan, another Nigel, a Brion still alive, as Morgan leveled the blade at eye level and slowly began to retrace Arilan's and Duncan's paths.

Light streamed from the tip of the blade as Morgan walked, scribing a ribbon of blue-white brilliance a handspan wide along the wall behind the altar. It floated with substance of its own where the tip of the blade bridged the southeast corner of the room, curving in a blue-white streak to follow all across the South.

Nigel watched Morgan's progress on toward the West until he could no longer follow without turning his body as well, catching just a glimpse of Richenda stepping closer to him, away from the West wall, so that Morgan could pass between it and her. The chamber was growing uncomfortably warm, as Duncan had warned, but he thought he could feel cold radiating from the ribbon of light. He shivered a little despite the sweat trickling between his shoulderblades and plastering his shirt to his back.

At the altar, their circuits completed, Arilan and Duncan replaced thurible and aspergillum on the altar, and backed off to stand directly in front of Kelson and Nigel as Morgan continued past the North and closed the ring of the circle in the East. The ribbon of light clung to the walls like a physical thing, pulsing slightly.

Saluting again, Morgan laid the sword back on the altar beside its sheath and came to stand behind Nigel, at Richenda's right. Nigel suddenly wondered what the circle looked like to Dhugal, standing just outside, in the doorway to the chamber—whether it floated across the doorway the same way it arched in the corners.

"We stand outside time, in a place not of earth," Arilan said quietly. "As our ancestors before us bade, we join together and are One."

"Amen," the others responded.

Nigel could feel the faint breeze of a flowing sleeve brush his back, and sensed the shadow of Richenda's hand raised between him and Kelson.

"Before us . . . *Ra-fa-el* . . ." Richenda intoned, chanting the syllables of the name with an odd inflection and holding the last note.

As the note died, he sensed her hand moving and saw a circle of black appear in the ribbon of light stretched above the altar. He stifled a little gasp, but the others seemed unperturbed.

"God has healed," Richenda said in a normal tone.

"God has healed," the others repeated.

Confused, he let himself be turned to face the south. Morgan was beside him now, Richenda behind Morgan. Again she stetched forth her hand.

"Before us . . . *Mi-ka-il* . . ."

Again, the prolonged note, the movement of her hand as the note died—only this time, a red glowing triangle pierced the ribbon of light, pulsing like a heartbeat.

"Who is like God," Richenda said this time.

"Who is like God," the others repeated.

Again they all turned, now facing the west. Beyond the ribbon of light, which *did* hang in midair where it crossed the recess of the doorway, he could just see Dhugal, looking very solemn.

"Before us . . . *Ji-bra-il* . . ."

A crescent of white light for the West.

"God is my strength," Richenda said.

"God is my strength," Nigel repeated with the others. He had suddenly realized that the phrases were translations of the names of the Archangels being invoked, the symbolism doubtless drawn from Richenda's eastern origins.

On to the North.

"Before us . . . *Au-ri-el* . . ."

A golden square here.

"Fire of God."

"Fire of God," came the response.

He started to turn again to the east, but Morgan pulled him back a step instead. Kelson also took a step away from him before turning, so that all at once everyone was facing toward the center. Richenda, her loose-fitting shift a luminous white by circle-light, spread both palms before her at waist level and closed her eyes.

"At our center and foundation is Spirit—that which endures."

As she moved her hands slightly apart and tilted them toward one another, a five-pointed star appeared in the air between them, etched in violet light. It floated to the floor as she parted them still farther, pulsing against the stone as she threw back her head and stretched her palms heavenward this time.

"Above us, the circled cross: defining and containing, unity of all contained within One."

As the symbol appeared, green fire hanging above their heads, she swept her arms to either side and held, eyes closing, but it was Arilan who spoke.

"Now we are met. Now we are One with the Light. Regard the ancient ways. We shall not walk this path again.

"*Augeatur in nobis, quaesumus, Domine, tuae virtutis operatio. . . .*" May the working of Thy power, O Lord, be intensified within us. . . .

"So be it. Selah. Amen," Richenda responded.

And as she lowered her arms, bowing her head over hands joined palm-to-palm in an attitude of prayer, the ribbon of light around the room quickly broadened and extended upward and downward until its edges met in the symbols above their heads and beneath their feet. Then all six symbols vanished. Glancing surreptitiously toward the doorway, Nigel could no longer see Dhugal except as a vague, shadowy form.

"*Lumen Christi gloriose resurgentis sissipet tenebras cordis et mentis,*" Kelson intoned steadily, signing himself in ritual gesture as the others did the same. May the light of Christ rising in glory scatter the darkness of our heart and mind. . . .

The motion seemed to release them from a former immobility. Suddenly Kelson was smiling at him, Arilan and Richenda withdrawing slightly to stand against the northern and western walls. Morgan took his elbow.

"Well, that's done," Kelson said softly. "The warding was drawn partly from the tradition that Richenda grew up in. Other than the Moorish elements that have crept in over the years, it's supposed to be fairly close to the form Camber might have used. Not that we'll ever know for certain, I suppose." He glanced at Morgan, at Duncan, who had moved to the altar, then back at Nigel.

"Are you ready?"

Nigel only inclined his head, afraid to speak.

"We'll get on with it, then. Come with me, please."

Three steps brought them to the altar. Duncan's small surgical kit lay open there, Duncan doing something with a wad of cotton wool and a small flask. As Morgan assisted Nigel to kneel, Kelson reached to his right ear and removed the great ruby fastened there. For the first time, Nigel noticed that Kelson also wore the Ring of Fire, the garnet-studded seal of Brion's power, great central cabochon surrounded by a dozen lesser, brilliant-cut stones that fractured the cold light of the circle like summer lightning. He did not think he had seen it since Kelson's coronation.

"So far as we know, the Eye of Rom has always played a part in the setting of the Haldane potential in Haldane heirs," Kelson said, handing the earring to Duncan for cleansing. "It and a ring seem to be important and constant elements in the power rituals of all Haldane kings. Because you aren't my heir in the usual sense, we'll only involve the ring marginally tonight, since it usually seals the ritual after the old king is dead, but I do want you to wear the Eye. I'll leave both in a place of safety here at Rhemuth before I go to Meara—just in case you should need them."

Nigel swallowed and managed a faint nod, eyeing the jewel as it was passed back to Kelson, and Duncan moved closer with the wad of cotton wool. As Morgan held his head steady from behind and Duncan swabbed his earlobe with something cool and pungent—welcome relief in the heat—Nigel braced himself for the bite of a needle, but it came as only a slight pressure and popping sound. He wondered whether Morgan had blunted that sensation for him. Intrigued now despite his apprehension, he watched Kelson remove the Ring of Fire and bring it close to his ear for a few brief seconds—marking it with his blood, he sensed—then lay it on the altar. Next, the Eye of Rom was brought close in a similar manner, though Kelson's hand came away empty this time.

Nigel felt a brief sting as Duncan threaded the earring's wire through his flesh, faint weight of the stone as adjustments were made to its fastening, but then Duncan did something else and the sting became a tingle and then nothing. As the bishop withdrew and Morgan released him, Nigel brushed the earring lightly with his fingertip. He was surprised to feel no discomfort.

"We've healed that for you," Morgan murmured, helping him to stand.

Somehow that did not surprise him. Nor did the piece of parchment lying on the altar, inscribed with all his royal names.

"I am told that the Deryni have a tradition of Naming their children by means of a brief magical ritual," Kelson said quietly, drawing the parchment nearer the edge and reaching for the tip of the sword with his right hand as Duncan steadied the hilt. "The child's mother generally performs this ritual between the ages of four and eight, depending upon the maturity of the child. Besides confirming the child's bloodline as Deryni, it is also the first formal ritual in which most Deryni children are involved."

He met Nigel's eyes briefly and managed a quick, nervous grin. "I daresay, I am hardly your mother, and you have a few more years than eight. Still, this *will* be your first true ritual experience. And it *does* provide a useful framework in which to shift the succession to your bloodline—if only for the present. As one might suppose, a shedding of blood is required."

He ducked his head at that. Nigel suddenly realized that Kelson was as nervous about the whole affair as he was. Holding the end of the blade over the parchment, grasped firmly between the thumb and first two fingers of his right hand, Kelson drew the tip of his left ring finger along the edge until blood welled from a fairly deep cut. His jaw tightened at the sight, whether from pain or some other emotion Nigel could not tell, but he made no sound, only touching the blood to the parchment beneath Nigel's name with solemn deliberation. He held the wounded finger curled into the palm of his hand as he surrendered his place to Nigel.

"Now yours," he said softly.

The blade itself held no terror for Nigel; as a soldier, he had sustained far greater wounds than was required now. Grasping the blade as Kelson had done, he drew his fingertip along the sharpened steel in a brisk stroke, letting the slight burning sensation of the cut help keep him from thinking about what might come next. When he had smudged his blood alongside Kelson's on the parchment, the king pressed their wounds together briefly in further symbolism of the joining of the two bloodlines.

"By this mingling of blood do I acknowledge thee Haldane: Nigel Cluim Gwydion Rhys, son of King Donal Blaine

Aidan Cinhil and only brother of King Brion Donal Cinhil Urien, who was my father and king before me.''

There was a bowl for rinsing off the blood after that, linen for drying, then Morgan's hand enclosing Nigel's wound briefly while Duncan ministered to Kelson. When Morgan released him, the wound was gone as if it had never been. As Nigel stared at his finger in the candlelight, Duncan wiped the sword clean with a linen cloth, then handed it off to Morgan, who reversed the blade and took up a guard position immediately behind Nigel, hands resting on the quillons. Nigel heard Kelson give a little sigh as Duncan pulled the thurible closer, still smoking slightly of incense, and opened it to the smoldering charcoal within.

"Be thou blessed by Him in Whose honor thou shalt be burnt," Duncan murmured, tracing a cross in the air over the incense boat before offering it to Kelson.

Kelson bowed over the incense, hands joined before him in an attitude of prayer, then took the spoon and carefully sprinkled a few grains of incense onto the charcoal.

"Welcome as incense smoke let my prayer rise up before Thee, O Lord. When I lift my hands, may it be acceptable as the evening sacrifice.''

The chamber was so still and silent, Nigel could hear the faint hiss of the resin beginning to melt. As sweet smoke started spiraling upward, Kelson took the parchment and creased it loosely into quarters, then touched one corner to the glowing coal.

"May this offering blessed by Thee ascend to Thee, O Lord," he said, laying the parchment full on the coal as it caught and began to burn. "And may Thy mercy descend upon Thy servants, both present and to come.''

When he was sure it was burning well, he turned once more to Nigel. Arilan had joined them at the conclusion of the prayer, and now took from the altar a thumb-sized brass container and a small ivory spatula.

"Bishop Arilan has offered to provide you with a little assistance for the last part of the ritual," Kelson said, as Duncan pushed back Nigel's right sleeve to expose the inner forearm and Arilan unscrewed the lid of the container. "The drug is sometimes used in the early phases of formal Deryni training to enhance psychic response. It also has a slight sedative effect.''

Wordlessly Arilan set aside the lid and dipped out a minuscule amount of viscous, butter-colored unguent with the spatula. This he spread in a thin film over a thumb-sized area of Nigel's inner arm, which Duncan then bound neatly with a strip of linen bandage.

"The drug is gradually absorbed through the skin," Duncan explained. "When we're done, we wash off the residue and the effect stops soon after. That makes it far easier to control than if you had taken a specific dose by mouth."

Nigel cradled the bandaged forearm close to his chest and fingered the linen nervously. He was beginning to sweat profusely, whether from the drug or not, he had no idea.

"It tingles a little," he said. "Sweet *Jesu*, it's hot in here!"

"You're feeling several effects already," Arilan replied, handing him a towel and watching him closely. "How's your vision?"

Nigel wiped his face on the towel and blinked several times, feeling slightly befuddled, then closed his eyes briefly and opened them again.

"I'm having trouble focusing," he whispered. "I feel a little—dizzy, too."

"Look at me for a moment," Arilan commanded.

Swaying a little on his feet, so that Duncan and Morgan had to steady him on either side, Nigel obeyed.

"His eyes are dilated," he heard Kelson murmur.

"Aye. Get him down before he falls down," came Arilan's low reply.

Nigel needed no encouragement to collapse to all fours. Light-headed and rapidly losing all sense of balance, he let them help him to a sitting position on the floor. His arms and legs seemed to have no bones in them. The stone floor was cool and soothing, and he wanted to lay his forehead against it, but Morgan knelt behind him and made him sit upright, providing a backrest for him to lean against.

He could not focus even as far as his toes. His hands lolled useless at his sides, but at least he could press the backs against the stone for relief from the heat now pulsing through his body with every heartbeat. The added warmth of Morgan's body against his back was almost unbearable until he felt the sword slip between them, the blade chill as ice along his spine. As he turned his head blearily to see what Duncan was doing, he glimpsed one quillon above his head and to the side.

Duncan had the thurible as he knelt to Nigel's right. Kelson was on his knees as well, but he loomed in Nigel's vision like a darkling giant, forbidding and austere. Far more slowly than seemed right, Kelson's reached into the thurible to crush a pinch of ash between thumb and forefinger, free hand burning Nigel's shoulder where it touched to steady him.

"Nigel Cluim Gwydion Rhys," Kelson breathed, touching Nigel between the eyes with a sooty forefinger and tracing a cross, "I seal thee Haldane and confirm thee as Heir until such time as I may produce an heir of my body."

Nigel trembled beneath his touch, tears welling in his eyes as Kelson reached again to the thurible to take another meager pinch of ash. The left hand shifted to his jaw, pressing his cheeks to make his mouth open—and he could offer not a shred of resistance.

"Taste of the ashes of our mingled blood," Kelson went on, sifting some of the ash onto Nigel's tongue. "By blood art thou consecrated to the Haldane legacy. If it should come to thee, *be* The Haldane. Then shall the power come upon thee."

The ash was bitter—bitter as the cup Nigel prayed he would never have to drink—and as the consecrated royal hands lifted slowly toward his head, Nigel felt a primal terror of the power latent there. In that interminable instant, the king seemed limned in fire—dread sovereign and master of all the power in the universe, not merely king and lord of the lands of their fathers—and Nigel feared that if Kelson touched him, he would die.

He had neither strength nor will to resist it, though; this cup, at least, must be drunk to its dregs—and the dregs were already bitter on his tongue. As the royal hands embraced his head, the thumbs pressing lightly on his temples, he closed his eyes with a shudder and surrendered any last resistance. The hands were hot, searing his flesh, making his fear boil up within him like molten lead, threatening to explode inside his brain.

But he did not explode. Not then, at least. The fire remained, but now another pressure began to build within him like a great wind, relentless and strong, scouring away the last vestiges of his will, pounding again and again in a rhythm a part of him only vaguely recognized as his own heartbeat.

The wind became a firestorm then, raging inside his mind and licking at his body, so terrifying that he was sure the very flesh must melt from his bones.

Water, then, quenching the fire but sweeping him away, out of his body, whirling and tumbling him in total disorientation, slamming him at last upon a stony beach where he seemed to lie and gaze numbly at a grey, fog-shrouded sky.

Until a face appeared against the fog: a kindly compassionate face framed by soft, silver-gilt hair; the eyes like windows to the fog beyond, calling him, drawing him, as a hand reached out to gently touch his forehead.

The touch sent him plummeting into nothingness.

# CHAPTER FIVE

*He shall direct his counsel and knowledge, and
in his secrets shall he meditate.*
—Ecclesiasticus 39:7

Nigel's vision stunned Kelson, but he kept both his reaction and the very fact that he had perceived the vision
carefully shielded from the others for the balance of the ritual. He suspected that Morgan and Duncan might have
glimpsed it as well, being part of the primary link, but if they
had, they followed his lead and gave no indication of it. Some
instinct warned that Arilan should not learn of it, so Kelson
forced himself to shutter away the information while he completed what he had started. With the unconscious Nigel now
open to his will, it was the work of only a few minutes to
finish keying in Morgan and Duncan, then to add Arilan and
Richenda to the chain that would enable them to trigger Nigel's Haldane potential in the event of Kelson's premature
death.

The process took energy, and the heat and closeness of
the room were taking their toll, but Kelson was not really
tired by the time he was finished. Still, he set Morgan to take
over monitoring Nigel's vital signs, himself standing apart
to watch in silence as Duncan and Arilan unbandaged Nigel's
arm and carefully washed off the residue of Arilan's drug.
He hoped that Arilan, at least, attributed his silence to fatigue and the need for introspection that often came after a
powerful working, for neither the vision nor his reticence to
tell Arilan of it had faded.

But Arilan seemed unaware. As soon as he and Duncan had finished, Kelson dropped heavily to his knees once more beside the still unconscious Nigel and bade the others close the circle. If Arilan read that as confirmation of fatigue, so much the better, for it might forestall further questioning later on; and in the meantime, the ritual kept Arilan too busy to pay close attention to him.

Kelson tried to keep his mind mirror-still as Arilan and the others wound the ritual to its proper conclusion, and he began shooing them out as soon as the last glimmer of the wards had died. He doubted anyone had much inclination to linger in the chapel overlong, for the hour's working in so close a space had made the temperature most uncomfortable, but he especially did not want to be left alone with Arilan. A chapel sacred to Saint Camber was no place to try to hide a vision of that saint from a high adept like Arilan.

With that in mind, then, he signed for Arilan and Richenda to precede him out, himself lingering only long enough to help Morgan and Duncan get Nigel on his feet. He trailed behind them as they half walked and half carried Nigel back into the study, giving Dhugal a fleeting smile and a brush of hand on shoulder as he emerged from behind the curtain his foster brother held.

Arilan was waiting just beyond, Richenda moving with Morgan, Duncan, and Nigel toward the chairs by the fireplace. Fortunately for Kelson, passing into the relative chill of the study set him to sneezing before Arilan could do more than open his mouth. At once, Dhugal was laying a cloak around his shoulders and insisting that he join the others by the fire, solicitous and almost a little alarmed. The grateful Kelson played the scene for its full distraction value, making a show of bundling the cloak around his body and wiping his sweaty face on the sleeve of his shirt. By the time he had huddled down in the chair next to Nigel's, he was not having to feign shivering.

"Are you all right?" Morgan asked, turning from Nigel long enough to lay the back of a hand against Kelson's forehead.

Kelson nodded, gesturing back to Nigel with his chin.

"What about him?"

"He'll be coming around in a few minutes," Duncan said, gently peeling back one of Nigel's eyelids. "The drug's almost worn off. He's going to want a lot of sleep, though."

Arilan grimaced and pulled his cincture from one of the piles of clothing shed earlier. The grimace became a scowl as he began wrapping it around his waist.

"Does that surprise you?" he muttered. "Whatever he experienced, it hit him like a wall. I don't suppose any of you can tell me what happened in there?"

Kelson shrugged noncommittally. "We did what we set out to do." He glanced at his uncle again. "And frankly, I would have been surprised if it *hadn't* hit him like a wall, as you so aptly put it. I suspect it's distinctly Haldane. Having been through it myself, I doubt anyone can appreciate the full impact unless he's also been through it. You can tell that to the Council if you like. That *is* where you're going when you leave here, isn't it?"

Arilan's mouth twitched in annoyance, though he tried to make it look like a grimace of frustration as he did up the collar of his cassock.

"Don't sound so accusatory, son. We may not have spoken of it directly, but surely you realized that I'd have to report on what you've done."

"Forgive me if it seems a lot like spying," Kelson countered. He nodded thanks as Richenda handed him a cup of pale wine. "They can't have it both ways indefinitely, you know. They've been vacillating for more than two years now, trying to decide whether I'm fish or fowl—and if *my* status is still in question, then Alaric and Duncan must still be in the insect category. God knows what they think of Dhugal!"

As he gestured curtly with his cup toward his foster brother, who was trying to become invisible before this increasingly heated exchange between king and bishop, Arilan glanced in Dhugal's direction, smiled wryly, and pulled his cloak from a chair.

"If we continue this discussion, we shall quarrel. And I'd have you at a distinct disadvantage, fatigued as you are." He slung the cloak around his shoulders and glanced around the room speculatively as he tied the ribbons at his throat.

"Now, I seem to recall that you have a Portal here somewhere, Duncan. I should like to use it, if I may. I *am* going to the Council now, Sire, but I assure you that I shall be as objective as possible in my reporting."

Kelson still had distinct misgivings, but there was no point belaboring the issue. Whether or not Kelson liked it, the

Council was going to know about Nigel before the night was out. He had known that from the moment he even considered asking Arilan's assistance. And at least if Arilan left now, Kelson would not have to risk him learning about the Camber vision.

"Show him the Portal," he said to Dhugal.

He turned his head away at Arilan's sardonic little bow of thanks, knowing it would irk Arilan just a little that even Dhugal knew of the Portal, where Arilan did not.

Arilan said nothing—merely acknowledged Dhugal with a curt nod and stepped onto the Portal when Dhugal had pulled aside the tapestry that covered the doorway; then he was gone.

Kelson sighed explosively and tossed off his cup of wine, stretching out his legs toward the fire to rest his boots on the raised hearth.

"Bloody Camberian Council!" he muttered.

Morgan raised an eyebrow, a little surprised at the king's outburst—though he quite agreed with the assessment.

"Come, now. This is hardly the first time Arilan has gone running back to the Council to report what we're doing."

"No—though in all fairness to Arilan, he's made no real secret of it, at least to me. In his way, I suppose he's trying to be open-minded."

"As an individual, that may well be," Morgan said guardedly. "You're certainly in a far better position to know about such things than I. From my own observation, however, I can't say that the apparent attitude of the Council as a whole has been anything but disturbing."

"I'd rather not talk about them," Kelson said quietly.

Morgan and Duncan exchanged glances, and Richenda withdrew unobtrusively to perch on a low stool beyond them and Nigel. Dhugal, still a little rattled by Arilan's comments and departure, took up a cautious post to Kelson's right.

"Kelson, we know you'd rather not," Morgan said quietly. "Unfortunately, your reticence to do so of late has hardly helped to reassure Duncan and myself. They may be courting *you*, but—"

"I don't know that I'd exactly call it courting," Kelson countered. "I may have made some progress with a few as individuals, but as a body they're still very, very conservative."

"I fear narrow-minded is nearer the mark," Duncan said. "I can only agree with Alaric. As far as we know, we're still half-breeds and outcasts where the Council is concerned—and as you yourself have pointed out, God knows what they think of Dhugal."

"Dhugal is a cypher," Kelson said, almost shortly, "and I intend that he remain so."

"And Nigel?" Richenda asked, speaking up for the first time.

Kelson set aside his cup, shaking his head. "Nigel himself can't have been any surprise to the Council. After all, they or their predecessors have been coping with Haldane heirs for two hundred years. Thank God that Arilan wasn't in the primary link, though." He shivered and looked up at Morgan and Duncan. "You do know what I'm talking about, don't you?"

The glances the two exchanged told Kelson that they knew precisely what he was talking about. Clearly Richenda did not—which meant that Arilan probably had not caught any inkling of Nigel's experience either. Dhugal, who would not have been expected to read much detail from outside the circle, even if trained—which he was not—looked predictably mystified.

Richenda's expression of speculation turned to comprehension as she laid a hand on her husband's forearm to share his memory of the experience.

"Ah, Saint Camber," she breathed. "I should have known."

Dhugal gulped and looked aghast at all of them.

"Saint Camber? What is she talking about?"

"Nigel had a—vision during the ritual," Morgan said, dragging his eyes from Richenda's to look at Dhugal. "Duncan and I caught a little of the spillover from Kelson."

"A vision? Of Saint Camber?"

Duncan nodded. "We've—ah—come into contact with him before. I must say, I certainly wasn't expecting him tonight."

"A—saint?" Dhugal only just managed to swallow.

Kelson sighed and gestured wearily toward Duncan. "Do you want to show him, Duncan?"

"Why can't *you* show me?" Dhugal asked plaintively, before Duncan could respond. "Unless you're too tired, that is. But I'm never going to learn if I only work with my father."

The request could not have been made a few months before, for it was only with the new year that Dhugal had learned to lower his shields even for Duncan. He had grown far more adept since then, working with Morgan, Kelson, and occasionally Richenda, but rapport with anyone besides Duncan still required far more effort on his part than he thought it should. Kelson knew that. So despite his fatigue, he smiled and held out his hand.

As soon as their fingers met, he could feel Dhugal's shields collapse—saw the sun-amber eyes go a little glassy as Dhugal slipped firmly, if not easily, into rapport.

He did not spare him, though. Cementing the link, he bore deep into Dhugal's mind and began to filter the memory through, beginning with Nigel's sensations as the drug took effect and his eyes began to go out of focus, and not letting up as the pain began to build along with other sensations.

Dhugal gasped and closed his eyes as the feed became more intense, inadvertently drawing back just a little, but Kelson merely shifted his hand around to grasp Dhugal's wrist and held the contact. As the link steadied, he fed the last set of images: the face against the fog, compassionate and kind; quicksilver eyes, silver-gilt hair; and the hand whose touch brought oblivion. With them he sent a montage of the other times he had seen that face, and the images of Morgan's and Duncan's sightings.

When he let the link dissolve, though not the physical one of hand to hand, Dhugal exhaled in a long, slow sigh and did not move or even open his eyes for several seconds. When he did raise his head to look at Kelson, his eyes were moist with tears.

"I—had no idea," he murmured, after a few more seconds, finally raising both hands to wipe surreptitiously at his eyes. "Do you—really think it was Saint Camber?"

Duncan smiled sympathetically and exchanged a glance with Morgan.

"Well, at least we know it wasn't Stefan Coram this time, don't we?" he said. "And I don't think it was Arilan, either."

"God, no!" Kelson said, sitting back with an explosive sigh and crossing his arms on his chest. "I don't think he caught any of it. Richenda didn't, after all. And after it was over, I was terribly anxious that he not pick up something about it from me or the two of you, before I could get rid of him. Somehow, I didn't want him to share that.''

"Perhaps because you knew he was going to the Council after he left," Morgan ventured.

"Perhaps." Kelson shook his head and sighed again. "What do *you* think, though? All of you. Was it Saint Camber?''

"Why not ask the man who saw it firsthand?" Duncan murmured, laying a hand on the forehead of the reviving Nigel. "Nigel, are you with us again? How do you feel?"

With a little moan, Nigel opened his eyes and turned his head toward Kelson, not fighting the light control Duncan extended to block any residual pain.

"Kelson," he murmured. "God, what an incredible experience! I had no idea. . . .''

Kelson grinned and laid his hand on his uncle's, glancing briefly at Duncan to shift control.

"I know. You weathered everything well, though. Do you remember any details?"

Nigel's lips parted in a slow, lazy half-smile, the grey Haldane eyes dreamy and still a little focused in some other world.

"I thought I was going to die," he said softly. "And then—you're not going to believe this—I think Saint Camber saved my life. Or at least my sanity." He turned his head to look at the rest of them searchingly, then back at Kelson. "He did. And I am *not* going mad now—am I?"

Slowly Kelson shook his head. "No, Uncle, you're not going mad. I saw him too. Alaric and Duncan—have seen him before."

"Somehow that ought to alarm me," Nigel replied, "but it doesn't. Your doing?"

"In part," Kelson admitted. "But in part, I think it goes along with what else has happened to you. Camber seems to have an affinity for us Haldanes. Now, perhaps, you understand better why I want to know more about him—maybe even restore his cult here in Gwynedd."

"I shan't argue that," Nigel answered, around a yawn. "'M too sleepy."

"The expected response," Kelson replied, giving the hand a squeeze and getting to his feet. "Are you ready to go back to your quarters?"

Nigel rose without help, if a trifle unsteadily, and gave another enormous yawn. "I think I'll sleep for a week."

"No, only until morning," Duncan said, grinning as he laid an arm around Dhugal's shoulders. "Dhugal and I leave for Kierney tomorrow, and you must see us off."

"Oh, aye," Nigel mumbled.

"Meraude's going to think he's drunk," Morgan muttered under his breath.

"Then, best she have reason to think he's been drinking," Richenda replied. Quickly she poured a cup of wine and put it in the swaying Nigel's hand. "Drink it down, Nigel. You'll sleep the better for it, too."

Nigel obeyed without hesitation, setting the empty cup back in Richenda's hand when he had finished. After he and Kelson had gone, Morgan sat down in the chair Kelson had vacated and pulled his wife down on his lap. She laughed lightly, and Duncan poured wine for all of them.

"Thank God that's over," Morgan said, lifting his cup in salute when everyone had wine. "Shall we drink to Saint Camber, King Kelson, and our fine Haldane heir?"

"To Camber, Kelson, and Nigel," Duncan agreed, raising his own cup as Richenda and Dhugal did the same.

"But how much will he remember?" Dhugal wondered, when the toast had been drunk.

"It's unclear just how much he'll remember," Arilan was saying at that very moment, addressing the other members of the Camberian Council. "He knows me as Deryni, of course, from the Portal construction at Llyndruth Meadows, but Kelson and I agreed at the time that a block should be placed to prevent him disclosing my identity to anyone else. That's held, of course."

Old Vivienne, even more irascible this evening than was usually her wont, allowed herself a sour smile. "Thank God you had the good sense to do that—and to erase that Warin person's memory of the incident altogether. I could have told you he would bolt again, once the immediate crisis of the war with Wencit had passed."

"It's true we've not heard much of Warin in the past year," Laran said, tapping his fingertips lightly together. "As a physician, I would like to have explored his healing gifts more thoroughly. Unfortunately, no one seems to know what's become of him."

"Good riddance, if you ask me," Kyri said with a toss of her flame-colored hair. "Healing by the power of God, indeed! We don't need *that* kind of superstitious nonsense!"

"However he does it, he does it," Arilan said dryly. "In any case, I hardly think Warin de Grey is the issue here. We came to discuss Prince Nigel, as I recall. I suspect that our Tiercel, at least, is bursting to hear more of the new Haldane heir—*though he will keep his peace until I have finished telling you of it, I feel certain,*" he concluded emphatically, flashing a brief but adamant glance of warning across the table.

Tiercel, on the brink of an objection, thought better of it and subsided, to the obvious relief of more than one person seated at the table.

"So," said blind Barrett, after a measured sigh at Arilan's right, "what *is* your understanding of what was done to Nigel? We must surmise that the Haldane potential was set, but was the king able to make the patterning reversible?"

"Such was his intention. However, since only Morgan and Duncan were included in the primary link, I have only Kelson's word on that."

Sofiana cocked her head to one side and studied Arilan thoughtfully. "Do you have reason to doubt him, Denis?"

"Not—exactly." He lowered his eyes, idly following the pattern he was tracing with a fingertip along the gold inlay of the table, his bishop's ring glinting in the chamber's dim illumination. "Oh, I don't doubt that the pattern was set. And we expected a powerful working. The Haldane rituals almost always are."

"Are you saying there might have been a transfer of power as well?" Tiercel asked, no longer able to contain his curiosity. "Some actual awakening of ability, I mean."

Vivienne glanced at him sharply. "Why *do* you insist upon belaboring the issue? Only one Haldane may hold the power at a time. We have gone over this time and again."

"And have never, *ever* truly answered the question!" Tiercel retorted.

"And *shall* not meddle in forbidden things!" Vivienne snapped, now openly glaring at the younger man. "Now, *will* you keep your peace, or must I invoke an official censure?"

Tiercel looked as if he might have been considering further defiance, but Sofiana, seated to his left, touched two fingers lightly to his lips in restraint.

"Enough, Tiercel," she murmured. "Now is not the time." She glanced back at Arilan, watching stoically a few places away. "What further can you tell us, Denis? By your expression, one might almost think Kelson *did* give his uncle at least a taste of power."

Arilan folded his hands carefully before him and shook his head. "It would have nothing to do with being Haldane, of course—and there are definite limits to what could be bestowed upon a human. We know of several such cases in recent years."

"Are you thinking of Bran Coris?" Laran asked.

"Aye—though one must almost wonder, in retrospect, whether he might not have been at least part Deryni himself. It hardly seems likely that Wencit would have bothered, unless there were something more to work with." He cocked his head at Sofiana in sudden speculation. "Do you know? *Was* Bran Coris Deryni?"

Sofiana gave an odd little smile that might have betokened either disdain or secret knowledge.

"If he *had* been, what does it matter, now?"

"It matters," Barrett murmured, "because he and Richenda had a son, your sister's grandson—a child who would be full Deryni, if Bran was. How old is Brendan now?"

"He will be seven in June," she replied quietly. "Unfortunately, his father was *not* Deryni."

Kyri sat back with a perplexed sigh. "You could have said as much. He's another rogue, then: Brendan, little Briony—young Dhugal MacArdry, from an even less explainable bloodline. Incidentally, Denis, how did the MacArdry boy behave? Have you any further speculations on that account?"

"None. He was door warden for the actual working. He never entered the circle. He seemed to keep his composure, so far as I could tell, but I *was* rather preoccupied." He frowned. "Come to think of it, he managed *not* to be next to me during our meditation time before things got started— whether by chance or design never occurred to me at the time. I had Morgan and Richenda to either side of me. He was between Richenda and Duncan."

Tiercel shrugged and gave an impatient sigh. "I hardly think that matters, since we're really supposed to be talking about Nigel," he said. "Touchy as Dhugal's shields are, I suspect he merely opted to minimize possible clashes. Kelson probably told him to. You certainly wouldn't have wanted that kind of distraction during the ritual."

"Thank you for bringing us back to the subject," Barrett said.

"And for refraining from your usual line of discussion," Vivienne added. "Denis, is there anything else that you can tell us about Nigel's reaction?"

Arilan shook his head. "Very little, I fear. As planned, Richenda and I were keyed in as facilitators on the secondary level—and what we were permitted to See seemed quite in keeping with what I expected." He raised an eyebrow wistfully. "Naturally, I can't give you any details of the actual process."

"Naturally," Vivienne said cynically. "He bound you by oath."

"I would think less of him if he had not," Arilan replied.

"Pray to every god in heaven that you are never forced to choose among your oaths," Kyri murmured. "We can accept your judgment that all was done properly for now, but if things should change, I do not think I should like to be in your place."

"Fortunately for all of us," Arilan said dryly, "none of you shall ever have to worry about that possibility." He shifted position in his high-backed chair and sighed.

"Now, is there other business for tonight, or may I go home and get some sleep? I must confess that keeping up with a seventeen-year-old king becomes increasingly difficult, even if he were not Deryni."

# CHAPTER SIX

*Thou hast given a banner to them that fear thee,*
*that it may be displayed because of the truth.*
                                          —Psalms 60:4

Keeping up with a seventeen-year-old king was enough to tax far younger men than Arilan. Though Kelson could have gotten little more sleep than any of the rest of those involved in the previous night's work, he was up at first light to see that Duncan's escort had begun to assemble in the castle yard, and summoned his bleary-eyed chief advisors to join him at table before another hour had passed.

Granted, it was the table in the great hall rather than the council table, for the still growing Kelson rarely missed a meal of late, but he seemed to take perverse delight in the yawns and long-suffering expressions of his lords of state, many of whom made no attempt to disguise their irritation at the early morning summons.

Nigel alone seemed to match the king for mood and freshness—which surprised Morgan and Duncan, given the ordeal Nigel had undergone only a few hours before. Even Dhugal, nearly two years Kelson's junior and by no means as involved as the others, propped his elbows on the table and occasionally leaned his chin on one hand while he ate and listened to the king's briefing. And Dhugal was eager for the day, for he and a handful of his clansmen rode with Duncan at noon to join the other MacArdry levies and the army of Cassan in the north.

Morgan studied king and prince as he and Duncan paused at the edge of the yard where the ducal escort was mustering.

67

Dhugal had gone ahead of them to be with his borderers, and the two Haldanes were inspecting the mounted men-at-arms, both resplendent this morning in Haldane crimson. The prince regent moved among the men with the same easy grace that had been his brother's trademark and was now Kelson's, even managing, with Kelson's connivance, to bring an occasional smile to the lips of Dhugal's dour border scouts.

"God, he's good," Morgan murmured. "Sometimes, watching him is like watching Brion at his very best. I think the men would ride to hell and back for him, if he asked."

"Oh, they would—though God grant that they never have to," Duncan agreed, tugging at the cuff of a gauntlet embroidered with the sleeping lion of Cassan. "He certainly seems to have weathered last night in good form, though. One would think he'd had a full night's sleep—which is more than I can say for myself. Do you think Kelson helped him with a fatigue-banishing spell?"

Morgan shrugged and smiled as he returned his attention to Kelson again, now examining a new battle standard that Dhugal and Jodrell were unfurling.

"I don't know. He may have done. It will be fascinating to see how much Nigel begins picking up on his own this summer, once you and Kelson and I are away." He sighed. "It's also going to be strange, having you and Dhugal off in the north."

"Aye. God grant that the war will be quickly won, and all of us soon reunited."

He did not reiterate—nor did Morgan—that grim possibility that every fighting man must eventually face, at least in some deeply buried, secret part of him: that for some of those who rode out on campaign, even on so glorious a spring day as this, there would be no reunion, at least in this life. That was an unspoken "given" that soldiers almost never voiced, lest the speaking invite the very thing they dreaded. As a bishop, Duncan might laugh off such a notion as superstition; but the soldier in him was more cautious. He was very much the soldier today, in appearance as well as demeanor.

No cassock or cope or other ecclesiastical accoutrement proclaimed his episcopal rank. The plain silver cross hanging from under his gorget might have belonged to any pious man, and his bishop's ring was hidden under its embroidered gauntlet. Over close-fitting trews of deerskin and knee-high boots, Duncan had buckled a trim, buff-colored jazerant of quilted leather studded with steel, the edges bound in bright McLain tartan and the McLain device picked out in silken stitches on the left breast. A sword and crozier crossed in saltire behind the embroidered shield gave hint of his dual status, but only at close range.

There was a helm that denoted his double rank more obviously, circled by a ducal coronet, and with a steel cross splayed above the eyes and extending down the nasal, but that was still hanging on the saddle of his palfrey: a cloud-grey mare chosen for stamina and smoothness of gait. A squire held her, over near Dhugal and Jodrell. The big, battle-trained destriers were with the baggage train and sumpter animals, along with the heavier armor, none of which would be needed for the swift dash across the plains to the Mearan border.

"The summer will fly; you'll see," Morgan said quietly, after a beat. "Richenda has promised to continue working with Nigel, and to send us progress reports. And when we exchange dispatches, I shall send you more of that excellent wine we drank last night, and you shall drink to all our very good health!"

As he clasped Duncan by the shoulder, he forced a smile which Duncan returned dutifully, then glanced past him to the men mounting up in the yard.

"But, I see the archbishops coming out to bless the troops. I suppose we'd best rejoin our respective contingents."

"Aye. You *are* still riding out with us the first few miles, aren't you?"

"Certainly. But this blessing is for *your* lot—unless you'd care to give *me* a blessing before you go. . . ."

Duncan raised one eyebrow in surprise, then grinned unabashedly. "I'm flattered, Alaric. You've never asked before."

"The last time we left on a major campaign, you weren't a bishop." Morgan flashed him a quick, self-conscious grin. "Nor were you even a priest in very good standing, as I recall—at least so far as the Church was concerned."

"Mere technicalities," Duncan muttered, quickly pulling off his right gauntlet and glancing around to see whether they were being observed. "I'm still flattered. I don't suppose we should call undue attention to ourselves, so you needn't kneel—but do bow your head."

Kelson and Nigel were returning to the great hall steps beside the archbishops, so most attention was focused on the king—which was fortunate, because the flash of sun on Duncan's episcopal ring triggered potent memories in both Deryni as he raised his hand slightly between them. Morgan caught his breath in an echo of the old awe, then as quickly dipped his head and averted his eyes. The memory was too intimate, too precious, to share with anyone but Duncan.

The ring had been Bishop Istelyn's until six months before: hacked from his hand at the orders of Edmond Loris and sent, still circling Istelyn's finger, as an earnest of Loris' intention, with his Mearan allies, to wage total war against the Deryni Kelson. When Kelson did not capitulate, Istelyn's head followed; and Duncan had declared he would be made a bishop with no other ring than the martyred Henry Istelyn's.

But the ring held power beyond the mere symbolism of a bishop's office; and as Duncan's consecration approached, the presumption of wearing a martyr's ring weighed increasingly on his conscience—until, on the morning of the ceremony, Morgan insisted he face his fear. Together they had used their Deryni abilities to read the psychic impressions the ring carried—and had experienced what they could only describe later on as a vision of Saint Camber, not the first nor the last of many.

Camber's magic was in the gold itself—which had been a communion vessel of some kind, before it was Istelyn's ring—and the metal seemed to have retained some whisper of its earlier sacramental nature, even through the fire of crucible and forge and the metamorphosis from holy cup to consecrated ring. A measure of that special magic surrounded both of them as Duncan lightly touched Morgan's bright gold hair.

"May Almighty God bless and keep you safe, now and forever," he murmured, tracing a cross on Morgan's forehead with his thumb. "In the name of the Father, and of the Son, and of the Holy Spirit. Amen."

Then the moment was past, and they were moving on into the yard, Duncan striding toward his waiting men and Morgan bounding up the steps by twos to join Kelson, a bright splash of green riding leathers against grey stone. Archbish-

ops Bradene and Cardiel, Bishop Arilan, Nigel, and a handful
of courtiers also waited to witness the departure. Not surprisingly, Queen Jehana was not present.

As Duncan neared the center of the front line, one of Dhugal's border drummers did a brisk drumroll. At that signal,
Baron Jodrell brought forward the new battle standard,
bright as a cardinal in his color-bearer's surcoat over mail
and leather, the silk of the standard spilling down the cross-
tipped staff and billowing over his gloved hands. Duncan
caught a handful of it as he and Jodrell continued to the foot
of the stairs and knelt on the bottom-most step, holding the
silk clear of the stone when Jodrell lowered the staff in salute
to the two archbishops coming down to bless it.

"*Omnipotens Deus, qui es cunctorum benedictio et trium-
phantium fortitudo . . .*" Bradene prayed, he and Cardiel
laying their hands on the standard as Duncan and Jodrell
bowed their heads.

*Almighty God, Thou Who dost bless all men, Who dost
give strength to those who triumph in Thee: in Thine infinite
kindness, hear our humble prayers and with Thy heavenly
blessing deign to bless this standard, meant for use in battle,
so that it may be a source of strength against aggressive
and rebellious peoples. Armed with Thy protective power,
may it strike terror in the enemies of Thine anointed, King
Kelson. . . .*

As Bradene continued, Duncan fixed his gaze on one of
the red roses scattered over the particolor of blue and white
that formed the tails of the standard. The roses symbolized
the McLain commitment to the coming venture, as the Haldane lion on its red field, next to the hoist, signified Kelson's
support as king and overlord.

Duncan touched the silk to his lips as Cardiel aspersed the
standard with holy water, and remained kneeling as Kelson
came down to join the archbishops. As the king laid his own
consecrated hands briefly on the standard, half a hundred
lances dipped in salute, swallow-tailed pennons of blue and
white almost brushing the ground.

"Receive this standard, blessed with the blessing of
heaven," Kelson said, helping Jodrell raise the weight of the
staff as the latter stood. "May its sight strike terror in all
our enemies, and may the Lord grant all who follow it grace
to break through the ranks of the enemy with it safely and
without harm."

"Amen," Bradene and Cardiel responded.

The Haldane lion danced in the breeze as Duncan released his handfuls of silk, and the azure and white of the standard's tails cloaked his shoulders in a mantle of McLain roses. Gravely he ducked his head to receive the flat-linked chain of gilt that Kelson laid around his neck, then offered the king his joined hands in token of his homage.

"Be our Captain-General in the North, Duke Duncan," the king said, clasping the ducal hands between his own and thereby raising him up.

"I will, my Liege, and shall serve you faithfully, upon mine honor and my life."

"Cassan!" shouted Duncan's men, rattling lances against shields as the two exchanged a formal kiss of peace.

Then Duncan was escorting Jodrell back to their waiting line, bracing the standard against his hip while Jodrell swung up on a mean-tempered blood-bay that had to be sharply curbed before it would move close enough to take the banner back. Beyond, Dhugal waited on a rust-colored mare that matched his hair and brigandine, the reins of Duncan's grey in his hands.

He grinned as Duncan mounted, raising a hand toward Kelson and Morgan, who were heading down the steps toward where their own horses and a small escort waited for them to accompany the troops for the first few miles. Behind them on the landing, Nigel had been joined by his three sons. They, the bishops, and a handful of lesser nobles watched attentively as king and champion fell in with Duncan and Dhugal, wheeling to follow the Cassani lancers already eddying out of the yard through the gatehouse passage.

"Well, then. They're away," Nigel said to Conall, who was looking very tight-jawed and upset. "Here—what's this gloomy face? I thought you were going to ride out with Kelson and Alaric for a way."

"He can't," said the thirteen-year-old Prince Rory, smiling primly. "Payne hid all his riding boots."

"Rory! You said you wouldn't tell!" Payne blurted, kicking his brother sharply in the ankle and then ducking hastily between him and his father as Conall whirled on him with fratricide in his eyes. "Papa, don't let him hit me!"

"Conall!"

At Nigel's warning, Conall reluctantly lowered his fist, but to be sabotaged by a nine-year-old was no mean affront to his adolescent pride. Several men who had overheard Rory's announcement were fighting to control snickers, and one had already walked away to keep from laughing. Conall could scarcely contain his anger.

"You'd better thrash him, Father," he said through clenched teeth, "because if you don't, I will. I swear it."

"You'll thrash *no one* without my leave, sir!" Nigel retorted. "You're a grown man, for God's sake! You're almost twice Payne's age and size. I'm sure it was only a childish—Here now!" he barked, as Payne poked his head from between Rory and his father long enough to stick out his tongue at his eldest brother. "Stop that before I *do* thrash you! You're not innocent in this matter, y'know."

As Nigel grabbed him by the upper arm and gave him a shake, Payne paled visibly and deflated, all the defiance draining out of him as Nigel went on.

"I can't say I blame Conall for being angry, if you're going to act like a spoiled brat. Perhaps I *should* let him thrash you. Now, why did you hide all his boots?"

"It isn't fair, Father," he whispered. "Why does *Conall* get to go on the campaign with Kelson? Why can't I go, too?"

Nigel sighed and released the boy's arm, and even Conall looked a little less angry.

"We've been over all of this before, son. Conall needs the battle experience. He's going to be knighted next spring. Your time will come."

"But Duke Alaric is taking Brendan, and he's not even seven!"

"Brendan will be serving his stepfather as a page," Nigel said patiently. "I need you and Rory to be *my* page and squire. You *know* I'm to be regent while Kelson is away. Do you understand what that means?"

Payne fidgeted and studied the toes of his pointed court boots, trying to hide his sniffles behind a scowl.

"Lots of boring courts," he muttered.

Nigel smiled. "I'm afraid that's a major part of the life of a prince, son. And it's a very necessary one. When a king has to go to war, it makes his job far easier if he knows that the 'boring courts,' as you put it, are being taken care of by someone he can trust. If you ask Kelson, I'm sure he'll agree. Rory understands that, don't you, Rory?"

Rory, the thirteen-year-old, managed a grimace of a smile. "Yes, sir. It isn't going to be nearly as exciting as being with Kelson, though. *I* could go with him. I'm almost as old as he was when he became king. And it *will* be glorious, won't it, Conall? You're going to have *all* the fun!"

Conall, mellowing as he realized what had sparked this minor rebellion on the part of his younger brothers, decided he could afford to be gracious.

"Ah, so it's *glory* you're worried about, is it?" he said, feigning amazement as he planted both hands on his hips and looked down at the two boys. "Are you afraid you're going to miss out?"

At their shy, grudging nods and murmurs of agreement, he glanced at their father and gave him a broad wink.

"Well, then, little brothers, if that's all that's bothering you, I promise to win enough glory for all three of us! Perhaps it isn't quite as exciting as actually coming along on the campaign, but it's better than nothing, isn't it? And Father *will* need your help while I'm away."

"They can help me right now, if they're interested," Nigel said, laying an arm around both boys' shoulders and flashing Conall a look of gratitude as he tousled their hair. "Gentlemen, did you know we're to receive a Torenthi embassy in the next few days?"

"So what?" Payne muttered under his breath, as Nigel began walking him and Rory back into the hall.

"Well, young King Liam of Torenth is coming to reaffirm his fealty to Kelson as overlord," Nigel went on. "His brother is coming, too. Liam's ten, as I recall, and Ronal's six. They'll probably be as bored as you are. Perhaps you can help me plan some interesting things for them to do while they're here."

Conall hung back as his father and brothers disappeared into the hall, paying no mind now to the few courtiers still congregated on the great hall landing. In retrospect, he supposed he could not blame Payne for his little prank. In fact, it was a compliment. Younger brothers were notorious for wanting to emulate their elders—and Conall *was* going to go after all the glory he could on this venture.

The last of Duncan's escort were long gone, however—and he had wanted to watch them ride out. But perhaps he could catch a last glimpse of them from the battlement. One day, *he* would lead an army out to crush the enemies of Gwynedd!

He ran across the yard, and was panting by the time he reached the top of the newel stair that led to the parapet beside the gatehouse, but he was rewarded with the sight he had come for: the Cassani warband winding its way onto the plain north of the city, bright banners undulating gently on the breeze that rose from the river. Beyond, a larger Cassani force waited for their duke to join them. They were too far away for him to make out much detail, but Kelson's red-liveried outriders at the rear of the march stood out against the green of the riverbank and the blue water beyond, and the crimson-clad speck of Kelson was a beacon all alone, far at the head of the procession.

Conall watched until the red speck and a barely discernable green one broke off from the rest and headed back along the line to rejoin the other red dots at the rear, and wondered who would watch *his* going when the second army left in a few days' time.

But before the glorious departure must come one of the boring courts about which young Payne had complained so bitterly—though, in fact, the court did not turn out to be nearly as boring as anyone had hoped for. The great hall was crowded, despite the departure of the Cassani forces a few days before. The child-king Liam of Torenth duly presented himself as specified, but the six-year-old Prince Ronal was nowhere to be seen.

"Prince Ronal was ailing with a cold that has lingered for some weeks now," his mother Morag informed the king, standing haughty and proud before the man who had killed her brother and her husband. "I felt it best not to tax his health further with a needless fortnight's journey. I have already lost one son in the past year."

And *that* was an allusion to the death of young King Alroy the previous summer, under circumstances sufficiently bizarre for many Torenthi nobles, his mother among them, to charge that Kelson had somehow contrived it, most probably by magic. Kelson, so the story went, had been fearful that young Alroy might constitute a renewed Torenthi threat, having recently come of age. In fact, the fourteen-year-old Alroy had broken his neck in a fall from a horse—not at all an unusual accident—and Kelson had not even learned of it for several weeks.

"We can understand your motherly concern for your youngest son, my lady," Kelson said gravely, glad that his own mother had declined to attend the ceremony. He was robed in full Haldane panoply, crimson lion surcoat over gold-washed ceremonial mail and the state crown on his head. "However, we must question the wisdom of leaving so precious a child without suitable protection. And you *were* commanded to bring both princes before us as a sign of your good faith."

"You need not fear for Prince Ronal," Morag retorted. "His uncle, the Duke Mahael of Arjenol, acts as his guardian in my absence. And the presence of myself and my elder son should be sufficient sign of faith, even for a Haldane!"

Murmurs of affront rumbled among the observing nobles, but Kelson refused to let himself be ruffled. Nor was there any point in asking the advice of Morgan or Nigel, standing to either side of the throne. Morag and the absent Prince Ronal had suddenly become two entirely different problems, only one of them of immediate urgency. Morag was Deryni, like her dead brother Wencit, and immune to any subtle pressure Kelson or Morgan might have applied to some human belligerent, but she must not be allowed to interfere with the taking of Liam's oath.

As for Prince Ronal—whether or not he was, indeed, too ill to travel, the fact remained that he was the next heir after Liam, and in the hands of Duke Mahael, who had no cause to love the man who had slain his brother. If anything happened to Liam, Mahael had the next King of Torenth in his control—and eight years to wield the power of the Torenthi Crown in young King Ronal's name.

"Very well, my lady," Kelson said quietly. "We shall take you at your word—for now."

His gaze shifted to young Liam, standing taut and defiant beside his mother, precociously regal in his heavy russet court robes and scaled-down crown. The boy had the same tawny coloring as Wencit, but his eyes were black, echoing Morag's darker beauty. And even though the boy was only ten, Kelson sensed the presence of rigid, powerful shields. Already, Liam of Torenth was becoming a Deryni to be reckoned with.

"Liam of Torenth, we welcome you to our court," Kelson said formally. "Are you now prepared, before God and these witnesses, to do homage for your lands of Torenth and to pledge us your fealty, as was specified in the treaty between your father and ourself?"

The boy inclined his head in a curt gesture of agreement. "I am prepared, my lord."

At his response, Kelson glanced aside at Bishop Arilan, who specifically had been asked to administer the oath because he was Deryni, and could shield completely against any deception Morag might attempt—and without revealing what *he* was. As Arilan came forward, little Brendan Coris gravely carrying the Gospel book, Liam cast an uneasy glance at his mother.

But then he approached the throne without prompting as Kelson stood, to sink gracefully to both knees on a cushion that young Payne placed at Kelson's feet. He took off his crown with both hands and gave it over to Payne as Arilan held the book before him, then laid both hands flat on the jeweled cover.

Kelson held up one hand before Liam could draw breath to speak.

"My Lady Morag, we shall ask you to kneel as well, in token of your support of your son's oath, as his regent."

He sensed Morag was all but biting her tongue behind clenched teeth, but she said not a word as she moved to kneel beside and slightly behind Liam. Her dark eyes glittered like obsidian as she clasped her hands firmly to her son's shoulders on either side, head raised haughtily in as much defiance as she dared in the court of her brother's conqueror.

"Will you require my assistance with your oath, young sir?" Arilan asked Liam, low enough that he could not be heard beyond the dais.

Liam shook his head, then lifted his eyes boldly to Kelson's.

"I, Liam, King of Torenth and all the lands therein, do enter your homage and become your vassal of life and limb. I will observe my homage and perform for you the services which I owe, in good faith and without deceit. So help me, God."

When he had kissed the sacred book, Arilan took it to Kelson, who likewise laid both hands upon it.

"And we, for our part, do make known to all those present and to come that we do receive this Liam as King of Torenth and all the lands therein, and take him as our vassal. And we shall guarantee to him the lands held of us, and protect and defend him against every creature with all our power, in good faith and without deceit. So help me, God."

He, too, kissed the sacred book, then took the crown Payne had been holding and raised it slightly above the kneeling Liam's head.

"Take from our hands this symbol of the fee we have confirmed to you this day," Kelson said, setting the jeweled circlet back on Liam's tawny head. "Wear it in faith and honor, that the oaths we have sworn may be nobly kept."

"All that I have promised today, I shall faithfully keep," Liam responded, lifting his joined hands to Kelson in the traditional posture of giving fealty.

Kelson enclosed the joined hands between his own and raised Liam up, but the hands were cold, even in the warm hall, and the onyx eyes of Liam's mother colder still. As he and Liam exchanged a frigid kiss of peace, and Liam turned to assist his mother to rise, Kelson conceived a prudent precaution regarding the two. He sent his intention to Morgan in a tight-focused flash of thought as he resumed his seat on the throne, and sensed emphatic approval in Morgan's shift a little closer to his side. The hands of his champion moved casually to the hilt of his broadsword, and even Nigel seemed suddenly more attentive.

"A moment more, your Highnesses," Kelson said quietly, stopping Morag and Liam stark in their tracks as they prepared to rejoin their entourage. "We must ask your indulgence in one further matter."

Two pairs of night-dark eyes fastened on him, Liam's merely curious, Morag's more suspicious.

"We have fulfilled the letter of our obligation to you, Kelson of Gwynedd," Morag said, daring him to deny it. "You will understand if I do not care to tarry at the court of my husband's and my brother's murderer."

Her hostility elicited a murmur of surprise and indignation among the watching nobles of the court, but Kelson refused to rise to the insult.

"I need not justify myself to you, my lady," Kelson said evenly. "I do not require your approval or your love. I do require your obedience."

"And I have obeyed!"

Kelson inclined his head patiently. "It is true that you have complied with my requirements before this court—but you did not bring your younger son as you were commanded. Nor have I any way of verifying that young Ronal is, indeed, too frail to make the journey. I shall therefore insist that you and your elder son remain in Rhemuth through the summer, as earnest of your brother-in-law's good behavior."

"What?"

"Duke Mahael has the Torenthi heir," Kelson went on, raising his voice to cut off her further outburst. "You will appreciate that I cannot risk his possible belligerence on my eastern border while I am subduing a rebellion on my western one. You and young Liam shall be kept in honorable custody by my uncle, Prince Nigel, and shall be permitted free communication with Duke Mahael to assure him of your safety, but you shall remain here at least until the fall, when I return from my campaign. Your brother would have been far more harsh, I think, had the circumstances been reversed."

He feared, for a moment, that Morag would continue to resist, but the sister of his old adversary was wise enough to know when she had met her match. She expressed the sort of indignation one might expect of any royal person suddenly become hostage against her will, and voiced additional objections when it was learned that Liam would be lodged in separate quarters, but Kelson suspected it was more on principle than with any real hope of persuading him to relent.

Still, he did not relax his vigilance until he and Morgan personally had seen her to the quarters Nigel hastily prepared. And he set Arilan to ensure that the Deryni Morag did not use her powers to engineer an escape before more permanent measures could be taken. He would place her in Richenda's charge as soon as that could be arranged. He put aside his court robes and crown and went with Morgan to find her, as soon as he was certain Arilan had things under control.

They found Morgan's duchess in the cool of the cloister garden, writing under a shade tree. Several letters and ancient-looking scrolls lay on the bench beside her, along with a pot of ink and paraphernalia for sealing letters. On a blanket spread underneath another tree nearby, a nurse supervised the play of Richenda's and Morgan's baby daughter Briony, a merry toddler of nearly eighteen months.

"Good day, my lord—Sire," Richenda said, starting to rise as Morgan and the king approached. "What stormy faces you wear. Is anything wrong?"

Grimacing, Kelson motioned her to sit down, himself sinking down on the grass at her feet and glancing sidelong at the nurse.

"I don't think so—now. I'm going to need your help, though. Alaric, let's keep this a bit private, shall we?"

At Kelson's gesture, Morgan went and gave the nurse leave to go, bouncing the laughing Briony in his arms as he returned. As he plopped down on the grass beside Kelson, holding the child in his lap and making faces to amuse her, Kelson sighed and lay back on the grass, hands clasped behind his head.

"I'm sorry to interrupt your writing," he said. "I've come to ask a special favor. I've just taken two Deryni hostages."

Richenda set aside her pen and parchment and smoothed the skirts of her gown over her knees. She wore the pale blue she often favored in summer—a shade that made her eyes look almost as light as the sky Kelson could see through the leaves overhead. Those eyes looked back at him now with surprise and frank curiosity, the mind beyond them as still and as calm as a pool of high lake water.

"Two Deryni hostages," she repeated softly. "I should have expected three."

Kelson raised his head long enough to look at her in surprise.

"You *expected* me to take hostages?"

Richenda shrugged delicately. "I expected three rather than two, if you did. Did you not receive Morag of Torenth and her two sons this morning?"

Kelson sighed and glanced aside at the towheaded Briony, now perched on hands and knees in the grass between him and her father.

"She only brought Liam. She said Ronal was too ill to travel, so she'd left him in the charge of Mahael of Arjenol. Liam swore his oaths dutifully enough, but something didn't seem quite right. With Ronal under Mahael's control, I was afraid he might use my absence as an excuse to raise trouble to our east. I can't risk that if I'm to be in Meara all summer."

"I quite agree," Richenda said. "You're concerned, then, that Morag and Liam are Deryni, and might work mischief here in Rhemuth while you're away."

"Or simply escape," Kelson answered, amazed, as always, at her immediate grasp of all the ramifications. "I've set Arilan to working out precautions against that for now—and I doubt Liam will be much problem, though he's going to be very powerful when he's grown. Right now, he's still a little boy; he'll be playing with Payne and Rory before a week is out."

"Aye, that's very likely true," Richenda agreed. "Morag, however, is *not* a child."

"Good God, no! And she hates me. If I had any doubts about *that*, I don't any longer. I suppose I'm most concerned that, in trying to escape, she might try to subvert the servants. I don't *think* she could construct a Portal without assistance—"

Richenda shook her head at Kelson's look of question.

"Nay, few could."

"So that means that any other kind of escape attempt would almost have to involve others," Kelson finished.

"That's easy enough to prevent," Richenda said.

Kelson smiled wanly. "I was hoping you'd say that. In the meantime, I should imagine she'll eventually want the company of other women—at least after a while. You'd be in a perfect position to see that she doesn't get out of line."

"So," Richenda said, in a tone that softened the potential bite of her words, "I'm to be the guardian of two Deryni queens. I don't mind," she added, at Kelson's look of dismay. "At least Morag isn't ashamed of what she is."

"Nor would she have any reluctance to use what she is to improve her lot," Morgan said, capturing a giggling Briony by one bare foot before she could crawl out of reach. "As Wencit's sister, her training was probably incredible. I want you to be careful, Richenda."

Richenda smiled and laced her fingers together on her knee. "With all due respect, my lord, I suspect the Lady Morag and I may have shared some of the same masters. I had finished a letter to one of them only moments before you and Kelson came into the garden." She picked up one of the scrolls and dropped it on Kelson's stomach. "I had that from him a few days ago. It's a contemporary account of Saint Camber's death at Iomaire."

Kelson lurched to a sitting position and opened the scroll. "Camber's death," he breathed, scanning the closely penned lines. "Any mention of his burial place?"

"The MacRorie family vaults at Caerrorie," Richenda replied, "now in ruins. The body isn't there anymore, of course."

"Destroyed when his sainthood was rescinded?"

Shaking her head, Richenda picked up another scroll. "No. At the time he was declared a saint, it was believed he'd been bodily assumed into heaven, as befitted one of the blessed. His son, however, claimed he'd moved the body to another resting place—though he never would say where. He was a priest. For some reason, though, he was always against the canonization."

"Bad blood between father and son?" Morgan asked, scooping the wiggling Briony under one arm as he scooted closer to inspect the scroll over Kelson's shoulder.

"Gracious, no. They were devoted."

"Listen to this, you two," Kelson murmured, reading from the scroll. "*So did Joram MacRorie and the Vicar of the Michaelines return from the field of battle with the body of the slain Earl Camber. . . .*" He looked up. "Who were the Michaelines?"

"A militant order of priest-knights," Richenda replied. "Joram and several other Deryni important in the Restoration are said to have been of that order. The vicar mentioned is Father Alister Cullen, later the last Deryni bishop."

"Well, not the *very* last," Morgan said with a grin, shifting Briony to his shoulder. "We know of at least two since then."

Kelson snorted and continued scanning down the scroll.

"Damn, I wish we didn't have to campaign in Meara this summer! This is fascinating. Who did you say had sent it?"

"I didn't, but his name is Azim. He's—" She cocked her head at the leaves above their heads as she searched for the right relationship. "He's my cousin's husband's uncle—which must make him some kind of relative by marriage, but I haven't the foggiest notion what he'd be. I've always called him uncle, but I know that isn't right. What's more important for our purposes is his affiliation with the Knights of the Anvil, down in Djellarda. Have you heard of them, Sire?"

Kelson nodded. "Hospitaller knights of some sort, aren't they? They guard the routes to the Holy Land. *Very* ferocious fighters, and not entirely Christian."

"Very good." Richenda smiled. "They're said to have sprung from Moorish interaction with fled Knights of Saint Michael after the Michaeline expulsion from Gwynedd in 917. Incidentally, Anviler tradition has it that Camber, at the insistence of his son Joram, was buried in Michaeline habit—which was dark blue," she added, glancing at Morgan. "And the Servants of Saint Camber, the religious order that was founded to venerate him, wore grey."

Morgan looked up abruptly and whistled low under his breath, and Kelson went a little pale.

"I know," Richenda murmured. "It fits the pattern of every instance of possible Camberian intervention that we know of."

Swallowing a little nervously, Kelson let the scroll roll back on itself and handed it back to Richenda.

"I'd better not read any more of this right now, or tomorrow I'll be heading east instead of west. This is incredible! Do you think the Knights of the Anvil know where Camber is buried?"

"No. But through them, we may eventually be able to find out."

"And this Azim is one of them?" Kelson asked.

She nodded.

"Well, when you next communicate with him, please tell him it's very important to me," Kelson said, gesturing toward the letters. "And send me progress reports while we're on campaign, if you can."

"I shall, Sire."

She would have continued, but Nigel came into the garden at that moment with Conall, Payne, and Brendan, obviously looking for Kelson. Both Conall and Nigel wore riding leathers. Brendan pretended to be very matter-of-fact about being included in the prince regent's entourage, stiff and correct in his page's livery, but he grinned ear-to-ear as Richenda and Morgan gave him grave nods of approval.

"I hope I'm not interrupting anything too important," Nigel said, as Kelson twisted to look up at him, "but those new lancers have finally arrived from Carthmoor. I thought you might like to inspect them and meet their officers before they unsaddle and scatter for the evening. I wasn't sure they'd get here in time to go with you tomorrow."

"Well, I suppose I'd better come and have a look, hadn't I?" Kelson said, setting Richenda's scroll aside and getting to his feet. "My lady, I apologize for dragging your lord away to play the soldier, but I think he probably ought to see them, too, since both our lives may depend upon them."

Smiling, Richenda reached out to take Briony from Morgan, she and Morgan both having to disengage the baby's hand from Morgan's captain-general's chain.

"I would not dream of interfering with my lord's duties, Sire," she said, standing. "Besides, I have duties of my own, I think. I shall be most interested to meet the Princess Morag and her young son."

She scooped up the sealed letters and held them out to Conall, who took them with a bow. "Please see that those go to a messenger at once, would you, Conall? You can do it on your way out with His Majesty. And Payne—perhaps you would be so kind as to return these scrolls and writing materials to my chambers."

Young Payne, clearly delighted to be included in the notice of the beautiful Richenda, flushed bright red and bowed.

And Conall, following Brendan and the adults out of the garden toward the castle yard, fingered the letters in his hand thoughtfully, turning them over and over in his hands.

# CHAPTER SEVEN

*For they have consulted together with one consent;
they are confederate against thee.*

—Psalms 83:5

The Haldane host left Rhemuth the next morning. Nor did
news of their advance toward Meara take long to reach the
rebel leaders in Ratharkin. Before Kelson and his army had
ridden a day's march west, rebel spies on fleet R'Kassan
steeds were carrying the news in relays across the western
Gwynedd plain and through the mountain passes of Cùilteine
and Droghera.

They already knew of the Cassani army massing in the
north, and were preparing to meet it. Mearan partisans had
been converging on Ratharkin since the first thaws, the
picket lines and bright pavilions of their encampments
springing up like strange, exotic wildflowers against the new
spring green of the surrounding meadows. Lured by the old
dream of a sovereign Meara, perhaps even restored to include Kierney and Cassan, zeal fanned through the winter,
first by promises of support from a militantly independent
ecclesiastical hierarchy and then by the news of the capture
and killings of Princess Sidana and her brother, they came
by the hundreds: from the northern strongholds of Castleroo
and Kilarden—always on uneasy terms with their Cassani
neighbors farther north—and as far west as Laas and
Cloome; from the central Mearan plains and the mountains
to the east; and from as far south as the Connait. By the
time word arrived that Kelson was on the move, more than

two thousand were camped before the gates of the Mearan capital.

Three hundred Connaiti mercenaries also swelled their ranks: the princely gift of Meara's self-proclaimed patriarch, Edmund Loris, the former Archbishop of Valoret—who could afford to be generous since, if the venture succeeded, he stood to gain as much as Caitrin, albeit on ecclesiastical rather than secular grounds.

And if Loris paid his troops with silver smuggled out of the treasury of Valoret by his henchman, Lawrence Gorony, what was that to Meara? If Kelson of Gwynedd had unjustly deprived Loris of his former office, what better retribution than to employ the assets of that office to defeat Kelson and restore Loris to what was rightfully his?

Others of former Gwynedd service Loris had likewise recruited: William du Chantal and Grigor of Dunlea, neighbors of the traitorous Brice of Trurill, both of whose defections would shock Kelson when he learned of them. And other men of even less savory reputation: the border chieftains, Tibald MacErskine, Cormac Hamberlyn, and Tigan O Daire—brigands to the man, all but outlawed in the days of Kelson's father—who would bring their clansmen to Meara's aid out of greed for the promise of booty and spite against Haldanes in general.

So had they come, for all the myriad reasons that usually draw men to war, and now prepared to embark upon the great venture that would either free them from Haldane sovereignty or else lay waste to the land for yet another generation. As the sun approached the zenith on that balmy day in May, the soldiers formed their ranks before the gates of Ratharkin and awaited the coming of their queen, banners lifting bravely on the breeze that swept south through the passes and off the nearby lake.

All was prepared for her arrival. Just outside the gates, beneath the shade of an open-sided white pavilion, an altar had been erected for celebration of a rite of blessing no different in intent from those rites celebrated in Rhemuth only days before—for surely the Mearan cause was just, and God was on their side. The priests gathering at the pavilion for Mass had told them so, as they made their way through the camps the night before and heard confessions.

Soon would come their archbishop to confirm that belief: Edmund Loris, who would also ride with the Grand Army

of Meara, to command his episcopal levies and the fierce
Connaiti mercenaries he had bought. His captain-general and
chief aide, Monsignor Lawrence Gorony, rode along the
ranks of the gathering soldiers even now, heartening the men
with his words of encouragement and blessing, giving final
instructions to the officers and lords who had come to free
their land.

Just inside the gates, the rebel bishops who supported
Loris waited to escort the Mearan royal family from the bishop's palace to the pavilion—the Bishops of Cashien and Ballymar, youngish men formerly sworn to obedience to Loris'
successor as Archbishop of Valoret, Bradene, and four ambitious itinerant bishops: Mir de Kierney, Gilbert Desmond,
Raymer de Valence, and Calder of Sheele, the latter an uncle
of Dhugal MacArdry. By day's end, only they and a small
garrison would remain behind to attend their sovereign lady
and await news of the Haldane defeat.

And in Ratharkin itself, the *soi-disant* Queen Caitrin of
Meara met with the remnants of her family and their key
leaders for one final conference before riding out to the open-
air Mass that would send Meara's hopes on their way. She
had gathered them in the solar of the bishop's palace, whence
she had kept informal court all through the long winter. This
morning, however, the scene was one more of domesticity
than of pomp.

Seated in a pool of sunlight near the chamber's largest
window, looking more like a nun than a queen in royal
mourning for her two slain children, Caitrin spent the tension
of her anticipation in the soothing, mind-lulling pastime of
mending, making a last-minute repair to a surcoat bearing
the sovereign arms of Meara differenced by the label of the
eldest son. Nearer the fireplace, the surcoat's owner, Prince
Ithel, occupied whatever predeparture jitters he might have
harbored by helping his father adjust a greave to support a
leg still weak from a winter fall. Both wore fine Connaiti
brigandines of leather and steel, Sicard's partially covered
by a surcoat quartered with his own arms and those of his
wife, the MacArdry border cats on crimson, bordured *or*,
and the sable dancing bear and crimson *etoilles* of Meara on
chequey of silver and gold.

"No, that will have to be tighter," he murmured, as Ithel
slid a finger underneath a strap and tried the tension.

Edmund Loris, looking far younger than his three-score years, lounged in a chair to Ithel's and Sicard's right, burgundy riding leathers and mail mostly covered by an ankle-length white surcoat embellished with a large blue cross on breast and back. He and the Mearan royals were listening, with varying degrees of agreement, to the impassioned rhetoric of an intense, able-looking man of half Loris' years, his war harness emblazoned with the arms of the Barony of Trurill. Loris, in particular, did not look pleased.

"I still maintain that Kelson's approach from the south is not nearly as great an immediate threat as what Cassan is doing in the north," said Brice of Trurill, who would lead the force about to head south under the nominal command of the sixteen-year-old Ithel. "I can harry Kelson; I can slow him down a great deal without sustaining major losses. I'll even lay waste to our own lands in the south and east to buy you time, if I must.

"But in the end, it all boils down to one incontrovertible fact: if your lot doesn't stop Bishop McLain's northern army before he joins the main Haldane force, we haven't got a prayer."

Loris' blue eyes smoldered with the low, dangerous fire of the fanatic as he twisted the bishop's ring on his right hand.

"Your arguments have long since passed the point of tedium, Brice," he muttered. "Can you speak of nothing but that jumped-up Deryni priest?"

Sicard gave a buckle at his knee a final tug and shot Loris a sharp look.

"For God's sake, let it be, Loris," he said irritably. "Brice isn't the only one who's becoming tedious. That 'jumped-up Deryni priest' is no less competent for your constant berating of the state of his soul."

"You speak as if the state of his soul meant nothing, my lord," Loris said frostily.

Sicard, his patience clearly stretched near the breaking point, straightened wearily and set both fists on his hips, and young Ithel eased himself quietly to a seat on the raised hearth to watch his elders have at it. Caitrin ignored them all, apparently intent on her sewing.

"McLain's soul," Sicard replied, "is not a factor in determining how hard a fight he'll give us. His cleverness and intelligence are. If McLain is anything like his father in the field, he'll be a most formidable opponent—and that's all that matters until the battle has been won.''

"He is a symbol of all that is evil in Gwynedd," Loris muttered. "Corruption of sacred as well as secular authority. His very existence offends me."

"As yours undoubtedly offends him, Archbishop," Sicard retorted, snatching up his sword belt and buckling it on. "Despite your sometimes overly simplistic view of what is good and what is evil, it's just possible that some things in this world are really shades of grey."

Loris' eyes narrowed dangerously. "Do you dare to suggest that there are instances in which one might *condone* what McLain has done?''

"Sicard is suggesting no such thing, Edmund," Caitrin said, knotting her thread and biting it off. "Don't be so quick to take offense. *We* aren't your enemies; nor are we Deryni—nor are we in sympathy with those who are. It simply becomes a little wearing when you constantly single out McLain for your anger, as if he alone were responsible for our present situation."

Loris drew a deep breath and let it out slowly, flexing and unflexing his fingers around the ends of his chair arms.

"You are right, my lady," he conceded. "I am sometimes intemperate in my hatreds. It is a failing."

"But an understandable one, I will grant you. Ithel, this is finished, my dear." She shook out the surcoat and extended it toward her son, who took it and began drawing it over his armor.

"I, on the other hand," Caitrin went on, "have had many years to bank my hatred of the Haldanes to a lower but no less vehement flame. I will concede that it was rekindled, however, when word came that they had slain my sweet Sidana and her brother."

"Ah, yes. As I recall, King Brion slew your first husband, didn't he?" Loris said softly, eyes narrowing to calculating slits.

Caitrin turned her head grimly toward the window.

"Aye. And my firstborn, who was but a babe suckling at my breast." She sighed and crossed herself, bowing her head. "But I was young then. I am no longer young. Now Brion's son has slain two more of my children. If he slays my Ithel as well, it will all have been for naught. Even if

Sicard and I were to survive, I am too old to begin yet a third family."

"God forbid that it should come to that," Loris said without much conviction, "but if it should, you still have a scion of the Mearan royal line in Judhael. And I believe there is a cadet line as yet untouched, is there not? Ramsay of Cloome, I believe?"

The sheer offhandedness of his remark left the entire Mearan royal family speechless. Caitrin blanched as white as her gown and coif; Sicard seemed frozen in his place. Young Ithel, his handsome face draining of color to be so lightly dismissed, sank back to his seat on the hearth and looked mutely to both his parents in appeal, the bright surcoat on his breast suddenly as much a potential shroud as a proud banner of war.

"Jesus, you're a cold bastard, Loris!" Brice muttered under his breath, laying a reassuring hand on the boy's shoulder and glowering at the archbishop. "What a thing to say."

Loris only shrugged and studied the nails of one well-manicured hand.

"Don't be impertinent, Brice," he said. "We must be realistic."

"Very well," said Sicard, beginning to regain his balance. "Let's *be* realistic, then. Judhael is a priest. Even if he *should* eventually succeed instead of Ithel, the line would end with him. And there's no question that the Ramsays are junior to Kelson's line."

"That needn't concern true Mearan partisans," Loris assured them. "And Judhael's unquestionably senior line need not end with him. It could continue in the same manner in which the Haldane line continued when Cinhil Haldane, a priest of the *Ordo Verbi Dei*, was restored to the throne of Gwynedd two hundred years ago."

"And what manner is that?" Caitrin asked.

Loris allowed himself a prim smile of satisfaction.

"His priestly vows can be dispensed, as King Cinhil's were. I have already spoken with him on the matter, and he has agreed."

As a resentful-looking Ithel exchanged tight-jawed glances with Brice and his father, Sicard hitched his thumbs in his swordbelt and turned away disgustedly.

"I don't suppose you feel that's just a little premature?"

"No, merely prudent," Loris said. "Unless, of course, you mean Meara's cause to end in the event of the present principals' demise." He smiled frostily. "Of course, *you* are not a Quinnell, are you, Sicard? You only married one. Three generations of Quinnells have fought to preserve a royal heritage that you have known for less than a score of years, and only, if I may gently point out, as the consort of a queen. One can hardly expect you to understand."

As Sicard whirled, aghast, Brice aimed a vicious kick at one of the logs burning in the fireplace, sending up a shower of sparks as he, too, turned on the archbishop.

"Loris, I don't care if you *are* an archbishop—you're a pompous ass!" he said, restraining Sicard with an arm across his chest. "No *wonder* they couldn't stand you in Gwynedd anymore."

"Watch your tongue, Trurill!"

"Brice, please!" Caitrin interjected. "Sicard, I beg you. . . ."

"Your pardon, madame, but he goes too far," Brice returned. "We're going to *win* this one, Loris. *If*, that is, you and your goddamn Connaiti mercenaries do what they're supposed to do."

"They will do what they are paid to do," Loris said icily. "And if the army under my Lord Sicard does what *it* is to do, McLain will be lured into a trap from which there is no escape."

"He'll not escape!" Sicard snapped.

"Just as that MacArdry boy did not escape, when you were responsible for his security last fall?" Loris retorted.

Young Ithel flushed bright red and jumped to his feet.

"*I* want Dhugal MacArdry's blood!" he cried.

"*You'll* ride with Brice and harry the Haldane army," his father replied. "*I'll* deal with my dear nephew—and Mc-Lain."

"You may *have* the boy," Loris said. "You may even deal with McLain in the field—though I hope you will not have to kill him outright. I have a special fate planned for our dear Deryni bishop-duke. If he's captured, he belongs to *me!*"

"You'd best capture him first, then," Sicard said, turning away in disgust.

They continued to bicker for several moments, tempers wearing ever thinner, until a page's knock on the door an-

nounced the arrival of Bishops Creoda and Judhael, both
wearing scarlet copes over their priestly vestments. Old
Creoda looked venerable and stately in the full panoply of
his bishop's regalia, but Judhael's cope seemed more the
royal mantle than the ecclesiastical trapping as he came forward to bend and kiss his aunt's cheek, prematurely silver
hair gleaming like a crown already as he passed into the sunlight surrounding her. If he noticed the coolly resentful looks
he received from Ithel and Brice, he did not acknowledge
them.

"Your Royal Highness," said Creoda, making Caitrin a
solemn bow, "the procession to escort you to the Mass of
Leave-Taking is ready to depart. Your loyal subjects await
you."

Flashing Loris a withering glance, Caitrin rose and shook
out the folds of her gown.

"Thank you, Bishop Creoda. We are ready to join them."

As she adjusted the coif veiling her grey hair, Sicard
brought her a casket from across the room, kneeling on one
knee for her to take out the crown inside. The rubies and
sapphires studding the golden circlet flamed in the sunlight,
endowing her plain, tired features with a classic and regal
dignity as she set it on her head. In that instant she looked
every inch the queen she hoped to be, and all in the room
sank to their knees to do her homage—even Loris.

"You shall rule a sovereign and reunited Meara, my
lady—I swear it!" said Brice, seizing her hand to kiss it
fervently.

"Aye, madame, you shall!" came Creoda's enthusiastic
agreement, and Judhael's, and Loris' more restrained one.

Then her husband was escorting her from the chamber,
Loris and his clerics preceding her, Brice and Ithel bringing
up the rear and muttering quietly between them as they
watched the proud archbishop go before them.

# CHAPTER EIGHT

*The horseman lifteth up both the bright sword and
the glittering spear.*

—Nahum 3:3

The weeks that followed quickly brought home the rigors
of war to rebels and Haldane supporters alike. Aware that
a joining of the Cassani and Haldane armies would spell an
end to Mearan hopes, the Mearan commanders proceeded
with their agreed strategy of harassment and potential en-
trapment, Brice and Ithel harrying and laying waste in the
south and east to slow Kelson's advance while Sicard and
the main Mearan army played a game of cat-and-mouse in
the north, beginning the maneuvers they hoped eventually
would lure Duncan's Cassani levies into a trap. The first
encounters were not what either Gwynedd commander had
expected, puzzling Kelson in particular.

"I thought we'd get more traditional resistance here in the
south," he told Morgan, when they had finished repelling
yet another nighttime raid on the periphery of their camp.
"We've never seen more than a few hundred men at a time.
I begin to wonder whether we're dealing with an army at
all."

Morgan set his teeth as he watched a lancer sergeant put
down a foundered chestnut mare, one of nearly a dozen
horses deliberately hamstrung by the enemy in the skirmish
just past. Blood fountained black in the torchlight, and young
Brendan buried his face against his stepfather's side.

"I don't think we are, my prince," Morgan said softly,
comforting Brendan with a hand stroking his reddish gold

93

hair. "Each new engagement shows signs of different leadership. My guess is that Sicard has split at least part of his army into fast, mobile raiding parties, hoping to wear us down with these hit-and-run raids. It's a typical border tactic."

"Sire! Your Grace!" Kelson's squire, Jatham, approached them at a run. "Duke Ewan took a prisoner, but he's failing fast. You'd better hurry if you want to get any information out of him!"

They ran with Jatham to where a battle surgeon was working zealously over a ghost-pale man in border leathers and plaids, trying to staunch a gaping belly wound. The man was sobbing for breath, rigid with pain, hands clawing futilely at the wad of bandage the surgeon was pressing to his wound. Archbishop Cardiel knelt at the man's head, putting away his holy oils, but he drew back, tight-lipped, and shook his head as Kelson thumped to his knees beside him and laid hands along either side of the man's head.

"He isn't going to make it, Sire," said the battle surgeon, Father Lael, catching the man's wrists and restraining them as Morgan crouched opposite and thrust one hand underneath the blood-soaked bandage, the other slipping smoothly inside the front of the leather jerkin to monitor the pounding heart.

The man's struggles weakened as Kelson began to block the pain, but it was as much from a deteriorating condition as any easing of his agony. Blood was pulsing from between Morgan's fingers with every labored heartbeat—so much that Morgan wondered how the man had lasted this long—and in a desperate attempt to at least slow the inevitable, he eased his hand deep into the wound, clear to the last set of knuckles, and began to call up his healing talent.

"It's no good. I'm losing him," Kelson whispered, closing his eyes as he tried to force his mind past the barriers of fading consciousness that, even now, were melting into the darker, more tenuous mists of death.

"So am I," Morgan answered.

He did his best to send healing across the link, and felt the power begin to stir in him; but abruptly he came up short, gasping, as if he were a fish flopping helplessly in a too-small container, and waterless besides. It was too late.

He stopped trying, and the sensation ceased. The man sighed softly, twitched, and was still. Morgan did not attempt to intrude on what Kelson was doing; only blinked and drew himself a long, steadying breath to reorient as he raised his head, paying no mind to the reactions of the others watching.

"So," Kelson whispered, taut and just a little indignant as he raised his head and blinked, focusing with difficulty on Morgan's face. "He was Grigor of Dunlea's man. God, I didn't know *he'd* betrayed me, too!"

Sighing, Morgan pulled his hand slowly out of the dead man's body. The stench of blood and sundered bowels made him particularly grateful for the basin of clean water and the towel that Conall offered him, kneeling expectantly between him and Kelson.

"Are you really surprised at that, my prince, given the border tactics we've been seeing?" Morgan murmured, mechanically washing his hands as he continued settling back into normal consciousness.

Duke Ewan crouched down beside the king and held out a piece of bloodstained tartan.

"Aye, an' here's another border token, Sire. D'ye recognize the sett, Alaric?"

At Morgan's negative, Ewan grimaced and tossed the bloody plaid contemptuously over the dead man's face.

"MacErskine. An' one o' my scouts swears he saw old Tegan O Daire. Sicard's recruited goddamn *outlaws!*"

"More likely, Brice of Trurill's recruited outlaws," Kelson retorted, getting wearily to his feet. "He and Grigor of Dunlea were always like two kernels on the same ear."

Morgan said nothing as he dried his hands and laid the towel over Conall's arm with a nod of thanks, but he relayed his and Kelson's growing suspicions to Duncan a few nights later, when they made one of their increasingly regular contacts via deep Deryni trancing.

*We begin to suspect the main Mearan army isn't in the south at all,* he told Duncan. *So far, all we've met are skirmish bands—no more than a hundred men or so at a time, and they never strike in the open. Sicard may have their main strength in the north, hunting you.*

*While Brice and his minions slow you down?* Duncan replied. *That could well be. We have yet to encounter an actual army ourselves, though we see occasional signs that large bodies of men have passed. They can't afford to let our two armies meet, though.*

*That's for certain,* Morgan agreed. *Where are you now?*

*South of Kilarden, well into the great plain. Like you, we're fighting a will-o'-the-wisp enemy that strikes in the dark and out of the setting sun—Connaiti mercenaries for the most part, though we see the occasional episcopal knight. Jodrell's gotten it into his head that they're under joint command of Gorony and Loris, though no one's seen them yet.*

"Then, where *is* Sicard?" Kelson asked aloud, when the contact had been broken, and he watched Morgan prepare to banish the Wards Major. "If *we* haven't seen him, and *Duncan* hasn't seen him. . . ."

Shaking his head to fend off further discussion until he was done, Morgan blew out the candle set on the camp table between them and put on the signet ring he had just used as a focal point for concentration. All around them, barely discernable against the redder glow of a lantern hanging from the tent pole, the dome of the warding he had raised to shield them glowed a cool, gentle silver. It pulsed briefly brighter as he raised both arms to shoulder height on either side, empty hands upraised, and drew a slow, centering breath.

"*Ex tenebris te vocavi, Domine,*" Morgan whispered, slowly turning his palms downward. "*Te vocavi, et lucem dedisti.*" Out of darkness have I called Thee, O Lord. I have called Thee, and Thou hast given light.

"*Nunc dimittis servum tuum secundum verbum tuum in pace. Fiat voluntas tua. Amen.*" Now lettest Thou Thy servant depart in peace, according to Thy will. Let it be done according to Thy will. . . .

As he lowered his arms, the doming light faded and died, leaving only four pairs of dice-sized polished cubes set towerlike, white atop black, at the quarter-points beyond their chairs. Two of the four sets toppled as Kelson leaned down to retrieve them, too precariously perched, on the straw matting of the tent's floor, to stand steady without the balancing effect of magic. Morgan sat back in his chair and sighed, wearily rubbing the bridge of his nose between thumb and forefinger, as Kelson stowed the ward cubes in their red leather case.

"It gets harder each time, doesn't it?" Kelson murmured, setting the box beside the blown-out candle.

"No, I just get more tired." Morgan sighed again and managed a smile. "It's never been easy, though, and this particular talent was never meant to be used regularly over this kind of distance—at least not this often.''

As he closed his eyes and began to run the beginning steps of yet another fatigue-banishing spell, trying to will away his growing headache as well, Kelson interrupted his train of thought with an explosive sigh.

''*Damn* Sicard!'' the king muttered under his breath. ''*God*, how I wish this stupid war were over!''

Lethargically, Morgan nodded and tried to regain the track of his spell, surrendering to an uncontrollable yawn. When, as he tried to keep from putting head down then and there and simply passing out, he nearly knocked the ward cubes off the table, Kelson reached across to seize a handful of his tunic.

''Are you all right?''

Morgan nodded yes, but he could not seem to make his eyes focus on Kelson's face.

''Just a little after-reaction,'' he murmured, and yawned again. ''It's been building over the past week. I don't sleep well after these sessions.''

''And of course you wouldn't dream of telling anyone, would you?'' Kelson released him only long enough to come around and hoist him to his feet, royal hands set firmly under one elbow.

''Too much fatigue-banishing, isn't it?'' the king went on indignantly, as he read the evidence at close range and propelled Morgan toward the camp bed set opposite his own. ''And you were about to do it again, weren't you? Well, you're going to sleep tonight if I have to fight you every step of the way.''

Morgan managed a wry smile as he let Kelson help him to the bed, but his knees all but buckled under him, and he lay down far faster than he had intended.

''No fight, my prince. I'll save that for the Mearans,'' he promised, a groan escaping his lips as he opened his mind to the king and let the pressure go.

''That's right,'' Kelson whispered, touching fingertips lightly to Morgan's forehead. ''Release it all and sleep. You've done enough for a while. You aren't the only Deryni around here, you know. In the future, I'm going to insist you let me share more of the burden.''

*Not if it impairs you*, came Morgan's groggy protest, only barely sensed, even mind-to-mind.

*We'll discuss it when you're rested properly*, Kelson replied. *Now go to sleep*.

And Morgan did.

They moderated their contacts with Duncan after that, letting Kelson carry the link alone from time to time and alternating the energy drain so that neither was too depleted from any single operation.

Meanwhile, the uncertainty of the tactical situation only increased, and frustration along with it.

"How can we fight an enemy we bloody never see!" Kelson complained, as they skirted the mountains west of Droghera and headed north, still encountering only token harassment from isolated warbands. "Having two thousand men doesn't do us a lot of good if we can only use a few hundred at a time."

Nor, as they penetrated deeper into the Mearan heartland, was the enemy's increasing scorched-earth policy reassuring.

"We haven't any real provisioning problem just now," General Remie reported at a staff meeting one evening, as he and Kelson's other key commanders gathered outside the royal tent. "As long as we can find forage for the animals, we can feed the men until, say, Midsummer or a little later with what we're carrying. This large an army moves slowly, though. I wonder whether we might not be better off to take a lesson from the enemy and break into smaller, more manageable warbands. In this part of the country, we could do it with very little danger, and far more effectiveness."

The general staff thought it a fine idea, and Kelson agreed. By the next morning, the army had been parcelled out among four semi-autonomous commanders: Duke Ewan, Generals Remie and Gloddruth, and Morgan, Kelson riding with the latter. By the end of the day, the warbands had dispersed half a day's march apart, stretched across the line of advance. Regular couriers kept the units in touch, and skirmishes with the formerly phantom enemy began to yield more definite results, and to produce more desperate countermeasures.

"I'm afraid we're going to see more and more of this," Morgan said to the king, one sultry June morning when they had been gone from Rhemuth for a full month.

They were riding a track through yet another field burned to keep it from Haldane use, approaching the outskirts of what once had been a prosperous village of some size. The stubble still smoldered to either side of the track, but smoke curled from behind soot-smudged walls and reeking roofs as well.

"I think this is the worst so far," Kelson agreed.

Thus it had been for the past week, enemy devastation no longer confined to ruined fields and ransacked storehouses, as in the beginning, but now being extended to the very citizenry of Meara. Each day had found the Haldane warbands passing through more gutted villages and towns, peopled by ever more pitiful refugees—common folk, the ultimate losers in any war—who must try to scratch out a living after both sets of soldiers were gone, and cared little what king sat on what throne, so long as they and their children might live unmolested and without hunger.

Kelson could feel the eyes of the survivors upon him as he, Morgan, and a small escort rode into the town, Jatham leading with the bright Haldane banner. A lancer unit had already swept in ahead of them to secure the area and deal with any enemy stragglers, and the townspeople were beginning to appear in doorways and windows. An old man spat at the sight of them, and a hollow-eyed woman suckling a baby at her breast glared at Kelson from the shattered doorframe of a burned-out cottage.

Sick at heart, Kelson lowered his eyes in helpless shame for his warrior caste, wishing there were any other way than war to keep the peace.

"This is almost the worst part of war," he murmured to Morgan, as they let their greathorses pick their way through the rubble-strewn street. "Why do the common people always have to suffer for the folly of their masters?"

"A grim but constant trapping of war in every time, my prince," Morgan replied. "If we were as desperate as the Mearans apparently are becoming, we might well—"

Suddenly he stiffened and broke off, standing in his stirrups to peer ahead.

"What's wrong?" said Kelson, following his gaze.

At the end of the street, a score of lancers' mounts waited by the foot of steps leading to the entrance of a modest but noble church, the building giving way to cloister walls and a domestic range off to the left. The wall was breached in several places, a gate of iron grillework dangling crazily from its hinges, and smoke curled lazily upward from the cloistral buildings beyond.

"I don't like the looks of that," Morgan murmured, as several agitated-looking lancers on foot came out a shattered postern door.

As one, he and Kelson set spurs to their mounts and moved out at the trot, splitting to either side of Jatham and the standard and clattering on with their escort trailing raggedly behind. The troop had regained some semblance of order by the time they reached the foot of the steps, but the faces of the lancers turning to acknowledge them were tight-jawed and grim. One of the younger men had sunk to a crouch to put head between knees, near to fainting, and their officer raised a tight-lipped and outraged face as Morgan reined to a halt, grabbing at the horse's headstall to keep from getting stepped on. Behind them, a greenish-looking Conall stumbled out ahead of Roger, the feisty young Earl of Jenas, who looked as if he cheerfully could have killed the first person who crossed him.

"What's happened?" Morgan demanded, swinging down from his mount and pulling off his helm.

The lancer captain shook his head, handing off the reins of Morgan's horse to one of his men and steadying Kelson's as the king also dismounted.

"Something for that traitor Trurill to be very proud of, I suppose, Your Grace. It's a convent—or was. What else is there to say?"

"How do you know it was Trurill?" Kelson asked, as he also removed his helm and pushed back his mail coif. By his tone, and the casual ease with which he cradled the helm under his arm, Morgan guessed that the implications obvious to a man more battle-seasoned than Kelson simply had not yet registered with the seventeen-year-old king. That Kelson might *not* fully understand apparently had not yet occurred to Roger, either, for the young earl charged blithely on to give the king the answer he had asked for.

"Oh, it was Trurill, all right, Sire," Earl Roger said, contempt for the name so thick in his words that Morgan could almost taste it. "The sisters don't know anything about coats of arms, but one of the monks described him to a fare-thee—Conall, goddammit, if you're going to be sick, do it somewhere else!" he snapped, suddenly clamping a gloved hand

on the prince's nearer forearm and giving him a stiff shake.
"These things happen!"

"What—*things*?" Kelson demanded, stunned, not wanting to believe what he was starting to realize. "Are you saying—"

"Kelson, they—raped the sisters," Conall whispered, too
numb with shock to object to the liberty Roger had taken
with his royal person. "They—even killed some of them.
And they d-desecrated the church! They—"

"They rutted in the aisles and they pissed on the High
Altar, Sire!" Roger said bluntly, outrage smoldering in his
eyes. "There isn't any pretty, noble way to say it, because
there isn't anything pretty or noble about it—or about men
who would do such a thing. If you've never seen something
like this before—well, it's probably time you did, just so you
know the kind of animal you're dealing with in Brice of Trurill!"

Roger's outburst left little doubt in Morgan's mind what
they would find inside. Tightly leashing his own anger, he
passed the earl his helm, with its telltale coronet of rank,
and bade the ashen Kelson do the same, catching an all-too-
vivid preview from the man's mind as their hands brushed
in the transfer.

Quickly he and the king shouldered between Roger and
the now shaking Conall and climbed the glass and stone-
littered steps. The distraught cries of the injured and bereft
floated on the still air with the stench of smoke and blood
and excrement as they neared the shattered doors. But even
the Deryni imaging that Morgan tried to relay was not sufficient to prepare Kelson for what lay inside.

Rape was a crime at no time condoned by any knight or
other man of honor, much less the desecration of a holy
place—though the former occurred all too often in time of
war for it to be regarded as uncommon. The rape of Saint
Brigid's, then, as Morgan soon discovered the place was
called, was all the more despicable because the chief victims
had been nuns, whose consecrated status generally pre-
served them from the fate more often meted out to their
secular sisters.

"We begged them to spare us, my lord," one of the blue-
robed women told Morgan, sobbing, as he and Kelson
paused in one of the less-damaged side chapels, currently
commandeered as a hospice for the injured. "We gave them

the foodstuffs they asked for. We emptied our storerooms to them. We did not dream they would violate the sanctuary of the church to—to take their pleasure of us.''

"Beastly, savage men!" another agreed, her anger at odds with her physical attitude of prayer as she knelt and watched a tattered and bruised old monk give Extreme Unction to a sister sprawled motionless in the doorway leading from church to cloister garth. "Like animals they were! May God forgive them for what they've done, for I never shall, an it cost me the bliss of paradise!"

Once past his initial, disbelieving shock, Kelson weathered the inspection reasonably well, he and Morgan passing all unrecognized among the survivors, if somewhat suspiciously received—though that was for being men, as much as anything. In the minds of most, Kelson's crimson brigandine with its golden lion apparently linked him vaguely with Haldane service in some way—perhaps a squire or young man-at-arms, by his age, or aide to the courteous, fair-haired lord in black and green—but that was all. And Morgan's own armorial bearings would not be expected to be familiar to a tiny community of women tucked away in the foothills of southern Meara.

"Oh, they were highborn lords as well as common soldiers," came the unanimous accusation of all questioned, with little variation. "Most of them wore fancy armor such as your own."

Others recalled border tartans and leathers, and eyed Kelson's border braid with some suspicion.

"Could you describe any of the tartans, or the designs on shields or surcoats?" Morgan always asked. "Even colors could help us identify who they were."

But most were too cowed, or too dazed, or both, to recall any truly useful details, and both Morgan and Kelson were reluctant to attempt Deryni persuasion under the circumstances. Not until they took their questioning into a corner of the ruined garden did the pattern of response shift.

There they found what at first appeared to be merely a repeat of the same grim story: a hysterically sobbing young girl with masses of curly blond hair who cowered in the arms of another at their approach. Both wore the pale blue habit of novices of the order, though the latter was decently coiffed. Neither looked to be above sixteen.

"Oh, what does it *matter* who he was?" came the un-expectedly defiant reply of the coherent one, as she raised a tear-streaked face to glare angrily at the two armored men. "He told her he was sick and tired of having to knuckle under to arrogant bishops and priests, and that he was going to show them he was a man.

"A man—ha!" Outraged fire flashed in her dark brown eyes. "Big, important man, to rape an innocent woman! *She* had nothing to do with these bishops who supposedly offended him. Now her betrothed will *never* have her!"

"Her betrothed?" Kelson asked, crouching down beside them. "And—bishops? But, is she not a sister?"

"The Princess Janniver?" The girl shot him an amazed look, blinking at his obvious surprise. "Ah, I thought everyone knew by now."

Grimacing, for the princess had redoubled her weeping at the sound of her name and title, the darker girl pulled off the pale blue coif covering her hair and pressed it into Janniver's hands to use as a handkerchief. A thick, blue-black braid tumbled down the back of her own rumpled and soot-streaked habit, and she pushed a damp tendril out of her eyes with the back of one grimy hand before looking back at Kelson a little less belligerently, one arm still around the weeping Janniver. Morgan guessed she had no idea who either of them was.

"Well, then, my lords. Where to begin?" she said, with a brave attempt at nonchalance. The lilt of eastern climes was in her voice, consistent with her dark hair and eyes and olive skin.

"She's the only daughter of a prince of the Connait," she went on. "She was on her way to be married to the King of Llannedd, and paused here to make a prenuptial retreat. It's customary for visitors to wear the habit of novices during their stay with us," she added. "That's why her attacker thought she was one of us."

As Kelson glanced up at Morgan in question, the Deryni lord also dropped to his knees beside them.

"Is she actually injured or only badly frightened, child?" Morgan asked gently.

The girl shook her head and drew the sobbing Janniver closer into the circle of her arms in a vain attempt to comfort her.

"Mostly frightened, I think," she whispered. "She—won't talk about it."

"And you?" Morgan persisted.

The girl sniffled and bowed her head over Janniver's golden curls.

"I was untouched," she murmured. "I was in the cellars with two other sisters when the soldiers came. We hid. They didn't find us, but they—brutalized Sister Constance. Four of them. She was very old, and she—died." She lifted her eyes defiantly. "What difference does it make to you?" she challenged. "Do you ask out of true concern, or to titillate your own male lust?"

"I ask because I have a wife and baby daughter at home," Morgan said softly, refusing to take offense. "Because I would pray that some other man might show similar compassion if *they* had suffered what you and the princess have endured. I thought I might be able to help. I have some ability as a healer."

"And *do* you, sir?" The girl's eyes flashed. "Well, we have some ability as healers ourselves. Has no one told you? We are a hospitaller order. We were founded to tend the sick and injured." Her eyes went softly unfocused and began to brim with tears as she quickly looked out at the ruined yard beyond him.

"We exist to give succor to the ill and injured, doing harm to no man. What more fitting reward could we ask than to have men—"

Her voice broke in a sob. As the tears began to flow, and she buried her face in one hand, Morgan eased a little closer and reached out to touch her arm, at the same time mentally warning Kelson to see to Janniver, who had cringed back and gasped at his approach.

"No! Please d—" Janniver began.

But Kelson was already seizing one wrist to keep the princess within reach, passing a hand gently but insistently over her forehead and willing her to sleep. Before she could even finish her plea, she was plummeting into blessed unconsciousness, Kelson scrambling closer to catch her before she could collapse into a rose bush, a dead weight in his arms.

But Morgan, attempting the same sort of approach with Janniver's companion, met an entirely different response: the surge of powerful shields springing up in reflex as his mind brushed hers—a trained, disciplined defense—and then quick shifting to a more neutral balance point as one Deryni mind recognized another and she read his benign intent.

"Who *are* you?" he murmured, as she sagged against his chest with a little groan of relief and abandoned any physical resistance, shoulders shaking in silent reaction as she tried to gulp back her tears.

"Rothana," she replied. "My—father is Hakim, Emir Nur Hallaj. Who—who are *you?*"

*She's Deryni!* Morgan sent to Kelson with an incredulous glance. *And kin to Richenda, if I'm not mistaken.*

"I'm Morgan," he said gently. "That's Kelson of Gwynedd. And I believe you and my wife are related by marriage."

"*Your—your wife?*"

He felt her stiffen at his revelation, but he could read nothing behind her now impenetrable shields as she drew back to look at him. Nor did she make any attempt to touch his mind again.

Kelson shifted the dead weight of Janniver in his arms to gape at both of them in amazement.

"Is she really related to Richenda?"

"Richenda?" Rothana whispered. "Richenda of Rheljan is your wife? She who was Countess of Marley?"

"Aye, among other things," Morgan said neutrally. "She is Duchess of Corwyn now, however."

"Oh, merciful God, of course," Rothana murmured, clasping both hands before her lips as she shook her head in disbelief. "Morgan—the Deryni Duke of Corwyn—and Kelson Haldane, King of Gwynedd. I should have known."

"Well, I knew our fame had gone before us," Morgan muttered, "but—"

"Oh, no, my lord, I meant no slight. But I remember Richenda from my childhood, before her marriage to Bran Coris. She used to play with me, and—"

She stiffened and broke off as she glanced from Morgan to Kelson.

"She had a son by Bran Coris, my lord. And Bran betrayed you."

"Aye," Kelson replied. "But his son did not. Surely you don't suppose I would have harmed—"

"Of course she didn't," Morgan said. "In fact—have you ever met the boy, my lady?"

Rothana shook her head.

"Perhaps you'd like to, then," Morgan went on, trying to put Rothana at ease and lighten the mood. "Sup with us this evening, and you shall. My stepson, Brendan Coris, serves as my page on this campaign. He's seven. Richenda and I have a daughter as well, over a year old. Briony, she's called. You hadn't heard of our marriage?"

"No, I had not."

Once over her initial surprise, Rothana seemed not at all dismayed at the news, and soon was asking eager questions about the children and Richenda, though she gracefully declined Morgan's supper invitation.

"I thank you, my lord, but I must not," she said softly, returning her attention to the sleeping Janniver. "It would not be seemly for me to partake of better than my sisters and the townsfolk may expect, even were I not needed to help tend the injured. Besides, the princess will need me when she awakens—and I thank you, Sire, for granting her such ease as should have been my duty, had I myself not been so shaken by this day's villainy."

"I'll send some of our battle surgeons to assist you," Kelson said quietly. "And provisions—to the town as well. And work details to help with the cleanup and any burials."

As he went to give the necessary orders, Morgan carried the sleeping Janniver into the church at Rothana's direction and left both in the care of the abbess. Later that night, after supping and hearing reports from their commanders and scout captains on the probable route of the raiders, Morgan and a coolly silent Kelson returned to the abbey to check on the progress both of their royal patient and the abbey in general.

"The men are doing a masterly job of cleaning up," Archbishop Cardiel told them, just coming out the door of the church with Father Lael, the wiry little priest who served as his own battle surgeon and chaplain. "They're nearly done in the church. I should be able to reconsecrate it before we leave in the morning."

"And the sisters?" Morgan asked.

Cardiel shrugged and sighed. "Not as easy a question as the physical surrounds, Alaric, though I suppose they're doing as well as can be expected. I've just gotten some actual figures from the abbess."

"How many killed?" Kelson asked.

"Fortunately, not as many as we first feared," Cardiel replied. "Casualties were highest among the men, of course. Five lay brothers and a monk were killed outright when they tried to defend the women, and a few more roughed up—the usual sort of thing. Only three sisters died, though: one during the assault and two more as a result of injuries. Actually, more escaped than not."

"Thank God for that," Kelson murmured, shifting his attention to Lael. "There were few deaths in the town, at least. What about the princess?"

The usually merry Father Lael, his surgeon's satchel slung jauntily over his shoulder, glanced back at the doorway through which he and Cardiel had just emerged and heaved a heavy sigh.

"I've given her a sedative, Sire. Physically, I'm sure she'll mend quickly. That old biddy of an abbess would hardly let me near her, of course, but she's young and strong—and the little novice who's with her claims there are no serious physical injuries." He sighed again.

"The *other* hurts are the ones that take so long to heal. It's too bad she can't just forget. Or, can she?" he added, glancing expectantly first at Morgan, then at Kelson, for he had seen both of them work often enough to surmise some of their potentials. "You could make her forget, couldn't you?"

As Kelson glanced at his feet, suddenly inaccessible—Morgan had no idea why—Morgan cleared his throat gently, bringing Lael's attention back to him.

"Within the bounds of propriety, we'll certainly do what we can, Father," he said softly, at the same time trying to ascertain the reason for Kelson's isolation. "However, if the abbess wouldn't let an archbishop's battle surgeon-chaplain touch her charge, you can imagine how she'll feel about a Deryni duke and a hot-blooded young king whose soul may also be somewhat suspect."

"What if she *won't* let us see Janniver?" Kelson murmured, still tight-shuttered when the two priests had gone on and he and Morgan were making their way toward the chapel where Janniver slept. "God, I should have done it while I had the chance, when we first found her."

"Done what?"

"Read her memory. Remember, Rothana said that Janniver's attacker ranted about arrogant bishops and priests. Suppose he was talking about Loris?"

"Hmmm, the description certainly fits," Morgan agreed.

"Of course it does. And even if he *wasn't* talking about Loris, he may have said something else that will give us some clue as to who's leading the rebel bands in this area. Besides, I want the bastard!"

"Ah," Morgan said, suddenly understanding Kelson's mood. "And what if Rothana's already done what the good Father Lael suggested *we* do?"

Kelson stopped dead in his tracks and looked at Morgan aghast. "Good Lord, you don't suppose she has, do you?"

Rothana had not; but her cool efficiency quickly turned to vehement resistance when Kelson told her what *he* wished to do.

"No, no, and a thousand times, no!" she whispered, as she and Kelson glared at one another across the sleeping girl and Morgan watched uncomfortably from the chapel doorway. The abbess had left Rothana in charge before setting out on her rounds, but the Deryni novice was quite sufficient a defender for the sleeping princess.

"Would that I had eased her of the memory already! And I *should* have, had I known what you would ask."

"My lady, it would be quickly done—" Kelson began.

"No! Can you not understand? It is not even seemly that you should *be* here. Has she not been sufficiently violated already? What purpose would it serve?"

"It would serve my sense of honor," Kelson replied. "I wish to bring the perpetrators of this deed to justice, if I can. I *will* read her, Rothana. Stand aside."

"Ah, then, do you mean to use physical force and overpower me?" she whispered, taking a step back as he started to raise a hand in entreaty. "Does *that* serve your sense of honor?"

"*What?*"

"If that is your choice, there is nothing I can do to prevent it, of course," she said, "for you are two armed men, and I am only a woman, and as defenseless to stop you as *she* was."

"My lady—"

"Go ahead and overpower me!" she taunted. "For I swear that is the only way you shall touch her. And I doubt even the two of you would dare attempt any—*other* force to overwhelm me." She raised her chin in defiance. "I do not know your training, but I know mine. Nor would you wish to risk what might be drawn down upon you!"

The taunt might have been a child's bravado, but Kelson could not be sure. Had he not been already somewhat in awe of her—for he had never met a Deryni woman near his own age—he might have simply gone ahead and done what needed to be done. He doubted that Rothana would *really* wage the full-scale psychic defense she threatened, right here in the church. And as for any small amount of physical force—

But that was not the answer. Both Rothana and Janniver surely had had enough of force for one day. He must try to persuade her, if he could.

"My lady, please try to understand," he explained patiently. "If I can find out who, specifically, was responsible for what happened here, it will tell me a great deal about my enemy. And I *shall* find him—mark me. And when I do, I shall mete him the fate he deserves."

"*Shall* you, then, my lord?" she replied, dark eyes flashing. "And shall you then take your vengeance upon him? Will that restore what Janniver or any of the others have lost?"

"My lady—"

"'Vengeance is *mine*, saith the Lord,'" she went on, primly quoting scripture at him. "'I will repay.' The Lord of Hosts will do this, Your Majesty—not Kelson Haldane, Lord of Gwynedd!"

Such impertinence was almost maddening enough to change Kelson's mind about force. Nearly speechless with anger, grey eyes narrowed in concentration, he set his balled fists on his belt and glanced for guidance at Morgan, who could give him none, then looked sourly back at Rothana.

"It is not vengeance I seek, my lady, but justice," he replied, keeping his voice low and expressionless. "'O Lord, with your judgment endow the King, and with your justice the King's son.' Do you think you are the only one who can quote scripture to support an argument?"

Her mouth opened and closed once in astonishment. She clearly had not expected that response. When she started to turn away, he bounded up the single altar step and seized her upper arm, whirling her around to face him again.

"You can turn your back on *me*, my lady, but you can't turn your back on sacred writ—not if you have any respect for what that habit means!" he said angrily. "'Let our strength be the law of the just,'" he quoted again. "'For that which is feeble is found to be nothing worth.' I want to bring him to justice under *law*, Rothana. I will *not* countenance this sort of behavior in my kingdom—and especially not in men formerly sworn to uphold my laws."

"Then, take your hand off of me, my lord," she said frostily, "if *you* have any respect for the habit that I wear."

He sighed and released her, sensing he was bested, but as he half turned to glance at the slumbering Janniver, and Morgan still filling the doorway of the chapel, he knew he could not quite let it drop. Not yet.

"I ask you one more time, my lady—for *her* sake," he murmured.

"No, my lord. She is under my protection. She has none other to defend her."

"Then, if you won't let me read her directly, *you* do it," Kelson pleaded, ready to grasp at any faint hope. "And then let me read the pertinent information from *your* mind. I *know* that I'm asking a great deal, but it's important to me to find out who did this—*all* of this!"

As he swept one hand to include all the violated abbey, reaching out to her with his mind as well, she seemed to recoil to an almost physical blow. Wincing, she turned away again, bowing her head and pressing clasped hands close against her lips in an attitude of prayer. But when she turned back toward Kelson, some of the stiffness had gone out of her shoulders.

"I—had lost the larger picture for a while, my lord," she said softly, not meeting Kelson's eyes. "I had—forgotten how many others suffered at the hands of those who did this work." She bowed her head again. "I will do as you request, but I—must ask that it be done in private. Duke Alaric, I mean you no disrespect, but—this will be very difficult for me. Not the procedure itself, but—"

"I understand," Morgan murmured, making her a little bow before glancing at the king. "Shall I wait outside, my prince?"

"No, go back to the tent," Kelson said steadily, not taking his eyes from Rothana. "I'll be along directly."

When Morgan had gone, closing the door behind him, Rothana sighed and came down to Janniver, looking suddenly like a frightened child, fragile and vulnerable as she sank down on the stone floor beside the low bed. Kelson would have gone to her, but she sensed his intent and shook her head, further staying him with a gesture.

"Please, my lord, I must do this alone," she whispered, her face strained in the wan light of the single votive light set on the bare altar. "You must not try to help, either myself or Her Highness. She would be angry and frightened as well as embarrassed, if she even guessed that *I* was about to know what she suffered. The touch of mind to mind can be more intimate than any violation of the body. When I have done, I will show you what concerns you."

Kelson only nodded and settled gingerly on the altar step, hardly breathing as Rothana took Janniver's nearer hand and clasped it in both of hers. He let himself center and settle as he sensed her entering trance, already preparing for his own rapport as he watched her dark eyes take on the softly unfocused sheen of deeper trancing.

Then her eyes were closing and she was shuddering, shaking her head, ducking to press her forehead hard against the soft edge of the mattress, shoulders shaking in silent reaction to what she saw.

He wanted very much to go to her, but his promise kept him firmly in his place. When, at last, she lifted her head to look at him, her dusky face was pale and drawn, her eyes bright with tears. She seemed to get herself in hand as she carefully laid Janniver's hand back at her side and brushed a gentle touch across the sleeping girl's forehead, composed once more when she looked up again.

"I didn't expect that she would know his name," she said quietly, "so there's no disappointment at that. I *can* show you his face, however—and the design on his surcoat. Will that be enough?"

Gravely Kelson nodded, not trusting himself to speak.

"Very well. Give me your hand," she said, holding out hers.

He came across the altar step and settled at her feet. Her hand was cool and passive in his, the skin soft in contrast to the calluses of his own. As their eyes met, he lowered his outer shields and allowed himself to be drawn into her directing without resistance, knowing that the control he permitted was only tenuous, that he could break it at any time, if necessary.

Drifting on the tide of her bidding, he sensed the outside world receding, his vision tunneling until all he could see was her eyes. Then even that was gone as he let his eyelids close and floated on the blankness—until suddenly he was in another point of perspective, and a form was taking shape before him.

The man would have been handsome, had his face not been contorted with rage and lust. He was young, too—perhaps only a little older than Janniver herself—but only general impressions filtered past her terror: brown hair barbered close in the common style of soldiers, matted with sweat from having been confined under the camail pushed back on the slender shoulders; a wet, leering mouth working obscenely as he raved about bishops and priests, and having to obey them.

The brown eyes burned with madness as the man stared at his victim. Kelson could feel himself trembling in an echo of Janniver's own terror, projected through Rothana, and a scream threatened to burst from his throat as a gauntleted hand bruised cringing flesh and the face came too close to be looked upon any longer.

Only as the free hand wrenched at a buckle, releasing the man's sword belt, and a sense of vertigo threatened to overwhelm him, did Kelson finally manage to rip his own attention through Janniver's memory and notice the arms emblazoned on the man's surcoat: the chequered field of silver and gold and the dancing bear and crimson *etoilles* of old sovereign Meara, all differenced with the label of the eldest son.

# Chapter Nine

*She entered into the soul of the servant of the Lord,
and withstood dreadful kings in wonders and signs.*
                                        —Wisdom of Solomon 10:16

That part of Kelson that remained dispassionate and uniquely Kelson recognized Janniver's attacker at once. He had never met Ithel of Meara face to face, but with memory triggered by the chequered surcoat, the family resemblance to Llewell and Sidana became immediately apparent—and only Ithel would dare to wear that coat of arms. The part of Kelson that was king and dispenser of justice noted the face and device with steely-willed calm, and marked Ithel of Meara for appropriate disposition when eventually they met.

But the part of Kelson that, through Janniver's senses, briefly relived the memory of Ithel's attack did not know or care that the armored boy-man roughly thrusting her to the ground was a rebel prince—only recoiled in disbelieving terror and tried, unavailingly, to shrink from the fear and the pain.

Adding to the outrage was Kelson's awareness, in the unassailable security of his own consciousness, that the fragment of memory Rothana passed on to him was only a minute part of what Janniver herself had suffered. Even filtered through Rothana's perception, truncated to only a few seconds' duration, the helplessness and pain and shame reverberated with such intensity that he felt momentarily paralyzed, powerless to break the link, even had his life depended upon it.

By the time Rothana ended it, his heart was pounding with Janniver's reflected terror. He was drenched with perspiration, panting, his hand clutching Rothana's so tightly that a part of him was amazed she had not cried out.

Moaning, he made himself release her, clapping his hands to his temples as he half-collapsed across the altar step and lay there shaking, his heart still pounding, gulping in great, shuddering breaths to regain his equilibrium.

Gradually, his measures had their effect. Yet even as his head cleared and his heart rate slowed to a more normal level, he realized that Rothana had given him not only the information he had asked for, if more intensely than he had dreamed, but also a glimpse of her own reaction to the outrage—and with that, almost without volition on her own part, a fleeting but intimate brush with her own soul. And as he raised his head to look at her, he sensed that both of them had responded to that glimpse, and were shaken by it.

"I'm not sorry for what I did," she whispered, flinching a little as their eyes met. "I had to make you understand what *she* felt. You're a man. You can't know what it means to be a woman, and to be—*used* that way. And Janniver had been so sheltered, so protected. . . ."

As her voice trailed off, Kelson glanced away, forcing himself to draw another deep, ragged breath as he rubbed both hands hard over his face. He hardly dared trust himself to speak.

"You're right," he finally managed to murmur, glancing furtively at the sleeping Janniver and suddenly very thankful that she was asleep. "I wouldn't have had any idea. If you—think it best to blur her memory, by all means do it." He swallowed with difficulty. "I only wonder who will blur yours—or mine."

Rothana squared her shoulders and let out a resigned sigh. "One who gives oneself to a life of healing must expect to bear such burdens, my lord," she said softly. "Just as one who wears a crown must ever feel its weight. Is it not so?"

It was. But acknowledgment of that universal truth did not make his own burden any lighter, or resolve the other emotions still churning just at the surface of awareness. When he had taken halting leave of her, he spent the best part of an hour wandering the quieting camp alone, walking the picket lines and brushing the velvet noses of the greathorses thrust out to nicker welcome and nuzzle his clothing for a treat. All of that blurred in the face of the memory that kept playing itself back in his mind, until finally he returned to his tent to seek out Morgan.

"Sire?" Morgan said, he and young Brendan rising as Kelson drew aside the entry flap and came inside.

They had been cleaning Morgan's harness while they waited—Brendan all smart and correct in his page's livery, polishing a spur; Morgan stripped to arming tunic and worn leather sandals, bare-legged, a sleeveless mantle of forest green silk drawn on against the faint chill of the late night air. The high boots and metal-studded brigandine he had worn earlier glistened in the light of the several lanterns that lit the enclosure, as did the sword with the belt coiled loosely around its scabbard, lying on the camp bed that was Morgan's.

"Brendan, you can go to bed now," Morgan said, sending the boy on his way after only a glance at the expression on Kelson's face. "We'll finish in the morning."

Eastern silks rustled in the lanternlight as Morgan poured a cup of wine Kelson had not asked for but needed very much, and Kelson gulped half of it gratefully before sighing and sinking down on a camp stool Morgan pulled beside the little table. Only after another deep draught did he feel ready even to think about speaking of what had happened.

"I had to walk for a while," the king said softly, setting his cup on the table and unbuckling his swordbelt, letting sword and belt slip to the straw mat beneath his feet. "I needed time to think."

Morgan said nothing as he settled on a stool in a rustle of silk, only waiting patiently as Kelson stared into the flame of the lantern set on the table between them.

"It was Ithel," Kelson murmured after a moment, not looking up. "There's no doubt about that. I'll make him pay for it, too."

Morgan only leaned one elbow on the little table and propped his chin gingerly on that hand. The other hand toyed with the stem of a silver goblet—unfortunately empty—but he did not even consider refilling it. Something more had happened than the mere discovery of the attacker's identity, but Kelson was not quite ready to talk about it.

After a very long, still silence, Kelson glanced up uncomfortably and then half-turned away on his stool to stare at the tent wall, in profile.

"Alaric, have you ever raped a woman?" the king finally asked in a very low voice.

Morgan raised one eyebrow, but otherwise allowed no outward sign of his surprise.

"No, I haven't," he said softly. "Nor, I think, have you."

Kelson flashed a grim, fleeting smile, then shook his head, clasping his hands on his knees. "No," he whispered. "I confess I've never even been tempted. It isn't through want of normal—appetites," he added. "I—wanted Sidana. . . . I think."

He swallowed hard, twisting Sidana's ring on his little finger, and Morgan nodded understandingly.

"I'm sure you did."

"That was—different, though," Kelson went on. "Rape is . . ."

"—Is, unfortunately, a harsh fact of war, my prince," Morgan said gently. "No honorable man condones it, but it—happens."

"I know."

Kelson swallowed again, then let out a heavy sigh.

"Alaric, have you—have you ever wondered what it must be like for—for the woman?" he said haltingly. "I confess I hadn't. But I—know now."

And as he choked back a sob and buried his face in his hands, Morgan nodded slowly, guessing what had happened.

"Rothana showed you Janniver's memory?"

Kelson raised a bleak profile to Morgan's scrutiny. "How did you know?"

"This is not the first time I've come upon a scene of rape, Kelson. Why do you think I didn't suggest we read the victims this afternoon?"

"Oh." After a few seconds' reflection, Kelson looked down at his intertwined fingers again, still troubled. "There's—something else," he said softly.

"Yes?"

"It—it was Rothana," he stammered, shifting uneasily. "I—I glimpsed a—I don't know—a flash of something I—I—" He shook his head vehemently. "It shouldn't have been there, Alaric. It wasn't right. She's vowed to God. I shouldn't even *think* such things!"

"Sharing another's memory is a very intense and intimate experience, under the most well-intentioned of circumstances," Morgan said neutrally, wondering whether Kelson truly could have touched the sort of rapport to make him be entertaining even semi-serious thoughts about a nun—and already assessing the potentials of a match with a trained Deryni like Rothana.

"And you're a normal, healthy young man, and she's a spirited and fascinating young woman, and Deryni as well—something you've not encountered before. It's not at all surprising that you should feel at least a twinge of interest. Besides, is she not a novice? That means her vows are but temporary."

"That's beside the point," Kelson murmured, shaking his head. "It's clear she has an honest vocation. Who am I to—to—"

"Kelson, if she truly *does* have a vocation to the religious life, I don't think you need worry about undermining it—if that's what concerns you," Morgan replied. "And if she *hasn't* a vocation—why, she may have much to recommend herself to you as a potential bride."

Kelson looked up in alarm, his expression shifting from shock through speculation to rejection.

"Bride? That's absurd! I couldn't possibly—"

"No, you're probably right," Morgan said, ending Kelson's protests with a nonchalant wave of one hand. "It's out of the question. Forget I even mentioned it."

But the seeds of speculation had been sown, whether or not Kelson would admit it to himself, and perhaps contributed to his next decision regarding the refugees now under his protection.

"I think it might be best to send the Princess Janniver back to Rhemuth," he soon informed Morgan. "And the rest of the sisters as well. They'll be safer there, as long as Ithel and his men are on the loose."

"Aye, that's probably true," Morgan murmured, being very neutrally agreeable and noting that the situation would also keep Kelson safe from temptation where Rothana was concerned.

"Janniver *is* a princess, after all," Kelson reasoned, rising to pace back and forth on the straw matting, and wrenching at the buckles that closed the throat of his brigandine. "And I don't know that it's a good idea to return her to her father—at least until I've avenged her honor. And God knows what kind of reception she'd get from the King of Llannedd. He was expecting a virgin bride."

"Hmmm, it *could* be awkward," Morgan agreed.

"Aye, they'll be safest at Rhemuth, until I've had a chance to sort things out," Kelson went on. "And Rothana can help Aunt Meraude, when the new baby comes. She's trained in healing, after all. Besides, it will be good to have another Deryni at court. I'm sure Richenda won't mind."

Morgan had to agree that she probably would not.

"I have it! I'll give Conall charge of their escort," Kelson continued, grinning as the thought came to him. "His first independent command—he'll love that!"

"So long as he doesn't see the duty as an exile—missing out on all the fighting," Morgan said lightly. "But I suspect that escorting two such attractive young ladies might soften the sting."

Kelson grimaced and made a disparaging wave of his hand. "Oh, really, Alaric! He has a lady-love at home. You've seen how he disappears for hours at a time. Besides, I can't spare anyone more experienced. We're going to need every good man we can get, before this is finished."

"Well, Conall is never going to *get* more experienced if you don't give him responsibility," Morgan pointed out.

"This *is* responsibility; it just doesn't require battle-sense. Someone has to do it. And quite frankly, he'll be far more use to Nigel, back in Rhemuth, than he is to me. He can be *so* tedious sometimes. I'll make it sound very important."

Fortunately, Conall also chose to see the importance of the mission. When called into Kelson's tent a little later and told what was required, he seemed almost relieved.

"My own command!" he breathed, allowing himself a tentative smile. "I confess, I'd hoped for battle experience, but that would have been under everybody else's supervision. This one is mine! And maybe we'll have to fight off brigands on the way home."

The news that he would also carry back dispatches to Nigel, and hold himself in readiness through the summer if Nigel should require a confidential messenger back to the king, also sweetened the assignment.

"I might not be in Rhemuth very long, after all," he said. "Father might have news to send back very soon."

"Or he may need you there to help deal with our Torenthi hostages," Kelson reminded him. "I'm afraid I've left him with a dreadful job. Do try to give him as much support as you can."

The interview had its desired effect, and at dawn the next morning, a happy and contented Prince Conall busied himself assembling the party that would return to Rhemuth. Less happy were the abbess and some of the other sisters, though most of them seemed resigned to the journey, once Kelson had explained the reason for his decision.

"I can't protect you here, Reverend Mother," he said, adjusting a stirrup leather on the abbess' saddle, and acutely aware of Rothana mounting another horse behind her. "The danger may not matter much to you and your order, but the princess has been through quite enough, I think; and I'd prefer not to send her on such a long journey without the comfort of other women. You'll be safe and welcome in Rhemuth, I assure you. If you wish, I'll even give you land to establish a new abbey nearby."

The abbess inclined her head curtly. "That is most generous, Sire, but our work is here. And as for our safety, what of the safety of the village women, who have not the advantage of a royal protector?"

Kelson sighed and made a final check of the horse's girth. He was already dressed for battle, the Haldane lion on his brigandine bright gold against crimson leather, night-black hair pulled back sleekly in a neat border braid. Behind him, Morgan was performing similar service for the princess, who sat weeping miserably on a dun-colored palfrey, pale face buried in her hands. Rothana urged her horse forward a few paces to comfort her, but Janniver wept on, her desolation beginning to shake the composure of some of the other sisters.

"I wish I had time to discuss the matter with you, Reverend Mother, but the decision has been made," Kelson said. "I'm sorry you don't agree. Conall?"

Conall had been giving last-minute instructions to his men, and continued doing so in passing as he strode toward the king, every inch a Haldane on this bright June morning. When he reached the royal presence, he gave smart salute with a gloved fist to breast, including the women in a sketchy bow. Kelson had rarely seen Conall so self-assured and content.

"Well, cousin, you seem eager to begin your new duties," he said with a smile, bidding Brendan forward with a thick packet of dispatches, which he passed to Conall. "You have good men, and I am certain they will serve you well. God grant you a safe journey to Rhemuth.''

Conall slipped the packet into the front of his brigandine with another little bow. ''Thank you, my Liege.''

''Just give that entire packet to Nigel,'' Kelson went on. ''I've included instructions to several others, but he can sort them out. Routine replies can be sent back by regular couriers. Richenda will know how to find us.''

Conall only nodded again, but Kelson surmised from his expression that he understood exactly how Kelson meant for her to do the finding. As he glanced up at the abbess, however, he put that from his mind, also trying to forget that Rothana watched from a horse nearby.

''Reverend Mother, I place you and your ladies in the hands of a most excellent commander: Prince Conall Haldane. Cousin, this is Mother Heloise.''

Basking in Kelson's recommendation, Conall made the abbess a courtly bow. ''I am most honored to be able to serve you, Reverend Mother,'' he said.

As he straightened, Kelson grinned and caught him quickly in a cousinly embrace.

''Good luck, Conall,'' he murmured so that only Conall could hear. ''Would that we were all going back to Rhemuth with you. I like not what I shall have to do in the months ahead.''

Conall flushed and also managed to smile as they drew apart, pleased but just a little embarrassed at being the center of royal attention.

''I shall do my best, Kelson,'' he said softly.

Then he was backing off to make Kelson a last, formal bow, mounting up and signalling his party to move out. The horses sidled and jigged in the cool of the early morning mist, bits a-jingle. The bright livery of the men showed almost garish against the pale, muted blues of the sisters' mantles.

As the last rider trotted out of the mustering space before the royal tent, Kelson turned to Morgan and let out a relieved sigh. Behind Morgan, his other officers were waiting for further orders.

''Well, that's done. Gentlemen, we're behind schedule. Let's finish breaking camp and ride. We have an appointment to keep with Ithel of Meara.''

As Morgan gave the orders, and the officers scattered to relay them, neither king nor general noticed a R'Kassan scout draw apart from his fellows and disappear beyond the picket lines, obscured by the bustle of breaking camp.

In the fortnight that followed, Kelson never did catch sight of Ithel himself, though his scouts reported glimpses of Brice of Trurill and other turncoat border barons. As they penetrated deeper into the rugged hill country which lay between them and Ratharkin, even the smaller battle groups Kelson had divided off became unwieldy, so he sent Generals Remie and Gloddruth and the heavy cavalry and foot in a more westerly direction, to press toward the Mearan capital over a slightly longer but flatter plains approach. Meanwhile, he, Morgan, and Ewan broke the remainder of the army, the light horse and lancer units, into even smaller warbands and pressed on through the hill country, hunting for Ithel of Meara and Brice of Trurill.

But though their northward progress continued, punctuated by increasing skirmishes with bands of a similar size and disposition, they fought no decisive battles and found no Mearan prince. Looted villages and burned-out fields abounded, and the increasing scarcity of forage for man and beast confirmed that Kelson had chosen wisely in sending the bulk of his army by another route.

Nor were the increasingly brief reports from the army in the north any more encouraging. Duncan continued to skirmish with the occasional warband, mostly episcopal and mercenary forces, and fought several larger engagements successfully, but Sicard continued to evade him—constantly on the move with, one presumed, the bulk of the Mearan army, location unknown.

*If it is Sicard directing their northern strategy, he's good,* Duncan warned them. *The suspense is almost worse than actual battle. The men jump at shadows—and that's mostly all there is to jump at. I'd almost be glad for an honest, full-pitched battle. This game of hide-and-seek is dulling our edge.*

Fear that the edge might be fatally blunted was Kelson's worst nightmare, as he collapsed on his pallet at the end of each frustrating day and worried. Eventually, the Mearans *must* stand and fight. He would be at the gates of Ratharkin in a week.

Rather less often, he wondered how things were going at home, and whether Conall and his charges had safely reached Rhemuth yet. He tried not to think about any of those charges in particular; and as the days passed, that part became easier.

But Conall and his charges reached Rhemuth without incident, and the prince received a hero's welcome as he escorted them through the gatehouse arch and into the castle yard. Nigel had quarters awaiting them, alerted to their coming by Richenda, several days before, and the sisters were quickly installed in apartments overlooking the castle gardens.

Duchess Meraude, delivered of a healthy daughter the week before, took the pale and listless Princess Janniver under her wing for mothering. Richenda, delighted to be reunited with the kinswoman she had not seen in so many years, insisted that Rothana take lodging in her own quarters.

Jehana, too, noted the arrival of the newcomers, and made interested inquiries when told that they were nuns. But she learned little, for everyone who knew much of the situation disappeared for the afternoon to digest the letters Kelson had sent, with Nigel scheduling a meeting of those contacted for that evening. Conall, to his great annoyance, was not invited, and soon sent his squire out of the keep to deliver a letter of his own.

"Well, it appears we know little more than we did before of the Mearans' actual battle strategies," Nigel said glumly, when everyone had reported. "Nor, unfortunately, does the affair at Saint Brigid's surprise me. Brice of Trurill has always been a ruthless man—though I would have thought this Ithel of Meara a little young to have grown so calloused. Meraude, has the princess settled down at all since she arrived?"

Meraude, nursing their infant daughter contentedly in the intimate surroundings of what was almost exclusively a family gathering, sighed and shook her head. Besides herself and Nigel, only Richenda, Arilan, and Meraude's brother, Saer de Traherne, were present.

"Poor child. She's convinced that her life is over," Meraude said. "She was calm enough when she first arrived, but I think the long ride simply numbed the import of what happened. After my ladies helped her bathe and put her to bed, she cried herself to sleep. She hasn't touched a bite of supper. . . ."

Richenda sighed and shook her head. "Poor lass. I don't know what's been done already, of course—I'll speak to Rothana about it in the morning—but it ought to be possible to ease at least some of the memory. I'd go into her mind myself and try to ease things, but it's always better if contact is made by someone already close." She smiled at Saer's raised eyebrow. "That's right, Saer. Rothana is kindred by more than marriage. I've not seen her since she was a little girl, but she may be even better trained than I am, by now."

"Ah, another Deryni," Saer murmured, too fascinated at the knowledge he had gained in the past few weeks to be surprised at much of anything. He and Meraude both now knew of Nigel's assumption of the Haldane potential, and Arilan's identity. And because of the other Deryni in the castle, both had voluntarily allowed Richenda to block their ability to discuss that information except in this company.

Arilan only snorted and toyed with his pectoral cross, running it back and forth on its chain with a soft, musical rattle of metal against metal.

"Let's investigate that, then," Nigel said, lifting several parchment sheets and transferring them from one pile to another. "No sense in letting her brood overmuch on what's happened, if there's a way to ease it. While we're on the subject of Deryni, what have you to report on Morag and young Liam, Richenda?"

Richenda managed a fleeting smile. "I do believe we've made our point with the Lady Morag," she said drolly. "It took her several days to realize that all the humans who come into contact with her have been protected, but she's stopped trying to tamper."

"She's probably regrouping for some other mischief," Arilan said darkly. "We mustn't forget she's Wencit's sister, after all."

"Oh, she's clever," Richenda agreed. "But perhaps not that clever. She knows what I am, but she hasn't a clue about you."

"And Liam?" Saer asked.

"Settling in nicely," Richenda said. "He and Payne and Rory are fast becoming inseparable."

Nigel frowned. "I've noticed that. You don't think he'd try to tamper with them, do you?"

"I don't think it's likely," Richenda replied. "I did a surface reading the first night Liam was here, while he was asleep. He has a great deal of potential, but less training than I would have expected—probably because no one ever thought he'd succeed his brother."

Saer furrowed his brow. "Doesn't he have shields?"

"Of course. Very good ones, too, as one might expect of the nephew of Wencit of Torenth. But one can read a great deal about a person's training and mental discipline just from the surface pattern of the shields. I think any attempt he made to influence Payne or Rory would be immediately obvious. In any case, I took the liberty of setting a few alarms in both boys, just to be on the safe side. If he tries anything beyond a simple Truth-Read, they'll come running right to me."

As Arilan nodded approvingly, Meraude shifted her baby to the other breast and allowed herself a great sigh.

"I'd be less than honest if I pretended I wasn't relieved," she said. "Do you think similar precautions should be taken with Conall?"

"That was going to be my next topic," Nigel said. "Unless anyone objects, I'd like to begin including Conall in our meetings, since I have him here for the summer after all. The responsibility will be good for him."

"So long as certain limitations are imposed," Arilan said dryly.

"Of course. Richenda, will you handle it?"

Richenda inclined her head thoughtfully. "Certainly. We're talking about a slightly more complicated situation than we had with the boys, or Meraude and Saer, but he seems to trust me—and I know he's fascinated by our powers. The prospect of being included in our deliberations ought to make him quite cooperative. I assume you'll want it done as soon as possible?"

"Please. It didn't occur to me earlier, but he's probably annoyed at being left out tonight—though I'm sure he must be tired after riding all day. He mentioned going directly to bed and not wanting to be disturbed."

"I'll see to it in the next day or so," Richenda said. "Let him get his rest tonight. What other business, my lord?"

"The reception of trade delegations, beginning next week," Nigel said. "I'm not anticipating any particular problems, but I'll want to review our procedures with such lords of state as are currently in Rhemuth before writing back to Kelson. We should do that tomorrow, I think. Incidentally,

I'll also want to tell him how Jehana's doing. What shall I say? The only time I see my dear sister-in-law is at Mass."

Richenda shrugged and traced a fingertip along the carving of her chair arm. "I'm afraid that's the only time you're likely to see her, too—unless, of course, the report of our newly arrived sisters brings her out of hibernation to investigate. Such time as she does not spend in solitary meditation, she spends with her chaplain and Sister Cecile. I fear she'll not get much sympathy from the ladies of Saint Brigid's, however. I've not pried, but I suspect Rothana may not be the only one with Deryni blood."

Saer whistled low under his breath and crossed himself before he even realized what he was doing, then offered Richenda and Arilan an embarrassed grimace. "I'm sorry. It's just that I keep discovering more Deryni."

"You needn't apologize, my lord," Richenda said, laughing gently. "It sometimes takes a while for old reflexes to die. You're doing very well for a man who'd had little contact with the 'godless Deryni' before a few months ago."

"Just be patient with me, lass. I'm working on it."

"So am I, Saer," Nigel said, himself permitting a small chuckle as Arilan looked pained. "However, if we've quite finished reassuring one another, I should like to finish this meeting before it gets too late. Incidentally, Richenda, I'll have our replies ready to send out by the day after tomorrow, so you'll need to locate Morgan before then."

"Tomorrow night," Richenda agreed. "You may observe, if you wish. And sometime in the next day or two, I'll make the opportunity to have a private chat with your son."

Nigel's son, however, was not getting the rest his father and companions supposed. Having received favorable reply to his missive of the afternoon, Conall readied himself to keep a long-awaited assignation. The faithful squire who had performed messenger duty slept obliviously on the pallet at the foot of his master's bed, assisted to that state of profound slumber by a strong sedative in the wine he had drunk but his master had not, following a light supper in the prince's sitting room.

Distractedly Conall crouched beside the sleeping lad and laid two fingers over the artery throbbing in the side of the upturned throat—pulsebeat strong, steady, and slow—then rose with a satisfied smile and donned a dark, hooded cloak.

Soon he was slipping down the tower stair and along a torch-lit corridor to another room.

It was the room that had been Kelson's as prince. Now it was Dhugal's. Conall wished it were his. The door was locked, but Conall had a key. It turned smoothly in the lock, the door swinging back soundlessly as Conall slipped through, closed it softly, and relocked it.

The room was dark after the torchlight outside, only a narrow line of light shining under the door, but that was sufficient to guide Conall to flint and steel. Soon a candle flame was steadying between his cupped hands. He held it aloft to inspect the empty room, satisfying himself that he was alone, then moved quietly toward the darkened fire-place, stopping a few paces to its left. There he lifted his right hand and with his outstretched forefinger boldly traced an ancient symbol. Softly a section of the wall withdrew to reveal a dark stairwell.

He stepped into it with no further thought for what he had done, only intent now on reaching his assignation. Descend-ing the narrow, rough-cut stairs, employing other signs to open other passages, he came at last to the doorway he sought: a shutterlike affair of rough-hewn timber.

He snuffed the candle and set it in a little niche before opening the door, resting his hand on the hilt of his sword and drawing his cloak and hood a little closer as he emerged in an alley well outside the walls of Rhemuth Keep. Heading toward brighter light, keeping to the shadows, he shortly passed through a small square, and thence up another street until he reached a tavern called the King's Head.

He was expected. The barkeep who approached him the moment he stepped inside led him immediately to a private room in the back of the establishment.

The room was dim, lit only by the fire on the hearth. Conall thought he was alone at first, as the door closed behind him and he pushed back his hood, yanking at the clasp of his cloak in consternation, but then a form stirred in the shadows beyond the fireplace and stepped into the light, smiling.

It was Tiercel de Claron, almond-colored eyes crinkling at the corners in mild amusement.

# CHAPTER TEN

*I have multiplied visions.*

—Hosea 12:10

"So, my prize pupil returns early from the wars, eh?" Tiercel said lightly, folding his arms across his chest and chuckling at Conall's obvious sigh of relief. "What's the matter? Didn't you think I'd come?"

Conall threw off his cloak and flung it over a bench near the door, grinning eagerly as he crossed to sit, at Tiercel's invitation, in a chair before the fireplace.

"Of course I knew you'd come. You've never broken your word to me yet."

"That you know of," Tiercel retorted, flashing another reassuring smile at Conall's fleeting start of uncertainty. "And I'll try never to give you reason to think I might."

As Conall made conscious effort to relax his reflex stiffening, Tiercel's almond-amber eyes warmed in the firelight. The balmy June evening had brought him out more casually arrayed than was his usual wont: a tawny green tunic open at the throat, richly worked with bands of interlace threaded red and gold and purple at cuffs, neck, and hem, and cool linen leggings of a dull vermillion, cross-gartered with ochre to the knee, with low, cuffed boots of walnut-hued leather, butter-supple.

He would not have ridden thus attired—not far, at any rate—which only confirmed Conall's theory that the Deryni lord had either lodgings or a Portal somewhere in Rhemuth town—perhaps both—though Tiercel had never admitted to

127

any details about his personal life. By firelight, the cords of his neck twisted in bold relief at the open throat of his tunic as he took two goblets from the high mantel and offered one to Conall.

"But, relax, my young friend, and tell me what brings you back to Rhemuth so unexpectedly," Tiercel said casually. "Is the war over already? That isn't what the Council tells me."

"Over? Hardly." Conall glanced into his cup as Tiercel sat on a stool partway between him and the fire. "It was just starting to get interesting when Kelson sent me home. I still haven't decided whether he meant it as a compliment or an insult. If it weren't for the fact that you and I can continue working together through the summer now, I think I might be really angry."

"Hey, then—whoa! What are you talking about?" Tiercel demanded.

"Well, there was this convent, and this princess—"

"All right. This obviously is more complicated than I thought." Tiercel set his wine on the floor beside him and dusted his hands together as Conall looked up at him in question. "I think you'd better show me."

As he set one hand on Conall's two, still clasped around his goblet, and reached the other across Conall's shoulder lightly to cup the back of his neck, Conall shivered just a little in anticipation and made himself relax. He and Tiercel had done this often enough that he had long ago stopped counting, but he suspected nothing would ever erase that eerie, fluttery sensation in the pit of his stomach just before he allowed the other to enter his mind.

"Look into your goblet and focus on the reflections on the surface of the wine," Tiercel murmured, his one hand tightening on Conall's while the other encouraged him to bow his head closer. "Lower your shields and let the memory run. That's right. . . ."

Conall was conscious of the beginning of the process, but not the end—only that one moment he was thinking back to the day they had come upon Saint Brigid's, and the outrage they had found there, and the next moment he was back in the shadowy room at the King's Head, Tiercel releasing his hands and gently massaging the back of his neck.

"Have some wine," the Deryni murmured distractedly, standing to lean one elbow against the mantel and stare at the fire on the hearth.

Conall sipped at the wine as ordered and watched his mentor with a detachment that would not have been possible when they first began working together, the previous winter. He felt far less light-headed than usual after one of Tiercel's deep probes, too.

Oh, there had been stretches of weeks at a time when both of them had despaired of ever tapping into the Haldane potential, but perseverance finally had begun to pay off after a while. Conall was by no means a functioning Deryni, Haldane or otherwise—not yet—but he was sure Tiercel was pleased. And would it not be glorious to go one day before the Camberian Council and prove that more than one Haldane *could* assume the Haldane legacy of magic?

Conall had already mastered several useful talents, like rudimentary Truth-Reading, and shielding, and how to use the sigils that operated the passageway he had used this evening. He had even gotten quite adept at making his squire forget where they went, when they rode out for Conall's training sessions with Tiercel. The young fool thought it was a lady Conall had been meeting, all those times they'd slipped away on various pretexts. Had it not been far too much trouble, Conall might simply have put the lad to sleep tonight; but uncertainty about the possible length of tonight's session had also dictated other, more direct measures.

He could have done it, though, if he'd wanted to.

He was congratulating himself on his improving prowess when Tiercel turned to look at him again, the handsome face somber above the tawny green tunic. The fire lit the dark cap of Tiercel's hair with reddish highlights, flaring behind his aristocratic profile like some satanic halo. Suddenly, Conall was a little afraid.

"We may have a problem," Tiercel said.

Conall swallowed and set his goblet on the floor beside his chair, all taste for wine suddenly gone.

"What—problem?" he managed to say without his voice betraying his apprehension.

"There are entirely too many Deryni at court, with you beginning to come into your powers. You know Lady Rothana, the sister who looked after Princess Janniver?"

Conall's jaw dropped, for he had rather begun to fancy the girl on the long ride back from Saint Brigid's. He thought she might even return his interest, despite her outward dedication to the religious life. Her quiet courtesy to him had

even sparked the rebuke of her abbess once, though nothing
untoward had passed between them. In fact, he had already
been considering a gentle wooing. She was only a novice in
religion, after all—and a princess herself, according to Morgan.

"She's—Deryni?" he breathed, suddenly realizing that it
followed, if Rothana was indeed related to Richenda, even
by marriage.

"Don't worry. She doesn't suspect you. I read very deep
to be sure you hadn't been touched. She'd be a good match
for you—"

"Damn you! Do you have to read my most intimate
thoughts?" Conall blurted.

"*Keep your voice down!*" Tiercel whispered, very softly,
but with such force that there was no question of disobeying.
"I apologize. I had to know whether she suspected you. It
wasn't the sort of thing you could tell me on your own."

"That doesn't mean I have to like it," Conall murmured,
his voice subdued but still a little petulant.

Tiercel drew in a deep breath and let it out patiently. "I
didn't *expect* you to like it. I don't like it that you'll be among
so many Deryni now, either: Rothana, Richenda, Jehana—
and Morgan, Duncan, and Dhugal, of course, when they
come back; not to mention Kelson."

"*Dhugal?*" Conall gasped, "He's Deryni? But how—"

"I don't know. All I can tell you is that he is—though
apparently untrained. I doubt he could spot you, even if he
were here. A far more immediate problem is likely to be your
father."

"My father?" Conall whispered. "What do you mean?"

"Kelson set the Haldane potential in him before he left,"
Tiercel said quietly. "Ah, I didn't *think* they'd told you. He
doesn't have all the powers, of course. They'd never do that
while Kelson's alive—and don't think it *can* be done; that's
where *we'll* prove them wrong one day—but he has *some*
powers. According to—friends, he's beginning to Truth-
Read, he can certainly link in with other Deryni for major
workings—and he may be able to detect shields. That's the
danger for you."

Conall managed to swallow noisily. He could hardly avoid
contact with his own father.

"What—what are we going to do? We've worked hard to
build my shields, Tiercel. Shields are the heart of almost
everything you've taught me."

"I know that. Fortunately, shield potential sometimes runs naturally in the Haldane line, even without being sought after. As long as your shields appear to be only rudimentary, I don't think even a trained Deryni would bother too much about them—*if* you can avoid doing anything to provoke a need to go deeper."

"Like what?" Conall wanted to know. "You're going to have to be a little more specific than that. And why would they even care about me?"

"Because you're Nigel's son, and he now has a partially activated potential."

"But—"

"Don't press me for details," Tiercel said, holding up a hand to stay further insistence. "If anything should happen to Kelson, and Nigel becomes king, you're next in line."

"I know that," Conall said faintly.

"Which means it's only natural that your father is going to want to include you on more of what's happening at high levels of government from now on."

"He didn't tonight," Conall muttered. "He's meeting with some of the privy councillors right now. I wasn't invited."

"Not this time, no. But you can bet that's one thing they'll be discussing; take my word for it."

"And?"

"And—" Tiercel sighed. "Conall, there are Deryni at court that you don't know about—and I can't tell you who they are. Nigel may choose to tell you, however—he almost has to, if you're to work at the levels you should, as his heir. And if he does, their identities will have to be protected."

"How—protected?"

Tiercel shrugged. "I can't tell you that exactly, because I don't know myself, but probably one of the Deryni he has access to—Richenda, most likely—will set limited blocks. Then you can be told who the others are—but you won't be able to use that knowledge in any situation that might betray their identities to outsiders. It's a rather neat trick, actually."

Trying to assimilate it all, Conall drew a deep breath and set both hands carefully on the arms of his chair.

"These—limited blocks—I take it they're dangerous for us?"

"Only the setting of them, and not if we prepare," Tiercel replied. "Fortunately, I have a very good idea who would need protecting, so I think I can set a facade over your shields that will leave that area accessible, yet hide what we don't want seen. Whoever does it will only be interested in getting in, doing the job, and getting out. Beyond that, it will be up to you to make sure you don't make someone want to see more."

"How complicated is that?—setting a facade over my shields, or whatever you said?"

"Not very, for me, though it will be a little rough on you—mainly because it will take a while. Because of that, I'll want to give you something to knock down any reflex resistance. We really ought to do it tonight, if you're up for it. It's getting late, I know, but God knows how soon it will occur to the rest of them that you ought to be included in what they're doing, and try to take precautions."

Conall made himself draw in a deep breath and hold it for several heartbeats before letting it out slowly. What Tiercel proposed sounded frightening, but not nearly as frightening as being caught before they had accomplished their goal. When he glanced up, Tiercel had not moved; only studied him with those faintly glowing almond eyes. Abruptly Conall wondered whether the Deryni was reading his mind.

"Tonight, eh?" Conall whispered.

Tiercel nodded.

"All right."

Immediately Tiercel pushed himself away from the mantel and went to the bench across the other side of the room. The little satchel he always brought with him to their sessions was lying under the heap of a dull ochre cape, and he rummaged in it for several seconds as Conall got up to join him.

"Pour yourself about half a cup of water," Tiercel said, conjuring handfire so he could sort through several parchment packets he pulled out of the satchel. "I'm giving you a heavier dose than usual, but I'll give you an antidote when we're done. You'll probably have a bit of a headache in the morning, but no worse than a mild hangover. That's better than going back to the castle with the first drug still working on you, though—just in case you run into anyone who shouldn't know what we're doing. I don't want you that vulnerable."

Conall brought the water and watched Tiercel empty the contents of one of the packets into it, wrinkling his nose at the sharp aroma as the powder dissolved. He remembered this one, though he couldn't have said what its name was. Even half a packet had always been enough to leave him groggy for several hours. As Tiercel gave it a stir with the blade of his dagger, Conall took off his sword and coiled the belt around the scabbard, wondering vaguely, as he set the weapon aside, whether a person could die from too much of the drug. He had no idea what this much would do to him.

"You'd better sit down before you drink this," Tiercel said, answering the unasked question as he gestured with the cup toward the fireside chair. "If you don't, you may fall down before you can finish it. In this concentration, it's going to hit you like a mule. Once you're under, however, I promise you won't feel a thing."

"Small consolation," Conall murmured, sitting and gingerly taking the cup. "Any special instructions?"

"Only the usual. Take a nice, deep breath and try to relax. Drop your shields as much as you can. Then toss it down."

"Easy for you to say," Conall muttered.

But he did as he was instructed, consciously relaxing his body as he breathed in, then willing his shields to subside as he let his breath out in a slow sigh. When he had breathed in again, he tossed off the contents of the cup in a single gulp, managing to bypass most of the terrible taste.

He had time to swallow once and close his eyes to prepare, and was aware of Tiercel taking the cup from his hand. Then the room began to spin, and he had to hold tight to the arms of the chair to keep from being sucked into—nothing.

He squeezed his eyes shut tighter, gasping. He felt disembodied hands clamp down on his head, welcome cool across his forehead and quivering eyelids and around the back of his neck— reassuring, supportive—but already the pressure was building behind his eyes, threatening to explode his very skull. There was a roaring in his ears, and a sharp bile aftertaste in the back of his throat.

Then a black tide washing over him and carrying him away—and nothing, and spinning into nothing, and touching and touched by nothing—and blessed oblivion.

It was not the first morning after, but the second, that Conall had cause to try the success of what he and Tiercel had done. He remembered little of what had passed between them after he drank the cup, but he had become faintly aware, in the previous twenty-four hours, that he seemed to be functioning on a dual level now, his most intimate thoughts sequestered away in some less accessible dimension while the humdrum of the everyday continued on the surface.

He was heading toward the castle yard. He had a packet of letters his father had asked him to collect this morning, ready to be delivered to the courier about to leave for Kelson's camp. He was cutting through the garden, thinking he might catch a glimpse on the way of Rothana at her morning office, when Richenda and Rothana came around the corner of a hedge. A look of speculation flitted across Richenda's face as they all exchanged greetings—enough to make him suspect the moment might be upon him, if Tiercel had been right in his suspicions.

"Ah, the rest of the letters for the courier," Richenda said, drawing another out of her sleeve and extending it to him. "May I add another one?"

"Of course, my lady."

As he slipped it under the leather band securing the others, he saw Richenda glance at Rothana.

"Incidentally, I wonder if I might prevail upon a moment of your time, Conall," she said. "Is it important that you go immediately to the yard with the letters?"

"Well, the courier will be waiting—"

"Of course he will. Would you perhaps permit the Lady Rothana to take them in your stead? Nigel would not mind, I think."

He started to decline—he was sure now that Tiercel had been right—but Richenda laid her hand on the letters, her fingers brushing his own, and her touch sent all thought of resistance out of his head.

"Very well," he found himself saying, as Richenda took the letters and handed them to Rothana. "I thank you, my lady."

In a daze he watched Rothana walk on past, letting Richenda guide him a few paces farther along the path until they could step into a tiny arbor recessed between the hedges.

"Please don't be alarmed," Richenda murmured, turning him to face her, still maintaining contact, hand to hand. "Your father has asked me to speak to you. He intends to begin including you in the most intimate of his counsels, but certain safety measures must be taken before that may occur.

Kelson has awakened a portion of the Haldane potential in him, so that he may govern more effectively in Kelson's absence, and has given him the counsel of several Deryni you do not know about, here at court.''

For the first time, he was consciously aware of the brush of another mind against his own, though only at the surface levels Tiercel had isolated. The surface levels did not seem to elicit any surprise in Richenda, however; and he found himself able to react on two levels at once, only the surface responding with the curiosity and slight apprehension that should be expected of one in his position.

"I—do not know what you're talking about, my lady," he murmured haltingly, unable to drag his eyes from hers.

She smiled gently and brushed her free hand down his forehead, fingertips coming to rest on his trembling eyelids.

"That will all become clear, in due time," she whispered. "Relax a moment, Conall."

A wave of vertigo swept over him, making him sway a little on his feet, but her hand still resting on his kept him steady. Her fingers were cool on his eyelids.

After a few heartbeats, both her hands dropped and he could look at her again. She was smiling, her blue eyes lit with satisfaction, and he knew that both she and Tiercel had accomplished what they intended.

"Good. That's done. Nigel will ask you to join us this afternoon. How do you feel?"

"A little—confused," he said, cocking his head at her. "What did you do to me?"

"I set up a block to protect what you'll be learning later today. Did you know, by the way, that you have the beginnings of excellent shields? Not that I'm surprised. You're Nigel's son, after all."

"Shields? Oh . . ." Conall murmured. "But, I—"

"Don't worry." She brushed his hand again in reassurance. "As I said, it will all become clear, in due time. Did you want to see the courier off? I'm sure he hasn't left yet."

It took the entire brisk walk to the castleyard to clear his head and regain his full equilibrium, and he was glad Richenda did not accompany him. Rothana was already gone when he arrived. He stood at his father's side as Saer de Traherne gave final instructions to the courier, and only nodded casually when Nigel asked whether Richenda had spoken with him. His acknowledgment of the invitation to join the council that afternoon was equally casual, which seemed to reassure Nigel that all had gone as it should.

He thought about notifying Tiercel, as he watched the courier ride out of the courtyard and disappear through the gate, but their next session was only a few days away; the news could wait. Besides, he suspected there would be more to tell, after this afternoon's meeting.

So he thought about Kelson instead, and wondered what was happening on campaign, a part of him longing to be out there, too, covering himself in glory. By now, the Haldane army must be approaching Ratharkin, and Duncan's army closing in from the north.

Well, with luck, the whole thing would soon be concluded. No sense prolonging things, if Conall could not be there to share in the victory. He hoped Kelson gave the rebellious Mearans what was coming to them—especially that swine of a Prince Ithel!

"God *damn* the Haldane!" Ithel was saying at that very moment, safe within the walls of Ratharkin since a few hours before, but well aware that Kelson and his army were but a day's march away, and only the lake and a river to stop him. "Mother, we've harried him, burned out our own people, niggled at his heels, and *still* he comes! I say we should pull back to Laas!"

He was staring out a small, south-facing window of the highest tower in Ratharkin palace, Brice of Trurill fidgeting slightly behind him. Both men were still fully armored except for helmets and gauntlets, sweat-stained arming caps pushed back from their heads, faces streaked with dust. A shocked Caitrin stood near the doorway to the sparsely furnished chamber, Judhael and Archbishop Creoda flanking her. She wore her crown, having come from the formal welcome of her son back to Ratharkin, but she and the bishops looked frightened. Judhael took her arm in a gesture meant to reassure, but she shook it off and left them to join her only remaining son.

"We'll make a stand," she said, touching his armored shoulder with a tentative hand. "Sicard will stop McLain in the north, and then come to our aid. We can outwait the Haldane. We can. You'll see."

"A chancy undertaking, Majesty," Brice said wearily, making her a placating bow as she turned to glare at him.

"We're better off at Laas. We'll be on the coast. We might be able to bring in more mercenaries. The water supply is better, too. And we can fish. If it comes to siege, we can hold out almost indefinitely."

"He's right, Mother," Ithel said, yanking at the buckles of his brigandine to ease his neck. "If we stay here, we may not be able to hold out until Father comes to relieve us. Laas will buy us and him time. Brice and I can mount a rearguard action and slow down the Haldane some more, while you and Judhael and the bishops head west."

"And leave you here?"

Ithel sighed and rested his hands patiently on the splayed sides of the window slit, glancing out across the plain again. He was a man now, and growing old before his time—not the callow boy who had ridden out so confidently but a few weeks before.

"Am I your heir, Mother?"

"What sort of thing is that to ask?"

"Then let me do what I was born to do!" he snapped, turning on her to lift a fist in supplication. "If there's any chance to take back and hold our land from the Haldane usurper, then I must stand! *You* must escape—and Judhael! Brice and I will follow if we can. If I have to, I'll burn Ratharkin to the ground to slow your pursuers! But we cannot stay here, brought to ground like foxes before the hounds. You *must* give Father time to relieve us from the north!"

"And suppose Sicard *cannot* relieve us? What then?" she demanded. "Am I to lose *both* of you? Ithel, I *cannot!*—I *will* not see you cut down like your brother! We *must* persevere. We must!"

"We *shall*, Majesty," Creoda said soothingly, daring to intrude on the family argument for the first time. "The Lord Sicard *will* come to our rescue. Even now, my lords Loris and Gorony are drawing McLain and his army nearer their doom. Once the Cassani forces are crushed, Loris and Sicard will join us. But their aid will be of little avail if we have stayed in Ratharkin and perhaps fallen to the Haldane invaders."

Caitrin listened to his speech, one small foot tapping impatiently against the stone floor, then glanced tight-lipped at Judhael.

"Well, Creoda is against me. How say you, Judhael? If we retreat, and Ithel is lost, *you* are King of Meara after I am gone. Is that what you want?"

Blanching, Judhael averted his eyes. "I wish only to serve you and your son after you, my Queen," he whispered. "I have all that I have ever wanted. But Archbishop Creoda is right. For the sake of your cause, you *must* fall back to Laas. You *must not* be taken."

"I see." Slowly Caitrin's shoulders slumped and she bowed her head. "It appears I cannot sway you." She took a deep breath and let it out with a sigh as she looked up at them again.

"Very well. I place matters in your hands, my son. Tell me what to do, and I shall do it."

As Ithel glanced uneasily at Brice, the border baron braced his shoulders and set his hands on his swordbelt.

"You and the bishops should leave at once, Majesty," Brice said softly. "We'll give you the household guard to escort you, and part of the castle garrison. The rest of the garrison will join us. They're fresh, and can provide a more vigorous rearguard."

"And we're to go to Laas," she said dully.

"Aye. You've a reserve garrison there as well. If we— shouldn't be able to join you, they'll be able to protect you until Sicard and Loris can come to your aid."

"Very well," she murmured, not looking at any of them. "I—would like a few moments alone with my son, however, before I must leave."

The others went out immediately, leaving only Caitrin and Ithel standing near the narrow southern window. Sighing, she took off her crown and turned it idly in her hands.

"I—do not regret what I have done," she said softly. "The dream *might* have been—*still* might be, I suppose."

Smiling bravely, Ithel set his hands gently where the crown had been and rubbed his thumbs along the line where the metal had rested on her forehead, bending down to kiss her brow.

"It still *shall* be, Mother," he said quietly. "You *are* the rightful queen of this realm, and we both shall live to see you take your rightful place."

As he drew away to look down at her, she lifted the crown between them, reaching up to put it on his head.

"I pray that it shall be, my son—but do not pull away!"

"The crown is yours, Mother," he whispered. "Please don't."

"Just for a little while," she said, "so that you shall have worn it if—"

She did not go on, but he knew what she had almost said. Before that plea, he slowly sank to his knees so she could set the jeweled circlet on his sweat-plastered chestnut hair. He flinched as he took the full weight of it on his brow, but then he caught both her hands and kissed the palms in fervent homage. A sob escaped her lips as he did so. After that, she held him to her breast a final time, not minding that her cheek pressed against the cruel metal of the crown's jeweled points.

Caitrin wore the crown again when they left the tower, a few minutes later, she and Ithel both with heads held high. A little while after that, the Queen of Meara and a small but loyal escort rode out of the gates of Ratharkin and headed north, Prince Ithel and Brice of Trurill remaining behind with the Mearan rearguard. By nightfall, the remaining defenders had melted into the hills to await the approaching enemy, all sign of the royal passage was gone, and Ratharkin was burning.

The fire of Ratharkin was seen in the south, as the sun dipped beyond the vast central Mearan plain and Kelson and his army made camp for the night. Standing atop a little hillock looking north and east across the far lake that separated them from the Mearan city, Kelson followed the directing finger of the scout who had brought him and Morgan up here to see. The glow was still faint in the shimmering twilight, but growing brighter by the minute as dusk settled its mantle over the land.

"I suppose it has to be Ratharkin," Morgan said, lowering his glass and handing it to Kelson with a perplexed sigh. "Jemet, is there *anything* else of size in that area?"

The R'Kassan scout shook his head. "Nothing, Your Grace. We've been several hours' ride closer, and there's no mistaking. The Mearans have torched Ratharkin, plain and simple. We think a party might have headed west around midday, but it could have been a caravan. It was already far out on the plain when we spotted it—too far away to be certain."

"More likely, it was Caitrin, high-tailing it for Laas," Kelson muttered, studying the brightening glow through Morgan's glass. "She can't have taken her army with her, though. You would have been able to see that many men."

"That's true, Sire," Jemet said. "Our guess is that they've stayed behind to slow us up. Or maybe they haven't *got* that many men left. We've been saying all along that the main army isn't with Ithel and Brice at all."

Kelson lowered the glass and telescoped it down with a solid snick of nested brass fittings.

"Then where the bloody hell *is* it? *Duncan* hasn't seen it. *We* haven't seen it."

"Maybe it doesn't exist," Morgan muttered, taking the glass from Kelson and slipping it back into its case. "Maybe Caitrin just wants us to chase our tails all summer. It's the sort of war *I* might fight, if I had a very stubborn dream and very few men."

With a snort, Kelson hooked his thumbs in his swordbelt and continued to look out at the stain on the northern horizon.

"You might, and I might—but Loris wouldn't. And we know he isn't doing so. *I* think he's giving cover to Sicard and the real Mearan host. Duncan may not have seen a full Mearan army, but he's certainly seen signs of its passage. I think it's out there somewhere," he swept his arm across the north, "between him and us. And if we let ourselves be drawn to Laas in pursuit of Caitrin herself, Sicard just might manage to do some heavy damage in the north."

"I agree absolutely," Morgan said.

"Very well, then, we'll clean out whatever Caitrin's left to harry our tracks in the Ratharkin area, then head north to help Duncan," Kelson said, dismissing the scout with a wave of his hand. "Thank you, Jemet. You may go. If there *is* a Mearan army, maybe we can pincer it between us."

Morgan nodded agreement as the scout slipped into the darkness down the hill. "I think that *is* the more serious threat."

"In the meantime," Kelson went on, "I want Ithel and Brice. I want both of them badly, Alaric."

"I know you do."

"And then I want Loris, and Sicard—and that toadying little priest, Gorony!"

"Now, then!" Morgan said with a chuckle. "I think a few of our closest friends might object to that last remark about toadying priests. Cardiel, in particular, would be crushed. I've asked him to dine with us this evening."

"I would hardly call it dining, considering the dwindling state of our provisions," Kelson quipped, as he turned to start down the hill, "but at least the company will be civilized. Are you ready for a wash? I am."

Morgan's silvery laughter accompanied them as they descended, floating on a little breeze that had finally risen to relieve some of the day's heat, and mingling with the reassuring sounds of camp being made. They walked back along the picket lines opposite the officers' tents, wading midcalf through a stream already muddied by the watering of scores of horses, and chatted briefly with a few of the squires and men-at-arms tending the animals before making their way up the little promontory to the royal pavilion.

Young Brendan had clean towels and basins of warm water waiting for them, and tankards of ale already chilled in the nearby stream. Idle banter turned to grunts and sighs of sheerest animal relief as Brendan and Kelson's squire, Jatham, helped divest both king and champion of their armor. Fresh clothing followed ablutions, all interspersed with draughts of cool ale, so that by the time Cardiel came to join them, both men were considerably restored in body and in spirits.

And far to the north, in another loyal campsite, Duncan, Dhugal, and Dhugal's rangers concluded conferences very similar to the one Kelson and Morgan had just held, though with far less confident an outlook—for they had been harried all day along their flanks by Connaiti raiding bands and the crack episcopal strike forces commanded by Lawrence Gorony. They had suffered few casualties, either dead or wounded, but the constant skirmishing and the unaccustomed heat had taken their toll on frazzled Cassani tempers. Now Duncan's vast campsite was ringed with watchfires, sentries posted along all the perimeters, the bulk of the men still armed, ready to defend against night attacks while the rest of their fellows slept in shifts.

Duncan was also still fully armored, save for helmet and gauntlets, and sat sipping a cup of cool water on a camp stool outside his tent; it was yet too hot to sit inside. Nearby, Dhugal sprawled half-reclining on another stool and tried to brace himself so that Ciard O Ruane could hammer on one of his greaves, jammed at the knee joint during one of the day's several skirmishes.

As Ciard cursed under his breath and gave the offending piece of armor yet another blow with the hilt of his dagger, the joint unlocked with a screech of tortured metal.

"*Got* the little bastard!" Ciard muttered, as Dhugal let out a whoof of relief.

"Any damage to the knee?" Duncan asked.

Dhugal shook his head as he and Ciard undid the buckles and pulled the greave off his leg, flexing the knee to test it. His boots came almost as high as the greave had, and he ran a finger inside the top edge to ease out a crease.

"I think it's all right. It's a bit stiff from not being able to bend all afternoon, but a little walking should take care of that. Ciard, can you fix the thing before morning?"

As Ciard grunted assent and wandered off with the damaged greave, Dhugal removed its mate and stood, grinning wanly as he hobbled over to his father, favoring the suspect knee.

"I feel really stupid, getting clipped like that," he said, as Duncan set aside his cup and bent to run both hands over the stiff joint. "Can you sense anything through the trews?"

"Just give me a moment," Duncan murmured, extending his Deryni senses through the leather to the knee. He surrounded the joint with healing warmth for several seconds to increase the circulation, feeling Dhugal's mind reach out in fond caress and returning the affection, then permitted himself a relieved sigh as he straightened and glanced up at his son.

"Nothing serious," he said, "though I might not be able to say the same if you hadn't been wearing that steel. I suppose it's days like this that justify the heavier armor, despite the heat."

Dhugal flexed his knee again, smiling at the improved mobility, and pulled his stool closer to sit beside his father. He had a grime-streaked towel draped around his neck, and he used one end to wipe his sweaty face yet again. Duncan, when he noticed the condition of the towel, offered him a cleaner one that had been lying across his own shoulder.

"What do you think is going to happen next?" Dhugal asked softly, when he had unbuckled the front of his brigandine to mop at his neck and fan a breeze into his soggy undertunic.

Duncan shook his head, retrieving his cup to sip at it again. "I wish I knew. Have some water?"

Grinning, Dhugal took the cup and poured the contents over his head, basking in the cool as the water sluiced over his hair and into his armor. Duncan only chuckled and took the cup back as Dhugal toweled off again, refilling it from a pewter ewer at his feet.

"Waste of good water," he muttered, as Dhugal sighed and slumped contentedly on his stool. "Doesn't it get rather soggy in there?"

"No soggier than it was from my own sweat," Dhugal retorted with another grin. "You should try it."

"Hmmm, thank you, no."

"If we can't get out of our armor tonight, it's better than nothing," Dhugal ventured.

Duncan chuckled and shook his head. "Dhugal, do you know how much I *despise* being filthy? It isn't so bad during the day, but not to be able to get clean at night—uck!"

"And you call yourself a borderman!"

"I do *not* call myself a borderman; I happen to be chief of a border clan, but I am a duke, and a son of a duke, and a prince of the Church, thank you very much," Duncan said in mock indignation. "And neither dukes nor sons of dukes nor princes of any sort whatever should have to put up with being grimy after a long day of fighting for their king." He grinned. "On the other hand, complaining about it does provide diversion after such a day, doesn't it?" His manner sobered abruptly. "Sweet *Jesu*, I wish I knew where Sicard's army was! I'd give a great deal to face an enemy that would stand and fight."

"I know," Dhugal said bleakly, propping his elbows on his knees and resting his chin on his hands. "It's getting to be more than just annoying, isn't it? Do you think we should try to contact Morgan? Maybe he and Kelson have got Sicard occupied, down in the south."

"You know they haven't. Anyway, I'm too tired to try a contact tonight." He yawned and stretched as he stood. "Besides that, they won't be expecting contact for another three days. Are you about ready to see what Jodrell has managed to scare up for supper? I don't know about you, but I'm famished."

"I suppose. Only—"

"Only, what?" Duncan asked, setting his fists on his hips to peer at his son as Dhugal also stood.

"Well, I was just wondering what you would do if we *had* to contact Morgan, and he wasn't expecting us."

"Hmmm, considerably more difficult than a planned contact," Duncan murmured, glancing around to be certain they were not overheard. "However, if it *had* to be done, I'd wait until it was very late, when I was sure he'd be asleep. He'd be more receptive asleep. We'd probably get through." He cocked his head in question. "Does that answer your question?"

"I suppose," Dhugal murmured. "There isn't much point to it just now anyway, is there? We *know* who's been giving us fits for the past two weeks: Loris and Gorony."

"That's right," Duncan agreed. "And when we catch up with them, I intend to thrash them both for every bath I *haven't* had during this campaign. Now, come on and let's find supper. It's bad enough to have to sleep in our armor. I'm *damned* if I'll do it on an empty stomach!"

# CHAPTER ELEVEN

*Now a thing was secretly brought to me, and mine
ear received a little thereof.*

—Job 4:12

"*Angelus consilii natus est de virgine, sol de stella,*" Richenda quoted, sitting at her loom the next morning as she
and Rothana capped verses back and forth between them.
"The angel of counsel is born of a virgin, the sun from a
star. *Sol occasum nesciens*, a sun that knows no setting, a
star that is always shining, always bright."

Rothana, following the text from a scroll in her lap, rocked
back and forth with delight.

"Yes, yes! I know that one. *Sicut sidus radium, profert
virgo filium, pari forma.* As a star puts forth its ray, so the
virgin puts forth her son, in like manner. . . ."

They were alone in the ladies' solar. Rothana was perched
cross-legged in the shade of a window seat, pale blue habit
tucked demurely around her knees and bare feet. Here in
the privacy of the women's quarters, she had taken off her
veil, and the heavy braid of her hair gleamed blue-black over
one shoulder, the end brushing the manuscript unrolled
across her knees. Her fingers fluttered in emphasis like the
wings of the doves that nested in the eaves above the window, her face lighting dreamily with the rapture of the ancient verses.

"*Neque sidus radio, neque mater filio fit corrupta.* The
star does not lose virtue by giving forth its ray, or the mother
by bearing a son."

There had been a time when Richenda, too, had felt that adolescent rapture. Now the words brought a deeper enjoyment, tempered with the wisdom and experience of nearly twice Rothana's years. The half-decade of marriage to Bran Coris had been a resigned suspension of the scholar's life Richenda had enjoyed as a young girl, for Bran had not thought it seemly that a woman should be too learned. That life had been revived with Bran's death, not only tolerated but actively encouraged by Alaric, and fed by Duncan's and Kelson's even more avid interest in the things she found to share with all of them. It was Duncan who had managed to locate the scroll Rothana now held, though it had been Alaric who paid the exorbitant sum the scroll had cost.

"I remember a related text from *Ecclesiasticus*," Rothana was saying, running an eager finger down the columns of fine-penned script. "'I am the mother of fair love, of fear, and knowledge, and holy hope. . . . My memorial is sweeter than honey, and mine inheritance than the honeycomb.'"

Richenda smiled encouragement and made a sound of concurrence, but her shuttle never missed its rhythm as Rothana resumed reading.

The solar was warm already, though it was only just past Terce, the "Third Hour" of the ancient world, when the Holy Spirit came down upon the Apostles. It would be warmer still, before the evening brought relief. Longing for the blessed cool of the lakes of her mother's Andelon, or even the brisk sea breezes that swept into Coroth, Richenda paused in her weaving to readjust a pin in her coiled, flame-gold hair; like Rothana, she had shed her veil on returning from early Mass. Her gown this morning was a soft rose rather than the blue she usually favored, out of deference to the azure habits of Rothana and her sisters. The shade suited her, but it played up the high color in her cheeks that the heat brought out, and drained off the fire from her bright tresses.

The heat would be even worse in Meara, Richenda reflected, as her fingers resumed their patient, steady rhythm, casting the carved bone shuttle back and forth hypnotically across the pattern she was working.

But no sense worrying about Alaric; that would do neither him nor her any good whatsoever. And the poetry Rothana recited was pleasant, the cadence only reinforcing the easy spell she wove into her threads. She found herself slipping into a light, pleasant trance as the words dropped into the morning stillness like polished pebbles into a shaded pool, and she was glad they had come here early, before any of the other women thought to join them.

"'Hail, Queen of heaven; Hail, Lady of the Angels,'" Rothana went on. "'Salutation to thee, root and portal, whence the light of the world has arisen.'"

A tangle in the thread required Richenda's closer attention, and as she bent closer to her canvas to work it free, a part of her mind continuing to follow the spell Rothana was weaving with her poetry, she suddenly became aware that someone else had entered the room and stood now behind the carved screens set before the entryway, listening—and that the someone was Deryni, shields tight and unreadable.

Glancing curiously over her shoulder—for the interloper must be one of only two royal ladies, to enter without knocking here, in the women's quarters—she caught a glimpse of white through the screens that confirmed her suspicions: Jehana, obviously not recognizing Richenda from behind, in rose rather than blue. If the queen chose to come closer, this might prove most interesting.

*Don't stop*, she sent to Rothana, as the younger woman, too, became aware of their visitor, though not her identity.

Rothana continued with hardly a break in her rhythm, only shifting the scroll a little on her lap. Richenda bent more intently to her canvas and kept her face averted as Jehana came around the edge of the screens.

"I beg your pardon," Jehana said softly, as Rothana looked up and stopped reading. "I was drawn by your beautiful poetry, and I—are you one of the sisters who recently arrived? You're very young."

"And out of habit, I fear, my lady," Rothana said, smiling sheepishly as she picked up her veil and rose to make the queen a polite curtsey. "It's very warm, and as a novice, my sisters often overlook my childish lapses."

"Nay, it *is* warm, child. I shan't tell on you," Jehana said with an answering smile, only then glancing at and recognizing Richenda, who had also risen at her approach.

"*You!*" she whispered, after a little gasp.

Richenda inclined her head in acknowledgment and dipped in dutiful curtsey.

"Majesty."

"Majesty?" Rothana echoed, cocking her head at Richenda in question.

"Jehana of Bremagne, mother to the king," Richenda said softly, not taking her eyes from the queen. "Your Majesty, may I be permitted to present my kinswoman Rothana, daughter of Hakim, Emir Nur Hallaj, a novice of Saint Brigid's."

As the speechless Jehana darted her gaze from Richenda to the startled-looking Rothana, who was replacing her veil with all possible speed, Richenda lifted a hand in invitation for the queen to join Rothana in the window seat. The queen would refuse, of course, but Richenda found herself taking an almost perverse pleasure to be making the offer.

"Please join us if you wish, Majesty," she said. "Perhaps you would care to hear more poetry. Interspersed with more traditional material, Rothana was reciting from the works of the great Orin. He was Deryni, like the three of us."

Jehana swallowed audibly and went nearly as pale as her white robes, looking as if she might bolt at any instant, green eyes darting fearfully to the silent Rothana and then back to Richenda.

"But, she's a nun!" she whispered, shaking her head in denial. "She *can't* be D-D— She simply *can't* be! Not and be in religion. . . ."

Richenda had all she could do to keep her anger from flaring visibly. "Why not? That's what *you* wish to be, isn't it? What makes you think you're the only one?"

"That's an entirely different matter," Jehana said weakly. "You know it is. I turned to the Church to help me *cast out* my evil; you *celebrate* yours!"

"Nay, madame! We celebrate our closer kinship with the Creator," Rothana answered. "You yourself commended Orin's verses—"

"*Deryni* verses!" Jehana snapped.

"Verses that were perfectly acceptable before you knew their author," Richenda countered. "Do you fear to be contaminated simply by listening, madame? I assure you, if it were possible to win acceptance of our race by the mere speaking of Deryni poetry, then all the hilltops of this land should resound to Orin's verses! Alas, for those of us who must endlessly continue trying to prove ourselves pious and upright servants of the same God you serve, things are not that easy."

"You speak blasphemy! I will not listen!" Jehana murmured, shutting her eyes tight and turning away, trembling.

"Aye, fly from the truth, madame!" Richenda went on, truly angry now. "But you cannot fly from Him who made both human and Deryni!"

"Would that He had not!" Jehana sobbed.

"And if He had not," Richenda hammered on, "then *we* should not have been. Not you and I, not your son—nor even a Haldane Brion for you to marry! Why must you continue to persecute us, Jehana? Why must you persecute *yourself*?"

The final accusation was too much for Jehana. Tears streaming down her face, she fled from the room, almost bowling over Conall, who had been just about to knock on the door. Glancing back over his shoulder in astonishment, Conall thrust his head around the edge of the screen and knocked on that as Jehana's running footsteps receded down the corridor. He had a letter sealed with scarlet in his hand, and wore riding leathers and a look of amazement that quickly changed to faintly amused understanding as he ventured farther into the room and spotted Richenda still standing at her loom beside the window.

"Good God, what did you say to my aunt to make her run like that?" he asked with a chuckle, making her a little bow. "One would have thought demons, at least, were after her!"

"Only the demons that she herself allows," Richenda said weakly. "Sometimes I think we make our own hell on earth, and need no threat of demons in the afterlife. But, enough of that. You have some missive for me?"

"Oh, aye—and the messenger who brought it, too. Forgive the intrusion, but there's a peddler in the yard who claims to have letters from a Cousin Rohays. He calls himself Ludolphus, if you can believe *that*. Frankly, he looks quite the brigand—a Moor of some sort, so far as I can tell—but he said you'd recognize this seal." He handed over the letter in his hand and grinned and bowed again as he noticed Rothana in the window embrasure behind Richenda.

"Anyway, he wouldn't let me bring the rest," he went on, more self-conscious now that he had seen Rothana. "He insisted he had to deliver them himself. Do you want to see him?"

Richenda ran a fingertip over the seal and smiled as she sat at her loom again, aware that Rothana was becoming increasingly embarrassed by Conall's sheepish glances.

The seal did, indeed, come from Rohays, but—Ludolphus, indeed! Given the seal, Richenda had a fair idea what messenger Rohays *had* sent, and it was no peddler named Ludolphus!

But Rothana would be as pleased to see him as herself—and receiving him would extricate Rothana from an increasingly uncomfortable situation.

"Yes, thank you, Conall, I do. I've been expecting him. And would you please see that we're not disturbed?"

"Very well, if you're sure. Ah—" He glanced at Rothana hopefully. "May I, perhaps, escort the Lady Rothana elsewhere?—assuming that you wish to see the fellow privately, of course."

"No, no, that won't be necessary." Richenda glanced up from breaking the seal just in time to see Conall erase a crestfallen expression. "Rohays is kin to Rothana as well as myself," she explained, shards of scarlet wax exploding across her lap as she unfolded the stiff parchment. "Besides, if the fellow is as much the brigand as you say, perhaps I shall need a chaperone."

Rothana flashed a smile both wistful and relieved and sank down on the seat in the window embrasure, making a self-conscious adjustment of her veil.

"Very well," Conall said doubtfully.

As soon as the prince had bowed and made his exit, Richenda cast a droll glance at Rothana and stifled a giggle, raising the letter between herself and the doorway to shield her growing mirth.

"Rothana, have you been leading Conall on?" she whispered. "He could hardly take his eyes off you! It must have been a *very* interesting journey back to Rhemuth."

"Oh, Richenda, I was only *polite*," Rothana protested, clasping her hands tightly in her lap and blushing furiously. "He *is* rather nice, but—I'm under *vows*, for goodness' sake!"

"Well, I don't suppose you can help how *he* reacts, can you?" Richenda replied, dismissing the subject with a smile as she began scanning her letter.

"No," said Rothana in a very quiet voice. "Maybe I just have that effect on Haldanes."

Richenda raised an eyebrow in surprise, wondering whether she had just heard what she thought she heard.

"Any Haldanes in particular?"

Rothana blushed and gave a furtive nod, twisting a handful of pale blue skirt in her lap.

"Aye. I wasn't going to tell you," she whispered. "It's probably nothing—I *hope* it's nothing."

"Go on," Richenda murmured, lowering her letter.

"Well, it was the king," Rothana admitted. "He—wanted to read Janniver to find out who'd attacked her. I told him no. Then he asked *me* to read her, and to show him what I saw."

"And did you?"

Another reluctant nod. "Yes. But I was angry, Richenda. I know I should be able to forgive those who hurt me and the people I love, but I was outraged at what the soldiers had done to Janniver and my sisters, and—and maybe a little guilty that I'd escaped their fate. So I—took out some of my anger on the king. After I showed him what he wanted to know, I—made him feel a little of what it was like for—for *her*, to be—*used* that way."

"I see," Richenda said gently. "And you don't think that's something valuable for a king to know?"

"Oh, I suppose it is," Rothana said with a perplexed little sigh. "I certainly thought so at the time. Only—something else happened, just before I broke the contact; a—a deeper touching than I'd planned—far more intense."

"On whose part? Yours or his?"

"Both, I suppose," she whispered. "I shouldn't have let it happen, though. *I* was supposed to be in control. And I don't know why I responded that way."

"Perhaps because you're a woman and he's a man?" Richenda asked.

"Richenda, stop it!" Rothana blurted, standing abruptly to turn and look out the window, arms hugged across her chest. "I didn't do anything to encourage either him *or* Conall!"

"No one said you did," Richenda replied. "On the other hand—well, if you should ever decide you don't want a religious life after all, you could do far worse than either young man."

"Richenda!"

"All right! Forget I ever mentioned it," Richenda said drolly, ducking and raising a hand in surrender as Rothana turned to stare at her in shock. "You're a body as well as a soul, however. Don't ever become so wound up in Orin's poetry that you forget that.''

Any further objection Rothana might have been contemplating was cut off by another knock at the door, followed by the tentative peering of Conall around the entry screen.

"May we approach, Your Grace? My lady?''

With a quick nod of assent, Richenda and then Rothana stood as Conall moved aside to admit a slender, wiry man dressed all in dusty black, about Conall's height. So skilled was his shielding that even Richenda, who knew what to look for, could not detect any hint that the man was Deryni.

She had no time for a close look at his face. He wore the flowing robes she had expected from Conall's description, with a bulging black satchel slung across his left shoulder on a leather strap, but the swathings of his turbanlike headdress allowed only an impression of dark eyes and a closely clipped heard and mustache before he made her a sweeping, graceful bow in the eastern fashion, fingertips brushing heart, lips, and forehead in salute. He kept his eyes averted as he straightened from his bow, his right hand returning to his breast. He did not appear to be armed, but Richenda knew he had no need to be.

"This is the peddler Ludolphus, Your Grace,'' Conall said doubtfully. "If you should need me, I'll not be far away.''

"Yes, thank you, Conall,'' Richenda murmured, giving him dismissal with a nod of her head and extending a hand in invitation for the visitor to approach. "Please be welcome, Master Ludolphus, and tell me the news of my cousin.''

Not until the door had closed behind Conall once more did Richenda allow her formal demeanor to slip, darting across the short distance between herself and the visitor with a stifled little cry to fling her arms around him in delight.

"Ludolphus, Ludolphus, what is this *Ludolphus* nonsense, my lord?'' she whispered, letting her mind answer his psychic greeting even as he returned her physical embrace. "Rothana, do you not see who it is?''

Rothana's breath caught in a little gasp as she got a closer look at him, but because he set a finger across his lips in warning, her scarcely breathed "*Uncle Azim!*'' was more a psychic whisper than a spoken name as he came to embrace her as well. Though he brushed both women with the caress of his mind, he did not speak aloud until he had drawn them into the greater privacy of the window embrasure.

"Do not give me too glad a greeting, children," he cautioned, grinning as he set his satchel on one of the window benches and swept one arm in gesture for them to sit opposite. "I fear I might not be welcome if my true identity were recognized outside this room. Fortunately, my alter-ego Ludolphus only arouses the suspicion one must expect of a Moorish peddler come to request audience of a Christian lady."

"Nay, my lord, that is not true!" Richenda protested.

"Ah, do not try to lie to save my feelings, child," Azim chided, the white flash of his grin softening the rebuke. "Ludolphus the peddler arouses only human fears; Azim, brother of the Emir Hakim Nur Hallaj and precentor of the Knights of the Anvil, has been all too open that he and his Order both harbor and recruit Deryni.

"Even so, I should have had no hesitation in coming more openly to see you if Kelson were here. But with the king away at war—well, I think you have enough Deryni and near-Deryni to contend with, until he returns."

"I think I'm acquainted with all the Deryni," Richenda said dryly, giving him a dubious expression as she folded her arms across her breast. "You've obviously heard about our Torenthi hostages, and Queen Jehana. However, I wonder what you mean by 'near-Deryni.'"

Azim shrugged noncommittally and opened the mouth of his satchel, searching among the ends of half a dozen leather scroll tubes. "Why, your Haldane princes left here to manage things in Kelson's absence: Nigel, and the suspicious young Conall waiting in yonder corridor, hoping for another glimpse of my lovely niece." He smiled to see Rothana blush. "Tell me: how much time do they spend in the company of your Torenthi hostages?"

"Why, hardly any," Richenda replied, puzzled by a faintly brittle edge to his question. "The two younger boys play with little Liam, of course—and we're quite aware that Liam's mother is a potential threat, so proper safeguards have been taken on *that* front—but I've also patterned the boys to warn us if Liam should attempt anything. Are you just worrying on general principles, or is there something else I should know? Is *that* why you played messenger, rather than sending a servant? Nearly anyone could have delivered letters and scrolls."

Azim shrugged and handed one of the smaller scroll cases across to Richenda with a wistful look. "More of that in a moment, child. First of all, is Prince Nigel expecting a Torenthi trade delegation in the next week or so?"

"I really couldn't say," Richenda said softly, suddenly developing a heavy feeling in the pit of her stomach. "Why do you ask?"

"In a moment. Does he have audiences scheduled for this morning?"

"No."

"Good. Then we have a little time. First you must read the letter." He gestured toward the leather case. "I shall warn you now that it's a blind copy of another I *know* to have been sent. I do *not* know to whom it was sent, or what other documents there may be to support it. I *can* say that my source on this particular letter is impeccable. It is for you to decide what action is to be taken—and Nigel."

Not wasting further time, Richenda yanked the end off the leather tube and shook out the contents. As she skimmed the angular lines, the lead in her stomach rose to her throat.

*. . . plans proceeding . . . liberate the royal prisoners . . . safety of the king of utmost importance . . . rescuers to pose as traders . . . access to the Haldane regent . . . assassination. . . .*

She had read enough. Stunned, she raised her eyes to her old master, handing the letter to Rothana to read.

"They're going to try to kill Nigel?" she whispered. "When?"

"That, I do not know. Not this morning, at any rate. I gather you've had no inkling that anything of this sort was afoot?"

"No."

"But you *did* permit the Lady Morag to send and receive correspondence?"

"Kelson allowed her to write to Mahael, informing him of her hostage status through the summer. I myself dictated the words."

"And she sent no further messages, in the seals, perhaps?"

Richenda shook her head. "I would have known, even if I could not read the messages themselves. Besides, there has been no time for a further exchange of letters."

"Well, then, perhaps something more direct," Azim guessed. "She will have been well trained, being Wencit's sister. And Mahael of Arjenol is perhaps even craftier than his brother Lionel."

"You think Mahael responsible?" Rothana asked, looking up from her own perusal of the letter.

"Or one of his minions," Azim agreed. "If Mahael, however, the plot may extend even further than we think. Young Liam himself may not be safe."

"*Liam?*" Richenda said.

"Think how I have taught you, Richenda," Azim murmured, leaning forward to rest both hands on her shoulders and look into her eyes, fingers entwined around the back of her neck. "Mahael stands to lose nothing if ill should befall the young king while he lies hostage, having the next heir in his governance, but loss of the Princess Morag is another matter. Suppose that someone has reminded him how he might increase his own fortunes, could he but marry his brother's wife, she being heiress of Torenth after her two remaining sons? If Mahael were wed to Morag, whether or not with her consent, all he need do is fall back to his own lands of Arjenol for ten or fifteen years and breed heirs, much as the Mearan pretender has done; your Kelson could do nothing to stop him. And if, somehow, a convenient 'accident' were to befall his stepsons . . . ?"

"As befell King Alroy," Richenda continued, seeing it all through the mirror of Azim's mind, "then Mahael would rule Torenth with Morag, and his sons after them. Sweet *Jesu*, do you think that's what he really plans?"

"That, I do not know," he replied, releasing her and sitting back. "You will have to discover that for yourself. I have given you the warning, however, and tell you that Mahael is capable of such a plot, whether or not this particular plot is of his crafting. But a plan does exist to attempt the rescue of the Torenthi hostages, with Nigel targeted for assassination. *That* is what you must act upon at first. The rest remains to be discovered."

"I must go and tell him right away," Richenda said, starting to rise.

Azim smiled and caught her by the wrist, shaking his head. "Not yet, little one. He is safe enough for now. You have already told me that he has no audience this morning, and I dare not stay much longer. The official reason for my visit has yet to be fulfilled. You *do* still wish the scrolls I've brought you, I believe?"

"Yes, of course."

Schooling release of tension the way Azim had taught her so many years before, Richenda sat again and helped brace his satchel while he removed half a dozen more scroll tubes, several of them long enough that he had to force the ends free of the satchel's mouth.

"First of all, I've had no luck locating the transcripts you asked for," Azim said, "though I've not yet given up hope. There's precious little about Saint Camber in anyone's archives, even our own, and finding accounts of his canonization simply may not be possible."

"What have you found, then?"

"Well, this one is the most interesting," he said, handing her the most weathered-looking of the cases. "It's an account of the proceedings of the Council of Ramos—badly damaged in spots, and probably not complete even when it came to us, but perhaps it will be of use. God alone knows how it got into the Djellarda archives, knowing how our Michaeline predecessors felt about the ecclesiastical hierarchy of that time."

Richenda glanced at the markings on the outside, then passed it to Rothana as Azim handed her another.

"Disappointing to me, but Arilan will be fascinated—and Duncan. Nothing directly relating to Camber?"

"Not to him, but to his children," Azim replied. "That one is an order to pay stonemasons for work done on a chapel—signed by Camber's son Joram, who was a Michaeline priest and knight. It's dated in the reign of King Rhys Michael Haldane, however, which puts it at least fifteen years after Camber's supposed death. What makes it interesting is that the remnants of the seal reflect traces of a message once set there—which puts its importance beyond what one would expect of a simple bill for masons' services. Maybe what they built for him was special."

"Like a chapel to house Camber's remains?" Richenda said, raising an eyebrow in speculation.

"The thought had occurred to me," Azim admitted dryly, "though I've not been able to read anything in the seal. Perhaps you'll have better luck."

"What about the others?" Richenda asked, as Azim passed the remaining scrolls to her.

"Some poetry I thought you might enjoy, and a text that could be part of a Healer's manual from the old times. Knowing of your Alaric's burgeoning healing talents, I thought that might be of particular interest. It could even be Gabrilite—though I warn you, they were fond of cloaking everything in at least two levels of double-meaning. The two of you should have a merry summer puzzling at them.

"And finally," he handed her a slender packet of letters, "missives from Rohays and the stewards of your remaining estates in Andelon. The spring plantings were very good, I'm told, but instructions are required on repairs needed to the roof at El Ha'it."

"El Ha'it. . . ." Richenda smiled and laid the rest of the letters on the seat for later reading. "Would that I could transport the lake here to Rhemuth for the summer. 'Tis times like these that the temptation of weather-working is almost too great to resist."

Azim closed up his satchel and rose, smiling.

"If I thought it a true temptation, I should scold you as your mother did when you were a child," he said softly, "but I know you are my true student—and you, R'thana," he added, brushing the curve of Rothana's cheek with a fingertip as his eyes softened with affection for both of them.

"But I must go now. Consider well how you use what I have told you, Richenda. Foiling the Torenthi plan seems simple enough, but we do not know the extent of Morag's involvement, and she is very powerful. Be careful."

"I shall, master," she promised, as first she and then Rothana kissed his hand in formal farewell, student to teacher.

Then he was striding out of the solar, resuming the humbler demeanor of the peddler Ludolphus as Conall approached to escort him back to the courtyard, reading the faint uneasiness of those they passed in the corridors, even though Conall's presence reassured them that a Moorish peddler had a guarded right to be here.

Once, just before they reached the yard, a young priest hurrying in the same direction all but collided with them, too preoccupied with leafing through the pages of his breviary even to see them until he had nearly run them down. In their mutual juggling to keep the book from falling, Azim instinctively brushed the man's mind as well as his hand—and was astonished to find that the priest was Queen Jehana's chaplain!

He could not resist the temptation. Holding the link just an instant longer, even though physical contact had been only the most fleeting, he set a swift but irresistible compulsion in the man's unconscious that just might bear fruit. The priest hardly faltered as he clutched his book to his breast, murmured hurried thanks, and dashed on across the yard, already late for chapel.

The Deryni master put it from his mind then, for they had reached the yard. Conall dogged his heels, polite but taciturn, until he had mounted his dust-brown mare and trotted her and the laden pack mule toward the gatehouse arch. Even then, the prince and his squire followed on horseback all the way to the city gates, presumably to see that he was, in fact, leaving; the squire had been waiting with horses saddled already.

Azim easily could have misdirected them, had he wished, but he was ready to leave Rhemuth anyway, so he did not bother. Let the young Haldane play at being the zealous guardian of the women left in his father's protection; he would be tempered all too soon by more serious contention, if Azim's suspicions about Mahael proved well-founded.

As Azim headed south along the river, to rendezvous later that night with transportation more fitting his station—one of his Order's galleys out of Kharthat, though flying Fianna's colors in these Gwynedder waters—he thought about the task he had left for Richenda, regretful that she must be the one to deal with it, but confident of his student's ability to handle the situation.

He would keep close tabs on this one. Not only family honor was at stake, but the slowly recovering honor of Deryni in Gwynedd as well. Not for the first time, he wondered at the odd assortment gathered at Rhemuth, now that Kelson, Morgan, Duncan, and young MacArdry were away.

Richenda would be rock-steady as she had been trained to be, of course—the perfect plant in a land predominantly human—and also Rothana; Arilan would provide maturity and depth, if a trifle overfussy at times; and Nigel, though something of an unknown so far as his Haldane potentials were concerned, was at least a man of intelligence, caution, and even temper. Together, they ought to be able to balance Morag without difficulty, if she was the only Deryni to be reckoned with.

Of course, he must not totally discount Jehana—even more of a question mark as a Deryni than Nigel was as a Haldane, in all truth—but Azim doubted she would change much from her stand of the past few years, despite the bit of whimsy in which he had just indulged with her young priest. Still, he found himself wishing, as he urged his mare along the path atop the riverbank, that he had thought to spend more time in Bremagne during his youth. Contact with Jehana at that time, forcing her to see and deal with what she was, might have saved unthought-of problems now.

But he was not going to indulge in the game of "what if." That was altogether too tempting and fruitless a pastime for any of his race. He turned his thoughts instead to the challenge of a new conundrum his grand master had vexed him with at their last meeting in Djellarda. Rocail *said* it had been a favorite of the R'Kassan adept Sulien, but Azim was convinced Rocail himself had fashioned it—not that the work was beyond Rocail's capabilities. It was quite brilliant, actually. . . .

And as Azim amused himself with linguistic gymnastics, whistling a desert air under his breath for the benefit of his mare and the plodding mule following behind, the most recent subject of his contemplation—but one—knelt in a side chapel of the basilica within the walls of Rhemuth Keep and buried her face in her hands.

Jehana had not been able to find Sister Cecile, after her soul-shaking encounter with Richenda. Around her, several of the newly arrived Brigidine sisters also bowed at prie-dieux set in neat rows across the little chapel, but it was their first Mass of the day; it was Jehana's second. Father Ambros wore the crimson vestments of a martyr's feast day as he chanted the Introit from before the altar.

"*Scio cui credidi, et certus sum, quia potens est depositum meam servare in illum diem, justus judex. . . .*" I know Whom I have believed, and I am certain that He is able to guard the trust committed to me against that day, being a just judge. . . .

The Introit was that of the Commemoration of Saint Paul the Apostle—not one of Jehana's favorites, but since she had already heard it once today, she could let her thoughts edge reluctantly to consideration of the earlier confrontation with Richenda.

How could she not have noticed the fair-haired Deryni woman sitting at the loom? And how could the seemingly pious Rothana also be Deryni, deliberately damning herself by entering religion when she knew herself to be of the evil of their race?

On the epistle side now, the Introit, *Kyrie,* and *Gloria* concluded, Father Ambros was opening his lectionary to read the first lesson, fumbling a little with the stiff pages.

"*Dominus vobiscum.*"

"*Et cum spiritu tuo,*" Jehana responded automatically with the others.

"*Sequentia sancti Evangelii. 'In diebus illis: Saulus ad huc spirans minarum, et caedis in discipulos Domini. . . .*'" At this time: Saul, with every breath he drew, still threatened the disciples of the Lord with massacre; and he went to the high priest and asked him for letters of commendation to the synagogues at Damascus, so that he could arrest all those he found there, men and women who belonged to the way. . . .

As Jehana automatically translated the Latin of the reading, she suddenly realized that it was not the same epistle read earlier in the day; in fact, it was not the expected passage from *Galatians* at all, but a text from the *Acts of the Apostles.*

"'*Et cum iter faceret, contiget, ut appropinquaret Damasco: et subito circumfulsit eum lux de caelo. . . .*'" And on his journey, when he was nearly at Damascus, a light from heaven shone suddenly about him. He fell to the ground and heard a voice saying to him, Saul, Saul, why dost thou persecute me . . . ?

She clapped her hands over her ears in horror. What was Father Ambros saying? The epistle he read was for the feast of Saint Paul's Conversion, not his Commemoration. How could he have made such an error?

But a part of her already considered the possibility of a higher work in what he did, and perhaps the why of it, if not the how. Though she tried vainly to shut out his words, shaking her head and closing her eyes against the sight as well as the sound of him, another figure seemed to rise up in her mind before the red-clad after-image of Father Ambros, cowled grey of the Other overshadowing the red vestments of martyrdom.

*No! That could not be!*

She had tried to avoid even hearing about the long discredited saint who purported to concern himself with the welfare of the curst Deryni race—*his* race—but somehow she knew it was he who seemed to hold out his arms to her and call her, in the vision that forced itself upon her tortured mind.

*Saul, Saul, why dost thou persecute me . . . ?*

Only, in the prison of her mind, it was not Saul he accused, but herself—not the Christ who called, but the dreaded Deryni heretic, Saint Camber! She could not turn away or shut *him* out, but only listen as he seemed to stretch out his hand to her and touch her brow.

*Jehana . . . why dost thou persecute me . . . ?*

And the voice of Father Ambros, continuing unperturbed with his redirected reading, floated on the air like an angel's, inescapably underlining her fear.

"*'Et tremens, ac stupens, dixit: Domine, quid me vis facere . . . ?'*" And he, trembling and dazed, asked, Lord, what wilt thou have me do?

And the Lord said to him, Rise up, and go into the city, and there thou shalt be told what thy work is. . . .

# CHAPTER TWELVE

*Then thou scarest me with dreams, and terrifiest me through visions.*

—Job 7:14

"Sorry I'm late," Conall said, as he and his squire drew rein in a forest clearing not far from the city walls of Rhemuth. "Did you get the message I sent yesterday?"

"I did, indeed. It seems we anticipated your father's intentions only just in time."

Casually, Tiercel de Claron came and set a hand on the bit of the squire's horse, fixing the boy with his eyes. "Come down from there and have a nap, young Jowan," he ordered, catching the boy under the elbow with practiced ease as the lad nearly tumbled from the saddle, half-asleep already.

As Conall also dismounted and took charge of the two horses, setting them to graze with a sleek chestnut already browsing at the other side of the clearing, Tiercel walked the stumbling Jowan to a shady spot underneath a birch tree and eased his collapse to the ground. The lad was snoring blissfully by the time Conall came back across the clearing. Tiercel dusted his hands together and breathed a sigh of satisfaction as he rose and glanced at Conall.

"So, Richenda set the blocks as we suspected, did she? And caught not hide nor hair of what we'd done to prepare for them?"

"Nothing! I could sense that she was doing something—though I couldn't tell what—and I certainly couldn't have stopped her. But I also knew that there was another part of me she wasn't even seeing!"

"Indeed?" Tiercel said, his tone encouraging further details.

"And later that day," Conall went on eagerly, "Father let me attend my first real privy council meeting. I don't mean just the formal privy council, but a *private* privy council meeting! They told me all kinds of things, only—I can't talk about some of them. I mean, I literally *can't*. I think they must be in some other kind of secondary level, only *she* set that one."

"Behind her block, I should think," Tiercel said, gesturing toward the shade of another tree where a small wineskin, a spread-out cloak, and his ubiquitous satchel already lay. "I'll have a look in a bit. Why are you so late? It's nearly noon."

"I had to deliver a letter to Richenda," Conall said, plopping down on the spread cloak at Tiercel's invitation. "It was from some cousin in the Forcinn—a lady. I wish I could have read it."

Clucking his tongue in gentle scolding, Tiercel sat down beside Conall.

"Do you, now? Just curious, or a particular reason? In general, it's best to stay out of the affairs of ladies, Conall. They have a world all their own. Besides, I don't want you in a position where Richenda might be tempted to try a deeper reading on you."

"Well, I suppose." Conall wrinkled his nose doubtfully. "You should have seen the man who brought the letter, though. In fact, there were several letters. He insisted he had to deliver those in person. He *said* he was a Moorish peddler, and he dressed the part, but I'm not sure that's all he was."

"Oh? What makes you say that?"

As Tiercel lay back on one elbow, he unstoppered the wineskin and directed a stream into his open mouth.

"Hmmm, just something about him," Conall answered slowly. He leaned against the tree trunk and propped his wrists on his upraised knees as he thought about it. "I honestly wasn't sure she'd even see him, him being a Moor and all—especially since it was just her and Rothana alone in the solar.

"She said she'd been expecting him, though, even before she opened the letter, and that she and Rothana would receive him in private. Then, when I showed him in, he moved more like a courtier than a peddler. You should have seen the bow he made her. Do you think he's a secret lover or something?"

Tiercel smiled around a mouthful of wine and let the smile turn to a chuckle when he had swallowed. "I strongly doubt that. It isn't at all uncommon for peddlers to act as ladies' messengers. Their occupation takes them many places. And if they make a profession of messengering as well as peddling, and hope to be employed by high-born ladies, they've usually acquired fairly polished courtly manners as well. What did this fellow look like?"

"Hmmm, dark and swarthy, as you might expect of a Moor; about my height, but very wiry, compact. Later on, when I was escorting him back to the yard to leave, he struck me as a man with battle training. He had incredibly fast reflexes."

"What did you say he called himself?"

"I didn't—but it was Ludolphus."

Tiercel, in the process of having another swallow of wine, nearly choked.

"*Sancta Dei Genetrix,* I think I know who it was," he whispered, when he had recovered. "What's *he* doing in Rhemuth? Did he touch you? Show me what he looked like."

Surprised at Tiercel's reaction, Conall only cocked his head and stared as his mentor lurched to a sitting position and reached across to touch his forehead, without giving him any time to prepare. Resisting never crossed his mind, but Conall suddenly decided that, rather than simply surrendering passively to Tiercel's probe as he always had in the past, he would try to consciously give Tiercel what he wanted to know. He almost faltered before the onslaught of Tiercel's sudden *presence* in his mind, but he managed never to lose consciousness or even close his eyes as he spread the images of his recent encounter for Tiercel's inspection. The surprised Tiercel clapped him on the knee in distracted congratulation as he withdrew, a strained little smile playing at his lips.

"So," the Deryni murmured, almost to himself, "someone is sending in the heavies. And you're hardly in the butterfly-weight category yourself anymore, either, are you, my young friend?" he added, glancing at Conall. "You've never managed to stay with me that way before."

Conall grinned and ducked his head briefly, suddenly a little shy.

"It seemed important," he replied, looking up at Tiercel again. "For the first time, it seemed that maybe *you* needed *me*, for a change. Who was he? By your reaction, it's fairly clear that he's Deryni—and perhaps even more highly trained than you are."

"He's—ah—an acquaintance," Tiercel hedged. "Not an enemy, I assure you," he added, at Conall's look of concern, "but I can't explain further. Let's just say that he's an old friend and teacher of Richenda's and leave it at that, shall we?"

"I suppose."

"Good. And that being said," Tiercel went on, tapping Conall's boot to reengage his attention, "I'm now interested in returning to what *you* just did. I think you've made a major break-through. You went from being a passive subject to an active participant. I've been hoping for that."

Conall smiled, pleased. "Did I do well? I think it started after our last session, when you set me for Richenda's blocks. I knew *something* had happened."

"It certainly did." Tiercel thought a moment, then slapped Conall's boot in resolution. "I think we'll follow up on something you mentioned earlier, too. How would you like to learn to read without your eyes?—like the letter for Richenda, that you were wishing you could have read today."

Conall's eyes widened and he swallowed visibly. "You could teach me that?"

"I think so—now. A blind friend of mine does it all the time. Not as fast as visual reading, but it does have its advantages—and some additional applications, if you can master this one. All very useful talents for a prince." Tiercel drew a dagger from his boot top and arched an eyebrow at Conall. "I assume you *would* like to try?"

Conall eyed the drawn weapon with some misgiving, but he grinned and gave a very positive nod as Tiercel merely gestured with it toward a patch of bare earth at the edge of the cloak they sat upon. As Conall scooted closer to sit cross-legged at Tiercel's left, the Deryni began scratching a maze-like pattern into the earth with his blade.

"Now, what I'm drawing is sometimes called a 'staring pattern,'" Tiercel explained as he drew. "Later on, you probably won't need the physical pattern—not for this particular procedure, at any rate—but it helps in the early visualizing. I think I'll have you start by using it with a pendulum. Are you wearing your Camber medal today?''

"Aye.''

As Tiercel put the finishing touches to his design, cleaning the blade of his dagger deftly against the side of his boot before resheathing it, Conall drew a silver chain out of the neck of his tunic and looped it off over his head. The medal caught the dappled sunlight under the tree like a jewel as he handed it to Tiercel by the end of the chain.

"That's fine,'' Tiercel said, holding the chain between thumb and forefinger so that the medal hung a handspan above the design, stilling its swing with his other hand.

"Now: I've had you use a pendulum before as a point of focus. This time, instead of letting the movement of the pendulum carry *you*, I want *you* to direct the movement of the pendulum. With your mind, though—not your hand.''

"Mmmm?''

"Just watch. Notice that the pattern is all a single, continuous line, gradually spiraling toward the center. We begin with the pendulum hanging quite still, just above this outside end of the pattern, and then we concentrate on the medal—on making it start to swing so that it follows the pattern toward the center. See? It's starting to move, but I'm not deliberately doing anything with my hand. . . .''

"I see it,'' Conall murmured, already reaching for the chain. "Let me try.''

Nodding, Tiercel handed it over and helped him still its swing.

"All right,'' he said, removing his hand. "Now, focus on the path the pendulum follows, rather than the pendulum itself. Imprint that pattern on your mind and let yourself be drawn toward its center. The end-result is called 'centering,' aptly enough—regardless of how you arrive at that state.''

As Conall obeyed and the pendulum immediately began to swing, Tiercel quietly slid one hand around the boy's shoulder. Even before he made mental contact, he could sense Conall coupling in with the path of the pendulum as he concentrated, the raven head beginning to nod, and he extended the lightest possible tendrils of control to enhance relaxation as he cupped his hand around the back of the bent neck.

"That's fine,'' he murmured. "Just relax and flow with the pattern.''

But Conall had no need of his help. He was already well into trance, going deeper by the heartbeat—and consciously aware, on some level not quite clear to Tiercel, that the other's controls were present.

That awareness startled Tiercel, even though Conall made no shred of resistance. As startling as the awareness was the quarter whence it came. To learn to recognize another's psychic probe was one thing; humans who worked regularly with Deryni often learned to sense such a touch, and to cooperate consciously to facilitate results. What Conall had done when Tiercel read his memory of Azim fell into that category—a commendable achievement, but not wholly unexpected, given the length and intensity of their interaction.

But to be aware of *controls* exerted by another was quite a different matter, even if Conall was unable to resist them—though perhaps not all that unexpected after all, in light of what Conall had told him of his encounter with Richenda.

He probed the barriers *he* had set, to see whether Richenda had, indeed, skimmed over them unawares, but all seemed intact. Sequestering and burying Conall's memories of himself and their training sessions had been tricky enough a proposition, knowing his work must stand before Richenda's scrutiny, but apparently he had succeeded. Though he could not broach the blocks Richenda had set—and had not expected he would be able to—neither did it appear Richenda had even tried to probe beyond the limits of her own blocks. Thank God for that!

But as Tiercel held Conall momentarily in balance and continued to scan, he realized that some of the secondary levels he himself had partitioned off in preparing Conall for contact with other Deryni were now obscured, almost like a secondary shielding system—almost like a Deryni! It also appeared to be the source of Conall's new ability to recognize controls.

Now, *that* was interesting—though Tiercel decided not to take the time now to look more closely at the phenomenon, lest they not accomplish what they had set out to do. Conall was nearly deep enough for the next phase, his hand holding rock-steady over the maze while the medal at the end of the chain swung with ever-increasing accuracy over the pattern, nearing the center.

Impressed, Tiercel pulled back and merely observed as Conall settled deeper still, himself dropping into supportive trance to guide the prince through the next phase.

"Good," he said, touching Conall's forehead lightly between the eyes, which closed, and then taking the pendulum and pressing Conall's hand gently down to rest on the ground. "Now relax and follow the images I show you. Just let yourself drift and observe. . . ."

An hour later, an elated Conall had not only mastered the new mode of sightless reading, but he had come up with several additional applications on his own.

"One could use this for opening locked doors!" the prince breathed, wide-eyed. "Maybe even for seeing behind closed doors—"

"A little beyond your ability yet, I think," Tiercel said, chuckling gently, "though who knows how far you'll go now that you've passed this hurdle?"

Conall merely grinned and set his concentration to a blade of grass between his fingers, watching one end slowly curl and loop around itself until it had formed a knot.

And Tiercel, watching fondly from a supine position on the spread cloak, laced his fingers behind his head and dreamed of bringing his pupil in triumph before the Camberian Council.

Meanwhile, the Haldane intrusion into Meara continued. The following dawn, in the foothills southwest of Ratharkin, Kelson and Morgan stood in the meager privacy between their saddled greathorses and listened to the excited report of a dusty R'Kassan scout.

"I know they didn't see us, Sire," the man said. "I think they're a skirmish band split off from the Mearans' main van. If we send a like force in the next hour, we can cut them off and take them before they know what's happened."

"How many?" Morgan asked.

"Jemet counted nearly sixty horses, Your Grace. An additional twenty might be hidden in a box canyon we couldn't get to, but certainly no more than that. And we're certain they're all cavalry. No commander in his right mind would leave foot soldiers that far behind the main van."

"You're assuming that Ithel of Meara is in his right mind," Kelson said dryly, fiddling with a harness buckle, "but you're probably right. How far did you say?"

"Perhaps two hours' ride, Sire. But I—think, though I couldn't swear to it—I think the commander may be Prince Ithel himself!"

Instantly the animation drained out of Kelson's face, only the eyes blazing with life as he glanced quickly at Morgan.

"I hear, my prince," Morgan said softly.

At his raised eyebrow and Kelson's answering nod, almost imperceptible, Morgan drew the scout farther between the horses with a gesture, better shielding them all from curious eyes as he started to pull off one of his gloves.

"I think we'll have a little closer look at what you saw," he said easily. "I don't doubt your reporting, but if it *is* Ithel, we wouldn't want to miss anything."

But before Morgan could carry through with his intention, Kelson's revised order snapped in his mind like a brittle twig underfoot in autumn:

*On second thought, I'll read this one.*

"Stand here between us, Kirkon," Morgan added, deftly turning the man to face Kelson as the king stripped off mailed gauntlets and jammed them into his belt.

Kirkon gave no sign of resistance as Morgan braced him from behind with hands set on shoulders and Kelson moved closer. All the scouts knew that being read was a possibility, whenever they came to report to the king or his champion, if clarification was in order—and most had learned not to mind, and certainly not to fear. They had also accepted the growing convention, deliberately fostered by Kelson and Morgan, that Deryni always must touch their subjects on the head or neck in order to read their minds, preferably bare-handed. In fact, a hand or wrist or any other part of the body would do as well, and Deryni *could* read through gloves or other clothing if they must; but Kelson had felt that if humans at least *thought* the Deryni limited in this regard, it might ease some of the apprehension attached to actually dealing with them on a regular basis.

So now, though the scout succumbed to a few nervous blinks as his eyes met Kelson's, he did not flinch as the king touched fingertips to his temples.

"Take a deep breath, Kirkon," Kelson murmured.

It was over almost before the scout could draw breath a second time. He was left swaying a little on his feet, but otherwise only faintly relieved as Kelson withdrew mind and hands.

"Your orders, Sire?" Morgan asked quietly, continuing to steady the scout for a few seconds more.

Kelson turned away abruptly, to lean an armored elbow against the side of his horse's saddle, that fist pressed briefly to his teeth. If anything, the Haldane face was even more masklike than before.

"You can go, Kirkon. Thank you," he murmured. And did not lift his eyes or speak again until the scout had gone.

"I'll want all of Nigel's new lancers for this little escapade, Alaric," he said softly. "And your Corwyn heavy cavalry as well. This time, I think we've got him."

"Ithel?" Morgan asked.

"Aye." The whisper was harsh, the eyes gone even colder with the one word. "Aye, 'tis Ithel—and may Saint Camber be the hammer of our retribution!"

"There may be a reason he's apart from the others," Morgan cautioned. "It could be a trap. . . ."

Kelson shook his head. "No, no trap. We *know* the location of the rest of the Mearan van. And we know that Sicard, wherever he is, is not within striking distance of us. No, Ithel has finally made his fatal error. And now he's *mine*!"

"Very well, my prince," Morgan murmured, wiser than to contradict the king in this sort of mood. "Shall I call your captains, so you may give your orders?"

Kelson's nod was curt, his gaze wolf-keen, as he looked out toward the rolling hills of the plain south of Ratharkin and dreamed of vengeance.

Dreams of vengeance occupied a queen as well as a king that brightening July morning, though Jehana, unlike her son, felt herself the subject of vengeance rather than the author of it. She rose early—or, rather, left her quarters early—for she had not slept all night, nor found respite from the vision that had haunted her thoughts since the previous noon. The accusing image of Camber of Culdi seemed to loom in her presence every time she closed her eyes, his words taunting, torturing.

*Jehana, Jehana, why do you persecute me?*

Nor had she been able to rationalize what had happened, even when, later that afternoon, she had confronted Father Ambros about his choice of texts.

"Why, did I read the wrong lesson, Majesty? I don't remember doing so. Was it not the same I read at the early Mass?"

"Don't mock me, Father!"

"*Mock* you, my lady? But I don't understand."

Their exchange had occurred in the basilica, before the Blessed Sacrament. Surely he would not dare to lie to her there. But lying would have been welcome, compared to what did occur. For though he clearly was shocked by her accusation, she had found herself extending her powers to Truth-Read him anyway, to her helpless horror.

"Do you mean to tell me you didn't realize?" she snapped. "Don't lie to me, Father! Do you think I can't tell when you're lying? Did someone put you up to it?"

"My lady, I don't know what you want me to say. . . ."

"*Why are you doing this to me?*" she insisted.

Alarm flickered in his eyes as he lifted both his palms in entreaty, and she knew at once that he was innocent, but she had already gone beyond any stopping point by then. Not content merely to know that he was telling the truth as he perceived it, she seized his wrist and captured him with her eyes, invading his mind with such force that he moaned a little at the shock. He sank to his knees before the onslaught, stunned and frightened but unable to resist, a prisoner of her will.

She held him thus for several seconds, compelling his exacting recall of the events preceding the reading of the offending scripture. But she found only innocence in his heart as, in memory, he opened his book where the marker made it fall and read the words, oblivious to their difference from the morning's reading.

Sweet *Jesu*, he had *not* realized! But if his action had not been deliberate, how had such a thing happened? What agent of Fate had intervened?

A sob rose in her throat as she released the reeling Ambros, for the conclusion was inescapable, filling her with dread. Oblivious to the young priest's trembling after-reaction, face buried in his hands, she sank to her knees before him, blinded by tears.

The heretic Deryni Camber had driven her to this. Why was he pursuing her? Was it not enough that he must disturb her meditations and haunt her dreams? Must he also tempt her to use her God-forbidden powers even here, in the very Presence of the Lord, in an effort to escape him?

And she had yielded to the temptation! God, how she despised herself! Not only had she dared to use her long-denied powers, but she had used them to force entry into another's mind, and caused him pain in the forcing.

And her innocent victim was a priest! Oh, Blessed Mother and all the saints, even if Ambros eventually forgave her, God would not!

"My God in heaven, what have you done?" Ambros murmured, as she dared a guilty glance at him.

He had hardly moved from where she released him. Dazed and bewildered, more than a little frightened still, he sat huddled on the step at the base of the altar rail, leaning weakly against one of the carved supports, the blue eyes still pain-shadowed and accusing.

"What have you done?" he repeated. "I felt like you were looking into my very soul. . . ."

"I d-didn't mean to hurt you, F-Father," she managed to stammer through her tears. "I was so afraid. . . ."

"But, daughter—"

He was trying to understand, but the residue of fear mirrored in his eyes once more triggered her desperation.

"Forget what has just happened," she commanded, lifting her tear-stained hands to either side of his face and imposing her will once more, even though he tried to shrink from her touch this time. "Forgive me if you can, Father, but you must forget. Forget and sleep."

Resistance was not possible. Even had he wished to share her torment, he could not but obey. As his eyes closed and he slumped helplessly beneath her hands, she touched his mind once more, relentlessly reshaping his memory to hide her guilt.

Then she left him sleeping, to remember only that he had dozed while he meditated in the basilica, and fled with her conscience to the solitude of her own quarters. She saw no one for the rest of the day, and took no meal that evening. Nor did she sleep that night.

But not fasting nor prayer nor even mortification of her body could drive what she was and had done from her mind, or allow her the peace she so desperately sought. Oppressed by her guilt, she even debated whether she dared attend Mass the next morning, for surely she was damned for her sin; but neither did she dare *not* go. She always went to the early morning Mass that Father Ambros celebrated for herself and Sister Cecile, and they would wonder if she did not go. Also, some tiny corner of remaining innocence still hoped that the very act of hearing Mass and receiving the Sacrament might somehow bring her the healing she sought. Surely God would not smite her for seeking Him, even in her frailty and failings.

But forcing herself to turn thought to action and actually cross the seemingly vast expanse of yard between her quarters and the basilica with Ambros and Cecile was an ordeal she had not reckoned on. Though Ambros showed no sign of remembering anything of their previous encounter, she imagined she saw accusation in his every glance; and Sister Cecile seemed far more solemn and silent than was her usual wont.

Jehana was halfway across the yard with them before she began to be aware how her self-imposed deprivations of the night had further diminished the rigid checks she habitually maintained on her detested powers, lowering her resistance to temptation. The yard bustled with merchants and tradesmen already assembling to seek later audiences with the regent Nigel; but as she made her way among them, she began catching the occasional psychic impression as well as actual snatches of their conversations.

". . . told Ahmed that the grain was mostly chaff, but he pleaded a poor harvest and . . ."

". . . get a fair hearing from Prince Nigel, at any rate. He's as honest as his brother was . . ."

*. . . God, it's going to be another hot day today. I wonder if I can slip away while the master is having audience. . . .*

". . . all we need to do is get that trade concession and . . ."

Jehana ducked her head deeper into the shadow of her light cloak—worn for anonymity rather than any need for warmth, for it was already uncomfortably warm in the widow's weeds she wore—and continued on through the yard, consciously trying to shut off the psychic input.

". . . Get that pack mare over here, Ned! If those silks are damaged . . ."

". . . and then we'll see what happens to the Haldane. . . ."

*. . . images of blood . . .*

". . . and three tuns of Fianna wine . . ."

Jehana stumbled and nearly fell, so startled was she by what she was not even certain she had heard. Ambros rushed to assist her, steadying her with a supporting hand under her elbow, but as she glanced in the direction she thought the Haldane reference had come from, she was already looking for its source with mind as well as eyes.

". . . So I told old Rechol that his blades weren't worth half what he was asking, and he said . . ."

No, farther to the right. . . .

A silver merchant and his servant were unpacking a pannier on a packmule, two clerks reviewed an account scroll in the shade of an overhang, and three grooms were chuckling over some secret joke shared among them. Instinctively she opened her senses wider and cast for more information—and *knew* that neither the grooms nor many of the supposed merchants milling in the yard were at all what they seemed. They were men of Torenth, come to kill Nigel and take control of the castle and the captive Torenthi king.

*Only a little while now . . .*

With a little sob, she cowered back inside herself and clung to Ambros' arm, suddenly shocked and horrified as much by how she had gained her knowledge as by the knowledge itself.

"Oh, take me away from here, Ambros!" she whispered, burying her face against his shoulder.

"But, my lady," he breathed, "what's wrong?"

She would not answer him, though. Not until they had gained the safe haven of the basilica and he had drawn her insistently into the shelter of the little side chapel and closed the door, shutting out even Sister Cecile, would she even do more than weep almost hysterically.

"What *is* it, Jehana?" Ambros whispered, stroking her hand with trembling fingers as she huddled at his feet and wept. "Tell me, daughter. Surely it cannot be as bad as all of that."

"Oh, God, I am damned! We are all damned!" She wept.

"You, damned? Nonsense."

"Don't you mock me, too, Father," she managed to whisper between sobs, withdrawing her hand from his. "*He* mocks me already. First he made you read the wrong lesson yesterday, and now he shows me what I would not know—only, only—"

"Daughter, what are you talking about?" Ambros asked, taking her by the shoulders to look her in the eyes. "*Who* made me read—"

Jehana shook her head and snuffled loudly, pulling a hand-kerchief from her sleeve to dab ineffectually at her eyes.

"I—I can't tell you."

"Nonsense. Of course you can tell me. I'm a priest. I'm your confessor."

"No, I can't! I've hurt you enough already."

"You've *hurt* me? Jehana, what *are* you talking about?" Ambros gave her shoulders a shake. "What happened out there? Get hold of yourself! I can't help you if I don't know what's wrong."

Snuffling forlornly, Jehana sat back on her heels, twisting her handkerchief in anxious fingers, eyes averted.

"You'll hate me," she murmured.

"Hate you? Certainly not!"

"But, I've committed terrible sins!"

"Surely none so terrible that God will not forgive them."

"You would not say that with such ease, did you know what I have done."

"Daughter, daughter, it surely cannot be as serious as that! Tell me what's wrong. Surely I can find a way to help you."

Swallowing noisily, Jehana dared to glance up at him through her tears.

"Will you keep what I shall tell you under the seal of the confessional, Father?"

"Of course."

"Do you swear that, by your office as priest?"

"Certainly."

"Put on your stole, then," she demanded.

With a sigh of only partially concealed exasperation, Ambros fetched a stole draped across the altar rail and touched the violet silk to his lips before looping it around his neck.

"Now. Tell me," he ordered.

And she did—though she would not let him touch her, lest she again succumb to the temptation to use her illicit power. When she had blurted out the entire story, beginning with the vision of Camber the day before and ending with the ominous hints she had caught of a plot against Nigel, not sparing him the account of the assault she had made upon his mind, Ambros was shaken but resolute.

"Sweet *Jesu*, you must not concern yourself for *me*, Jehana—or even for this vision of Saint Camber which you may or may not have had," he whispered, his handsome face as pale and drawn as hers with the weight of the knowledge. "You must warn the prince. Even now, it may be too late!"

"No. I must not. Think how I learned of it, Ambros! 'Tis forbidden knowledge! Have you and I not spent two years now, trying to stamp out its taint? Even *you* have not escaped its curse!"

Ambros swallowed audibly, but he did not allow himself to shrink from her gaze.

"I—seem to have survived unscathed, my lady. Perhaps the taint is not so virulent as you have always feared."

"No?"

With a flick of her mind, Jehana released his memory of what she had done before, watching tearfully as he blanched and turned even paler than he had been—though beyond his initial gasp, he showed little other outward sign of fear.

"I dare not ask for forgiveness for what I've done, Father, but perhaps now you understand its enormity."

Ambros clasped his hands tightly before his bowed head for a few seconds, then looked up at her again.

"My lady, I think I do understand at least a part of why you felt yourself compelled to do what you did," he murmured. "But you must not chastise yourself overmuch for it."

"But, I *hurt* you, Father! Think back to it. Remember it. You can't deny that I did it."

"I—cannot deny that I experienced—some discomfort," he admitted haltingly, the remembered pain showing on his face. "But I—think that is as much my fault as yours."

"What?"

"I—think that if I had been able to overcome my fear, when I realized what you were doing—"

"Are you saying that what I did was *right*?" she gasped.

"It is not—so much a matter of right or wrong, my lady, but—Jehana, you, too, were in fear! You perceived a mortal threat in the visions you have received, and you used the most powerful means at your disposal in an attempt to discern the true nature of that threat."

"But I hurt you," she repeated dully.

"Not intentionally," he replied. "It wasn't intentional, was it?"

As she shook her head, he went on.

"Then, listen to me. Jehana, I don't know anymore whether the power you have is evil. Your control of that power is sometimes uncertain—and perhaps you applied it with more force than you might have, had you not been oppressed by your own fears. Perhaps that's why you hurt me.

"But now your power has revealed this plot against Nigel. And because of your power, we have learned of the plot in time to prevent it. There's nothing evil about that, Jehana!"

"But I shouldn't have found out," she whispered dully. "Decent, God-fearing people don't find out things that way."

"Jehana, they're going to kill Nigel!" Ambros blurted. "You can't just stand by and let that happen."

"God help me, I don't know *what* I should do." She wept, hugging her arms across her breast. "The knowledge is evil—"

"The knowledge can save an innocent life, for God's sake! How can that be evil? If you don't warn him, I—"

"You'll *what*," she challenged, looking up at him angrily. "You'll tell him yourself?"

"Well, I—"

"Of course you will not," she went on, her voice gentling a little as she broke their eye contact and turned forlornly toward the altar. "You are bound by your office and your oath. And you would never betray the faith betokened by that which hangs about your shoulders."

Ambros recoiled as if struck by a physical blow, one hand going automatically to the purple stole he still wore, and she knew the temptation had crossed his mind. Closing her eyes against even that knowledge, though it had come from no Deryni source, she choked back a sob and shook her head.

"Please, Father. Leave me now. You have done your duty to advise me. This decision I must make on my own."

"But, my lady," he pleaded. "I can help. Please let me stay."

But as he reached out to touch her shoulder in compassion, she shrank from him and shook her head.

"No! Do not touch me. If you touch me, I may contaminate you further."

"I am not afraid," he began.

"Perhaps not, but I am," she replied. "Go, now, *please*! Do not add to my temptation. You will *not* betray your office, for my sake or anyone else's. Do you understand? I must discern the reason I have been given this knowledge, and I alone may make the decision as to how it shall be used."

# CHAPTER THIRTEEN

*The king's strength also loveth judgment; thou dost
establish equity, thou executest judgment and
righteousness.*

—Psalms 99:4

Ithel of Meara set his shoulders stubbornly, chin held high,
sullen and resentful as he and Brice of Trurill rode with their
bodyguard through the silent streets of Talacara town.

The stupid peasants had *better* stay inside, if they knew
what was good for them! How *dare* they question his right
to do what he had done? He was risking his life to delay the
invading Haldane army, buying time for his father, covering
the strategic retreat of the brave and loyal men taking his
mother to Laas for safety, and what thanks did he get? Since
the burning of Ratharkin three days before, even his own
Mearan people had begun to turn against him. And Talacara
had been the most belligerent so far.

Talacara. The sharp, acrid bite of woodsmoke hung on the
air with the sweeter, more distinctive smell of burning grain
as Ithel jerked irritably at the chinstrap of his helmet and
pulled it off. He was sweating like a pig inside his armor.
He saw two men emerging from a house with their arms full
of plunder, but he felt no inclination whatever to stop them.

The town had it coming. The stiff-necked folk of Talacara
had not only refused to provision him; the town bailiffs had
actually shut the gates against him, and the mayor had dared
to shout his defiance from behind the shelter of the walls!
Did they not understand that men must have food to fight,
or even to flee, and that anything Ithel left behind might be
seized by the enemy?

Not that there had been any question of prolonged resistance, of course. Talacara's "walls" were a crude palisade of sharpened stakes, its gates an impediment only to unarmed peasants on foot—not to an armored warband. On Brice's orders, their men had piled summer-dry brush against the gates and palisade and torched it. Once the structure itself began to burn, breaching the walls was hardly the work of an hour. When their provisioners had taken what they needed from the town's granaries and other storehouses, Ithel turned his men loose on the town before ordering them to burn what was left. Nor was further belligerence dealt with leniently. He would teach these cheeky peasants to defy *him*.

Being preoccupied, then, with cheeky peasants and the lesson he was teaching them, Ithel temporarily lost sight of the possibility that another master more canny than himself might be preparing to teach *him* a lesson.

"I want that mayor found," Ithel said to Brice as, in the town square, they watched several of their men make rough sport of two of the captured bailiffs of the town, stripped naked and made to run at the end of ropes around their necks. "We may be in retreat, but I'm still his better!"

"I believe suitable chastisement can be found to humble the fellow, Your Highness," Brice replied blandly. "However, we'd best not delay too long. Retribution may be sweet, but steady retreat is still our wisest course. It wouldn't do to be cornered here in Talacara."

Hardly were the words out of his mouth when one of his own Trurill scouts came galloping through the smoking ruin of the town gates from outside, rowelling his horse's sides until the blood ran, waving an arm frantically.

"Raise the alarm! To horse! To horse! Battle force approaching!"

Men with their arms piled high with booty scattered before him as he came. Ithel went cold despite the day's heat, craning fearfully back the way the man had come, but Brice was already bawling orders, trying to rally their scattered and much preoccupied troops to flee.

"Armed riders approaching from the south, Your Highness!" the scout shouted, setting his horse on its haunches as he drew up before them, breathing hard. "Scores of men, moving fast. Oh, God, I think they're Haldanes!"

"Haldanes!"

"Sergeant, get these men moving!" Brice yelled, urging his horse among the booty-laden soldiers now milling in panic. "Drop that, if you value your lives! It may be too late already!"

He drew his sword and began using the flat of it to underline his order as another man came galloping up from the opposite direction, even more agitated than the first.

"More men, m'lord! They're closing us in! We're trapped!"

And Kelson Haldane, drawing tight the noose he had set about Talacara town, set his crowned helm firmly on his head and drew his father's sword, grey eyes cold as ice in the midday sun.

"Men of Gwynedd," he shouted, raising the blade above his head. "I want Ithel of Meara. Alive, if possible, but I want him. And Brice of Trurill as well! Now—for Gwynedd!"


And in Gwynedd's capital, Kelson's mother began an action equally important for Gwynedd.

"Father Ambros," Jehana whispered, almost weak with relief as she came out of the basilica and found him still waiting there, against her instructions. "Thank God you're still here. Come with me, quickly! I still don't know whether I'm doing the right thing, but I cannot let Nigel be killed."

Breathing a fervent prayer of thanksgiving, Ambros took her hand and kissed it tenderly.

"You are a true queen, my lady!" he whispered. "I prayed that you would have a change of heart."

"It is not a change of heart," she replied, as she led him toward the back corridors that would take them to the great hall without going through the crowded yard again. "I still must expiate my sins, but Nigel is my husband's brother. Besides Kelson, he's all I have of Brion anymore. I owe him this. I owe it to Brion. And if I can save Nigel's life today, perhaps it may not be too late to save his soul another time."

"Nigel's soul?" Ambrose said. "But, he isn't Deryni."

"No, but they want to *make* him Deryni, Ambros—and can, or nearly so, if they put Brion's magic on him," she answered.

"*They?* What are you talking about?"

"Morgan. And Kelson, too, unfortunately. But perhaps I can make him see the danger. Perhaps it isn't yet too late."

"I only hope it isn't too late today," Ambros muttered, running a few steps to keep up with her as she took an unexpected turn. "Never mind any other day."

But it was already too late for Ithel of Meara. He was sixteen years old, and he knew he was going to die. Even though he and Brice managed to rally their men before the Haldane attackers actually came into sight, gathering them in the empty market square to make a final stand, he had no illusions about their chances. They numbered scarcely two hundred now, most of them still on foot. The ragged square formation that the battle site allowed would only be whittled away, little by little, by the vastly superior Haldane foe.

Sword in hand, then, Brice of Trurill at his side in the center of their men, Ithel watched his doom approach: silent, steely-eyed lancers in Haldane crimson, closing the ring simultaneously from all directions. All at the walk they came, stirrup to stirrup, lance points set in a glittering wall before them—scores of them. And a second line followed close on the first, with swords at ready—more heavily armored knights, another hundred, at least.

And beyond the second ring, heralded by the crimson and gold Haldane standard, came King Kelson himself, backed by half a dozen officers and aides, crowned helm gleaming in the sunlight and a fair sword resting across his armored shoulder. At his side rode a man in black, bearing a green gryphon on brigandine and shield and a ducal coronet on his helm: surely the infamous Alaric Morgan, the king's Deryni.

Ithel hardly dared breathe. For an interminable few seconds, the only sounds in the square were the jingle of bits and harness, the checked huffing of the greathorses, eager to be released to the charge, the dull stamp of iron-shod hooves on the trampled earth—that, and the pounding of Ithel's pulse in his ears, seeming to echo inside his helmet.

Hardly anything moved. The deadly certainty of the ring of Haldane lances shimmered in the heat like a moment snatched from hell. A breeze stirred the pennons on the lance-tips, the Haldane standard, wisps of the battle chargers' manes and tails, but it did not reach Ithel, stifling in his brigandine and helm.

Then a heavyset man with tartan pleated baldric-wise across his breastplate broke from the knot of men surrounding the king, kneeing his mount carefully forward to ease between the ranks and join the front line, sword in hand. The coronet on his helm proclaimed him a duke; and when he raised his visor to speak, a bushy red beard and mustaches bristled from the opening.

"Ah, yes," Brice muttered through gritted teeth, close at Ithel's side. "Yet another nail in our coffins."

"Who is he?" Ithel asked.

"Ewan of Claibourne."

"Is that bad?"

"It isn't good," Brice replied.

"Well, it can't be worse than Morgan," Ithel muttered, gathering what shreds of courage still remained him, as Ewan let his mount move half a horse-length closer still, and halted.

"Men of Meara, throw down yer weapons!" Ewan commanded in a broad border accent, pointing to the ground with his sword and sweeping the listening soldiers with his gaze. "Ye stand in arms against yer lawful king, Kelson of Gwynedd, who has come t' reclaim what is his. Ye canna' escape his justice, but if ye surrender now, ye may hope for his mercy. Ye need nae throw away yer lives for these who hae led ye astray."

Before Ithel could stop him, Brice of Trurill raised his sword in defiance.

"We have not been led astray!" Brice cried. "The destiny of the borders rightly lies with Meara! The Haldane usurper—"

At Brice's first word, Kelson's sword had raised in warning. Now the tip of the blade dipped in curt signal toward the nervous Mearan troops, his voice cutting off Brice's diatribe.

"Duke Ewan and the first rank, one horse-length forward—move!"

Instantly the first rank obeyed. The distance between them and the surrounded Mearans closed perceptibly, to the extreme consternation of the men crowded around Ithel and Brice, most of them on foot and ill-armed. Appalled, Ithel struck at Brice's arm for silence. The idiot was going to get them cut down like so many sheep at the slaughter!

"*I* speak for these men of Meara—not Brice of Trurill," he said, beginning to work his mount toward the edge of his troop, closer to Kelson. "Surely you do not mean to butcher them where they stand!"

"That is your choice, and yours alone," Kelson replied, for the first time turning his gaze directly on the Mearan prince. "I hold you and your officers entirely responsible for what has happened here—and in other places. You have much to answer for, Ithel of Meara."

"If I have, it is not to *you*!" Ithel retorted, though his answer carried not nearly as much conviction as he would have wished. "You have usurped the legitimate succession in Meara. I answer only to my sovereign Lady, Caitrin of Meara, she who is lawful successor to Prince Jolyon, the last Mearan Prince to rule this land independently."

"Aye, so your brother also maintained, until the day he died," Kelson said. "That did not save him, however; nor will it save you."

"You murdered him, because he was the lawful heir to Meara after me!" Ithel cried. "And you murdered my sister!"

The sword in Kelson's hand started to lift again, but then he stopped and let it rest across his shoulder once more.

"I *executed* your brother, because *he* murdered your sister—despite what you may prefer to believe," the king said evenly. "And I shall do the same to you—not because of what you are, but because of what you have done."

"You have no authority to try me," Ithel said bravely. "I can be tried only by a court of my own peers."

But his blood ran cold as the king's crowned helm moved slowly back and forth in a gesture of negation.

"I almost pity you," came the royal answer. "But I am King of Gwynedd and Prince of Meara, and I can afford no pity when justice must be done. My writ must run in all my lands. And I have with me all the authority I need to carry out my justice."

As he swept his sword to include the men surrounding Ithel's forces, Ithel felt himself flush with shame and fear.

"I am not a despot, however," Kelson went on. "I shall not hold your men culpable for carrying out the orders of their superiors. Men of Meara, if you will throw down your weapons, I give you my word that only the guilty shall be punished. But if you force me to order the attack, I swear that I shall execute ten for every one of my men who is slain. Now, which is it to be?"

Their answer came not in words but in the sound of weapons being cast to the ground, until only Ithel and Brice remained armed, watching dumbly as Kelson's men began riding into the square of surrendering men, cutting off groups of six or eight at a time and herding them into custody.

Finally, when only Ithel and Brice remained within the ring, Kelson and Morgan rode in, weapons sheathed. Brice started to raise his sword, but a glance from Morgan stopped him in mid-motion, frozen until Morgan rode close enough to relieve him of his weapon. Ithel, too, found himself unable to move; only sitting numb and motionless until Kelson had reached casually across to take his sword as well, helpless before the Haldane gaze.

"Bind them and bring them before my tent when camp is made," Kelson ordered, not even bothering to look at Ithel anymore as he and Morgan turned to leave the ring of steel.

Meanwhile, two more rings of steel were readied to close on their unsuspecting targets. The first was in the crowded great hall at Rhemuth Castle, where Nigel Haldane presided from a throne-like chair on the dais, flanked by tables of busily writing clerks, and pretended to listen to the petitions of diverse merchants.

"When Lord Henry brings his wool to market at Abbeyford, however, he pays no tithe to the monks, the town, or any other local lord," a bailiff was reading. "If Lord Henry believes he is above the law . . ."

Nigel knew, of course, of the ring of steel prepared for him—and had prepared his own counter-ring after Richenda warned him the night before. It was the Torenthi agents who would be caught when the trap was finally sprung—not Nigel.

Nigel had even sweetened the trap by allowing young King Liam to attend court, ostensibly to receive the greetings of the Torenthi trade contingents and gain experience in statecraft. Even now, the boy was fidgeting on a stool at Nigel's right, uncomfortable in the stiff, formal clothing that court protocol decreed for a king, beginning to be bored with the seemingly endless petitions. He had grown increasingly biddable since being taken from his mother's influence, however; and Morag herself was safely under guard in another part of the castle, lest she attempt to lend Deryni aid to the plot about to unfold.

And if there were other Deryni in the surprise contingent that Nigel was expecting, he was prepared for them as well.

Richenda and Rothana sat unobtrusively in the musicians' gallery at the far end of the hall, and Bishop Arilan watched from behind an arras to the left. Nor was he totally without recourse himself, though he hoped he would not be called upon to test his meager skills.

As for the physical aspects of Nigel's preparations, an attentive Conall sat on a stool at his left, ready to command nearly a score of extra guards strategically stationed around the hall. Saer de Traherne lurked in the withdrawing room right behind the dais with another twenty men. Archers manned the side galleries as well, posing as servants, and Haldane agents comprised one entire trade delegation waiting just outside in the yard.

Having made due preparation, then, Nigel felt ready to deal with whatever might present itself. What he had *not* expected was the timorous appearance of Jehana and her confessor in the doorway of a side passage leading from the hall, off to the right. What was *she* doing here?

At her urgent signal that he should join her, he sent a page to inquire—young Payne, who had been attending Liam. A few seconds later, Payne came back.

"She says it's very important, sir," the boy whispered in his father's ear. "You're to come immediately. She says it can't wait until after court."

A glance in her direction confirmed the insistence in her face, and the priest looked anxious as well. The chamberlain reading the current petition was just winding up, so Nigel leaned closer to Conall.

"Make the appropriate noises about taking the petition under advisement," he murmured. "I'll be right back."

As Conall straightened importantly, delighted to be delegated this additional responsibility, Nigel rose with a murmur of apology and went out through the side passage. As soon as he had come through the door, Ambros closed it behind him.

"Are you sure this couldn't have waited?" he asked, eyeing both of them impatiently.

Emphatically Jehana shook her head, her white widow's coif floating on the air.

"Please don't make this harder for me than it already is," she murmured, avoiding direct eye contact. "You're in terrible danger. Don't ask me how I found out. There are men in the hall determined to kill you—or will be. I don't know if they're inside yet. I think they want to kill you and rescue the little king.''

"Oh?" Nigel immediately gave her his undivided attention, wondering how she *had* found out. "Who are they? Do you know?"

She shook her head. "Not specifically. Torenthi agents, I suppose. They've infiltrated one of the trade delegations."

"I see." Amazed, he turned his attention to Ambros, standing rigid and nervous against the door. "Do you know anything about this, Father?"

"Only what Her Majesty has told me, Your Highness," he murmured. "But I believe you would do well to heed her warning."

Frowning, Nigel turned his Truth-Reading talent on the priest, wondering whether Jehana, too, had used Deryni talents to gain the information.

"I'll see to it, then," he murmured. "I don't suppose either of you have any idea which of the trade delegations is involved."

But both of them shook their heads at that; and Ambros, at least, was telling only the truth as he knew it. Jehana's shields were far too rigid for him to read through, but her shielding tended to confirm her source; and her reticence to reveal that source would certainly make sense if she *had* stumbled upon the plot as a result of her powers.

But, he must get back to the hall. He doubted the attack would come without his presence—the delegations he suspected were still several places down the order of presentation—but he did not want Conall to have to handle the situation alone, if he was wrong.

"We'll speak more of this later," he promised Jehana, as he moved grimly back toward the door. "I'll do what needs to be done. And I thank you for the warning. I have an idea what it may have cost you."

She blanched at that, and he knew that he was right. He set his expression as if nothing had happened as he went back into the hall, though he made eye contact with all three of his Deryni allies by the time he had taken his seat again. A Kheldish merchant was presenting his felicitations now, and Nigel let a part of himself listen and make appropriate facial expressions and nods of agreement as he leaned closer to Conall after a few seconds.

"Apparently your Aunt Jehana has gotten wind of the plot too," he whispered, allowing himself to smile at the Kheldish merchant as a compliment was made. "I'll let you guess how. We'll pretend we didn't know and appear to be taking protective measures. Smile now. I've only made a jest."

Conall grinned and picked up a cup of wine, raising it in salute before sipping at it casually, apparently completely at ease. As Nigel settled in to wait, he caught the most fleeting brush of a mental touch and knew it was Richenda's, from where she watched in a gallery. Soon the hunters would become the hunted, and Nigel would spring his trap.

The second trap about to be sprung was not at all to the benefit of Haldanes. Far from Rhemuth, and more than a day's ride north of where Kelson prepared to try the rebels he had captured at Talacara, Duncan and Dhugal were leading a crack Cassani strike force in fast pursuit of Lawrence Gorony's episcopal troops, gradually drawing ahead of the main Cassani host. Cassani warbands had been skirmishing with Gorony off and on for days, the episcopal troops gradually giving ground and making even more desperate withdrawals from disputed territory. And now the renegade priest seemed to be leading his men into a mountain-ringed plain from which there was little chance of escape.

Only, suddenly Gorony's supposedly cowed force was turning to stand and fight, hundreds of unexpected men beginning to pour from the shelter of myriad valleys and defiles opening onto the Dorna plain—Connaiti mercenaries, well-armed and freshly mounted, backed by more episcopal troops. And to the west, emerging through cover of the dust Duncan's own passage had made, a bristling wedge of heavy cavalry was driving toward a point well behind Duncan's advance unit, threatening to cut him off from his main army.

"Damn!" Duncan muttered, stretching in his stirrups to gain a better vantage point as their danger became apparent. "Dhugal, I think we've just found Sicard's main army."

Sicard's son, however, stood captive at that moment before Duncan's king, with Brice of Trurill at his side and some forty officers of various ranks bunched behind them, waiting for the judgment of the king's tribunal. Two dukes flanked Kelson behind the camp table set before his tent: Corwyn and Claibourne. Each had already signed the documents to which Kelson now affixed his signature and seal.

"Brice, Baron of Trurill, step forward," Kelson said, looking up coldly when he had laid aside his quill and wax.

The men on trial had been divested of all military accoutrements and stripped to their undergarments before trial began, their wrists bound behind them, even Ithel and Brice. Brice had also been gagged, having tried the patience of the already sour-tempered Kelson once too often with his defiant outbursts.

When the rebel baron did not move, only glowering defiantly at the king from behind his gag, two guards hustled him forward none too gently and thrust him onto his knees. In sight of the impromptu court, but well-guarded by watchful Haldane troops, the ordinary Mearan soldiers who were not on trial watched and listened anxiously from a large holding area, straining to hear the king's verdict—which might give some indication as to their own fates.

"Brice, Baron of Trurill, you have been found guilty of high treason," Kelson said, setting his hands precisely on the arms of his camp chair. "Not only have you broken faith with your sworn liege and king, giving allegiance to a suzeraine in unlawful rebellion against her rightful overlord, but you have aided enemies of this realm and victimized its innocent subjects without mercy. Therefore, it is the sentence of this tribunal that you be hanged by the neck until dead—and be thankful that I do not have you drawn and quartered, as your 'sovereign lady' had done to my bishop. Sergeant, take him to that tree across the clearing and carry out sentence."

Ithel gasped, and Brice struggled wild-eyed in his bonds, outraged, as his guards pulled him roughly to his feet, for to hang a man of his rank with so little ceremony was almost unprecedented.

"Will ye no' allow the man a priest, Sire?" Ewan asked quietly, from the king's left elbow. "Wi' such sins on his soul—"

"He receives the same solace of religion that he allowed his victims," Kelson said coldly.

"But, laddie—an eye for an eye—"

"That's right, Ewan. This is Old Testament justice. I will not discuss it further. Sergeant, hang him."

And as the guards, the sergeant, and two men with ropes coiled on their shoulders began dragging the condemned man toward the indicated tree, Kelson turned his attention to the stunned Ithel, ignoring the continued but now muted rumblings of Ewan and the cool shielding that was Morgan, sitting silent and neutral at his right. The officers standing behind Ithel had been murmuring fearfully among themselves, their watching subordinates across the clearing similarly shocked, but all speech ceased as Kelson summoned Ithel to his judgment.

"Ithel of Meara, step forward."

Unnerved already by the stark harshness of Brice's sentence, and praying that his royal blood would mitigate at least a little of the king's wrath, Ithel meekly obeyed, not daring even to think about the activities now beginning at the tree across the clearing behind him.

"Ithel of Meara." Kelson drew careful breath and let it out slowly. "I find you likewise guilty of high treason and assign the same sentence: death by hanging."

"But—I'm a prince!" Ithel gasped, stunned, tears welling in his eyes as the finality of the words registered and two more guards laid hands on his rigid shoulders. "You—you can't just hang me like a common felon!"

"You *are* a common felon," Kelson said evenly. "By your heartless destruction of towns like Talacara and others too numerous to mention, your rape of defenseless women—"

"Rape?" Ithel blurted. "I had no part in rape! Ask my men. I was never even off my horse!"

"I believe," Morgan said quietly, "that His Majesty is referring to a certain abbey farther south of here, where you personally violated religious sanctuary and raped at least one of the women who had taken refuge there."

The color drained out of Ithel's face so suddenly that he looked as if he might faint.

"Who told you that lie?" he whispered.

"Is it a lie?" Kelson answered, standing at his place. "Shall I ask Duke Alaric to ascertain the truth?"

Morgan did no more than flick his glance dispassionately

down Ithel's rigid form, but the Mearan prince blanched even whiter, if that were possible, and swayed on his feet. Not a man present could be unaware of the reputation of the king's Deryni champion; and the Mearans, whose fear of Deryni had doubtless been fanned by Loris, surely harbored wildly exaggerated ideas of what he could and could not do, even by a look.

"At least let me die by the sword," Ithel pleaded, finally managing to tear his fascinated gaze from the Deryni duke. "Please don't hang me. You granted my brother—"

"No," Kelson said, with a finality that surprised even Morgan. "There is honor in death by the sword. Your brother, despite his crime of murder, truly believed he acted in honor, for the honor of his family. That is why I granted him an honorable death. Your acts had no honor, for yourself or your family."

"But—"

"The verdict has been given. Sentence will now be carried out. Guards, take him away."

Brice of Trurill was already twitching at the end of the first rope as the guards obeyed, escorting the stunned and stumbling Ithel across the clearing to join him. Some of the watching Mearan soldiers gave salute as their prince passed, but most had already turned their attention to the forty officers remaining before the king. At the urging of the guards, these moved forward uneasily to kneel in the dust before the royal tent.

"Now," said Kelson, casting his grey Haldane gaze over their number as he sat down again. "What to do with you? It is poor military discipline to punish subordinates for obeying the orders of their superiors. But nor, on the other hand, can I dismiss the excesses that were sometimes countenanced by some of you, far exceeding the scope of your actual orders. You were dealing with your own countrymen—not a conquered people. The murder and rapine committed with your knowledge and consent, and sometimes with your assistance, is inexcusable."

"Please, Lord King!" one of the kneeling men cried. "Not all of us had a hand in that. For the love of God, have mercy!"

"Mercy? Yes. I will grant you far more mercy than some of you showed your victims," Kelson replied, his face hard and set. "However, I must also mete out justice. And unfortunately, I have neither the time nor the stomach to determine the precise degree of guilt of every one of you. And if I *did*, I doubt there is a man among you who can claim total innocence."

Not a sound came from any of them as he continued.

"I therefore intend to impose an ancient form of justice: your number shall be decimated. One man in ten shall be hanged. That's four, to be chosen by lots. The rest will be flogged twenty lashes and left to the mercy of the townsfolk remaining here in Talacara—*with this exception.*"

He let his gaze scan their stunned faces, aware that Morgan was not entirely satisfied with the sentence he was imposing, but not caring.

"Other than the four condemned to hang," he went on, "I shall grant a full pardon to any man who will swear me complete and unswerving fealty from this moment on—and believe me, I shall know if any makes me oath falsely."

Consternation rippled among the prisoners, for the king's final statement touched far deeper fears than mere death for some. The black-clad man seated at the king's side was Deryni, and could read men's minds—everyone knew that—and the king himself was rumored to be not without power.

Even Morgan was forced to concede that the latter part of Kelson's judgment was masterful. He himself could not have contrived a finer justice than to make mercy contingent upon a moral trial that would also underline the power of the king.

The method of singling out those slated for execution disturbed him, though. And when he could not probe beyond Kelson's shields to ascertain a reason for the measure, he leaned physically closer to Kelson's chair, casually raising one hand to screen his mouth from the watching prisoners.

"My prince," he murmured, "I do not question your right to impose this sentence, but might not the web of your justice catch innocent men, if you choose the condemned by lots?"

Kelson lowered his eyes, only resistance smoldering across the surface of still-adamantine shields.

"Are you going to argue with me, too?" he muttered.

"You heard what I said. Would you have me Truth-Read all forty? No, actually, I'd have to Mind-See them, to determine the degrees of guilt. Would you have me use my powers that blatantly, for the sake of such as these?"

As he jerked his chin angrily in the direction of the prisoners, Morgan shook his head.

"Of course not, Sire," he soothed. "But you could allow *me* to choose the worst four. I assure you, my culling would be far more just than lots. As for the blatant use of powers, they already know that *I'm* an evil Deryni sorcerer. That enables you to keep them guessing about yourself."

Kelson scowled, but he gave a reluctant nod.

"Very well," he murmured. "Be quick about it, though."

"Thank you, Sire. And believe me, I relish the task even less than you do. May I use the tent?"

"Do what you like," Kelson said, as he stood and glanced across the clearing to where two bodies now swung from the gallows tree, and Morgan and Ewan also rose. "I'm going for a walk. When I come back, I want to see four more bodies on that tree."

Morgan had never seen Kelson in so bloodthirsty a mood, but he knew better than to push any further. As the king strode off, Ewan falling in at his side, the Deryni duke sighed and cast his eyes wearily over the still-kneeling prisoners.

They were afraid of him, of course. Morgan needed no recourse to his powers to read human fear. They had no idea what had transpired between himself and Kelson; only that the king apparently had left a Deryni to decide which four of them were to die. He could imagine what Loris had probably told them about him.

For that matter, some of the men guarding the prisoners looked none too happy about the veiled references to Deryni powers, so Morgan summoned two of the scouts who had adjusted easily to Deryni methods of working.

"Jemet, Kirkon, I'll require your assistance for a little while. Go into the tent, please."

And as the two obeyed, only curious, not fearful, as to why he had singled them out, he hooked his thumbs in his swordbelt and turned to scan the prisoners. By what he had said to them before he began, he could also do a great deal to set the prisoners' attitudes in more positive directions.

"All right, you know who I am," he said, his voice stern but without deliberate menace. "I'm going to have a private little chat with each of you. While you're waiting for your turn, I suggest that you give careful thought to which four of you most deserve to die for what you've done—because I'm going to ask you that, and I'll know if you're lying. That's the fairest way I know to see that justice is done—though I'm sure His Majesty is right, that more than four of you probably deserve to hang.

"So, I'll have you first," he concluded, singling out a burly, greying man in a second rank whose face betrayed his honesty even at that distance, and crooking a finger at him. "Guards, get him on his feet."

The man went white as two Haldane lancers came to do Morgan's bidding, trembling and afraid, not resisting as they laid hands on him.

"Oh, God," he managed to whisper. "Not me. I wasn't the worst. Please, m'lord. . . ."

"Fine. Come in and tell me who was. Guards, he'll walk in on his own, I think. And have the next man ready when this one comes out."

He did not even look to see if the wretch was following, for he knew he had judged his man correctly. Though he had exerted not a jot of force to compel the man's obedience, he could hear the faint foot-treads, bare feet on sand, as the man staggered reluctantly after him. He doubted any of them would put up much of a fight now.

"Kirkon, can you write?" he asked the R'Kassan scout, as he entered the tent and both men came to attention.

"Aye, m'lord, but only my own native tongue."

"That will do well enough for names, I think," Morgan replied, setting a stool in the middle of the floor and gesturing for the prisoner to sit on it. "You'll find writing materials in that chest behind you. Jemet?"

"Sir."

"I'll ask you simply to stand behind the prisoner and make sure he doesn't fall off his stool. Now, you, soldier," he added, distracting the prisoner's attention before he could twist around to look up at the scout. "Suppose you begin by telling me your name."

"R-Randolph, m'lord," the man managed to whisper, though he flinched as Jemet's hands came to rest heavily on his shoulders. "Randolph of Fairhaven."

"Randolph of Fairhaven," Morgan repeated slowly.

Pulling another stool close to the man's knees, Morgan also sat, much to Randolph's obvious consternation.

"Very well, Randolph of Fairhaven. Now tell me about your fellow officers."

# CHAPTER FOURTEEN

*The snare is laid for him in the ground, and a trap for him in the way.*

—Job 18:10

In the great hall at Rhemuth, another loyal Haldane man also labored in the service of his king: Nigel, continuing to act the unaware potential victim. After nearly three solid hours of court, he was beginning to wonder whether both his Deryni sources could have been mistaken about a Torenthi plot to kill him, for not one but two Torenthi delegations had already been presented, made their petitions, and gone their way without incident.

A Bremagni embassy was presenting credentials now, its ambassador making much of handing over what seemed like an endless array of documents, each ragged and weighty along the bottom edge with bright-hued waxen seals. Another group of monks would be next, and then one from Fathane, on the Torenth-Corwyn border. Perhaps *that* was where the attack would come from.

The hall was warm and stuffy. Nigel loosened the throat of his tunic and nodded agreeably to the clerk passing the last of the Bremagni scrolls to the scribes ranked at the side of the hall. Conall was growing restless with inactivity. Little Liam was yawning in his chair. Saer had come in twice to bring him "messages," but actually to satisfy himself yet again that all was in readiness.

Nigel was just reflecting on how ideal a time this would be for the attack to come, while everyone's edge was blunted by the tedium of the warm afternoon, when it came, indeed, erupting without preamble, not from the suspicious Fathane merchants, but from the midst of the monks approaching to present their petitions.

The first men were already at the foot of the dais when they made their move. The "abbot" and his "chaplain" were halfway up the steps before even Nigel, watching for an attack, realized that this was it. As weapons, not petitions, appeared from beneath robes and a sea of brown-clad figures surged forward, the first two making for Liam, legitimate merchants began screaming and scurrying like mice to get out of their way.

Conall saw it at the same time and exploded into motion, shouting for Saer as he shoved young Payne out of harm's way, sword clearing scabbard just in time to block the first attacker's determined lunge at his father. Simultaneously, Nigel threw himself over backward in his chair and yanked the startled Liam right off his stool, somersaulting both of them off the back of the dais and clamping one arm hard across the boy's throat to send him swiftly into unconsciousness if Liam tried using his Deryni powers to help his would-be rescuers.

Deryni powers were not an issue in the battle concurrently being waged between Duncan McLain and his Mearan attackers on the plain of Dorna. Deryni magic could not reverse the momentum of the wedge of heavy cavalry that Sicard of Meara had driven into the main Cassani army, cutting off Duncan's overextended strike force from his support.

Nor did there appear to be much chance that Duncan's commanders could break the widening Mearan wedge and effect a rescue. General Burchard and Jodrell would be gnashing their teeth and frantically contemplating actions Duncan never would have even considered, but Sicard's army was far larger than they had dreamed. No wonder Kelson had met only token resistance in the south. Already, the armies were evenly matched in strength, and more Mearan troops continued to pour in from the west.

Duncan's own situation was hardly any more promising, squeezed between Sicard and Gorony with only a few hundred men and trying desperately to dash ahead of the Mearan wedge and yet foil the Mearans' plans. They were some of his best, and might have hoped to hold against Gorony alone, but they would have no chance of surviving the onslaught of fresh troops now pouring in from the northeast to reinforce him—more episcopal knights now joining the Connaiti mercenaries surging off the fells, all of them mounted on grey battle chargers. And the man who led them, a blue cross emblazoned across his white surcoat, wore a mitre, not a helmet, on his proud grey head.

"Dear God, it's Loris!" Dhugal murmured, shocked, as he and his father reined up at the top of a little rise and looked around wildly for the next angle of flight.

"Aye. And it appears he's brought his own little episcopal death squad," Duncan replied. "How could I have been so stupid as to let us fall into this? *God*, he must want me badly!"

"I doubt he'd mind getting his hands on me, either," Dhugal muttered, clearly awed, for he had never seen so many armed men before. "What are we going to do?"

"What else *can* we do? Try to fight our way out, I suppose, for all the good it will do, though I don't see how we can hope to get through *that*." He swept an arm toward the main Mearan force, now engaging in fierce battle with his own army, then shifted his attention to a possible opening between Gorony's troops and the Mearan left flank, away from Loris. "Let's try over that way. They may take us anyway, but we're not going down without one hell of a fight!"

Their enemy appeared prepared for such a fight, however, and spent wave after wave of men ensuring that Duncan and his immediate warband should not escape through any possible bolt-hole. Again and again, their desperate dashes for freedom were cut off, until no choice remained but to stand and fight. The ducal guard surrounding Duncan fought valiantly, Dhugal and his MacArdry levies putting up a fierce defense at their backs and for a while even holding against ever-increasing numbers, but it gradually became clear that even border bravery was not going to be enough to save them. When yet another assault by fresh Mearan troops drove a new wedge into their midst, cutting off Duncan from Dhugal and his MacArdry borderers, Duncan began to acknowledge the inevitable.

He still had his ducal guard around him, and knew they would defend him to the death, but it was only a matter of time. Loris' knights were working closer and closer. They were going to get through to him eventually. As he tried to think how to sell his life most dearly, hacking mechanically at one attacker after another, he could catch the occasional glimpse of Loris sitting silently on the next ridgetop on a snow white horse, his episcopal banner floating above his head, directing ever more men in his direction.

The battle was taking Dhugal and his loyal MacArdry henchmen farther and farther away from him, too. The little knot of borderers was holding its own so far, but he had no idea how long that could continue. And as if that were not enough, he saw more riders joining Loris: lightly mounted and armored, but carrying short, deadly little recurve bows.

*Archers!*

"Archers, take aim!" Conall shouted, as he engaged his first assailant and kicked the second in the groin, ducking aside to evade and parry a curved Saracen blade in the hands of a third.

The shock value of thirty archers leveling their bows at every stranger in the hall had its desired effect, at least for a few seconds. Saer's men continued to pour through the doorway beside the dais, but only they and Conall's men, already grappling with the first of the attackers, did not look up, though the fighting lessened hardly at all. The poor merchants innocently caught up in the midst of the battle were thrown into even greater panic as they realized their danger, and scrabbled even more urgently to get out of the way.

"Get that man," Nigel shouted, as he saw one attacker shed his monk's robe surreptitiously and take off behind one of the legitimate merchants fleeing the hall, trying to pass himself off as one of them in the confusion.

But at least if there were Deryni among the attackers, as Nigel had feared, they did not betray themselves as that by trying to strike back with their powers. Perhaps, seeing that their intended victim had not been at all as unprepared as they had expected, they hoped to hold those powers in reserve for a later escape attempt, if their initial attack failed. Or perhaps the physical menace of armed defenders simply precluded the concentration needed to focus those powers.

"Everyone drop your weapons and freeze!" Nigel shouted, struggling to a sitting position with the terrified Liam pinned against his chest. "Archers, at the count of three, I want you to shoot anyone who's still armed and moving, unless you know for *certain* that he's ours. One—two—''

Weapons began clattering onto the floor well before Nigel said, ''Three,'' but not all of the attackers were ready to admit defeat. No rain of arrows materialized, but for several seconds, the hall echoed to the twang of bowstrings and the dull thump of arrows into flesh, grunts of struggle changing to screams of pain, as the archers methodically picked off five individuals who yet refused to give it up. Two more attackers had to be physically wrestled to the floor and overpowered, being too closely engaged with the defenders for the archers to get a clear shot. One innocent bystander was also wounded, though not seriously, when his panic got the better of reason and he attempted to bolt for freedom.

Liam wailed throughout, struggling hysterically, weeping and hiccoughing until Richenda, at Nigel's signal, came down to take him in her arms and soothe his terror, finally persuading him to drink a mild sedative she had prepared against just such a likelihood. Rothana was given the task of taking him off to bed, and staying with him until she was sure he slept.

Soon Conall and Saer had everyone in custody who was not personally known to themselves or to Nigel: seventeen, by Conall's first reckoning, of whom nine had been definitely involved in the murder plot, five of them wounded. Of the remaining eight, Saer was able to identify two more as having borne arms during the fray—leaving six of undetermined status, whose guilt or innocence would have to be winnowed out by more elegant methods.

As Nigel's men disarmed and bound the prisoners, clearing the hall of all unnecessary personnel as surgeons arrived to tend the wounded, Bishop Arilan also slipped into the hall, anonymously clad in the plain black working cassock of an ordinary priest. To forestall trickery by any unknown Deryni among the prisoners, he produced a jar of ointment similar to what he had used on Nigel, not many weeks before—though it was the human Saer de Traherne who, at Arilan's quick direction, passed among the prisoners and dosed each with a smear of the drug at the base of the throat.

''It contains *merasha*,'' the Deryni bishop told Nigel, as Richenda trailed after Saer to observe their subjects' reactions. ''Not a very large dose, but enough to disrupt Deryni functions just enough that even a trained one won't be able to feign the proper responses to Truth-Reading. For the humans among them, it will only make them a little drowsy."

"*I* should have thought of that," Nigel murmured, nodding his understanding. "What happens next, then? I suppose we interrogate them all?"

"Not a pleasant prospect, but it has to be done," Arilan replied. "You needn't take part unless you really want to. Richenda has offered to front the procedure, in case anyone feels compelled to talk about the fact that Deryni—ah—'persuasion' is being used. And I'll help out. They won't know who I am. The innocent ones can be culled quite quickly, and the humans among the guilty won't be difficult. Would you rather just observe?"

"No, this is just another facet of what I've seen Kelson do many times," Nigel murmured, though his voice betrayed a slight edge of nervousness. "I need as much firsthand information as I can get, if I'm to deal with this properly. No sense having the responsibility of what I've been given if I can't enjoy some of the benefits, is there? Do you suppose Jehana would like to observe?"

As he flicked a wry glance toward the doorway where Jehana had been watching surreptitiously for the past few minutes, she ducked out of sight. Richenda had heard the end of their exchange, returning with Saer from her inspection of the prisoners, and smiled wanly.

"Shame on you, Nigel. You know she isn't ready for that yet. It could be quite interesting, however. Several of our prisoners are showing distinct signs of disorientation."

"Just what we need at Rhemuth," Nigel said with a snort. "More Deryni. Ah, well. Conall, I'll ask you to secure the hall. No one in or out without my knowledge."

"Yes, sir."

"And Saer, we'll need the prisoners brought in one at a time."

"Aye."

As son and brother-in-law went to do his bidding, Nigel added, "I only wish Kelson were here. And Morgan and Duncan."

Duncan, meanwhile, would have been glad to be almost anywhere besides where he was. As battle raged around him, more and more of his men falling to Mearan swords, and Loris' white-clad death squad worked its way inexorably closer, the fatality of his error became more and more apparent. With luck, the bulk of his Cassani army might escape to fight another day, but he would not. Nor would his death even help the king. Sicard's army was far, far larger than they had been led to believe—and Kelson might never know until it was too late.

A battleaxe came whistling toward his head, and he managed to turn it aside, sword to haft, but the shock reverberating down his arm nearly unseated him from a saddle that was already slick with the blood of the horse slowly dying beneath him. One of his men finished off the man with the axe while Duncan recovered, but the horse was not going to recover. A McLain man drew alongside so that Duncan could lurch across to mount double behind him, but the situation was worsening by the minute. He sensed Dhugal's alarm across the sea of combatants, momentarily panicked at not seeing Duncan astride the familiar grey anymore, but there was nothing Dhugal could do for him—though Duncan did raise his sword so that Dhugal could see that he was still alive.

But though it might be too late for Dhugal to do anything for him, perhaps it was not yet too late for Duncan to buy a last chance for Dhugal—and if Dhugal somehow managed to escape, perhaps *he* could get a warning through to Kelson. It would involve a desperate gamble, and would surely seal his own fate if he were taken instead of perishing on the field of battle, but at least Duncan would not have spent his life in vain.

He had never used his powers to kill, and he could not bring himself to do so now, but he had no qualms about using them to create the necessary diversion—and Dhugal would not obey him without the impetus of what Duncan was planning.

The man in front of him took a fatal blow meant for him, and carried Duncan with him as he toppled from the saddle, but Duncan spared him little thought as he scrambled to his feet, sword still in hand, and centered all his concentration for one last, desperate gamble. What he planned would deplete him greatly; but he was not riding out of Dorna anyway, so it hardly mattered—so long as Dhugal escaped and could warn Kelson.

He whoofed as a horse shouldered him into another, nearly knocking him down, but it was one of his own men. Grabbing onto the stirrup, he let the horse shield him as its rider wheeled, lifting him away from another attacker. And drawing deep breath, he braced himself and set his call.

*Dhugal, leave NOW and ride for Kelson!* he sent across the din of battle, driving the order ruthlessly into his son's mind. *Do whatever you have to do, but GO! You can't save me.*

At the same time, he set another magic in force, raising the image of a wall of fire roaring in the midst of the men between himself and Dhugal, ostensibly driving toward the astonished and horrified Loris and his death squad, but also cutting Dhugal off from even trying to rejoin him—or Loris' men from preventing Dhugal's escape.

He could not hold it long, but he hoped it would be long enough. It died as the attackers closest to him recovered their composure and closed on him with renewed vigor, Loris screaming imprecations and almost frothing at the mouth.

"It's only a Deryni trick!" he heard Gorony roar. "Take him! He can't hold it if you press him!"

And press him they did. He could not see whether Dhugal was obeying him, but he renewed his physical fighting with all the strength he could muster, laying about him with his sword, inflicting as much damage as he could. They might, indeed, take him, but he would make them pay dearly for him. Perhaps they would even kill him. Better that, than to be taken by Gorony and Loris, though he could not deliberately seek his death.

Apparently they were not going to oblige him, however. They had him spotted now. He lost his shielding horseman, though he quickly fell in with two McLain men on foot and they tried to fight as a unit. Several times, when one of the attackers pressing closest to him *could* have killed him—and Duncan killed one of *them* without a second thought—they did not close for that fatal blow, though they killed one of his McLains. They had their orders to try to take him alive; he could read it in their eyes.

Finally someone dealt him a ringing blow to the back of his helm, and a shield slammed into his back. They tripped him as he staggered, and more swarmed in to pummel at his helm and set his ears to ringing. The chinstrap of his helmet gave, and a sword hilt smacked him above one ear as the helm came off.

As his vision began to grey at the edges, and he felt them wrenching the sword from nerveless fingers, someone hit him again at the base of the skull, very precisely. Pain exploded behind his eyes and then along every nerve ending of his body, just before the blackness swooped in on him. Then there was nothing.

Dhugal was already making the most of the opportunity Duncan had bought him so dearly, when he felt the last of the link with his father dissolve. He had reeled under the force of the order Duncan sent, both from its sheer strength and the action it required, but there was no question of disobeying. As the Mearans closest to him faltered, momentarily panicked by the fire suddenly roaring in their midst, he jerked his horse's head around to bolt through an opening their indecision had created, half a dozen of his clansmen at his heels. He would not let himself think about what his father's sudden silence meant, though he refused to believe that Duncan was dead.

Nor was there time to explain what he must do to the few men who managed to stay with him as he fled. Ciard looked at him as if he were crazy when he frantically led them away from the Cassani banner, and the three others surely thought him a coward for running away, leaving their commander to be killed or taken. Until his dying day—which would be soon, if he could not pull this off—he would remember the look of disgust on old Lambert's face when, as he rode, he wrenched off his helm, with its telltale earl's coronet, and cast it away, shouting at them to follow.

They followed, though, flanking him and covering his rear, he and the four of them cutting a grim swath as they raced south and west, away from the heat of battle. They followed, but Dhugal knew he would be a long time regaining their respect—if he *ever* did.

For nearly an hour, they galloped like men possessed, playing a deadly game of evasion, not slowing until the horses were nearly spent and Dhugal *knew* he had eluded the last pursuing Mearan skirmish band. But when, as they pulled up in a defile to let their horses blow, he threw away his targe and even his MacArdry tartan and ordered them to do the same, he almost had a mutiny on his hands.

"Just *do* it!" he snapped, stripping off his earl's belt and the badges of his chiefship as well. "We're not out of this yet. If a Mearan patrol catches us, and thinks we're important, this will all have been for nothing. We've got to pass as common soldiers."

"You insult the term, laddie," Ciard muttered, though he dutifully removed his plaid with the rest and tossed it contemptuously across a bush. "Even the commonest soldier will not leave his commander to his death, if he be a man of honor!"

The remark wounded Dhugal, already feeling lower than the dust beneath his charger's hooves, but he made himself harden against reacting as he peered back the way they had come and saw their chance to ride on.

"I can't discuss it now, Ciard," he murmured. "I'll try to explain later. Are you coming or not?"

"We 'common' soldiers will stay by our liege," Ciard said, "even if he doesn't deserve it."

"I said *later*!" Dhugal snapped, eyes flashing warning.

They followed again as he led them cautiously out of the defile and toward the south again, but he could feel their loathing like a physical pressure at his back, beating against the growing numbness of not knowing what had happened to Duncan. When they reached a place of greater safety, if he could get them to listen, he really would try to explain. But meanwhile, he must decide how he was going to stretch his untrained powers far enough to obey his father and warn Kelson—which was out of the question until well after dark, when the sleeping king might be more accessible to his inexpert probe. And he did not know whether he could stay alive that long.

His most immediate duty, then, was to stay free until it was time to try. Until then he could only keep riding, closing the physical distance between himself and the king—and putting more distance between himself and the man who, unknown to the men who followed him, was his father as well as his commander.

His father, meanwhile, was in more desperate straits than even Dhugal dreamed. Duncan was not dead, but he almost wished he were. His first awareness, as he fought his way back to consciousness through the red fog of pain reverberating inside his skull, was of hands plucking at his body, removing his weapons and armor—and someone forcing his jaws apart.

"Make sure he swallows," he heard a familiar voice say, just behind his head, as bitter liquid sloshed into his mouth.

Gorony! And there was *merasha* in the drink!

Sheer survival instincts jolted Duncan instantly back to full consciousness. Despite the pounding in his skull, he threw his head violently to one side and spat out what was in his mouth, at the same time arching his body in a desperate effort to break free.

Rough hands only slammed his shoulders back against the ground and pinned him. All he could see, as he thrashed and struggled to escape, were hard-eyed men in mail coifs and blue-crossed white surcoats, and hands bringing a cup toward his face again.

"No!"

He sprayed his captors with the next mouthful, but they only forced another past his lips. He tried to close his throat against it, determined not to swallow, but someone jabbed him expertly in the solar plexus. His reflex gasp sucked part of the drink into his windpipe, setting him to choking and hacking, but some of it went down. He gagged and tried to bring it back up again, but a gloved hand clamped across his mouth and nose so that he could not even breathe, another clamping down on carotid pressure points.

He was still fighting them as his vision began to go grey and his limbs started twitching. Worse, he could feel the *merasha* extending its insidious tendrils to undermine his control.

"One more time, I think, Father," the hated voice said in a mocking tone, as hands once more forced his jaws apart and bitter liquid filled his mouth. "You're *going* to swallow it."

And with perceptions blurring from the drug, and his nose pinched shut as they continued to pour, he found himself helpless to resist. His body was convinced that he was suffocating. To his horror, his throat contracted several times in painful swallows. The drug in his stomach was an icy serpent, relentlessly extruding coils of disruption into his system.

They let go of him at that, laughing cruelly among themselves as he curled, coughing and choking, on his side, cradling his forehead in his hands. As his perceptions blurred worse with every heartbeat, scenes of another dealing with Gorony and *merasha* rose in his clouding memory.

Gorony in a burning chamber beneath Saint Torin's Abbey. And a stake set ready to burn any Deryni heretic hapless enough to fall into his clutches.

Only it had been Alaric who was Gorony's helpless prisoner that time, and Duncan who had managed to save him from the fire. Even drug-fogged, Duncan knew that there would be no reversal of roles this time, with Alaric to save *him*. Unless Dhugal somehow managed to work a miracle, Alaric would not even know about Duncan's predicament until Duncan was dead.

Hands rolled him onto his back at that, efficiently stripping him to his breeks and twisting his bishop's ring off his finger. He was helpless to stop them; could hardly even turn his head without being overcome with waves of nausea and dizziness. They did not even bother to restrain his arms as a new white-clad figure stepped into his range of vision at his feet and stared down at him. Wispy grey hair showed around his head like a halo, and his blue eyes blazed with triumph above the blue cross on his breast. He smiled as Gorony handed him the bishop's ring, turning it several times in his fingers before slipping it on his hand next to the one he already wore.

"So, my elusive Deryni priest," Edmund Loris said quietly. "I believe it is time we spoke of many things. You and your Deryni colleagues have caused me a great deal of trouble. I intend to return the compliment."


"I don't much like what I had to do today," said one of those Deryni colleagues.

Morgan was standing in the doorway of the tent he and Kelson shared, where not so long before he had finished interrogating the last of the forty Mearan officers. Across the square, the fruits of his labor dangled, still twitching, beside the long motionless bodies of Ithel and Brice.

Kelson, picking joylessly at his sparse camp fare at the table behind Morgan, pushed his plate away with a snort of disgust.

"Do you think *I* did?"

"I don't know."

"You don't know?" Kelson repeated, aghast.

Morgan glanced aside at the king's reaction, then coolly returned his gaze to the gallows tree outside, where a burial detail was waiting to cut down the four executed officers.

No one knew better than he that those particular men had deserved to die for their excesses against the Mearan citizenry, but he resented the fact that Kelson had forced *him* to judge them.

Kelson caught an echo of that resentment and stood up abruptly, crossing to pull a curtain angrily over the opening, shutting out the sight.

"Does that really help?" Morgan asked.

Kelson wilted visibly, clinging to the edges of the closed curtains and bowing his head.

"I should have let Ithel and Brice see a priest first, shouldn't I?" he whispered.

"It would have been a noble gesture," Morgan answered.

Kelson sighed miserably and raised his head, eyes bright with tears he refused to let himself shed.

"Henry Istelyn was not allowed that grace," he said, not looking at Morgan. "Do you—do you think he will go to hell because he died unshriven?"

"Do *you* think that a just and merciful God would condemn His faithful servant, simply because he was not permitted to observe the outer form required for salvation?" Morgan countered.

At Kelson's quick headshake, he went on.

"By similar reasoning, I think we can safely assume that if Ithel and Brice were truly contrite over the crimes for which they were executed, God will not condemn them wholly out of hand." He paused to take a cautious breath. "In the future, however, and just in case I'm wrong, I might suggest that mercy is as admirable in a king as it is in Our Lord—and mercy need not clash with justice. It would have cost you nothing to at least give them a few moments to prepare for death—though I know why you refused, in the case of Ithel and Brice."

"Would you have?" Kelson asked.

"I don't know," Morgan said honestly. "That was not my decision, so we shall never know."

"What about the other four?" Kelson asked, clasping his hands behind his back and awkwardly turning halfway between Morgan and the curtained entryway. "I should have allowed *them* the last rites. *You* would have."

"Yes. And, in fact, I *did* allow it, since that *was* my decision—though I would that no part of the decision had been mine."

"What?"

Kelson looked up in shock.

"You told me to select the guiltiest four for execution, my prince," Morgan said quietly. "I did so. But when you gave me their deaths, you also gave me the authority to determine the circumstances of their deaths, within certain limits. I gave them five minutes with Father Laughlin. *Then* I had them hanged."

"As *I* should have ordered," Kelson added, biting at his lip. "You don't have to say it."

"Have I said anything, my prince?"

Kelson swallowed hard and bowed his head again.

"You do right to reproach me," he whispered. "I let vengeance impede my honor. I was so elated to have captured Ithel, and—oh, *God*, I wish Father Duncan were here!"

"Is Duncan your conscience?" Morgan asked, not ready to let up until he was sure Kelson understood his mistake.

"No, of course not, but he helps me listen to my conscience," Kelson replied. "I *should* have been more merciful! By giving Ithel and Brice the same as they gave Istelyn, I lowered myself to their level!"

"It is an understandable failing in one of your years, my prince," Morgan said softly.

"Kings can't have the luxury of falling back on that excuse!"

"But young men can," Morgan replied, "at least so long as they learn from their errors. Not a man alive has but made his share of youthful misjudgments as he grew to manhood."

"The men will hate me," Kelson insisted, flouncing into his camp chair.

"The men understand," Morgan countered. "This was a very emotion-wrought situation. Henry Istelyn was well respected in all of Gwynedd. He did not deserve the fate the Mearans gave him. Furthermore, all of your own officers know what we found at Saint Brigid's and elsewhere, and the brutality that was done and permitted by Brice and Ithel. Nor do they blame you for reacting more with your heart than your head. All of them have wives or sisters or mothers, Kelson. You will find little sympathy for Ithel's and Brice's fate."

"I would have done the same to the four Mearan officers," Kelson said, making a last, halfhearted attempt to continue berating himself.

"Perhaps you would have. But you did not."

"No. I made you do my duty for me. I shouldn't have done that, either."

Morgan sighed. At last they had reached the final point he had wanted to be sure Kelson understood.

"That is true, my prince," he said quietly, resting a hand on Kelson's nearest shoulder and kneading at the taut muscles beneath. "But I accept that burden, knowing that you have learned from my labors. Next time, you will do better. Meanwhile, there is no great harm done. Believe me."

"I suppose you're right," Kelson allowed.

Exhaustion began to take him soon after that, and he gratefully let Morgan's physical ministrations shift to more esoteric ones, finally surrendering to the sweet oblivion that Morgan urged upon him.

# CHAPTER FIFTEEN

*Behold, I know your thoughts, and the devices*
*which ye wrongfully imagine against me.*

—Job 21:27

By the time Dhugal and his sullen escort pulled up in a sheltering grove of trees, it was nearly full dark and Dhugal was weaving in the saddle, both from physical exhaustion and from the more draining emotional trauma he had suffered since abandoning the field at Dorna.

Only Ciard and three others had managed to keep up with him. Their reproach lay around him like a pall, stifling and oppressive, and he could hardly blame them. They did not know of Duncan's orders to leave him and ride for help; only that their young lord had deserted his commander in battle and ordered them to do the same. Nor could they guess what obedience had cost Dhugal, or how the cost had multiplied each time he tried to cast his mind back to Duncan, and encountered only deadly silence.

Fighting back the despair born of his own bereavement, Dhugal slid to the ground and loosened his horse's girth, crouching to glance under the animal's belly for Ciard as his horseman's hands slid automatically down sweat-sleek legs and fetlocks to check for injuries. The gillie's silence of the past four hours hurt almost as much as his father's. Ciard and the other three men had taken their horses far to the other side of the clearing to unsaddle, vague shadow-shapes in the forest gloom, but Dhugal did not need to see them clearly to read their contempt. And he had never known Ciard to be so angry with him.

He shivered and pulled back his Deryni perceptions, unable to bear their psychic isolation along with their physical withdrawal. When he had pulled the saddle from his stallion's sweaty back, staggering a little as he eased it to the grass, he began rubbing the animal down with twists of grass, scouring the sweat and grime from the once-silky coat and losing himself, at least for a few minutes, in a different kind of physical exertion than had already left his body aching. The stallion's pleasure in the simple procedure, and the affection displayed in the gentle buffet of sweaty head against ministering hands, welled into Dhugal's mind like soothing balm, helping him shut out the hostility of the others performing similar functions across the clearing.

He had no idea what he was going to do when he was finished. He knew he had to try to contact Kelson, as his father had ordered, but he would not let himself think very much about the man who had given him that order. Enough to acknowledge that if he had not been able to reach Duncan, who had been far closer physically, at least in the beginning, he probably had little chance of reaching Kelson. But he had to try. And if he had to try it alone, with his men still radiating their disgust and anger all around him. . . .

He lingered over his grooming task until all the others had gone. Then, while he let his horse drink sparingly in the little stream, he sluiced cold water over his face and forearms, even dunking his head for good measure. He was going to need all his wits about him if he hoped to win his men back to his side.

He shook the water out of his ears like a wet puppy as he led the horse back to graze with its fellows. He still felt grimy and exhausted, but the water that ran off his braid and inside the neck of his brigandine was blessedly cool. Gathering his courage, he hefted his saddle over his shoulder and carried it, staggering, to the tiny fire that old Lambert had kindled in the lee of a rocky outcropping.

The others were already there, reclining on their saddles and sharing meager provisions: Lambert, Matthias, Jass—and Ciard. No one even looked up as he put down his saddle and sat among them, though Lambert did pass him a cup of ale and a hard chunk of journey bread. Ciard actually turned his back. He could feel the rest of them pointedly *not* looking at him as he ate and drank, and the food lay in his stomach like lead. Nor did the fire warm the chill radiating from the four.

None of them had spoken to him since well before dusk, other than to acknowledge his orders. Ciard was a glittering point of fire and ice, barely contained; the usually ebullient Jass MacArdry, who was hardly older than himself, looked as if he might cry at any minute. Matthias and old Lambert simply ignored him, always looking to Ciard for confirmation before following his own instructions.

Yes, Ciard was the key—and the one man among them who might be able to understand and accept the full truth. And if Ciard could be won over, the other three probably would follow without question.

Dhugal set down his cup and dusted crumbs from his fingers, all appetite fled.

"Please don't do this to me," he said softly. "I need your help."

Ciard turned his grizzled head dutifully toward his young master, but his eyes reflected only pain and bitter disappointment.

"You need our help. Aye, laddie, you do, indeed. And Bishop Duncan needed *yer* help. But he didna' get it, did he?"

"If you'll only let me explain—"

"Explain what? That The MacArdry turned tail and ran? That he left his commander t' be cut down or captured by the enemy? Thank God yer father didna' live to see this day, Dhugal! He would've died o' shame."

Dhugal started to blurt out that *Duncan* was his father, and that he had fled at Duncan's order, but he made himself bite back his words. This was not the time to tell them of his true parentage, when they believed he had disgraced the MacArdry name.

But he needed desperately to get them back on his side. He had *not* turned craven! Perhaps a part of the truth would satisfy them.

"My father would have listened to my side of the story before condemning me," he said coldly. "Things are not always as they appear."

"Perhaps not," old Lambert said, speaking for the first time. "But it *appears* that ye got scared an' ran, Young MacArdry. Not much other way t' look at that."

Dhugal flushed, but he refused to back down from their accusing looks.

"It's true that I ran," he said unsteadily, "but it was not by my choice." He drew a deep breath to brace himself for their reaction. "Bishop Duncan ordered me to go."

"Ordered ye. Wi' his magic, I suppose?" Ciard said contemptuously. "Dinna' compound the cowardice wi' lyin', laddie."

"I am *not* lying," Dhugal said evenly. "And don't call me *laddie*. As a matter of fact, Bishop Duncan *did* use his magic—though apparently, you'd prefer to believe me a coward!"

Ciard set his jaw and turned his face away at that, not saying anything, and Dhugal knew this was going to be even harder than he had thought. The others looked anywhere but at him, angry with him, embarrassed for him, ashamed of him, their minds made up as well. And he could not afford to waste much more time trying to explain. He *must* begin trying to reach Kelson, and he was frantic with worry about his father. He wondered whether he had enough skill yet to *make* them listen to him.

No, definitely not all of them, he decided. But perhaps Ciard alone. Surely the old man did not really *want* to believe him a coward—Ciard, who had served him since his birth.

"Ciard, may I speak with you alone?" he asked quietly, after a few heartbeats. "Please?"

"I ha' nothin' to say to ye that canna' be said before my kinsmen," Ciard answered coldly.

Dhugal swallowed his pride to try again.

"You can tell them, after," he said softly. "Please, Ciard. For the love you once bore me."

Ciard turned his head slowly, his eyes full of ice and contempt, but he got up and went with Dhugal to where the horses cropped grass in the forest clearing. He stopped beside Dhugal's grey, throwing one arm over the animal's withers to lean against its shoulder as he glanced sidelong at Dhugal in the dimness.

"Well?"

Dhugal moved close enough to stroke the stallion's neck, choosing his next words carefully. With what Duncan and Morgan had taught him, he felt fairly confident that he could force the necessary rapport to make Ciard see the truth, but he knew he was not skilled enough to do it without physical contact—and that, Ciard would never permit, feeling betrayed, as he did, by his young master. Nor could Dhugal's lesser size and strength stand up to any physical contest with the experienced Ciard, who had taught Dhugal much of what he knew.

But physical contact he must have, if his ill-trained powers were to be of any help in the matter. There simply was not time to try to explain verbally, with each answer leading to yet another question. Still stroking the stallion's silky neck, Dhugal found himself wondering whether the living mass of the horse between them might be made to function as the physical link he needed—at least long enough to get past any physical resistance.

"Ciard, I'm sorry for the pain I've caused you," he said softly.

"I'm sure ye are, Dhugal, but it's a wee bit late tae be thinkin' o' that now."

"Perhaps." He began meshing his consciousness with the stallion's, extending tendrils of control along equine synapses toward the man leaning against the animal's other side. The big warhorse only shuffled softly and continued grazing, unconcerned with this new sort of partnership his master was building. A part of Dhugal found himself wondering if this was how he'd come to be so good with horses in the first place, doing by instinct what he had lately been learning to do by design.

"Ciard, I—there isn't time to explain as well as I'd like," he went on, "but I—there's a kind of magical communication that Deryni can do sometimes. When the king was at Transha last fall, he taught me a little about it. That's how Bishop Duncan gave me his orders."

He could just see Ciard's grimace of skepticism as the old gillie twisted a strand of the horse's mane between his fingers, unaware of the tendrils of power easing through the animal's body and beginning to wind about him as well.

"A convenient explanation, after th' fact, son, but hardly convincing," Ciard murmured. "They're Deryni—the king and Bishop Duncan. You're but border blood."

"Border blood—aye," Dhugal breathed, his free hand darting out to seize Ciard's arm across the horse's back, even as his mind surged across the link already made through his own contact with the animal. "But only through my mother's line. I am also Deryni!"

Even as Ciard gasped, Dhugal was in his mind, pulling him down into unconsciousness before he could draw another breath. As Ciard went limp, sliding slowly down the horse's neck despite Dhugal's attempt to slow his collapse, Dhugal released him long enough to duck under the horse's belly and catch his helpless form, himself sinking to the grass under Ciard's dead weight.

He hoped the stallion would watch where it put its feet. He had only done this a few times, and always under supervision by Morgan or his father, and he did not relish the idea of getting stepped on while he tried to work with Ciard.

But his trusty equine friend only stood with all four feet firmly planted and whuffled once, softly, in his ear, before returning to its grazing. And Dhugal's work seemed amazingly simple, once he began and let the process flow at its own speed.

"Listen to me, Ciard," he whispered, underlining his words with the fuller pictures from his mind, as he clasped Ciard's head between his hands. "Father Duncan is my father in fact as well as title. Old Caulay was my *grandfather*."

Swiftly the images passed then, of a Duncan only Dhugal's age, wooing Caulay's daughter Maryse. Ciard had known and loved the girl.

But he had known young Ardry MacArdry, slain by a McLain man in a drunken brawl, and had loved him, too; and well he remembered the blood feud that had threatened to erupt between the two clans, even though Ardry's murderer was executed by his own people—and the tension when The MacArdry and Duke Jared McLain, Duncan's father, had returned from campaign and agreed to go their separate ways, lest bloodshed erupt anew.

And Duncan and Maryse had been as much the victims of that fatal brawling as Ardry and the McLain man—whose name Dhugal never had learned—for well did they know how futile it would be to ask permission of their fathers to marry, after all that had occurred.

Thus had the pair exchanged secret vows in the deserted chapel late that night, with only God for witness. And when Maryse rode out of Culdi the next morning with her father and clan, intending one day to wed Duncan according to more orthodox rites, little did either she or Duncan dream that their brief union would bear fruit. The son born to Maryse late the following winter, but a few weeks after her mother bore a daughter, had been claimed by the mother and presented as Caulay's son when he returned from winter court and spring campaigning—for Maryse had died of a fever.

And no one had known that Caulay's youngest son was, in fact, a McLain replacement for the slain young Ardry MacArdry. Even Dhugal had pieced together the true story only the previous winter, when a cloak clasp left him by his "mother" had released a devastating flood of long-dormant memories in Duncan, who recognized it as his own and had put all the clues together.

Dhugal spared Ciard nothing of what he had learned, saving that which was private between father and son, for Ciard himself had been almost a father to him. Very soon, Ciard's eyes were fluttering open, to gaze up at Dhugal with awe and new understanding.

"Are—are ye still in my mind?" he asked.

Dhugal shook his head. "I wouldn't have gone in at all, except that I didn't know any other way to tell you. And I won't again, without your permission. Will you help me? I have to try to contact Kelson."

"Of course, laddie." Ciard sat up and dusted dead leaves off his shoulders and elbows, then let Dhugal help him to his feet. "I dinna' think we should tell the others everything, though. Especially not the part about yer not being Caulay's son an' all. That's—goin' t' take a bit o' gettin' used to."

Dhugal shrugged and grinned. "I'm still his grandson, Ciard."

"Aye. An' still the heir and rightful chief, for that matter—though yer heir to a duchy as well, now. My, my, now, won't *that* set the cat among the pigeons? You, a bishop's heir, an' all!"

"I just hope I haven't already inherited my ducal title," Dhugal murmured. "Ciard, I haven't been able to touch him at all!"

"Well, mayhap it's difficult o'er any distance."

"No, I have to accept the possibility that he may be dead," Dhugal murmured, not accepting that possibility at all, but knowing he must not let his fear keep him from doing what he *could*, since he could *not* do anything for Duncan just now.

"And if he *isn't* dead," Dhugal went on steadily, "he's almost certainly a prisoner—which, in some respects, is even worse. I know, firsthand, what Loris is capable of doing to a human prisoner—or one he thinks is human. A Deryni, like my father—''

He shuddered and made himself put the thought aside, not wanting to even consider what that might mean.

"Anyway, I have to try to reach Kelson," he went on bravely. "It's what my father wanted. And if he *is* still alive, and—and in Loris' power, then only Kelson and the main army have a chance of rescuing him in time."

"Then, we'd better get to it, lad," Ciard said, taking his arm and starting to march him back to the fire where the others waited.

"I believe that Bishop Duncan did order him t' leave," he told them, as he guided Dhugal to the bedding beside his own saddle and crouched down as Dhugal sat. "What we saw—the fire an' all—was cover so we could escape t' warn th' king. He used th' same magic t' tell Dhugal t' go."

The men seemed taken aback at that, but they were disinclined to doubt Ciard, even if they still had some misgivings about their young master. All of them had seen the outward results of Duncan's magic. Why not another part they had not seen? Certainly the visible part had been to their good.

"Fair enough," old Lambert said. "It appears we owe ye an apology, young Dhugal."

"Accepted," Dhugal murmured, ducking his head in acknowledgment. "I don't blame you for what you thought. I know my explanation seemed farfetched."

"No farther fetched than the other task th' good bishop has laid upon ye, lad," Ciard said, settling behind Dhugal with an elbow resting on his saddle. "Gather closer, lads. Our young laird needs our help."

They listened incredulously as Ciard told them what Dhugal wanted to attempt, but to Dhugal's amazement, they did not seem to take it amiss.

"Ye say the king's taught him how t' do this?" Matthias asked, reclining against his saddle and listening avidly.

Ciard nodded. "Aye. An' it's magic—make no doubt about that. But 'tis summer-white, I *know*. Difficult, though, not knowin' how far the king may be from here, so we must lend him our strength."

"How do we do that?" Lambert asked, not batting an eye.

Dhugal managed a reassuring smile as he leaned back against Ciard's chest, settling in the circle of his arms.

"Bonnie MacArdry men, an' true! Your strength will lend me wings to send my thoughts to the king. Just stay with me," he said, stretching out his hands to Lambert and to Jass, who were closest, and taking strength already from their firm handclasps. "Be at ease. Lie close, where I can touch you. There's no danger. You may even fall asleep."

"What if someone comes?" asked Matthias, shifting closer so that he, too, could join the link.

Dhugal flicked a tendril of thought out to scan the area, but there was nothing alive for miles, besides the horses and the five of them.

"Guard, if you'd rather, but no one will come."

But Matthias only shook his head and crawled closer, to lay his head trustingly on Dhugal's knee, curling on his side. Nor, to Dhugal's amazement, did any of the others have anything else to say.

"Wha' happens next?" Ciard whispered in his ear, watching awed as Dhugal's breathing began to slow and shift to the early stages of trance, the tension leaving his face.

"Just go to sleep," Dhugal murmured, yawning.

And within seconds, all of them were yawning, too, and settling drowsily around him.

He let himself sink deeper, his awareness of the clearing, the fire, and the men around him fading with every breath. It was different, doing it all alone, without Duncan or Morgan or Kelson to guide him, but he found himself gathering the strands of the men's potentials with little effort—and sensed their psychic strength ready to be tapped if he needed it.

The thought drifted across his consciousness that he really *ought* to find out more about the Second Sight his border folk had always claimed—perhaps it *was* some vestige of Deryni gifts long forgotten—but after acknowledging it, he made himself set that aside. Other matters were more important now.

When he had gone as deep as he dared without guidance, only just aware of his body slumped limp and defenseless in Ciard's arms, he cast out briefly for his father. And when, as expected, that brought no discernable result, he settled down to the more delicate task not only of locating Kelson, but of trying to touch his consciousness.

For a long time, nothing at all happened. But then he thought he began to detect a stirring, not in the sleeping men around him and not within himself.

His probe reached no one on any conscious level. Deep asleep after Morgan's earlier ministrations, Kelson had floated dreamlessly for several hours, so still that Morgan, too, had finally lain down on his own cot to try to get some rest. Sleep did not come easily, but when it did, Morgan dreamed about Duncan, and Dhugal, and the two of them battling their way through wave after wave of knights who never tired. It was Kelson's cry that jolted Morgan from his own nightmare.

"Kelson, what is it?" Morgan whispered, instantly out of bed and at the king's side, grabbing his wrists to restrain his thrashing.

Almost at once, Kelson was wide awake and still, his eyes a little glazed looking as he cast back for what had frightened him, confident now that Morgan was with him.

"I was dreaming—about Duncan," he whispered, gazing beyond Morgan's eyes as he sought still. "They were after him."

"Who was after him, my prince?" Morgan urged. For he, too, had dreamed of danger for Duncan.

"Knights with blue crosses on white surcoats. Loris', I think. Gorony was there, too. He was urging them on. What an awful dream!"

Drawing deep breath, Morgan sat down on the edge of the royal bed, shifting his grasp from Kelson's wrists to his hands.

"Go back," he whispered, locking his eyes to Kelson's and starting already to forge an old, familiar link between them. "Let me take you as deep as you can go, and try to capture it again. I don't think it was a dream. I dreamed it, too."

"Oh, God, I think you may be right," Kelson breathed, already plummeting to a more comfortable working level with such speed that he had to close his eyes. "I—I think it may have been Dhugal. Can something have happened to Duncan?"

*We can't worry about Duncan for now,* Morgan replied, shifting to mind-speech as both their levels deepened. *First, try to reestablish the link with Dhugal. He won't be able to hold it for very long. Stretch yourself to the limit, but touch him. I'll be with you all the way.*

And Dhugal, nearly a day's ride away, felt the answering probe of two familiar minds—not just one. He shuddered in

Ciard's arms as he drew strength from the men around him and flung his mind back across the miles. This time, they were able to lock on and hold him; and all three of them knew it was no dream.

Images of battle: Dhugal and his men fighting at Duncan's side . . . white-clad knights drawing nearer, nearer, directed by Loris. . . . Gorony's crack episcopal troops, closing the trap. . . .

Duncan's curtain of fire sending consternation into their ranks—at least long enough for Dhugal and his men to slip through and escape—and the order, swift and unmistakable and not to be questioned—for Dhugal to leave him to his fate and ride to warn Kelson. . . .

. . . that Loris had been found at last, and Sicard of Meara, and all the Mearan grand army, all lying within striking distance by the following noon, if Kelson's were away within the hour. . . .

The details were exchanged with a speed only possible in mind—a briefing that would have taken hours, face-to-face, but Dhugal was able to impart his knowledge in the space of a few dozen heartbeats.

He was gasping when he came out of it, struggling to sit up and get his bearings, making certain they were still safe from intruders. His companions stirred groggily to stare at him in awe, aware that power had coursed through him from somewhere, and had been drawn from them, but uncertain of anything else.

"The king will come," Dhugal whispered, his eyes still other-worldly and a little unfocused. "We'll meet him at dawn. Rest a few minutes now," he added, reaching out to brush each one in swift but insistent control.

And as they succumbed, he sealed each with his psychic order: *Sleep and remember nothing that will alarm you.*

Morgan, meanwhile, found ever more reason to be alarmed, as Kelson left him to give orders for march and Morgan himself settled back into trance. He cast for Duncan until Brendan and his squire came to arm him, stretching his own resources far thinner than was prudent, alone and unmonitored, but he could touch no trace of his cousin. The Deryni priest was either dead or drugged to senselessness.

"Do you think he really doesn't know where Kelson is?" Sicard asked, from somewhere out of sight, the voice wavering and hollow as it filtered through Duncan's crippled senses.

"Of course he knows. He's Deryni, isn't he?"

A hand turned Duncan's head roughly to one side, and Lawrence Gorony's face loomed in his vision, leering and obscene, watching from a stool close by his head. The sudden movement set up a wave of vertigo, bordering on nausea, that was almost welcome after the pain pulsing in his feet.

Duncan was fairly certain that Gorony had now pulled out all ten of his toenails, though he had lost accurate count at around seven. The little pile of them lay on his bare chest, bloody and pathetic. He had seen some of them, one time when his neck arched upward in his agony. Knowing Gorony, his fingernails would probably be next.

He shut his eyes against the thought, one of his hands contracting a little in reflex withdrawal from the threat, but further movement was checked by the shackles restraining his wrists. Others banded his ankles, all of the chains pegged into the dirt floor of the tent so that he lay spread-eagled and helpless on his back.

*Like Saint Andrew*, he thought dully, attempting to distance his own pain by thinking about another's. *He suffered as Our Lord suffered, only he was nailed to a saltire cross.*

At least Duncan lay on the ground, not a cross. Nor did he think they would crucify him. Unless some miracle intervened, Loris would almost certainly kill him eventually, but the Deryni-hating archbishop would never allow a heretic Deryni priest to take comfort from suffering the same death given the Christ, or even one of His sainted apostles.

No, Loris would find some other, more degrading form of dying for the Deryni Duncan McLain, who had dared to become priest and bishop in conscious defiance of the laws Loris served. Already, he and Gorony had been trying to get Duncan to confess to all manner of perversions and sacrilegious practices regarding his priesthood, interspersed with the more practical questioning regarding Kelson's whereabouts.

Loris was reviewing the records of interrogation regarding both subjects now, scanning the account of Duncan's answers with the clerk who had taken it all down. As he came to join Gorony and Sicard, an expression of long-suffering patience and solicitude on his narrow face, Duncan twitched feebly at his chains and longed for even one chance to blast all three men with a taste of the magic they so feared.

Not that he really could have done much to help himself, even released from his fetters of iron. The *merasha* locked away his powers far more inaccessibly than the chains locked away his physical freedom.

His captors knew how long *merasha* lasted, too. Just when the effects of the rather uncertain first dose had begun to wane to an almost tolerable level, Gorony had dosed him again—this time, without his being able to offer even token resistance.

It had only been a little, for apparently they knew that too much would either put him to sleep or kill him—out of reach of their pain in either case—but it was more than enough to keep him in thrall to the drug's disruptive effect. As his empty stomach rebelled at the new intrusion, and self-preservation made him fight to keep it down rather than choke on his own vomit, he found himself wondering where Gorony had gotten his obviously fine-tuned knowledge of *merasha*. But, then, torturers through the ages had always had their sources of information. . . .

His chief torturer was playing with one of his instruments of torture now, fiddling with the bloody pincers he had used on Duncan's feet, letting the meager torchlight in the tent catch and flash on the red-stained metal. Loris saw how Duncan was watching Gorony and his toy and crouched down beside the captive priest in a most comradely fashion.

"You're being very unreasonable, you know," he purred, his halo of wiry grey hair making of him a grim, avenging angel as he gently moved a tendril of sweaty hair off Duncan's forehead. "You have only to confess your heresies, and I shall grant you the swift and painless death you desire."

"I do not desire death," Duncan whispered, turning his eyes away from Loris'. "That is not in my choosing, as you know well. I will not risk the damnation of my soul by seeking my own demise, however much suffering it may save my physical body."

Loris nodded thoughtfully and turned one of the rings on his hand. It was Istelyn's ring, Duncan noted with a little start, and he found himself wishing that the power of Saint Camber might manifest through the ring as it had in the past and blast the obscenely confident Loris—not that Camber would sully his holiness on the likes of Loris!

"Aye, there is a certain, twisted logic in your reasoning," Loris went on. "Why speed your entry into the eternal fires of Hell, to which you are already damned by your heresies? What Earthly pain can possibly match that endless torment to which God will surely condemn you?"

"I have loved my God with all my heart and with all my soul and with all my might," Duncan whispered stubbornly, grasping for comfort in the familiar words as he closed his eyes against the sight of the mocking archbishop. "I have served Him as well as I could. If He demands my life, then I offer it freely unto Him, trusting in His infinite mercy."

"There shall be no mercy for Deryni!" Loris retorted. "If you die unrepentant, you are surely damned. Only if you confess your heresies and seek absolution may you hold any hope of forgiveness."

Duncan moved his head very slowly from side to side, letting the vertigo it produced help to block out Loris and the pain throbbing in his feet.

"God knows that I am repentant for any offenses I have committed against Him or any other. I admit me to His justice alone."

"You blaspheme with your every word and breath, McLain!" Loris replied. "Confess your heresies!"

"No."

"Admit how you have profaned your sacred office with every breath you drew—"

"No," Duncan repeated.

"Do you deny that you have often celebrated the Black Mass, in service of the Lord of Darkness?"

"I deny it."

"I shall burn you, McLain!" Loris shouted, little drops of spittle dotting Duncan's face. "I shall send you to the stake that you helped the heretic Morgan escape, and I shall scatter your ashes upon the dungheap! I shall give you such pain that you will weep for death, admit anything, deny all that you hold dear—just for an instant's respite from the wrath I shall bring to bear upon you!"

There was more, but Duncan only bit at his lip and deliberately curled his mangled toes against the earth, letting the sensory input of pain of his own choosing help blot out the sound of Loris' ravings. The threat of burning was the worst yet, but he had expected it would come eventually. If he was fortunate, perhaps Loris might become deranged enough to plunge a dagger into his heart and release him that way, before the stake could claim him. If he was to die, he did not think God would mind if he hoped for the quicker mercy of the blade. He knew, with unshakable faith, that Loris could not touch his soul.

"You shall writhe in the flames!" Loris ranted on. "But I shall be certain that the fire is slow, that your suffering may be prolonged. Shards of your roasted flesh will fall from your bones while you yet live! Your eyes will melt upon your cheeks!"

The horror Loris invoked cut through even the pain Duncan had managed to divert to himself, whirling and embellishing in his imagination, shaking his resolve, setting his body to quivering with a terror that would not be stilled.

He was actually glad for the sharp torment of Gorony's instruments, wrenching and twisting at his right hand. It seemed somehow fitting that the first of his fingers to suffer the torturer's ministrations was the one that, until lately, had worn the ring of a martyred bishop. He only hoped he could be as steadfast as Henry Istelyn.

# CHAPTER SIXTEEN

*He hath also prepared for him the instruments of
death; he ordaineth his arrows against the
persecutors.*

—Psalms 7:13

"So, are you going to execute him or not?" Sicard of
Meara asked, buckling a gorget at his throat as a squire adjusted steel greaves and tassets on his legs.

Loris, a white cope over his war harness, flicked the end
of a riding crop against his armored thigh in annoyance and
glanced down at the prisoner still spread-eagled on the floor.
Duncan lay in a faint, his breathing labored and shallow,
bloody hands and feet twitching occasionally in their shackles, his bare chest criss-crossed with welts from Loris'
whip. Gorony sat on a low stool near the prisoner's head
and watched for signs of returning consciousness. Neither
blood nor sweat nor even smudge of dust from the night's
work marred the snowy livery he wore over his armor.

"What's the matter, Sicard?" Loris said. "Have you no
stomach for the Lord's work? The man is a heretic."

"Well, burn him and be done with it, then."

"I need his confession first."

Snorting, Sicard took the sheathed sword his squire offered and thrust it into a hanger at his waist, dismissing the
lad with a curt nod.

"Listen to me, Archbishop," he said, when the boy had
gone. "You may know about saving souls, but I know about
saving lives."

"I see only one life in the balance here," Loris replied. "What does it matter to you whether he burns now or this evening?"

"It matters because I have the entire Mearan army camped outside this tent," Sicard said. "My wife—my *queen*—entrusted them to me, to use in the cause of Mearan victory. McLain's men may be scattered and demoralized for the moment, but they are not stupid. They know where we are, and they know we have their duke. Give them time, and they'll attempt a rescue, even if they can't possibly hope to succeed."

"If they can't possibly hope to succeed, then why do you fret?" Loris countered. "Have faith."

"I'll have faith when I know where Kelson and his army are!"

"We'll find out."

"Yes, but *when*?" Sicard slapped a mailed gauntlet against his thigh with a clash of metal links against plate as he glared down at the motionless Duncan. "Why hasn't he broken? That Deryni drug was supposed to make him talk."

"His will is strong, my lord," Gorony murmured. "Sometimes the drug alone is not sufficient. But he *will* tell us what we want to know."

"Easy to say, Monsignor. But I need some answers *now*."

"There *are* more stringent measures I could take," Gorony suggested.

"Aye, and with no more useful results."

"Do you question my methods, my lord?"

Sicard set his fists on his hips in a gesture of distaste and turned slightly away.

"I don't like torturing priests," he murmured.

"Ah, but executing them is quite another matter, isn't it?" Loris interjected smoothly. "Tell me, do you recall whether Henry Istelyn suffered any torture before his execution?

Bristling, Sicard drew himself up self-righteously.

"Henry Istelyn was hanged, drawn, and quartered because, in his secular capacity, he was a traitor to Meara," he replied. "His sentence did not reflect upon his sacred office as priest and bishop."

Loris permitted himself a chill smile. "Then, think of McLain's secular office as Duke of Cassan and Earl of Kierney, a prisoner of war with valuable information needful of extraction," he soothed. "So far as *I* am concerned, he is no longer even a priest, much less a bishop."

"You know I cannot argue the fine points of canon law with you," Sicard muttered. "I do not know what makes a bishop in the sacred sense. But this I know: a priest is a priest forever! At his ordination, his hands are consecrated for the purpose of holding the Body of Our Lord. Look what you've done to his hands!"

"*Deryni* hands!" Loris spat. "Hands that have profaned the blessed Sacraments every time he dared to offer Mass. Do not presume to lecture *me* regarding the proper treatment of Deryni, Sicard!"

Duncan, drifting feverishly at the brink of returning consciousness, moaned aloud as Loris punctuated his words with a cut of his whip across the already welted chest. The pain reverberated up and down his body in a wave of fire and chill dread.

He tried to push himself back down into the blessed blackness where he did not hurt, but full awareness welled and flooded back upon him in a rush of old pain, throbbing in his hands and feet. The hard edge of psychic distortion from the last dose of *merasha* had waned but little—certainly not enough to give him any real measure of control.

He did not open his eyes. But even as he sensed Loris bending closer to look at him, and someone else waiting near his head, any chance of maintaining the pretense of unconsciousness was obliterated by the sharp pressure of a boot compressing his wounded right hand against the dirt beneath it—not hard, but it did not need to be. His groan, as he curled to the limits of his bonds in an effort to evade the torment, was almost a sob.

"He's coming around, Excellency," Gorony murmured, from close beside Duncan's left ear.

Loris snorted and moved back, and the pain in Duncan's hand receded almost immediately to a dull throb.

"Amazing how much pain can be bought from the tip of a finger—even in so willful and obdurate a priest as our Duncan. Pay attention, McLain."

Loris underlined the order with another cut of his whip across Duncan's chest, and Duncan gasped and opened his eyes. He was burning with thirst, his throat so parched and swollen that he might almost have welcomed even another draught of *merasha*—for they had given him nothing else to drink since his capture.

"So, you *have* returned to us," Loris said, smiling with satisfaction. "You really must try to be more attentive. Can it be that you do not appreciate Monsignor Gorony's ministrations?"

Duncan only dragged his swollen tongue across dry lips and turned his head aside, bracing for Loris' next blow.

"Why, Father," Loris purred. "You clearly do not yet understand. What matters a man's body if his soul be damned?"

The end of the whip only tapped lightly against one raw fingertip, but the leather might as well have been red-hot steel, for the agony it produced. Duncan clenched his teeth against the pain, but he would not let himself cry out. Suddenly the lash flicked hard against his bare chest, raising yet another welt among the dozens already there, and he did let out a gasp at that.

"Answer me," Loris said sharply. "I am doing this for the good of *your* soul, not my own."

"A noble sentiment," Duncan whispered, almost managing a wry smile. "From a most noble and godly man."

The whip snapped across his face this time, laying open a bloody split in his lower lip, but Duncan was already braced, and only grunted at the blow.

"I believe I have just lost patience with you, Deryni!" Loris muttered through clenched teeth. "I wonder what kind of song you will sing when you taste a proper lash. Your tongue needs discipline as well. Gorony?"

Gorony rose immediately and disappeared to another part of the tent, where Duncan could not see, and for just an instant, he feared a literal fulfillment of the threat: that Loris meant to have his tongue cut out. Gorony would do it, too, if Loris ordered it.

But it was a cup, not a knife, that Gorony brought back with him: more *merasha*, then. God, how they must fear him, to risk another dose so soon.

He did not even try to resist as Gorony raised his head and put the cup to his lips. Whether he fought or not, they would get it down him eventually; struggling would only compound his discomfort. And perhaps they *would* miscalculate and overdose him. At worst, the drug's disruptive effect might help him blunt the other pain.

He swallowed thirstily, almost welcoming the nausea and vertigo the drug produced. Even this tortured near-oblivion of mind was preferable to what they were doing to the rest of his body. And if they burned him . . .

"Bring him," Loris said.

They left the shackles dangling from his wrists and ankles even when they unpegged the chains that had held him to the ground. Duncan groaned as guards wrenched him to his feet and led him, staggering, from the tent, Loris and Gorony following with a tight-lipped Sicard.

He saw the stake almost at once. They had set it atop a little hillock in the center of the camp, but a short distance from Loris' tent. Silhouetted against the early morning sky, it seemed hardly imposing enough to promise so horrible a death as Duncan knew awaited him—only a piece of a tree trunk, roughly hewn, with even a few branches still spiking from the top.

He stared at it in dread fascination as they drew him toward it, ignoring the jeers and taunts of Loris' troops drawn up to witness his humiliation, as he stumbled along a gauntlet of staring, hissing soldiers who wore a blue cross on their pure white surcoats. They did him no physical harm, but he could feel their hatred burning against his flesh in anticipation of the flames that soon would seek his life. Beyond the episcopal knights and men-at-arms, the massed troops of the Mearan army stretched as far as the eye could see, most of the signs of the night's camp already gone. The nervous Sicard obviously was preparing to move out as soon as Duncan's death was accomplished.

The chains on his ankles dragged at him with every agonizing step; his raw and bloody toes throbbed, making of the short journey to the stake his own personal Calvary, like walking on flames already. He found himself wondering whether the Christ had found His last journey so difficult. It all seemed just a little unreal.

The chains hanging from the stake were real enough, however—and the piles of faggots stacked neatly around the base, with only a narrow passageway left for him and his guards to stumble through. To either side of the stake, stripped to the waist, two soldiers waited with leather scourges, the knotted thongs moving restlessly in their hands, corded muscles rippling in brawny shoulders and chests.

He expected and received no mercy as his guards yanked him across the final steps and, without ceremony, drew his arms around the stake in a rough embrace, locking his wrists a little above head-height. Ragged chunks of bark and stubs of branches dug painfully into his chest; and when he tried to shift his stance a little wider-splayed to brace himself against the scourge, he jammed a nailless toe against a piece of kindling with such force that his eyes watered and he nearly fainted from the pain.

When he had mastered himself again, he opened his eyes to see Gorony's face only inches from his, the priest's hands slowly turning the handle of one of the scourges between them.

"Behold, the instrument of your salvation," he heard Gorony murmur, through the pain throbbing in hands and feet.

He flinched as the priest flicked the knotted thongs lightly across his bare shoulder, feeling the dread crawl in his mind despite his intention that he should *not* allow Gorony that satisfaction.

"Nay, do not shrink from your salvation," Gorony went on, his voice obscene in the pleasure it conveyed at another's suffering. "You must let each stroke drive the evil from you, that your death may be an expiation of your many sins."

When Duncan only turned his face away, welcoming the rough caress of the bark against his cheek, he could sense Gorony's disappointment. Battling the *merasha*-enhanced despair beginning to well in his mind, he tried to distance himself from what was about to happen. His torturers spent what seemed like hours testing their scourges on the ground behind him, making sure he heard the whistle of the leather rending the air and the dead snap the weighted thongs made as they struck the ground, but all too soon they paused.

Only a prior scourging could have prepared him for what came next. Even though he was expecting it, the first actual stroke of the lash caught him totally unready for the agony it produced. Biting back his first cry of pain and shock, he clenched his fists and tried to grind his raw fingertips against the rough bark of the stake, hoping to dull the new pain with an older, better tolerated one. It did not help.

Each individual thong of the scourge laid a fiery welt across his back, blotting out all other sensory input—and there were two scourgers. His torturers never seemed to tire. After the first half-dozen lashes, blood began to run, min-

gling with the sweat pouring from his pain-wracked body;
and after a few more, time began to blur as well.

He sagged more and more heavily against his chains as
the scourging continued, no longer able to see for the pain.
His wrists were numb and slick with his blood, but that was
as nothing compared to what they were doing to his back.
He had heard of men being flayed to the bone by the scourge.
Perhaps *he* would die. Loris would never break his spirit
with the scourge, but facing the fire was a different kind of
trial.

"He can't take much more," he heard Sicard say to Loris,
the words only barely filtering through his agony. "Unless,
of course, you prefer a cremation to an execution."

"He is stronger than you think," came Loris' cold reply,
as another stroke drove Duncan even nearer the brink of
blessed oblivion. "Still, I would not cheat the fire of its living
sacrifice. Gorony?"

The scourging ceased. As the half-fainting Duncan stirred
feebly, trying to get his feet under him again, rough hands
seized his biceps and supported him while someone unlocked
his wrists. His hands throbbed worse than before as circulation returned, but when they turned him and set his back
hard against the stake, stretching his arms behind him to
embrace its rough surface against his flayed flesh, he knew
that all his previous pain had been but prelude. The metallic
click of the shackles locking around his wrists was underlined by the clank of the chains Gorony then began winding
across his chest, binding him to the stake so that even the
fire would never release his body from the fate Loris had
determined should be his. He tried to ride with the pain, tried
to will himself to succumb to it, to pass into blessed unconsciousness, but he lacked sufficient control.

As the men set bundles of faggots closer around his feet,
filling in most of the opening they had left for access to the
stake, Duncan's sight grew preternaturally clear. Now there
would be no new pain until the flames. Beyond Loris and
Gorony, he saw and noted many of the men who had turned
against him and the Haldane cause in the past six months:
Grigor of Dunlea, a powerful neighbor of the traitor Brice
of Trurill and old Caulay MacArdry.

Old Caulay was dead, of course—though he never would
have forsaken his oath to the Haldane kings. Loyal and
steadfast Caulay, who had raised Dhugal as his own son.

Duncan swallowed hard at the realization that he would never see Dhugal again, and prayed that the boy had gotten to safety.

And then there were Tibald MacErskine and Cormac Hamberlyn, two of the border chieftains of his own vassalage who stood to gain by his death—and an outlaw from his own border regions called O Daire.

And Sicard MacArdry, kinsman to his son and husband of his enemy, and Kelson's enemy, standing with armored forearms crossed on his chest and a look of distaste on his bearded face.

Fire caught Duncan's attention then, far out at the periphery of his vision—a torch in the hands of a cowled man approaching slowly from the direction of Loris' tent. Against his will, Duncan found his eyes locking on the flame in horrid fascination, unable to look away even when the man passed the torch to Loris' gloved hand.

An awed hush fell upon the assembly then, for it was not often that the Church burned a priest and bishop, though Deryni aplenty had burned in the past. The silence was so profound that Duncan could hear the hiss and crackle of the burning brand as Loris approached, holding the torch aloft like the crozier that was his usual accoutrement. The prelate's cross on his breast reflected both heat and light as he stopped within an arm's length of his prisoner and looked him up and down.

"Well, well, dear Duncan, we have come to an ending at last, haven't we?" he said, so softly that only Duncan could hear him. "It is not yet too late to confess your sins, you know. I still can save you."

Duncan shook his head carefully.

"I have nothing to say to you."

"Ah, then you prefer to go to your death unshriven and excommunicate," Loris said, raising an eyebrow in mocking agreement. "I had hoped that mortification of the flesh might help you to master your pride and to repent." His expression hardened. "Tell me, Deryni, have you ever seen a man burn?"

Duncan shivered despite the heat of the day and the menace of the flame in Loris' hand, but he was determined not to allow his tormentor the satisfaction of any further response. Turning his head slightly away, he raised his gaze to the line of sun-glazed hills stretched across the eastern horizon. The bright rim of the rising sun dazzled his eyes as he fixed his attention on it, helping him turn his mind away from awful memories and the knowledge of what lay ahead for him.

*I will lift up mine eyes unto the hills, from whence cometh my help*, he thought dully.

"Well, I can tell you that burning is not a pleasant way to die," Loris went on. "And I can make it less pleasant, still. You will note that the kindling is set to burn very slowly, giving your body ample time to taste the full torment of these earthly flames before your soul must face the flames of Hell. It will be more terrible than you can even contemplate. But I could be merciful. . . ."

Duncan swallowed dry-mouthed and closed his eyes briefly, but the afterimage of the sun-rim persisted, presaging the fire to come, and he shifted back to physical vision almost immediately.

*My help cometh from the Lord, which made heaven and earth. . . .*

"Yes, I could be merciful," Loris repeated. "If you will recant your heresies, and denounce your cursed Deryni powers, I could see that the fire is quick and hot. And for the additional favor of giving me the information I desire on Kelson's whereabouts, I could be more merciful still."

As he glanced back at the men knotted around Sicard and gave a nod, Tibald MacErskine drew his dirk. The harsh rasp of metal against metal as it left the sheath called to Duncan, promising release, but he knew he dared not buy his body's ease at the cost of betrayal, either of his own conscience or of the faith he kept and would always keep with his king.

"Look you. His blade is sharp," Loris whispered, as Tibald came to join them. "See how it flashes in the sun, in the light of the flame. . . ."

As Tibald brought the blade to eye level before him and turned it, smiling obscenely, Duncan found himself watching with horrible fascination, squinting as the torchlight dazzled his sight.

"Yes, the fire is hot, but the release of steel is sweet," Loris whispered, taking the weapon in his own free hand.

As he set it gently against Duncan's throat, letting the flat of the blade lie cool and seductive across the pulse point, Duncan closed his eyes, trembling.

*So easy to succumb. So easy. . . .*

"It would be very easy, Duncan," Loris' voice purred on. "Very little pain. Far less than you have already suffered. They say that a tiny nick, just here, behind the ear. . . ."

He felt the momentary pressure of the metal like a caress, though flat-bladed still, but even that was withdrawn before he could have leaned into it. The heat of the torch beat upon his closed eyelids, leaving the brief memory of the cool blade the sweeter still.

*Oh, blessed Jesu, have pity on Your servant!* came his quick and desperate prayer.

"What, so eager?" Loris whispered, stroking the flat of the blade across his throat again. "Ah, but it *would* be a welcome exchange, wouldn't it, Duncan? The quick mercy of the blade balanced against the fire. Why, even in your weakened state, you could surely manage that, before the flames reached you. If you tell me what I wish to know, I will give you your mercy."

*YOU could manage. . . .*

Duncan forced his eyes to open as the trap suddenly became apparent, even to his dulled senses. Loris had tried to lure him to a far more lasting torment than the fire. It was not the *coup de grâce* Loris offered him—the stroke of mercy, to spare the recipient further agony. The alternative Loris offered to death by fire was death by Duncan's own hand—which would carry far heavier consequences than mere death of his body when he stood before God's judgment in the hereafter.

Nor, even if Duncan were fool enough to accept the terms, was there any guarantee that Loris would keep his part of the bargain. Did Loris really think he would betray his conscience and his king so that he might be permitted to commit the mortal sin of suicide?

"Ah, so you don't care for my little offer," Loris said, shaking his head in mock regret as he gave the dirk back to Tibald. "Well, I don't suppose I ever really thought you would. I do have a care for your soul, though—if Deryni even have souls, of course. And even if suicide is not among your faults, I am sure you will welcome the time to contemplate your other sins. The fire will take a long time to kill you.

"And that is all to the good of your immortal soul," he went on, as he began slowly backing off. "Your body, of course—"

He gestured with the torch, the fire passing so near a bit of brush-kindling that Duncan caught his breath in horror.

"But, you have surely seen others purified by the flame," Loris continued. "The blackened, twisted forms—the hands contorted into claws as the heat contracts the muscles. Of course, you may be dead by the time that begins to happen. . . ."

Duncan's imagination began filling in its own gruesome details long before Loris reached the edge of the kindling and his voice fell silent. As the fiery torch sank lower and lower in Loris' hand, finally setting the first edges of brush alight, a roar went up from the watching men. They rattled swords and spears against shields in approval as Loris trailed the torch slowly around the outer perimeter and the flames spread to follow in his wake.

All but despairing, Duncan wrenched his gaze above the growing flames and concentrated on the hills beyond, praying that he might be granted the grace to die as well as Henry Istelyn—steadfast and true, faithful unto death to himself, his king, and his God.

*Judge me, O Lord; for I have walked in mine integrity: I have trusted also in the Lord; therefore I shall not slide. Examine me, O Lord, and prove me; try my reins and my heart. . . .*

And his trying would be ruthless, Duncan knew—deadly, at least to his body. The flames leaped ever higher, beginning to eat toward him, but the heat that drove Loris and his minions back with its intensity would not reach him for some time—perhaps as long as half an hour. Not hot enough to kill, at any rate. He could feel the sting of sweat drenching his lacerated back, streaming down his limbs, but that was as much from his nerves and the beating sun as from the fire.

*In thee, O Lord, do I put my trust; let me never be ashamed: deliver me in thy righteousness. Bow down thine ear to me; deliver me speedily. . . . Into thine hand I commit my spirit: Thou hast redeemed me, O Lord God of truth. . . .*

Beyond the flames, Sicard and his officers began returning to their units and preparing to move out, cavalry and foot bristling with lances and pikes and bows as they formed up, mounted scouts already scattering to the west to reconnoiter.

The camp had nearly disappeared around him, even Loris' tent all but dismantled as his men packed the canvas onto sumpter mules. Farther out, the white-clad episcopal knights were mounted already, the mettlesome battle chargers fidgeting and anxious at the flames leaping up ever stronger around the condemned Duke of Cassan.

*I will lift up mine eyes unto the hills, from whence cometh my help. . . . The Lord is my shepherd; I shall not want. . . .*

So rapt was Duncan in his devotion that he did not even notice, at first, that the light of the eastern sky had begun to reflect from the points of hundreds of lances, or that the eastern glare masked the steady approach of Haldane banners.

But Sicard noticed—and Loris. And as their officers began bawling frantic orders to arm and mount, the dust of the Haldane advance roiled on the plain like the coming of an avenging angel.

# CHAPTER SEVENTEEN

*And I saw, and behold a white horse: and he that
sat on him had a bow; and a crown was given unto
him: and he went forth conquering and to conquer.*
— Revelations 6:2–3

"*A Haldane!*"

Suddenly the hills to south and east were abristle with
lances and raised swords, the Haldane host streaming down
onto the plain of Dorna to sweep the Mearan army before
them, crimson banners flying. Through the flames rising
higher around him, Duncan was dully aware of the Mearan
panic and its cause, but that knowledge was a thing apart,
a theoretical change of circumstances touching him hardly
at all; because he knew the flames would reach him before
his rescuers could.

Around the pyre, the Mearan forces so recently drawn up
to watch him burn were milling in confusion and panic, their
composure not aided by Loris, shaking a crozier at the attacking Haldane forces and screaming for a horse. White-
surcoated ecclesiastical knights boiled around the renegade
archbishop as one was brought, but their greathorses, skit-
tish with battle fever, only made it more difficult for Loris
to mount, and he ranted at them while Gorony tried to rally
the Connaiti mercenaries.

The secular levies were somewhat better disported, for
Sicard commanded with a logic unheated by the passions
that had impelled Loris, but even with his reasoned direction, some of the Mearan levies milled in confusion as their
officers tried to order them for a counteroffensive. Ragged
formations were beginning to charge across the plain to in-

tercept the attacking Haldanes, but isolated bands were already fleeing in disorder, streaming westward along the only avenue of escape not already menaced by Haldane attackers.

None of it was to Edmund Loris' liking—and even less, the possibility that his victim might yet escape his vengeance. Cursing and muttering in his mitre-crowned helm, he yanked his horse's head around and gigged it with his spurs, forcing it nearer the flames, and pointed his crozier at the half-fainting Duncan as if he wished it could strike him dead.

"God damn you, Duncan McLain!" he shouted above the crackle of flames and the din of battle being joined. "God damn you to eternal Hell!"

The sound of his name roused Duncan a little from his pain-dulled stupor, but lifting his head toward Loris only made the horror of his situation all the more terrifying. The flames leaped ever higher as they ate at the edge of the pyre, their heat an increasingly stifling oppression threatening to choke him even before the fire could consume his flesh. Beyond the fire and the white-clad renegade archbishop, the glad, welcome sight of Haldane and Cassani banners fighting their way toward him only taunted, for he knew they could never reach him in time. He tried to believe they would, and to shutter off his fear—as he had done so many times in the past half-day—but the *merasha* in his body still raveled his concentration. Dully he watched as Gorony returned to Loris' side, two nervous episcopal knights in attendance.

"Excellency, we must flee!" he dimly heard Gorony shout, as the priest kneed his mount into the side of Loris'. "Leave McLain! Let the flames do their work."

Stubbornly Loris shook his head, the blue eyes blazing with the single-minded fanaticism that had brought all of them to this event.

"No! It burns too slowly! They will save him. He must die!"

"Then, put an end to him some other way!" Gorony begged, signalling his episcopal knights to throw themselves between Loris and the first Haldane attackers now beginning to penetrate the former Mearan campsite. "We must be away, or they will take us!"

Shaking with indecision, Loris stared through the flames at Duncan, his hate distorting his reason even as the heat distorted his vision. The sounds of battle crashed ever nearer, but Loris did not seem to hear.

"Fight through to the duke!" Duncan heard someone cry, from beyond the pyre's opposite perimeter.

"Save the bishop!" someone else shouted hoarsely.

Face contorting with rage, Loris pointed his crozier toward the nearest of the Connaiti mercenaries still remaining in the immediate area.

"Archers, I want him dead!" he screamed, ignoring the pleas of Gorony and other of his episcopal knights to come away to safety. "Kill him *now*! I will not leave until he is dead!"

Instantly three of the men detached themselves from their fellows and began working their way to Loris' side, drawing deadly little recurve bows from saddle cases.

"Kill him!" Loris ordered, gesturing toward the feebly struggling Duncan as the archers drew rein before him. "Slay him where he stands. We cannot wait for the flames to finish him!"

"Your Excellency, you *must* come away!" Gorony muttered, again sidling his horse closer to Loris' snorting stallion, this time close enough to seize the near rein. "Let them do their work. You must not be taken."

Loris jerked the rein out of Gorony's grasp.

"No! I will see him dead!"

The end was very near now. Duncan knew it as surely as he knew Loris would pay for what he had done—though Duncan would not be there to see it. As the flames leaped higher, smoke stinging his eyes, and the heat began to scorch at his bare legs, he watched the archers fitting feathered death to bowstrings, trying to hold fire-skittish horses steady with knees and legs as they maneuvered close enough to take aim.

Both Dhugal and Morgan saw the Mearans' intent, though from much too far across the field to make a difference. Dhugal, fighting a heated encounter with Mearan lancers, Ciard and other of his MacArdry clansmen at his back, could only rage inwardly, redoubling his efforts to reach his father. Morgan was no less pressed, but his greater experience conceived a plan that just might buy Duncan a little time—but only if he could find Kelson.

"Jodrell, to me!" he cried, standing in his stirrups to look for the king. "Guard my back!"

He spied Kelson almost at once, sword in hand but relatively unpressed behind a phalanx of Haldane bodyguards and officers. Attackers swirled around the king's party, drawn by the Haldane standard Ewan bore behind him, but Kelson himself was virtually in the clear, as Morgan was not.

Fending off a Mearan spear thrust that got past Jodrell, Morgan focused all his concentration on touching the king's mind, if only for an instant.

*'Ware for Duncan!* he sent, faltering briefly while he took time out to plunge his sword into the throat of an attacking Mearan foot soldier. *Kelson! Remember the archery yard!*

But Kelson had already noted Duncan's increased danger—and grimly reached the same conclusion as to what must be done. He disliked making public display of his powers, but none of his archers were in range to handle things more conventionally. Nor could Morgan assist him, for working the delicate magical balance required was next to impossible when one was physically fighting for one's own life. Morgan's very warning was something of a miracle, under the circumstances.

Glancing around quickly to confirm that he was well protected physically, Kelson rested his sword across his saddlebow and drew deep breath to center, stretching his mind tentatively toward the stake and its helpless captive. He could feel the strain, for the distance was nearly twice that to which he was accustomed. Nor was working the spell under battle conditions the same as the light diversion of a quiet practice yard. It was one thing to guide an arrow of one's own sending, where the stakes were only points in a game—quite another to deflect another's shaft from feathered death, and not once but many times.

But the proper connections locked into place in time to deflect the first-loosed arrow. He saw the archer mouth a curse as the shot went wide, and shifted his attention to the next, just then setting the nock to his ear.

Even above the sounds of battle, he seemed to hear the twang of the second shot; and the feathered shaft again zinged harmlessly past Duncan's head. He could see the look of dismay on the archer's face, and the determination in the stance of the first as he and the third man nocked and drew simultaneously. Beyond, Duncan had closed his eyes, and only flinched as the third and fourth arrows thudded home in the stake itself, fletching tightly interlocked, less than a handspan above his head.

"The priest defends himself with magic!" one of Loris' men cried, pointing at the stake as a fifth arrow whizzed harmlessly past Duncan's shoulder.

"That's impossible!" Loris shouted, looking wildly around from the back of his rearing horse. "He *can't* be working his magic—not with the drug! He *can't* be!"

"It's Morgan, then," Gorony muttered. "But he can't do it if he's fighting for his life."

And with an oath, he wheeled his charger and took off in Morgan's direction, two score of his episcopal knights giving him support.

Only a handful of men remained to Loris himself, most of them shaken by the merest suggestion that Deryni magic might still be operable, whether from Duncan or some other Deryni. All but three turned tail and ran, one of the archers among them. But at Loris' even more vehement exhortations, the remaining bowmen only increased their efforts—though to no better effect.

It was Sicard who, fighting his way ever closer to the Haldane standard, finally connected Kelson's motionless stare, concentrated on the chained Duncan, with the extraordinarily poor showing of the Connaiti archers.

"Kill the king!" Sicard shouted, motioning his men with his sword to charge the royal position. "Break his concentration! 'Tis *he* who works magic to save the Deryni priest!"

The distraction had its effect. As Sicard and his shock troops swept up the hill in attack, and Kelson's warband must begin more vigorous defense, Kelson himself faltered—and a Mearan arrow skittered along Duncan's side, deflected by his ribs but opening a painful gash. Duncan's cry of pain further unnerved the king, and before he could recover, a second shaft thudded home in Duncan's right shoulder.

"*Father!*" Dhugal screamed, not caring who heard as he and his bordermen continued hacking their way toward the stake, though most would have taken the epithet as reference to Duncan's priestly office.

Kelson knew his control was gone as another arrow smacked into the fleshy part of Duncan's right thigh, but Sicard's attack had all but ended any possibility of continuing. Swept suddenly into a running battle with Sicard and his men, Kelson was able to spare only one last, desperate plea to Morgan, before physical survival became the highest priority, even for a Deryni king.

But Morgan was closer by half than he had been before. Though beleaguered himself by Gorony's new assault, he barely managed to slide into the protective link even as Kelson abandoned it altogether. The distraction from his own defense cost him a bruising blow to his side, but the brigandine held, and the next arrow meant for Duncan only grazed an ear, rather than burying itself in his unprotected throat.

Morgan was able to hold his defense long enough to make the difference. After a few more diverted shots, when it became apparent that someone besides Kelson was now protecting the prisoner, one of the remaining archers spotted Morgan standing in his stirrup and surrounded by men determined to give him respite from the general fighting—and galloped off, taking his companion and Loris' last mounted guard with him.

Loris raged at the abandonment. And as Sicard drew the king farther from the pyre, and Gorony forced more aggressive defense by Morgan and his men, the rebel archbishop suddenly reined in at the edge of the fire and threw himself from his horse. Cursing, he thrust his crozier into the burning bundles of kindling and began wrenching them aside.

"Watch Loris!" Morgan bellowed, blocking a blow to his head and cleaving a Mearan knight through the shoulder as, unable to do anything himself, he watched Loris toss aside the crozier and begin pulling and kicking bundles of kindling out of his way, tearing at them with his gloved hands in order to reach his prey.

Dhugal saw the new danger, too, and set his charger bolting toward the flames, counting on surprise to give him some advantage. With Ciard and several other MacArdry men at his back, as well as a few Haldane knights, he managed to penetrate deep into the thinning Mearan host before his momentum was broken. As he fought like a wild man, Ciard and the others fanning out to help him cut through the defending episcopal troops, he could see his father's face contorted with pain, blood running down his tortured body from several wounds—and Loris, working his way ever nearer his helpless victim, eyes wild, gauntleted right hand drawing a long dagger in triumph as he all but gained his prize.

"Lor-i-i-i-s!" Dhugal screamed.

Loris' abandoned mount bolted past with mane and tail aflame as Dhugal gained the outer perimeter of the pyre. Dhugal's horse reared and screamed, shying from the flames. Loris' once-white cope was streaked with soot, smoldering along one edge, his mitred helm discarded, only a few feet now separating him from his weakly struggling victim.

"*Lor-i-i-i-s!*"

Brutally, Dhugal raked his spurs along his horse's sides, trying to force it to leap the flames, but the animal reared up with a squeal of defiance, pawing the air and nearly going over backward, all but pitching Dhugal himself into the flames. Nor did Loris, clambering over the rough kindling, even glance at him, though Dhugal's men, scrambling after him on foot now, seemed to spur his progress, and more Haldane knights were drawing rein and dismounting also, having routed the last of Loris' men.

"Loris, damn you, no!" Dhugal swore, panting as he wrenched the horse's head around and again demanded the jump, this time flat-blading the beast across the rump to underscore his determination.

Again, the animal refused, this time exploding in a series of mighty bucks that cost Dhugal the grip on his sword and nearly his seat, showering burning kindling inside the ring of fire as well as without. The commotion distracted Loris' single-minded advance toward his prey, but only momentarily. As his cope snagged on a bundle of kindling and he had to stop to rip it free, staggering, he spared but a single glance for Dhugal before lurching on, the dagger still gleaming in his hand, rising above his head.

Only an instant remained. Dhugal's men would not reach Loris in time to stop him, and Loris knew it. All too clearly, Dhugal saw the blade drawing back to strike, the look of numb disbelief on his father's face, that rescue should fail by so little. In desperation, Dhugal grabbed a handful of mane and sent his mental command into the horse's panicked mind, knife-sharp, demanding obedience regardless of the cost.

"*Lor-i-i-i-s!*" he cried, as the animal gathered itself in a shuddering, terrified leap and launched itself across the wall of fire surrounding Duncan—and died in midair as its mighty heart gave out with the strain.

The horse was dead meat under Dhugal even before it landed, legs all akimbo, but Dhugal somehow managed to throw himself clear just before impact and get a hand on Loris' cope.

"God *damn* you, Loris!"

His desperate wrench at the handful of linen was just enough to deflect the killing blow. Instead of plunging into Duncan's heaving chest, Loris' stroke skittered harmlessly along the stake with a shower of bark and stopped against a branchlet.

The archbishop howled with outrage as the younger, slighter Dhugal began grappling with him for possession of the blade, the two of them rolling over and over in the rough kindling, both crying out when burning brands connected with bare flesh. Roger, Earl of Jenas, was one of the two Haldane knights who finally pounced on Loris and overpowered him, twisting the arm with the dagger until Loris screamed in agony.

"Drop it right now, or I'll break your arm!" Roger demanded, wrenching the dagger out of Loris' hand.

Ciard hurried to help his young master to his feet, brushing glowing embers from leather as his companions scrambled over Dhugal's dead horse to assist in securing the prisoner. The scattered fire was beginning to die out.

"Father?" Dhugal breathed, as he pulled away from Ciard to stagger toward the stake.

Duncan raised his head at the sound of Dhugal's voice, still hardly comprehending, in his pain, that he was still alive.

"Dhugal—" He winced and gasped as Dhugal's unsteady approach jarred glowing sticks of kindling against his raw and bloody toes. "Dear God, I thought I'd never see you again."

"Did you think I could let you die?" Dhugal answered.

Duncan shuddered and shook his head as Dhugal began urgently shifting debris out of the way to reach him, Ciard assisting. Bright blood seeped from around the arrow in Duncan's shoulder, and from his other wounds, and he moaned as Dhugal reached him, closing his eyes and shrinking from Dhugal's touch as gloved fingers brushed the shafts protruding from shoulder and upper thigh. Dhugal was estimating the damage, quickly surveying the other injuries, noting the nailless fingers and toes with a sibilant intake of breath. He stripped off his gauntlets as Ciard attacked the shackles binding Duncan's arms around the stake behind him, but Duncan shook his head when Dhugal would have made a closer examination of his wounds.

"No! *Merasha!*" he warned weakly, dully noting Roger helping to support him under his left arm as Ciard picked at the shackle locks with the point of a border dirk. "Tell Alaric—important—"

But the exertion cost too much, after what he had already been through, and he mercifully passed out. And when the locks did not yield quickly enough to Ciard's manipulation, Dhugal set his hand on one and sent his mind into the stiff, dust-clogged mechanism, not caring, in that moment, who saw the result and learned what he was.

"Lord Dhugal? *You?*" Roger gasped, as the first one gave, though Ciard did not bat an eye.

As the second sprang open, setting both of Duncan's wrists free now, and Ciard and Roger caught Duncan's dead weight between them, Loris craned in his bonds just in time to see Dhugal open the ankle fetters with a touch.

"A Deryni! Oh, God, you're Deryni, too!"

Dhugal hardly spared Loris a glance as he helped Ciard and Roger ease Duncan into a careful carry-hold, avoiding the protruding arrows.

"That's right, Loris. I'm Deryni. Bishop Duncan is my father. And you'd better pray he lives," he added.

"So the Deryni heretic has himself a Deryni bastard!" Loris muttered, before one of Dhugal's borderers cuffed him into silence. But his outburst partially covered the astonished doubletakes of those others who had not known.

Dhugal did not even care, as he helped Ciard and Roger ease his father's limp form down off the kindling around the stake, that the revelation would be the talk of the camp before nightfall.

Meanwhile, the battle around them had not abated, only moved on to other venues as Kelson's army shattered the Mearan command and routed the surprised Mearan levies. Once the enemy was in retreat, Kelson employed the same tactics he had used at Talacara, albeit on a larger scale, his highly mobile lancers and heavy cavalry gradually cutting off and isolating groups of Mearan warriors for slaughter or surrender, mounted archers backing them to reinforce the options.

Morgan, seeing Loris foiled by Dhugal's amazing feat of heroism, made it his special mission to run Gorony to ground—and managed to restrain both himself and his men from doing the traitor-priest any serious harm once he was finally taken. And it was Kelson himself who led the band of knights that eventually brought Sicard to bay.

"Give it up, Sicard!" Kelson shouted, as Sicard wheeled his tired greathorse in a tight, snorting circle, he and his men searching frantically for an escape route.

A score of knights remained to Sicard, two-thirds the number in Kelson's band, some of them men of rank, minor lords in their own right. Wary and desperate, they milled around him in a tight, well-ordered ring, facing outward. And though they bristled with weapons, and appeared ready enough to put up a last fight to the death, Kelson decided there had been enough killing for one day and determined at least to attempt some more moderate solution.

"I said, give it up!" Kelson repeated. "Your cause is lost. You cannot hope to escape, Sicard. If not for yourself, then surrender for the good of your men, whose only crime is loyalty to the wrong leader."

Sicard was bleeding from half a dozen painful wounds, his face sickly pale as he slowly removed his helmet and tossed it aside, but he raised his eyes defiantly to Kelson, his blood-streaked sword a little wobbly in his hand.

"I cannot do that, Haldane," he said softly, weaving slightly in the saddle. "I swore an oath to my liege lady—that I would defend her cause to the death."

"Do you seek your death, and the deaths of these men, then?" Kelson asked. "For if you persist in armed defiance, you shall have it."

"Then, face me in single combat!" Sicard blurted. "I am not afraid to die. If I win, I go free. If not . . ."

Coolly Kelson surveyed his foe. Though he could almost pity the man, Sicard MacArdry had already cost too many lives. While he pursued Sicard, the fighting had diminished to only a few odd pockets of desultory skirmishing, but the dead and wounded of both sides lay all too thickly on the plain of Dorna. And if, by some freak of physical endurance, the older and more experienced Sicard managed to wound or kill him—

"No, Sicard," he said at last.

Sicard seemed almost unable to comprehend what he had just heard. Blankly his gaze flicked over the surrounding knights to Ewan and the other Haldane nobles gathered around the king, to the Haldane standard spilling over Ewan's gloved hand, limp and motionless in the stifling summer stillness, to the bright sword resting on Kelson's armored shoulder.

"What do you mean—*no?*"

"I mean *No*, I will not give you single combat," Kelson said quietly.

"Not give—but—"

Despair flickered in Sicard's dark eyes as the full implications of Kelson's statement registered. Breathing harder, he turned his horse a full circle on its haunches, glancing desperately at Kelson's officers for some appeal. But the swords and lances leveled at him and his men did not waver, and he found only hard-eyed resolution on the faces of Kelson's knights..

"I—will not surrender," he finally said. "You will have to take me by force."

"No," Kelson said again, even more quietly than the first time. And then, over his shoulder, as he quietly sheathed his sword, he added, "Archers, attend. And someone bring me a bow."

Sicard's face went grey, and his men began murmuring urgently among themselves as Kelson also removed his helmet and gauntlets and handed them to a squire.

"You—you can't *do* that!" Sicard rasped.

"Can I not?" Kelson replied, not looking back toward the scout working his way closer with a bow and a quiver of arrows, or the troop of mounted archers that followed, interspersing themselves between the knights ringing Sicard and his men.

"But, there are conventions of war—"

"Oh? I had not noted a marked observation of conventions by the Mearan army," Kelson said. "Or can you have been unaware that the Duke of Cassan was tortured while a prisoner under your protection?"

"He was *Loris'* prisoner!" Sicard protested.

Without answering, Kelson took the bow the scout brought him and kneed his horse a few mincing steps to the right, to stand sideways to the Mearan commander as he tested the string.

"But you—you can't just cut me down like a dog," Sicard said weakly.

"Indeed?" Kelson said, calmly laying an arrow across the bowstring. "Sicard, I can and shall cut you down *precisely* like a dog, if I must. For, like a rabid dog, you have ravaged my lands and slain my people. Now, will you and your men surrender, or must I do what I would rather not?"

"You're bluffing," Sicard whispered. "What will the world say, if the great Kelson Haldane cuts down an enemy in cold blood?"

"They will say that a traitor was executed for his treason, without further endangering honest men," Kelson replied. Raising his bow arm, he began a slow, smooth draw. "*I* say that enough lives have been spent on you and your misguided cause. Are not three of your own children sufficient price to pay?"

"*Three?*" Sicard gasped. "Ithel—?"

"Is dead," Kelson said, as he sighted down the shaft at Sicard's heart. "I hanged him and Brice of Trurill yesterday. Now, throw down your sword. My arm is getting tired. And archers, if I have to shoot him, and his men do not immediately surrender, stand by to cut them down the same way. What's it to be, Sicard? If you say no, I let fly."

The head of the war arrow leveled at his heart gleamed dead black in the afternoon heat, but it no longer held the dread it once had. Numbly Sicard stared at the man who had now killed both his sons, as well as bringing about the death of his only daughter. It had all been for naught.

Then, as the Haldane archers nocked arrows, maneuvering their horses for clear shots at his men, Sicard MacArdry slowly raised his eyes above Kelson, toward the western hills and the queen he had lost—he, who had dreamed of a throne beside his Mearan queen—and whispered a single word.

"No."

Before any of his men could utter a word, Kelson's arrow took him cleanly through the left eye—a last-second change of target, lest Sicard's armor deflect the barbed arrowhead and prolong Sicard's final agony. The Mearan consort died without a sound, sword falling to the sand from lifeless fingers, toppling silently until his body hit the ground in a clash of armor. The sound seemed to release his men from their awed and stunned observation of the act; and as Kelson took another arrow and his archers began choosing targets, a murmur of protest rippled among the Mearan knights, quickly dying as all eyes fastened on the king.

"I now require *your* decision, gentlemen," Kelson said, as he nocked his second arrow. "Your commander was a brave man, if a foolish one, but for all that he was steadfast to the end in his loyalty to his lady, I shall see that he receives honorable burial—as I had already determined to give to Prince Ithel. You will now surrender, and face whatever just penalties your individual actions may have incurred, or else suffer the same fate as your late master."

The Mearans were not made of the same stuff as Sicard. Muttering there was among them, but almost at once, weapons began hitting the ground, empty hands rising above armored shoulders.

"Ewan, take them into custody," Kelson murmured, handing off his bow as he stood in the stirrups to gaze back toward the site of the stake where he had last seen Duncan chained. "We have our victory, but pray God that Bishop Duncan's life has not been part of the price."

General Gloddruth took the Haldane banner from Ewan and fell in with Kelson as the king urged his horse back toward the center of the former Mearan camp to find out. Battle surgeons had begun ministering to those who could be helped, priests to those who could not, and the cries of the wounded and the dying surged and eddied around the king on the stifling summer air as he picked his way back across the battleground.

Closer to the stake, a few Haldane scouts guarded the bodies of dead Connaiti mercenaries and episcopal knights. A little farther on, Baron Jodrell rose at Kelson's approach to give salute, grim triumph in his eyes as he gestured toward a middle-aged man gasping on the ground between a squire and a battle-surgeon priest bandaging his wounds, armor and a bloodstained white surcoat discarded to one side.

"Do you recognize him, Sire? Unfortunately for him, he's going to live to stand trial."

Kelson frowned. "One of Loris' minions?"

"His *chief* minion," the surgeon-priest muttered, silencing his patient with a precise blow to the jaw as, at the sound of Kelson's voice, the man opened his eyes and began cursing and squirming.

"Lawrence Gorony," Jodrell supplied, as Gorony fell back, unconscious. "It's too bad Duke Alaric didn't finish him off, but since he didn't—"

"Alaric? Oh, God, where is he?" Kelson interrupted, swinging an armored leg over his horse's rump and dropping heavily to the ground. "And Bishop Duncan? Is he alive?"

"Over there, Sire."

# CHAPTER EIGHTEEN

*The skill of the physician shall lift up his head.*
—Ecclesiasticus 38:3

Like a man possessed, Kelson ran toward the billow of canvas that Jodrell pointed to, dreading what he would find. Heat and fatigue dragged at his limbs, weighted by armor, and his breath burned in his lungs as he ran, but he did not let his steps slow until he had reached his goal, heart pounding with fear as much as the exertion as he staggered to a halt.

Partially under the shelter of the tent some men-at-arms were hastily erecting, familiar heads were bent over a supine, nearly nude figure who surely must be Duncan; but before he could make sure, Kelson had to duck his head between his knees, suddenly light-headed, until the throbbing in his temples eased. He tugged loose the buckles of his gorget as he straightened, still breathing hard, but no one even looked up. He tried to tell himself that things were not as bad as they appeared as he slowly stumbled closer to the crouching men.

It was, indeed, Duncan who lay there. Kelson's stomach threatened to revolt as he saw what had been done to him. A broken-off arrow protruded from his thigh, angry looking burns marked his bare legs, and his filthy, blood-caked toes were raw and nailless. What Kelson could see of his chest, past the men working over him so intently, was bloody and crisscrossed with welts, and at first seemed not to be moving.

But Morgan was one of those who knelt at his head, one hand across Duncan's closed eyes, the other rising and falling very slightly with Duncan's shallow breathing, his bright gold head bent close to Dhugal's more reddish one. Beside Dhugal, his back to Kelson, was Father Lael, Cardiel's chaplain; and Cardiel himself watched over Lael's shoulder, hands braced on his thighs.

The presence of the two priests sent a chill of dread through Kelson's already fear-numbed brain, and another wave of nausea made him stumble as he moved closer still.

"Dear God, he isn't dying, is he?" he whispered.

Cardiel turned and caught him by the shoulders before he could fall.

"Easy, son! He's holding his own."

"But, Father Lael—"

"Is here as a surgeon, not a priest—at least so far. And I'm just here to lend moral support."

Swaying on his feet with relief, Kelson let himself sag against Cardiel for just a second, fighting sudden light-headedness.

"Oh, thank God! How bad is he?"

"Bad enough—but I think he should make it. The burns are superficial, and the nails will grow back, and his back looks worse than it is. He took some arrows, though, and he's lost more blood than we'd like. The wound they're working on is the worst."

"Easy," he heard Dhugal murmur, as Lael cut deftly around the arrow embedded in Duncan's shoulder and Dhugal tried to work it free. "Are you sure it's missed the lung?"

Kelson moved around behind Lael as the little priest grimaced and slipped a fingertip along the shaft and partway into the wound, probing to free the barbed arrowhead.

"The angle looks good. I don't *think* we're in the lung. He's bleeding from somewhere, though. Be ready when this thing breaks loose."

"I'm watching," Dhugal breathed. "Easy—"

Suddenly the arrow came away in his hands, Lael's hand with it, and the wound began to pump bright red.

"*Damn!*"

As Lael slapped a compress over the wound, leaning most of his weight on the heels of both hands as he shouted for Ciard, Duncan moaned and went greyer around the lips, his breath rasping in his throat. With a whispered oath, Morgan shoved Lael off balance and ripped away the compress, shuddering as he rammed two fingers into the wound and shut his eyes, drawing a ragged breath.

"Alaric, no!" Dhugal cried.

He tried to pull Morgan off as Lael, too, clamped a hand around Morgan's bare wrist in an attempt to stop him, but Morgan only shook his head. Kelson dropped to his knees and stared, all but paralyzed by shock, and Cardiel tripped over him trying to get around to Morgan.

"Morgan, are you crazy?" Lael gasped, still fighting him.

"He's hemorrhaging!" Morgan answered, though he was beginning to shake with exertion. "I've got to stop it."

"There's *merasha* in his system, for God's sake! Get *out* of there!"

"I can't let him bleed to death!"

"He *won't* bleed to death if you'll let me at him," Lael retorted, still trying to pull Morgan away while he blotted frantically at the blood seeping around Morgan's fingers. "He'll die of shock, though, if you don't do something about *that*. And you *can't*, if the *merasha* gets to you. Ciard, where's that iron?"

Abruptly, Kelson became aware of Dhugal's gillie bending closer with a red-hot poker wrapped at one end with an insulating cloth—and that Lael's hand was lifting to take it.

"Morgan, get his blood off your hands *now!*" Lael ordered. "Sire, he needs your help!"

Somehow, Kelson knew that Lael meant Duncan, not Morgan. As Morgan withdrew with a little sob, plunging bloody hands into a basin of water a whey-faced squire offered, Kelson clamped his own hands to either side of Duncan's sweat-slick face and reached for rapport—and recoiled instantly as he nearly got intertwined in the *merasha* disruption Morgan had been fighting.

God, how had he stood it?

He made himself go back, though, and his body arched in shared response with Duncan's as Dhugal threw himself across his father's body to hold him steady and Lael thrust the tip of the glowing iron into the wound.

Kelson's scream intertwined with Duncan's weaker cry as the agony jolted his concentration. He tried to damp both their pain, feeling his own pulse rate soar in response to Duncan's, but the *merasha* muddling Duncan's controls interfered with his own functioning. The stench of scorching

flesh immediately catapulted him back to Duncan's memory
of the stake, and the flames reaching hungry fingers toward
his body, beginning to scorch—

Only Morgan's dripping hands forcing him aside enabled
him to break the link, Morgan's more experienced control
driving through even *merasha* fog to jar him back into his
own mind and keep him there while he moderated Duncan's
distress. Ciard caught the king by the shoulders as he reeled,
overcome by vertigo, and quickly hauled him back from the
three laboring over Duncan as he became aware he was
about to be violently ill.

He fell to his hands and knees and retched himself empty.
Then he shuddered with dry heaves until he thought he must
surely cough up his guts with the bile, though the reaction
gradually began to abate. But his vision went grey after that,
and then black.

When Kelson came to himself again, he was lying on his
side, the front of his brigandine unbuckled, and Archbishop
Cardiel was bathing the back of his neck with a cloth wrung
out in cool water. With returning consciousness, all the horror of the past few hours came flooding back as well, but
when he tried too soon to sit up, his vision blurred and the
bile rose in his throat again.

"Lie back and drink this," Cardiel murmured, easing him
back to lean against his knee and pressing a cup into his hand.

"What is it?"

"Water. You're exhausted from the heat. Drink it down,
and I'll give you some more. You'll be all right in a little
while."

Kelson rinsed his mouth to get rid of the bile taste and
spat weakly to one side. Then, as he drank more deeply,
praying for the pounding in his head to cease, he realized
that he was not where he had been. A curtain had been strung
between himself and the rest of the tent, and low voices
spoke of the presence of several people behind it: Morgan,
Dhugal, Father Lael, and—

"Oh, *Jesu*! Duncan—is he—?"

"He's alive," Cardiel said, closing a hand firmly around
Kelson's on the cup and topping it off. "And he's in good
hands. Now, drink up. There's nothing you can do to help
him until you've got yourself in order."

"But, Alaric—Dhugal—"

"They've stopped the bleeding. He was given some drug that interferes with Deryni power, so they have to wait before they can do much more."

"*Merasha.*"

"I think that's what they called it. Now, drink that, or I'm not telling you another thing. They *don't* need another patient to worry about. None of the surgeons do."

Shaking, Kelson drained the cup. There was no arguing with that logic. When Cardiel refilled the cup, Kelson drained it again.

He was beginning to feel waterlogged as the archbishop refilled it a third time, but he kept sipping dutifully, propping himself on his elbows as Cardiel balled up a cloak and shoved it under his feet. After a few minutes, with some careful nudging on his part, the pain in his head began to abate. Unfortunately, awareness of his other responsibilities came flooding back to replace it.

"I've rested enough," he said, setting his cup aside. "I need casualty reports. Where're Ewan and Remie? And Gloddruth?"

"Lie flat for a while longer, Sire," Cardiel said, pressing Kelson's shoulders back when he would have tried to sit up instead. "Actual losses were relatively light, at least on our side, though the surgeons will be busy through the night patching up the wounded. All the fight seems to have gone out of the Mearans. Most of the prisoners seem eager to reaffirm their allegiance to you."

"Prisoners . . . ?"

Kelson closed his eyes for a few seconds, remembering Sicard toppling from his horse, an arrow protruding from one eye socket, then sighed dismally and laid an arm across his forehead.

"Did they tell you what I had to do to Sicard?"

"Aye." Cardiel's voice was low, expressionless. "He was taken in arms against you, Sire, and he refused to surrender."

"So I shot him," Kelson muttered.

"Aye, he shot him," Ewan said sternly, poking his head through an opening in the flap that led to the outside, as Kelson lifted his arm to look. "An' don't ye dare let him wallow in self-pity for *that* little lapse, Archbishop. The lad has guts. He executed one traitor to force the peaceful surrender of many others."

Unconvinced, and suddenly deadly tired, Kelson lurched to a sitting position, not caring that the sudden movement made his head throb for a few seconds.

"I still should have tried to bring him to trial."

"That was *his* choice, Sire."

"But—"

"Kelson, he was a dead man already, an' he knew it!" Ewan said, crouching down to take the king's forearm and look him in the eyes. "Think on it. He was sore wounded. He'd been taken in rebellion, an' his last son already killed. D'ye think he didna' know what his fate must be? Is it nae better to die wi' sword in hand, than face trial and execution as a traitor? Is nae one arrow better than the rope, or the headsman's sword—or drawin' an' quarterin'—"

Kelson swallowed and glanced at the ground between his knees. "I—hadn't thought about it that way," he admitted.

"I didna' think ye had," Ewan muttered. "'Tis not an easy thing, growin' up an' bein' king all at once, is it, laddie? If it's any consolation, it was no easier for yer father, God bless 'im."

Kelson smiled bleakly. "I suppose not."

"Let's have nae more o' this, then."

Kelson nodded and drew a deep breath, making himself brace against Ewan's words, the logical part of him knowing that the old duke was right, even though he would have wished it otherwise.

But then he thought of Loris, who ultimately had brought about this whole sorry state of affairs, and set his jaw resolutely as he looked up.

"Aye. You're right, Ewan," he said. "And I know another who is even more to blame than Sicard for this day's work. Where is Loris?"

"Secure, Sire," Cardiel said promptly, locking down his hand on Kelson's shoulder when the king would have gotten to his feet. "And Gorony as well. I think it might be best if you waited until morning to see them, however."

Kelson's grey Haldane eyes went dark and cold, and he sensed it took all of Cardiel's strength not to quail before them, even though he extended not a jot of Deryni control.

"I saw Gorony and managed not to kill him in cold blood," he said evenly. "What's the matter? Do you think Loris would be too much temptation?"

"Edmund Loris is enough to tempt even a saint to may-hem, Sire," Cardiel replied. "I know I would not trust *myself* to see him just now, knowing what he has done to Duncan, and what he did to Henry Istelyn."

"I'm not going to kill him without a trial, Thomas! Nor do I torture prisoners, however much I might be tempted."

"No one said you would, Sire."

"Then, why shouldn't I see him now?"

Cardiel braced his shoulders against Kelson's continued hard gaze, refusing to be baited, until finally Kelson lowered his eyes, regretting his outburst.

"You aren't afraid of me, are you?" he whispered.

"No, Sire. Not for myself, at least."

"Th' Archbishop is right, though, Sire," Ewan inter-jected, hunkering down for more intimate conversation with the king. "Why *not* wait 'til mornin'? Bein' captured by De-ryni is torture enough for the likes o' Loris an' Gorony. Let 'em stew for a while! The longer ye make 'em wait, worryin' what yer goin' t' do to 'em, the weaker they'll be."

Pulled up short again by Ewan's unarguable logic, Kelson glanced aside at the flap leading out of the tent.

"I wish I had that option, Ewan."

"An' why not?"

"I need to know where Caitrin's gone to ground. This war isn't over until she's taken, you know."

"Ah, weel, if that's all," Ewan said, a sly grin splitting his bristling red beard as Kelson turned to stare. "Take 'em to Laas, an' try 'em there. That's where *she* is."

"Caitrin?"

"Aye. An' Judhael an' what little remains of the rest o' the rebellion as well—yer bishops, too, Cardiel."

"But, how did you find out?"

Ewan made a snorting sound through his nose. "D'ye think only Deryni can make prisoners talk, lad, or that Loris an' Gorony are th' only ones we took?"

"No, but—"

"Believe me, Caitrin an' the rest're in Laas. I wouldna' tell ye if I wasna' sure."

"We'll want to leave first thing in the morning, then," Kelson said, starting to get up again.

"Nay, Sire, we'll rest th' army tomorrow, an' ride for Laas the day after."

"But, she could get away—"

Ewan shook his head. "She willna' flee," he said. "She willna' even fight, if ye handle her the way ye handled Sicard."

"You mean, shoot her?" Cardiel asked, shocked.

"Nah. What has she t' fight for, wi' her bairns all gone, an' her husband slain? Mark me, Sire. She'll na' fight. An' yer army needs rest. An' its king needs his rest, too."

"There're still things to be done," Kelson said stubbornly, beginning to buckle the front of his brigandine again. "I need to get reports off to Rhemuth, and—"

"And on the other side of that curtain," Cardiel said firmly, "are men who you will not be able to help if you tire yourself out doing things others could do, Sire."

Kelson's eyes flew to the curtain, as if he could pierce it with eyes alone. He nodded. "Duncan."

"And Alaric and Dhugal," Cardiel added.

"But—they're not injured."

"No. In a few hours, however, when the worst of the Deryni drug has passed from Duncan's system, I believe Alaric means to try a more—satisfactory healing. He—seemed concerned that he have support from you and Dhugal when he attempts it. He won't be able to count on that from you, if you've pushed yourself too far. You already collapsed once from the heat and overexertion."

Sighing, Kelson let his hands fall away from the buckles and bowed his head, suddenly feeling very tired.

"You're right. Both of you are right. I've been pushing myself so hard, for so long, it's sometimes difficult to realize there's a time to rest, too."

"That's my braw lad," Ewan muttered approvingly, detaching the plaid from his shoulders and shaking it out to lay under Kelson. "Dinna' ye worry about a thing."

"Make sure a reports gets off to Nigel, though," Kelson said around a yawn.

Ewan only nodded patiently as Kelson laid back on the plaid, Cardiel tucking a folded corner tenderly under his head.

"I do have one last question, Sire," Cardiel murmured, glancing meaningfully at Ewan as Kelson closed his eyes and the old border chief leaned nearer. "Is it true that Dhugal is really Duncan's son?"

Kelson barely had the energy to open his eyes and look at the archbishop.

"Who said he was?"

"*Dhugal* did, Sire," Ewan said. "Everyone's talkin' about it. He said he was Deryni, an' that Duncan was his father."

Smiling, Kelson closed his eyes again and sighed.

"It's true, Ewan," he breathed. "And it couldn't please me more that it's finally out in the open."

"It *pleases* you that your foster brother is a bastard?" Cardiel gasped.

"He isn't a bastard," Kelson said around another yawn, "though damned if I know how we'll ever prove that to anyone else's satisfaction. There was a secret marriage. His mother died soon after he was born, and Duncan didn't even know there'd been a child until a few months ago. That was all long before his ordination, of course."

"Well, I'd realized *that* from the timing," Cardiel said, indignation in his voice. "I wasn't concerned for Duncan's priestly status. But the implications for Dhugal—"

"Tell you all about it in the morning, Thomas," Kelson murmured. "Ewan, don't forget that report for Nigel. . . ."

He was asleep before Ewan's reply could register, only vaguely aware of the buzz of their voices, as they continued to speculate about Dhugal, and gentle hands beginning to remove his armor as he slipped deep into dreamless, exhausted sleep.

# CHAPTER NINETEEN

*As cold waters to a thirsty soul, so is good news from a far country.*

—Proverbs 25:25

One Deryni who could not yet allow himself the luxury of sleep was Bishop Denis Arilan, back in Rhemuth. Nor had he slept much the previous night. As Richenda and Nigel went out of the room, he settled back in his chair and closed his eyes, wearily running a spell to banish fatigue as one hand absently fingered the cross around his neck.

He did not envy Richenda and Nigel their next task. Since breaking the Torenthi assassination plot the afternoon before, all three of them had taken turns interrogating the prisoners—though the Deryni among them, three in all, were kept apart in a specially warded cell until Nigel should decide what to do with them. The others even Arilan could interview with impunity, since their memories could then be blurred to keep his Deryni identity secret.

It did not take long for a pattern to develop to the answers, though no one man had full details of the plot. But careful correlation of all the information gradually confirmed a convoluted scheme to kill Nigel (and as many of his three sons as might conveniently be arranged), rescue the captive King Liam, and then lie in wait for Kelson's return, so they could kill him, too. Or perhaps it was to kill Nigel *and* young Liam and place Liam's brother Ronal on the throne of both kingdoms, with his Uncle Mahael as regent. There were even hints that Morag had, indeed, known of the plot and approved it, in all its permutations.

She would deny everything, of course. Richenda and Nigel were on their way now to confront her on the issue; but because she was Deryni, they would not dare to force her to the question. The notion that Morag might have condoned the murder of her own son was too monstrous for Arilan to give it very serious credence, but some lesser degree of participation in the plot was almost certain. Captive queens were ever wont to intrigue for their escape, and a Deryni queen would be more adept than most.

Oh, why could the Torenthi question not have lain dormant for a few more years? With Wencit dead, young Alroy dead, and a child-king now on the Torenthi throne once more—and another child-heir in the wings—would it have been asking too much for the Council's worries to be confined to Gwynedd for a change?

Sighing, Arilan pressed his palms across both eyes and took a last deep breath to set his spell, feeling the fatigue wash out of his brain like indigo running from fresh-dyed cloth in a mountain stream, finally clear. He sighed again as he got slowly to his feet. The Council would be waiting.

But as he headed for Duncan's study, and the Portal there, passing the dim-lit household chapel on the way, he found a different Deryni queen than the one who had been most lately on his mind: Jehana, veiled head bent in prayer, her white raiment washed palest azure by the glow of the votive lights that burned before a statue of the Virgin close by the altar.

Surprised, for the basilica was Jehana's more usual place for devotions when she left her apartments, Arilan paused in the doorway and cast out cautiously with his mind—and recoiled as quickly, as he read the guilt and spiritual anguish radiating from her.

The effort of shutting his shields to the disharmony set his head to throbbing just behind his eyes, all of it magnified because of too little sleep, undoing much of what he had accomplished with his fatigue-banishing spell. He considered simply moving on, pretending he had not seen her, for any delay would make him late for the Council meeting, but he knew he would regret it if he passed up this opportunity to find out more about her motivations of the day before. From what Nigel had told him, he had already deduced that she must have learned of the plot through some use of her powers, else the decision to tell Nigel of it would not have presented so anguished a proposition. He wondered how she had justified her action, if only at the time—for she obviously was regretting it now.

So he made his shields nearly transparent as he moved quietly into the chapel, trusting that measure to keep him from being recognized as Deryni if she was, indeed, beginning to use her powers. He saw her tense as the rustle of his cassock intruded on her meditation, but he kept his eyes downcast as he approached to within a few feet of her and sank to his knees at a prie-dieu.

He prayed for wisdom and patience as he bowed his head in a brief prayer of his own. When he looked up, she had just turned to glance at him furtively. She flinched as their eyes met; but his acknowledgment of the glance made it impossible for her not to acknowledge in return.

"Good evening, daughter," he murmured, rising gracefully to fold his hands benignly at his waist. "I had thought all the household would be abed by now—and you usually pray in the basilica. I hope I haven't disturbed your devotions."

Her mind was as tightly shuttered as any Council Lord's; but if the shields protected her from any would-be intrusion by him, they also protected him from closer scrutiny.

"It doesn't matter," she whispered, so low he almost could not catch the words. "I can't pray in the basilica anymore. It's all a sham anyway. God will not listen. I am evil."

"Oh?" He cocked his head and looked at her more closely, certain now that her part in the previous day's events had triggered this latest depression. "And why do you say that?"

Smothering a little sob, she sat back on her heels, bloodless fingers partially masking her face.

"Oh, God, don't you mock me, too, Excellency," she cried. "You cannot have forgotten what I am. And yesterday I—I—"

"Yesterday, you saved the prince regent from a most terrible threat," Arilan said smoothly. "I have just come from speaking with him. He is very grateful."

"Grateful that I discovered the plot by use of my cursed powers?" she replied. "Aye, that is like Nigel of late. He is too much among Deryni, and he cannot see the danger. What does he care if I endanger my immortal soul to save his mortal flesh? He is my husband's brother, and I could not fail to warn him, once I knew, but—but—"

"But you fear that to use the powers God has given you, even in a good cause, is somehow suspect," he ventured.

She looked up at him more directly, uncertainty and shock playing in her tear-bright green eyes.

"How can you, a bishop, even suggest that God has anything to do with it?"

He smiled gently and eased down to sit on the kneeler of the prie-dieu beside her, hands now folded carefully on his knees.

"Allow me to ask a question in return, daughter," he said. "If a man were granted extraordinary physical strength, and found his friend slipping over a precipice, and could save him by means of his strength, bodily dragging him back to safety, should he not do it?"

"Well, yes, but—"

"In fact, would he not be remiss if he did *not* do it?"

"Of course, but—"

"Another example," Arilan continued. "An innocent man is on trial for his life, accused by those who would do him ill. A king's magistrate has been told of an eyewitness who can prove that the accused is innocent. But the informant is a tax collector—honest and diligent in the performance of his duty, but despised by men. Even so, should the magistrate not use the knowledge given him to produce the witness, arrive at the truth, and set the innocent man free?"

"Do you mean to imply that the Deryni are honest and diligent?"

"Some undoubtedly are. But it is only a parable, my lady." Arilan smiled. "One more. If a woman learns of a plot against an innocent man, but has always believed the source of the knowledge to be wicked—if reliable—should she not, even so, give warning, and thereby save an innocent life?"

"You're making it sound so clear-cut, so logical. It isn't the same!" she replied, tears welling in her eyes. "Bishop Arilan, you can't know how I suffer with such knowledge— how I long to be the same as other mortals. How can I make you understand?"

Still smiling, shaking his head in compassion, Arilan cast beyond the doorway with his powers to be sure of privacy and projected a glamour to repel idle intrusion.

"Oh, believe me, I understand, child," he said softly, letting his shields fall away and the silvery light of his aura begin to glow around him.

She gaped at him, dumb with shock, as he cupped his hands before him and conjured handfire: cool, quicksilver light brimming in his hands and spilling in a sharp radiance that lit his face from below and cast his handsome features in light-limned relief.

"A child's trick," he conceded, as he let the light contract and closed it in one hand, quenching its fire—though the nimbus around his head remained. "But it serves a purpose. It's time you knew me for what I am—and that I view what I am as a blessing, an enhancement of my relationship with the Creator—not a detriment."

Bonelessly Jehana collapsed sideways to a sitting position, both hands pressed to the stones on either side of her, as if contact with the earth might help to ground her bewilderment and shock. Her colorless face seemed carved of alabaster as she stared up at him, appalled.

"You're Deryni, too."

"Yes. Nor, I think, is that a terrible thing to be."

Shaking her head, tears spilling from her lashes, Jehana glanced over her shoulder at the Virgin gazing down from her star-studded pedestal, carved hands outstretched in compassion.

"I was taught otherwise," she said dully. "I have believed it all my life."

"Does belief alter truth, then?" Arilan asked. "Or is truth a constant, whether we believe or not?"

"You're confusing me! You play with the words!"

"I don't mean to confuse—"

"Yes, you do! You twist the words to mean what you want them to mean! You even use holy writ to—sweet *Jesu*, was it *you* who made Father Ambros change the lesson yesterday?"

"What lesson?" Arilan asked blankly.

"The reading for Mass," she murmured, her eyes going a little glassy as she remembered back. "Ambros changed it. It should have been the Commemoration of Saints Peter and Paul, but he read Paul's conversion—and Saint Camber . . ."

"So, whether or not it actually happened," Arilan told the Camberian Council a short while later, "Jehana *believes* that she had a vision of Saint Camber, and that he rebuked her for persecuting Deryni.''

"Is that possible?" Laran asked.

"That Camber rebuked her?"

"Yes."

"I don't know. Saint Camber talks to Duncan McLain, and Morgan—and now Jehana, apparently. He doesn't talk to me."

"Really, Denis," Vivienne muttered.

"Well, he doesn't. He hasn't, so far, at least. But Jehana insists that *someone*—and she was convinced it was I, once she knew what I was—*someone* somehow induced her chaplain to read the story of Paul's conversion on the road to Damascus."

"Ah, how the guilty heart can embellish," Sofiana murmured. "And *Saul, Saul, why persecutest thou me?* becomes *Jehana, Jehana . . .*"

"Precisely," Arilan agreed, as Tiercel slipped quietly through the doors to the Council chamber and took his seat to Sofiana's right. "*I* can't explain it. Maybe she *did* see Camber, though."

Kyri, cool and tranquil as a summer forest at Arilan's left, fingered a green glass bangle on one wrist and glanced languidly at the tardy Tiercel.

"Denis has just come from revealing himself to Jehana," she said, disapproval edging her tone. "And now he would have us believe that the Deryni-hating queen has been graced with a vision of Saint Camber." She favored him with a droll, weary grimace. "You have missed little, Tiercel."

"Kyri!" old Vivienne murmured reprovingly, as Arilan bristled, Laran scowled, and Barrett de Laney looked decidedly uncomfortable.

Kyri only yawned delicately and leaned her head against the high back of her chair, bored.

"Is it not true?" she asked, gazing idly at the crystal sphere hanging above the table, sparkling and cool in the purpled moonlight that filtered through the faceted dome above. "Why must we continue to waste time and energy on Jehana?"

The remark produced a flurry of comments, pro and con, which did not diminish until Barrett rapped on the table for silence.

"Enough," he said. "We shall table all further discussion of the queen for the nonce. And of Saint Camber. More pressing matters require our attention. Denis, how stands the Torenthi question?"

Twisting the amethyst on his hand, Arilan shrugged.

"The prisoners have been questioned," he said.

"By?" Vivienne asked.

"By Prince Nigel, with the assistance of Richenda and myself."

"Prince Nigel *does* Truth-Read, then?" Tiercel asked.

Arilan nodded. "He does. Not as well as a Deryni, perhaps, but that could be as much from lack of practice as from lack of ability. He is yet new to what power he has been given. Time will temper him."

"What of the plot itself?" Laran ventured. "Is the Lady Morag involved, as we suspected?"

Again Arilan shrugged. "Difficult to say. It seems most unlikely that she could *not* have known what her brother-in-law planned. Still, if she continues to deny—as *I* would deny, were I in her place—it will be impossible to call the question without a dangerous confrontation. I think neither Morag nor Nigel is ready to take that risk. Morag's sons are young, after all—younger than Kelson. Time is somewhat on her side."

"I see," old Vivienne murmured, her grey head cocked in an attitude of speculation. "You do not believe a Torenthi campaign will be necessary for a while, then?"

"Not this season," Arilan replied. "And perhaps not for several years, though Morag and Liam must be close-guarded, and Mahael will undoubtedly conduct border skirmishes from time to time. We shall have no immediate war on two fronts, if that is what concerns you."

Old Barrett shook his hairless head slowly, the blind emerald eyes gazing into some unknown realm.

"It is not that which concerns *me*," he breathed. "It is the war in Meara. If the king should die—"

"The king will not die," Sofiana said, at Barrett's right. "At least, he *should* not, if he played his strategies as he ought. Today's battle should have brought him victory."

"*Today's* battle?" Arilan murmured.

"What talk is this?" Laran said, sitting up straighter.

Even Kyri watched a little more attentively as Sofiana seemed to pull herself back from some inner contemplation long enough to sweep them with her black eyes.

"I have an agent in the royal entourage," she said softly. "He has been reporting to me on a regular basis since the Haldane host left Rhemuth. I am awaiting his contact even now."

"Well, *that's* cheeky," Laran muttered, as Vivienne leaned across him to pass a whispered comment to Kyri.

Tiercel only watched Sofiana the more avidly, along with the other men. Once more, Sofiana and her desert ways of silence and stealth had caught them all off-guard.

"You have an agent in the royal entourage," Arilan repeated, stunned. "Then, you *know* what has been happening of late?"

Sofiana, her pale, exotic face framed by the snowy drapery of the Moorish *qiffieh*, raised her eyes to the crystal sphere above their heads, already centering for the contact she expected.

"Yesterday, the Bishop-Duke of Cassan made a grave tactical error. He found the main Mearan army he had been searching for—or, rather, they found him."

"*Sancta Dei Genetrix!*" Tiercel breathed. "Sicard's host. Was McLain defeated?"

"He, personally? Yes. But not his army," Sofiana replied. "Apparently he ordered them to scatter when he realized he had led them into a trap, reasoning that Loris would try to take *him* at all cost, and the army might escape to fight another day—which is precisely what happened."

"Was Duncan killed?" Arilan asked, grave dread turning his soul to lead.

Sofiana shook her head, closing her eyes.

"Not killed—at least, not outright. Captured. But if still alive, he is now in the hands of Loris and Gorony, who understand the weakness of Deryni when plied with *merasha*."

Even those with least cause to love the half-breed Duncan McLain shuddered at that, for all had experienced the effect of *merasha* in the course of training. Arilan's hands were actually shaking as he tried to fold them carefully on the ivory table before him.

"You said your agent was in the Haldane camp," he whispered. "Then, Kelson knows of Duncan's capture, and the rout of the Cassani host?"

"He does. Somehow, young Dhugal MacArdry contrived last night to contact him. The king immediately turned all his resources toward the relief of the Cassani host, and the rescue of Duncan McLain, in particular, if he was still alive. They rode all through the night, and would have engaged the Mearan host early today. It will have been resolved by now.''

"Dear Lord, it has all come to naught, even as we spoke," old Vivienne murmured, twisting her gnarled hands together in despair. "Sofiana, have you *no* idea how it went? Can you tell us nothing further?''

Without opening her eyes, Sofiana spread her arms to either side and took the hands of Tiercel and Barrett, drawing in another deep, centering breath.

"The moon has risen. My agent will be making his arrangements for the contact. If you will join with me in providing a channel to assist him, we shall have our answers all the sooner.''

He was slight and wiry in the manner of the desert folk of Nur Hallaj, unassuming and unmemorable in appearance, as became a seasoned scout of the Haldane eastern levies. He was physically tired, but the news he had for his mistress lent both vigor and urgency to his mood as he passed through the Haldane camp, glancing up at the moon. Time was nearly upon him.

"What ho, Raif!" a sentry called amiably. "Off on the king's business again?''

Raif raised a friendly hand in greeting as he drew abreast of the sentry, shaking his head bemusedly.

"No, the king is abed. I thought I'd check horses once more before I turn in. And you?''

The man shrugged. "I just came on watch. I'm here for another two hours. I intend to make up for the lost sleep when I *do* go off duty, though. Raise a few snores for me, friend.''

"I shall. Sleep well.''

Raif mulled what he had learned as he made his way softly between two barrack tents and headed toward the horse lines. The news was better than he would have dared to hope a few hours before. He had already been gathering information for several hours, as the encampment sprang up all around him over the ruins of the Mearan Grand Army, deftly questioning dozens of soldiers who would remember little of their conversations in the morning. He had shadowed the compound where the prisoners slept, ringed by wary Haldane troops, and he had braved the battle surgeons' encampment, with its tents full of wounded and dying men.

Now, as the homey sounds of finished meals and slumber replaced the harsher martial sounds of earlier in the day, he could turn his thoughts to more pressing matters. The man he sought would be by the lancers' picket line.

His passage aroused no special interest. Scouts were as familiar as grooms and squires along the picket lines, for scouts, like the armored knights and men-at-arms, depended upon good horseflesh for their lives and livelihood. A few men raised hands in greeting as he strolled among the horses, pausing occasionally to stroke a velvet nose or satin flank, but no one challenged him. He found Hoag propped against a saddle just outside the tent of the lancers' captain, drinking wine by light of a tiny campfire. No one else was within earshot.

"Hello, Hoag," he murmured, tossing his cloak beside the man and flopping down to share his saddle backrest.

"Ah, Raif. I wondered whether you'd show before I passed out for the night. Have some wine?"

"A few swallows, perhaps. Thank you."

He caught Hoag with his eyes as the wineskin changed hands and he made contact, taking the man so deftly into thrall that Hoag was completely unaware that anything had changed.

"So, how goes it?" Raif went on, lifting the wineskin to his lips. "Is the captain still abroad?"

Hoag blinked, glassy-eyed, his voice low and devoid of expression.

"Nay, he's abed."

"Good. I'm sure he needs the sleep."

Raif glanced casually toward the horse lines as he set the wine-skin between them, pretending amiable camaraderie for the benefit of anyone watching, then poked at the pile of kindling near the fire until he found a twig. He broke off a few projecting bits as he lay back against the saddle beside the dazzled Hoag, then gave the man a lazy, casual smile as he smoothed a patch of sand between them, next to the wineskin.

"You know, today's strategies were really quite brilliant," he murmured, beginning to sketch a pattern which, to the uninitiated, would appear to be a battle diagram. "Do you realize what the king did, when he ordered the charge from the east?"

Hoag's eyes had followed Raif's every move, and now they tracked the pattern he traced, with increasing attention, slipping unerringly into the deeper trance state that Raif demanded.

"But, perhaps that's too complicated, after a long day's fighting," he murmured, touching Hoag's hand with the end of the twig.

Instantly, Hoag's eyelids fluttered and closed, his breathing deepening to that of sleep, though he leaned on his elbow still.

"Ah, yes," Raif whispered, never taking his eyes from Hoag's as he tossed his twig into the fire, "you look very, very tired, Hoag."

Hoag's only sound was a tiny, relieved sigh as he collapsed back against the saddle.

Raif watched him carefully for several seconds, moving the wineskin into the circle of his arm, then glanced around again before himself settling slowly to a supine position beside his sleeping subject, head cradled on one arm. After a few more minutes, himself asleep to all outward perceptions, he shifted drowsily so that one hand sprawled across Hoag's arm around the wineskin, confirming the physical contact he needed in order to draw through the link he had created.

Then he set himself to trancing, pushing himself deeper, deeper, so that the glow of the firelight behind his closed eyelids gently receded along with the fading sounds of the camp around him, the warmth drew back to only barely discernable levels, and he was at last ready to cast his mind northeastward, toward the woman who awaited his call.

Images of the day's battle, bright and strong: Kelson's forces sweeping to the top of the last range of hills ringing the Mearan encampment, surging downward to surprise the Mearan host.

Duncan, his body bloodied from scourging and other tortures, chained groggily to the stake, the flames licking higher, nearer . . . magic to deflect the arrows . . . Dhugal's daring rescue . . . Loris and Gorony captured . . . Sicard choosing death at Kelson's hands rather than face trial and execution for his treason . . . the Mearan host brought to its knees in surrender—and plans to rest a day at Dorna before heading west to Laas, where the Princess Caitrin had fled to make her last stand.

Duncan's status? Rumors that, though grievously used, he would survive; that Morgan employed his healing powers alongside the surgical skills of young Dhugal MacArdry—and that Dhugal was Duncan's son!

Uproar swept through the Council when the link was released, strategic and military considerations giving way, as usual, to those concerns that were, in the Council's judgment, more practical.

"Why didn't you tell us about Duncan and Dhugal?" Laran demanded of Arilan, who was as astonished as any of the rest of them at the news. "Duncan's son! Why, the implications are staggering!"

"But, I didn't know!" Arilan protested. "As God is my witness, I didn't—but, the possibilities. . . . Good God, you don't suppose he could be a healer, too, do you?"

The mere suggestion was enough to send the Council into loud, agitated debate for several minutes.

Tiercel de Claron only laughed and shook his head, leaning both hands on the arms of his chair.

"Oh, this is marvelous! The rogue Deryni has a rogue Deryni bastard!"

"Tiercel!" Vivienne muttered, glaring at the youngest member of the Council.

But it was Sofiana who returned them to the more important point; Sofiana who had seen what the others had not, in their preoccupation with the immediate implications of the new information.

"And what of Kelson?" she asked softly, sweeping them with her bright gaze. "Should we not consider what he has done?"

As they muttered among themselves, she went on.

"This is not the first communication I have had from my agent on the new campaign," she told them. "I believe it was Lady Vivienne who complained, not many weeks ago, that Kelson must learn to be ruthless?"

"So I said," Vivienne conceded, matching Sofiana's gaze with one of challenge. "And so I still maintain."

"Nor do I disagree," Sofiana replied, smiling enigmatically. "However, I put it to you that the king has now accomplished a great many of the things we associate with mature, responsible, and, yes, ruthless kingship. He killed his enemies at Llyndruth Meadows, as was required of him. After trial, he executed Prince Llewell for murder, when he could have struck him down with impunity at the scene of the crime and no one would have said a word against him. He executed Prince Ithel and Brice of Trurill, also after trial, and decimated their officers.'' She drew breath again.

"Now he has cut down Sicard of Meara, as you have seen, rather than waste more lives bringing to justice a man who has already cost too many lives. It was a logical measure, and one that I must applaud, but it is not the merciful act of a child-king. I maintain that Kelson Haldane is now sufficiently ruthless even for our number.''

# CHAPTER TWENTY

*So he overcame the destroyer, not with strength of
body, nor force of arms, but with a word subdued
he him that punished.*

—Wisdom of Solomon 18:22

The following morning required that Kelson be more ruthless, still, as he and Cardiel approached the tent where Loris
and Gorony lay prisoners. Well-armed guards of the Haldane
lancers ringed the tent, and Ciard O Ruane, Dhugal's faithful
gillie, met them in the entryway, glancing back through the
tent flap before pulling the edges together with his hands
behind his back.

"Good morning, Ciard," Kelson murmured, as the gillie
sketched him and Cardiel a perfunctory bow. "A quiet night,
I take it?"

"As quiet as a tomb, Sair, once we stopped tha' madman
Loris' lyin' tongue," old Ciard muttered. "He wouldna'
cease his rantin', so we had tae gag him—he that brought
about th' Old MacArdry's untimely death. How is th' Laird
Dhugal this mornin'—an' his—father?"

"Ah, you've heard it, too, then," Kelson said. "They're
fine. Tell me, though, Ciard, does that bother you?—that
Dhugal is Duncan's son, rather than Caulay's?"

Ciard shook his grizzled head stubbornly. "I canna' speak
for the clan, Sair, but young Dhugal is *my* chief, an' will be
sae long as he lives, whether he's Caulay's son or only his
grandson. Th' borders inherit by tanistry. Dhugal was *chosen* as th' next chief, an' could hae been, even if he'd been
nae blood relative to Caulay at all. I dinna' think yon Duke
of Cassan can pass his title in th' same manner, however.

273

Methinks he'll need more proof than merely his word, that Dhugal is his legal heir. An' a bishop's son—"

"Duncan wasn't a bishop when Dhugal was born, Ciard," Cardiel said. "He wasn't even a priest. But you're right that it will take more than just his word to prove Dhugal's legitimacy. Maybe there's some Deryni way."

"Aye, that's problematical," Ciard agreed, apparently nonplussed by the prospect of Deryni magic, as many borderers were. "But even though ye believe he's tellin' th' truth—an' *I* do—it'll take more than that t' prove it to th' satisfaction o' most. Ye canna' be considered an unbiased witness, after all, Sair. An' I dinna' know what other Deryni ye might call upon, but if they count themselves yer friends, they canna' be considered unbiased, either. I dinna' envy ye yer task."

"I don't envy it, either," Kelson said, "but I'll figure out something." He sighed. "I suppose I ought to see the prisoners now."

"Aye, Sair. There's sommat ye should know, though, before ye go in." He reached into the front of his jerkin and pulled out a wadded kerchief which he opened to disclose two heavy gold rings set with amethysts. "I took these off o' Loris yesterday. There's sommat odd about 'em. I ken they're bishop's rings, Archbishop," he added, with a nod toward Cardiel, "but—weel, ye know that we border folk hae th' Second Sight sometimes. An'—"

"And you have more of it than most," Kelson murmured. "Dhugal's told me. Go on. You don't have to explain."

"Weel, then, ye willna' think it strange if I tell ye that I wouldna' touch th' rings bare-handed unless I was sure I was well warded—"

Kelson raised an eyebrow in surprise. "You know about warding?"

"Ach, o' course, lad. Hasna' Dhugal ever told ye?"

"No."

"Weel, 'tis old border custom. Ask him about it sometime. I dinna' ken that it's the same as yer Deryni warding, but it does the same job. In any case, be careful wi' th' rings. Would I be right in assumin' that one o' them belongs t' Bishop Duncan?"

Cardiel took the cloth with the nested rings and nodded. "Aye, and before that it was Henry Istelyn's."

"Ach, the puir, sainted man," Ciard muttered, crossing himself piously. "Mayhap that explains why Loris was a-cryin' out in his sleep last night, an' kept yammerin' about demons comin' t' get him. 'Tis he who had Istelyn murdered, was it not?"

"Aye." Cardiel wrapped up the rings and tucked them into the front of his cassock, as Kelson shifted uneasily from one foot to the other.

"We'll deal with that later, Ciard," the king said in a low voice. "Right now, I want to get on with my questioning."

"He willna' gie ye much help, I fear," Ciard muttered. "They've both got foul mouths on 'em, fer priests. Th' monsignor shut up after a few smart cuffs, but like I told ye, we had t' gag Loris t' get any peace at all."

"He'll speak civilly to *me*," Kelson said, motioning for Ciard to pull aside the tent flap. "I don't look forward to this, but he'll tell me exactly what I want to know."

He braced himself as he went inside. Guards snapped to attention as he appeared—four of the scouts who were accustomed to Deryni methods of working—and a disheveled Loris and Gorony bestirred themselves to sit up. The two were laden with chains, clad only in once-white linen singlets, stripped of all ecclesiastical pretense. Gorony looked lucid enough, and wisely held his tongue as Kelson and the archbishop paused to look at him, but Loris' blue eyes blazed above his gag with the undisguised hatred of the already doomed.

"Was it your idea to torture Duncan?" Kelson asked Gorony, without preamble, turning his Truth-Reading talent on the captive priest.

Gorony raised his eyes defiantly to Kelson's.

"No."

"Don't bother to lie to me, Gorony. I can read you like a book. Where has Caitrin gone?"

"I don't know—and I wouldn't tell you if I did."

"You do know—and you *will* tell me. Guards—"

At his signal, Jemet and Kirkon moved in to pin Gorony's arms.

"Don't you dare touch me, you filthy Deryni bastard!" Gorony ranted, lashing out with his feet as Kelson came closer, and nearly catching Kelson in the crotch. "Take your bloody—"

Without prompting, Raif came behind Gorony and thrust a riding crop cross-wise between his teeth, hands pulling back from either end to yank Gorony's head immobile against his chest, while the fourth man tackled Gorony's legs with his full weight to still them.

"Thank you, gentlemen," Kelson murmered, crouching to set his hands to either side of Gorony's head, and forcing rapport. "Gorony, stop fighting me!"

Immediately, Gorony's body relaxed, eyes rolling upward in their sockets, and Raif was able to lower his crop loosely across Gorony's throat, still supporting the prisoner against his chest.

"Now, whose idea was it to torture Duncan?" Kelson repeated.

The answer welled up in all its dimensions, read from the twisted mind, and Kelson nearly retched at the foulness of it. At his grimace, Cardiel knelt down beside him, though he did not touch him.

"Are you all right?"

Kelson nodded, his eyes a little glazed with shock, but he did not allow the rapport to slip.

"This is like taking a swim in the castle middens," he muttered, "in the summertime. He has a lot to answer for. Let's see if we can find out about Caitrin, before I lose my breakfast."

He found the information he needed, and sent Gorony relentlessly into unconsciousness before withdrawing. His hands were trembling as he pulled away, and he wiped them against his thighs in distaste as he glanced at his shaken scouts.

"You felt some of it, didn't you?" he murmured, as the scouts released Gorony and turned their attention to the cowering Loris. "Sorry, gentlemen. I'm afraid a little spill-over can be an occupational hazard for those who work regularly with Deryni. I suspect that's part of what makes you such good scouts. Unfortunately, we're going to have to repeat the process with Loris. If you'll release him as soon as I have control, that will make it easier for you."

"We'll do what makes it easier for *you*, Sire," Raif said in a low voice, signalling the others to pounce on Loris, who was trying to crawl out of their reach. "Will you want his gag removed?"

"Not necessary. His mind will be foul enough, without having to listen to his foul mouth."

Loris wriggled and squirmed as the scouts pinned him to the ground, a low, animal whimpering vibrating in his throat as Kelson knelt down beside him.

"I don't know why I bother doing this," he said softly, fixing the rebel archbishop with his grey Haldane eyes. "I have enough already to hang you several times over—I should never have allowed you to live, three years ago—but I won't send a man to his death unless I've seen the evidence for myself. I almost wish this process were more unpleasant for you, so you could feel a little of the anguish you've inflicted on others in the name of your hatred. Fortunately for you, the 'cursed powers of the Deryni' are benign in responsible use; and I hope never to succumb to the temptation to use them irresponsibly—though I confess that you push me very near the brink, Edmund Loris."

With that, he laid his hands across Loris' forehead, covering the blazing blue eyes, and forced rapport, allowing a small corner of Loris' mind to gabble on in hysteria and fear at the intrusion.

"I have him," he whispered, giving the scouts a chance to draw back before he began.

Reading Loris was even more loathsome than reading Gorony had been, for Loris, in addition to his other perversions, had revelled in the grisly death of Henry Istelyn, and had himself provided the specific instructions to the executioners as to how the killing should be accomplished. With dread fascination, Kelson found himself drawn into a precise and graphic recall of the execution, in all its gory details, and after that, an equally exacting recounting of Duncan's torture.

There had been other episodes as well, of which Kelson had known nothing: inquisitions and burnings of suspected Deryni in many outlying areas, while Loris was Archbishop of Valoret. Those, added to the expected psychic stench of Loris' long-standing and unreasoning hatred of the Deryni, contrived to leave Kelson gasping when, at last, he prepared to withdraw.

But then the king's attention was caught by something he had *not* anticipated. He was in Loris' nightmare of the night before—only, it was no nightmare to Kelson.

For Loris had dreamed of Saint Camber. Kelson was as sure of that as he was of anything he had ever seen. It was a demonized visual image of the renegade Deryni saint, colored by Loris' own hatred and fear of anything to do with magic and the Deryni race, but the face matched the paintings Kelson had seen from half a dozen sources, and the words of Loris' apparition spoke of temperance and tolerance, chastising Loris for his persecution. It had terrified Loris, and small wonder.

Kelson left Loris painlessly unconscious when he had read all he could stomach; no sense inviting further emotion-charged exchanges with a man who was half-mad. Coolly, and with no more regret than he might have given to crushing a poisonous serpent, Kelson knew what he would do to Loris, once they reached Laas. Far more important, for now, was the source of Loris' nightmare; and Kelson thought he knew what might have triggered the episode in the guilty archbishop.

"I've learned all I need to know," he said as he stood, calling the scouts to attention with a glance. "I'll deal with them when we reach Laas. Have them ready to move in the morning."

"To Laas, Sire?" Jemet asked.

"Aye, to Laas. That's where Caitrin is. Ciard?" he called, as he thrust aside the tent flap. "Pass the word to the commanders that we leave for Laas at first light. That's where Caitrin and what's left of the rebel army have gone. And no one's to have any contact with the prisoners except to see to their physical needs. Kirkon, you can gag them if they get too verbally abusive, but no one is to converse with them or answer any questions. I want them to sweat a little, wondering what I have in store for them. Is that clear?"

"Aye, Sire."

"Ciard, clear?"

Ciard chuckled appreciatively. "Aye, Sair. Guid lad! We'll make a borderer out o' ye yet."

"Coming from you, I take that as a compliment."

But Kelson's smile faded to weary wistfulness as he and Cardiel headed back toward the tent where Duncan lay, and he had Cardiel show him the rings again before they went in.

They found Duncan conscious and coherent, if still a little woozy from the headache that was always a legacy of *mer-*

*asha*, and weak from loss of blood, but otherwise reasonably healed of his wounds and the injuries he had received. He would have a scar from the cautery they had been obliged to do on his shoulder wound, and only time would grow new nails to replace those torn out by Gorony's pincers, but neither fingers nor toes were as raw-looking as they had been, and his healed wounds and burns looked thirty *days* old rather than thirty hours.

Lying on a camp bed in Kelson's tent, his head propped on a mound of pillows while Dhugal fed him soup, he looked almost his old self—pale and thin, if in need of a shave—but the brightness in his eyes came of returning strength, not fever. Both father and son looked up as Kelson and Cardiel entered, and Duncan managed a game smile that Kelson had feared never to see again, twenty-four hours before.

"Welcome, Sire," Duncan said around a mouthful of soup. "Forgive me if I don't rise to greet you more appropriately, but I fear my physicians might do me more harm than Gorony did, if I get out of this bed."

"Just because he's still alive," Dhugal said disapprovingly, "he thinks he should be able to dash right back into his old duties. Maybe if *you* tell him how close he came to dying, Kelson, he'll believe it."

"He'd *better* believe it," Kelson said, hooking a stool closer with a booted toe and sitting at the foot of Duncan's cot, nodding as Morgan emerged from behind a curtain beyond. "It's true. I was there. And I doubt Alaric is going to let you dash *anywhere* for a while, are you, Alaric?"

"No."

"I won't be left behind," Duncan said, warning in his voice as he glanced among the three Deryni.

Morgan, who had taken time out for a much-needed nap after working at Duncan's healing for most of the morning, stretched and sat down on a stool opposite Dhugal, gently taking Duncan's near wrist to monitor his condition.

"Don't worry, we're not going to leave you behind. You'll go on a litter for a few days, though. You're not riding for a while with those feet."

"Spoilsports, all of you!" Duncan muttered. "What would you do if I refused?"

"For once, you can't." Morgan grinned impishly as he released Duncan's wrist. "Don't you remember? You let me set control triggers while we were working the deep healings.

It was one of the few times when you were in your right mind. If I say sleep, you'll sleep, and no arguments. For that matter, both of your other physicians also have that authority. You can't even argue with Father Lael.''

After a moment's petulant consideration, Duncan grimaced and lay back on his pillows.

"Where *is* Lael? How's he taking all of this?''

"He's sleeping,'' Morgan replied, "with a little help from yours truly. He may not be Deryni, but he wore himself out doing things Deryni *can't* do, while you were still so full of *merasha*. And this morning, he let me pull energy while I was working on your healing.''

"Thank God he's so sensible about all this Deryni business,'' Cardiel murmured. "I knew he was a good man, or I wouldn't have had him as my chaplain, but one never knows how even the best man will react under extremes of stress.''

Dhugal grinned as he offered Duncan another spoonful of soup.

"Well, he survived his trial by fire beautifully—and *I* certainly learned a lot from him. He's a natural-born physician. Too bad he isn't Deryni. Don't ever let him get away, Archbishop.''

"Hmmm, I don't intend to do *that*.''

"He didn't even seem shocked when he found out about Father and me,'' Dhugal went on. "Incidentally, Kelson, I'm afraid that's the talk of the camp this morning.''

"What's the talk of the camp?'' Duncan asked.

"That you're my father.''

"Oh.''

"I hope you're not angry,'' Dhugal said. "I know we'd agreed to keep it secret until you had more proof than just your word, but I had to tell Ciard, to get him to help me contact Kelson, and I'm afraid I—blurted it out again when I was trying to fight my way through to you. I had to come up with *something* to divert Loris.''

"Well, I'm sure that diverted him,'' Duncan muttered. "What did he say? The Deryni bastard has a Deryni bastard?''

"You heard! Or did you guess?''

Duncan blew out breath through pursed lips. "I doubt you'd believe it really *was* a lucky guess. I wish it hadn't come out just yet, though." He turned his eyes to Cardiel. "Are you disappointed, Archbishop?"

"Disappointed? Are you joking?"

"But, it's a scandal for the Church—as if my being Deryni wasn't enough of a scandal."

"We've survived worse scandals," Cardiel answered. "I'm most concerned for young Dhugal—though Ciard doesn't seem to think illegitimacy would harm Dhugal as Chief of the MacArdrys. If you want him as your heir to Cassan and Kierney, though, *that's* going to take some doing."

"I know," Duncan whispered, collapsing back against his pillows and closing his eyes briefly as he winced. "I don't want to think about it right now." He drew a deep breath. "Alaric, I hate to ask this, but I can't play the stoic Deryni any longer. My head has started throbbing again from the *merasha* hangover. Could you please put me out for a little while?"

"Certainly. You shouldn't tire yourself anyway. Center the best you can, and I'll take care of it."

As Morgan laid his hand on Duncan's forehead, thumb and middle finger resting lightly on the fluttering eyelids, Duncan drew another deep breath and let it out slowly.

"I'll be all right when I've had some more sleep," he murmured, around a wide yawn. "They kept me so heavily drugged, though, for so long. . . ."

His voice trailed off as Morgan eased him into deep dreamless sleep, and Morgan kept the rapport for several minutes, strengthening other pathways and sending more healing energy into Duncan's weakened body until he was finally satisfied with the balance.

"*Merasha* must be terrible," Dhugal breathed, when Morgan had withdrawn and looked up at them again.

"It is. That's right—you've never been given *merasha*, have you? Either of you?" he added, with a glance at Kelson.

As both of them shook their heads, he went on. "Well, we'll have to remedy that—sometime this winter, perhaps, after we're back in Rhemuth. You should know what it's like, firsthand. Within limits, there are ways to fight some of the effects, if you know what you're doing—but you can't *know* what you're doing unless you've experienced it. I suspect that *merasha* actually helped Duncan withstand some of what Loris and Gorony put him through."

"I suppose that makes some kind of sense," Dhugal muttered, "though the logic escapes me just now. Is *merasha* worse than when my shields used to clash with anyone's besides Father's?"

"Far worse," Morgan replied.

"No wonder Duncan's in such bad shape, then," Kelson said. "How is he *really*, Alaric?"

"He'll be well on the road to recovery, once he's shaken the last effects of the *merasha*," Morgan replied. "Not that he'll be able to leap right back into action, however. He won't ride for a while with those feet, even if he were strong enough to stay in the saddle—which he isn't, with all the blood he lost. And any kind of glove is out of the question until his fingers have a chance to toughen up a little."

"Well, I don't think this will interfere with his tender fingertips," Kelson said, holding out his hand to Cardiel for the cloth-wrapped rings. "Having it back will probably give him some comfort. Ciard took these off of Loris yesterday, after he was captured. I've just come from questioning the slimy bastard."

"Why, what a thing to say about Ciard," Morgan chided, chuckling as he carefully unwrapped the wad.

"You know whom I'm talking about."

"Ah, yes, all too well." Morgan finally uncovered both bishop's rings and held them up, still grasping them only through several layers of insulating cloth, Duncan's in his right hand and Loris' half-forgotten in his left.

"Well, well, well. I'd wondered, in passing, what became of this. Ugh!" He shuddered. "Loris' psychic stench is all over it. I can't believe he actually had the audacity to wear Istelyn's ring."

Kelson grimaced. "I doubt there's much he *wouldn't* have the audacity to do. He got more than he bargained for in this case, however. *Something* gave him nightmares about Saint Camber."

"Indeed? Well, I can't say I'm surprised. Duncan will want it back, though. Duncan?"

Still keeping the rings insulated, Morgan lightly touched Duncan's wrist. Almost at once, the blue eyes fluttered open, gradually focusing on the ring Morgan held before them.

"Istelyn's ring," Duncan murmured, raising one raw-fingered hand to reach for it. "Where did you get it?"

"Where did you last see it?" Morgan countered, pulling it out of Duncan's reach. "I think it's going to want cleaning. Loris wore it."

A shudder passed through Duncan's entire body as the memory came flooding back.

"I know he did. At least he didn't cut it off my finger, as he did Istelyn's. I hope it gave him nightmares!"

"Actually, it appears it did," Morgan answered. "The question is, will it give *you* nightmares, after what it's been through? We know from past experience that it picks up strong psychic imprints."

Duncan grunted in the negative and shook his head, reaching for the ring again.

"Camber and Istelyn are stronger than Loris. Give it to me, Alaric. I promise not to do a repeat of the day of my consecration."

"For all our sakes, I hope you don't," Morgan muttered. But he gave the ring to Duncan, letting Cardiel wrap up Loris' again and replace it in his cassock.

Duncan held the ring between his thumbs and forefingers for several seconds, apparently staring through it, then blinked and grinned.

"I don't think Camber liked having this ring associated with Loris," he whispered.

"Oh?" Cardiel said.

"Alaric, bring Thomas into link with us. All of you, join in. It isn't a cleaning this ring wants. I think Camber has something to say to all of us."

As Cardiel blinked in astonishment, Morgan rose to give him his seat, setting one hand on the back of the archbishop's neck as Cardiel sat. Kelson and Dhugal moved closer to Duncan's other side.

"Close your eyes and relax, Thomas," Morgan murmured, gently extending control as Cardiel obeyed. "I know you've worked with Arilan before. Don't ask how I know. Just don't fight me. Let yourself float. I'll shield you, if anything gets too intense."

Cardiel's head nodded, chin sinking to rest on his chest, and when Morgan had made the link secure, he set his other hand on Duncan's forearm and slid into the rapport Duncan had already forged with Dhugal and Kelson. He did not close his eyes, so he saw Duncan slip the ring into place on his right hand.

Then another presence was in the link, besides the other four, and he had the impression of ghostly hands resting gently on his head in benison. It was the "Camber touch" he had learned long ago to associate with his healing gift, but it was also something more: a presence even more real than the apparition he had seen at Duncan's consecration; an impression of vast approval and support as well as blessing, filling him for a few seconds with an incredible sense of reasoned purpose and well-being.

Then the image was gone, the warm afterglow remaining only in memory, and Morgan was blinking as he let the links dissolve, absently kneading Cardiel's shoulder in reassurance as the human archbishop also blinked and raised his head to stare at them all in wonder, finally having shared a little of the magic in which he had long believed, but which he had never before experienced for himself.

"Was that—Camber?" Cardiel whispered haltingly, when at last he dared to speak.

Duncan cupped his left hand protectively over the ring on his right and cradled both next to his chest, careful not to jar his nailless fingertips.

"I'd ask who else you think it could have been," Duncan replied, "but I shouldn't like to sound facetious. One thing is certain: it wasn't Loris. *Now* do you understand why Kelson wants to restore Camber to his proper place of honor?"

"But, I'm not Deryni," Cardiel murmured. "I thought he only appeared to other Deryni. He's a *Deryni* saint."

"Yes, but he was originally the Defender of Humankind, as well as being patron of Deryni magic," Morgan said. "Nor do we know that he only appears to Deryni. We only know that a few Deryni in this tent have seen him before. Besides, he didn't exactly *appear* to you; you saw him through *our* link with the ring—not that that lessens the experience, to be sure. Duncan, do you think it was something new that has been added to the ring, or some residual from before?"

Duncan shook his head. "Hard to say. I don't *think* it was residual. Thomas, we're fairly certain that the ring was made out of a chalice or some other Mass vessel—apparently something closely associated with Camber himself, that he himself used. Do you happen to know who made Istelyn's ring?"

"I have no idea. I suppose it's quite possible that a piece of altar plate might have been melted down to make it, though. But, Istelyn wasn't Deryni—was he?"

"Not that anyone knows," Morgan answered. "And unfortunately, we'll never get a chance to find out. I'd be interested to learn more about his family, though."

"I'll see what I can find out, when we get back to Rhemuth," Cardiel replied. "And speaking of Rhemuth, will you be able to contact Richenda tonight, Alaric? Nigel should be told that this Mearan matter is just about resolved."

"It isn't resolved until I have Caitrin's surrender," Kelson interjected, before Morgan could answer, "but I agree that they ought to know what's happened so far. Besides, I suspect it will be easier to make the contact from here than from Laas."

Morgan sighed. "It won't be *easy* from *here*, given how tired we all are. But you're right; it won't get any easier. We'll try around midnight, after I've had time to sleep a little more. If I may, I'll ask all of you to assist me in the link—except Duncan, of course."

"Alaric, I'm not an invalid—" Duncan began.

"Yes, you are! And the sooner you stop being difficult, the sooner you *won't* be an invalid."

"I want to help!"

"You can help most by going to sleep."

The suggestion was backed by psychic insistence, and Duncan yawned hugely as he slumped back against his pillows, fighting to keep his eyes open.

"Alaric, that isn't fair," he complained around another yawn.

"*Life* sometimes isn't fair," Morgan countered, touching Duncan lightly between the eyes. "We all know that from bitter experience. Now, go to sleep."

# CHAPTER TWENTY-ONE

*He hath stripped me of my glory and taken the
crown from my head.*

—Job 19:9

They were not able to make contact with Richenda that
night; but they did the following—and learned of all the Torenthi intrigues that had been developing since their last contact.

"Now it's even more important that we bring this to a
speedy conclusion," Kelson told Morgan the next morning,
as they rode toward Laas, sweltering in the summer heat of
the plains. "It sounds like things are under control, but I
should be there to deal with the situation personally."

Nothing had changed in Rhemuth by the time they laid
siege to Laas, a week later. Duncan continued to grow
stronger with each passing day, finally abandoning his litter
for good on the day they arrived, though the toes of his boots
were cut out to spare his healing feet and he wore lightweight
gloves to protect his tender fingertips. He still tired easily
and would for some time, given what he had suffered, but
he knew how much it irked Loris and Gorony to see him
riding when he should have been consumed to ashes, and it
gave him satisfaction to watch them mutter to one another
as they rode in chains between their guards.

Meanwhile, Kelson and the grand army of Gwynedd laid
siege to the city of Laas, numbers swollen by the addition
of the Mearan partisans who had sworn Kelson their loyalty
after the battle of Dorna. The shackled Loris and Gorony
rode with a handful of other Mearan partisans who had re-

mained yet unwilling to swear the king their allegiance. The
bodies of Sicard and Ithel traveled in makeshift coffins in
the back of a sumpter wagon and had begun to stink in the
heat.

Just before noon on the day following their arrival, when
the city had had ample opportunity to worry about the camp-
fires of the Haldane host spread wide across the plain the
night before, Kelson rode under a parley flag to the edge of
bowshot from the city walls, escorted by Dukes Alaric,
Ewan, and Duncan. Archbishop Cardiel, Dhugal, and an
honor guard of six Haldane knights also accompanied the
king, Baron Jodrell and a further six guards shepherding
Loris and Gorony. At length, a lone herald rode out from a
postern door in the city gate, taut and professionally expressionless beneath his own white parley banner.

"My mistress bids me ask your intentions, King of Gwynedd," the man said, sparse but courteous in the salute he
rendered Kelson and his company.

Kelson, his open-faced helmet crowned with gem-studded
gold, studied the man quietly.

"Your mistress will have guessed that my intentions cannot be altogether peaceful, under the circumstances," he
said. "Surely, she will have noted that we hold captive her
former general, Edmund Loris, and the priest Gorony, and
that others formerly of her service likewise ride beneath Haldane banners. In addition there have been—other devel-
opments that I suspect she would rather hear from someone
of higher rank—no offense to yourself intended."

The man raised his head a little more proudly, but his
words were tempered with care.

"I am a knight and my lady's ambassador, Sir King. I
believe that betokens her trust in me, to carry what message
you will."

Kelson glanced at the reins in his gloved hands, red leather
stark against white. He and Dhugal had argued over the
choice of envoys to bring the Mearan pretender the news—
of husband and son slain, as well as Kelson's terms—but
Dhugal had spoken from the vantage point of kinsman and
had won, in the end.

"There are circumstances unknown to you, Sir Knight,
which are best entrusted to your lady's ears alone. Therefore, it is my desire to send my own envoy back with you,

to treat with your lady. I trust that she will guarantee his safe conduct?"

"Sire! My lady is an honorable woman."

"Aye, we all *try* to be honorable," Kelson said wearily. "Will you give my envoy safe conduct?"

"Of course." The envoy eyed Morgan and Duncan a little suspiciously. "Though I do not think my lady would be pleased to receive Deryni—no offense intended to your lordships," he added.

Kelson smiled wanly. "I had thought to send her an earl, not a duke," he said quietly. "And a kinsman as well, though I fear their last parting was not on the best of terms. Will she receive her nephew, Earl Dhugal MacArdry, do you think?"

The man gave Dhugal a long, measured look, then returned his eyes to the king, suddenly uneasy.

"Her offer of safe conduct will extend to the earl," he said haltingly, "only—do you know what has happened to Lord Sicard, Sire?"

Kelson nodded gravely.

"I do. But that news is for your lady first," he said, "and best come from Earl Dhugal. Will you take him to her now?"

Dhugal and the envoy exchanged hardly a dozen words as they rode toward the gates of Laas. There was little they could say. Dhugal was solemn with the weight of the news he bore to Caitrin, and the envoy could hardly be expected to welcome the bearer of terms which almost certainly told the end of assertions of Mearan independence.

Betokening his status as ambassador rather than warrior-earl, Dhugal wore riding leathers instead of war harness, with neither sword nor dagger at his belt. He had brooched a new MacArdry plaid across his chest to underline his kinship with the Mearan pretender, and a border bonnet bearing the three eagle feathers of a clan chief graced his head, border braid tied with a black ribbon. He moved at the Mearan envoy's side with brisk self-assurance as the two of them passed through the gates and dismounted in the castle yard, looking neither left nor right as he followed the envoy up the stairs and down a side corridor, rather than passing through the great hall.

Caitrin was waiting for him in a withdrawing room overlooking a cloister garden, flanked by Judhael, Bishop

Creoda, and the four itinerant bishops who had supported Loris and the Mearan bid for independence: Mir de Kierney, Gilbert Desmond, Raymer de Valence, and Calder of Sheele, an uncle on his mother's side—no, actually a great-uncle. Caitrin's seamed face went whiter than her raiment as she saw what ambassador the king had sent.

"How dare he send you, of all people?" she murmured, looking so pale Dhugal feared she might faint. "How can you even look me in the eyes?"

Dhugal made her a careful salute, king's ambassador to enemy sovereign.

"My lady, you cannot suppose that any Haldane ambassador will bring you news you wish to hear," he said quietly. "His Majesty thought you would at least prefer to hear it from a kinsman."

Carefully Caitrin composed her features as became a queen, setting her hands awkwardly on the arms of the chair which, in that moment, had become only a shadow of a throne.

"What—news?" she murmured. "Sicard?"

"Dead, my lady."

"And my—my son?"

"The same."

As her hands flew to her lips to cover an anguished, soundless wail, Judhael knelt by the arm of her chair and laid his head against her knee, and Creoda urgently moved a few steps closer to Dhugal.

"What of Archbishop Loris?"

Dhugal's manner turned colder, even though he knew he should try to maintain a strict neutrality as Kelson's spokesman.

"Taken, Excellency. And Monsignor Gorony as well. They await the king's justice."

"But, that isn't possible," Creoda whispered, more to himself than to anyone else, as Judhael paled and the other clerics buzzed among themselves, aghast.

"I assure you, it is not only possible, it is true, Excellency," Dhugal said coolly. "And frankly—"

He cut himself off, for it was not his place to speak of what Loris and Gorony had done to his father, or to intimate in any way that his relationship with Duncan was anything other than borderman to borderman.

"But, you will all be acquainted with His Majesty's feelings on that matter, in due time. For now, it is my charge to instruct her ladyship on the terms His Majesty is willing to offer."

"How *dare* he offer *me* terms?" Caitrin murmured.

Dhugal cocked his head curiously. "Why, because you have lost, my lady. Surely, you cannot think otherwise."

Drawing herself back to composure with a sheer act of will, Caitrin leveled her gaze on him again.

"I am secure in my own capital of Laas, young MacArdry," she said firmly, "Your Kelson cannot drive me from here."

"Drive you?" Dhugal glanced at the others in amazement. "Madame, you are under siege. Your chief advisors are captured or killed. Your army was bested in the field and has been sworn to Haldane loyalty, as should have happened generations ago. His Majesty has only to wait you out. And wait he shall, if needs be. You cannot escape. Your cause is lost."

Judhael laid a trembling hand on his aunt's and raised his eyes boldly to Dhugal's.

"What are the king's terms, cousin?" he said quietly.

"I shall read them to you," Dhugal replied, withdrawing the scroll from the front of his riding leathers and drawing a deep breath.

"Kelson Cinhil Rhys Anthony Haldane, by the Grace of God King of Gwynedd, Prince of Meara, and Lord of the Purple March, unto the Lady Caitrin Quinnell, *soi-disant* Pretender of Meara," he said steadily, as he unrolled the scroll. "Lady: Further resistance against your lawful sovereign will only result in the senseless spending of more Mearan lives; and each death of a loyal Haldane man will bring the eventual execution of ten Mearans, once battle is done. However, if your ladyship will surrender unconditionally, we are minded to offer the following terms:

"One. No further reprisals will be taken against the Mearan populace at large, though the nobility and all former military personnel will be required to swear allegiance to King Kelson of Gwynedd as their rightful sovereign and liege and will face summary execution if this oath is forsworn in the future. Individuals who have defied the law of Gwynedd in such a manner as to cause harm to others shall be dealt with on an individual basis.

"Two." He took another deep breath, not looking up as he read the next provision. "Permission will be granted for the bodies of Sicard MacArdry and Ithel of Meara to be given honorable burial here in Laas. The Lady Caitrin will be permitted leave to attend such ceremonies as are customary."

"How did they die?" came Caitrin's voice, cutting through the formality of the rehearsed speech.

Dhugal looked up, then slowly lowered the scroll.

"Are the details that important now, my lady?" he asked softly. "They will only distress you further."

"Tell me!" she demanded. "Otherwise, I shall not listen to another word of your lord's demands."

"Very well."

Uncomfortably, Dhugal let the scroll curl back on itself, trying to soften the truth a little by his choice of words.

"Your husband fell with a sword in his hand, madame," he said softly. "I—am told that he died bravely, preferring death to capture, when he realized he had lost your army."

"Yes," she breathed. "That would have been his wish. Did you see him fall?"

"No, my lady."

"But it was quick?" she urged. "Tell me he did not suffer."

"I believe he did not, my lady," Dhugal said, seeing in his memory the arrow protruding from Sicard's eye. "His wound would have been immediately fatal. I doubt he felt much."

"Praise be to God for that, at least," she whispered into clasped hands, before looking up again. "And my son?"

Dhugal swallowed, aware that this one would wound Caitrin even more than her husband's death had. But he could find little sympathy in his heart for Ithel.

"Two weeks ago, at Talacara, Prince Ithel was taken prisoner," he said. "That day, he and Baron Brice of Trurill were tried, convicted, and executed for their treason."

"How—executed?" Caitrin breathed.

"They were hanged."

There had been no way to soften the word, no way to prepare her for its starkness. As she closed her eyes, reeling in her chair, Judhael bent to comfort her, himself ashen with apprehension—for if Ithel, who was the heir, had been executed, what chance had he, as next in line?

"I—shall not press you for further details," Caitrin murmured, after recovering most of her composure. She took Judhael's hand as she gestured for Dhugal to continue, turning her eyes to gaze out the sunlit window through a film of tears.

"Three," Dhugal said, unrolling the scroll to read once more. "After giving assurance that she will never again rise in arms against the rightful sovereign of Meara, namely King Kelson of Gwynedd or his heirs, the Lady Caitrin will be permitted to retire to a convent of His Majesty's choosing for the rest of her natural life, there to spend her time as a religious of that house, doing penance and praying for the souls of those who died as a result of her rebellion."

"It is generous, my lady," Judhael murmured, tears welling in his own eyes as he stroked her trembling hand with his. "Dhugal, what of me?"

"Four," Dhugal went on, not daring to look at the young bishop. "In the matter of Judhael of Meara, nephew of the Lady Caitrin and sometime Bishop of Ratharkin: for his treason, both secular and ecclesiastical, and because His Majesty does not intend to allow another potential Mearan rebellion to form around said bishop, as heir to the Lady Caitrin, Judhael of Meara's life is forfeit."

A little gasp escaped Judhael's lips, and he swayed on his knees, going even paler. Caitrin moaned and hugged his shoulders convulsively. But before the other bishops could do more than mutter, Dhugal cleared his throat and stayed them with a shake of his head.

"However, for that Judhael is, by his descent from the ancient princes of Meara, a prince by birth as well as by episcopal elevation, King Kelson grants said Judhael the dignity of a prince's death by beheading with the sword, outside the public eye, and honorable burial with his kin here in Laas."

He looked up furtively at the stunned Judhael, avoiding his eyes, then glanced at the other clerics as he returned to his scroll.

"Five. After determination of any civil culpability, Bishop Creoda and any other dissident clergy who have been associated with the Mearan uprising shall answer to an ecclesiastical court to be convened by Archbishops Bradene and Cardiel, and the king shall abide by the recommendation of that court." He let the scroll curl back on itself as he looked up at last. "No further concessions are open to discussion."

There followed a harried few moments of recapitulation, with several clarifications of the exact terms offered, before Caitrin stood shakily to signify that the audience was at an end.

"Tell your king that his terms are harsh, young Dhugal, but we shall consider them, and give him our answer at noon."

"Aye, madame, I shall," he murmured, making her a polite bow of agreement.

"Thank you. And Dhugal—"

"Aye, madame?"

Swallowing, she signaled Judhael to withdraw with the other bishops and motioned Dhugal closer, drawing him into the partial shelter of the nearby window embrasure. The sun lit his tied-back hair like a helmet of burnished copper as he gazed at her awkwardly, and he started as she suddenly produced a little dagger from her sleeve.

"You are all unarmed, aren't you, Dhugal?" she said softly, her eyes never faltering as she read his apprehension.

"Aye, madame. I came as my king's envoy, all in honor, to treat with an honorable lady—for so she must be, to have married my uncle and borne him children to carry the blood of the MacArdrys."

With a sad little snort, Caitrin managed a tiny smile. "Brave words, nephew, when I could kill you where you stand—and probably should, for what you have done to me and mine. But you're right: he was a wondrous fair man, your Uncle Sicard. If I had allowed our children to carry *his* name instead of my own, how different things might have been."

"Aye, madame."

"He *was* a good man, Dhugal," she repeated. "And as I have heard of your deeds of valor these many weeks, I have often thought how different things might have been if *he* had been your father instead of Caulay."

He almost protested that Caulay had not been his father, but he still had no idea what she planned to do with the little dagger. He thought he could take it from her if she tried to use it on him—she was shorter than he and four times his age—but if she *did* try to use it, the others would come to her aid as well. It was not unknown for envoys to be killed for bringing the wrong news; and God knew, the news he brought had given her enough cause to hate him, if he himself had not given her sufficient cause before.

But she only fingered the dagger quietly for a few seconds and then offered it to him, hilt first, across her sleeve, a shy, almost wistful little smile faintly lighting her lips.

"A MacArdry gave me this, on our wedding day. I want you to have it."

"Madame?"

"I want you to have it. Go ahead." She pressed the hilt into his unresisting palm. "Indulge an old woman's fancies. Let me pretend, if only for a few seconds, that you were my and Sicard's son, instead of Caulay's. My children all are dead, and my dreams for them—and Judhael, my only other kin, will also shortly perish."

"But the killing can stop there," Dhugal ventured. "It doesn't have to go on."

She swallowed with difficulty. "You saw them all die, didn't you?"

"Who?"

"All my children."

"Not—Ithel," he murmured. "I saw Sidana—and Llewell. But it does no good to dwell upon it, my lady."

"I do not dwell upon it," she whispered, "but I do have to ask about Sidana. If—if Llewell had not—killed her, would the marriage have brought peace, do you think?"

"I think it might have. A joint heir would have answered most people's quibbles about the succession."

"And Sidana—would she have been happy with your Kelson?"

Dhugal swallowed dry-throated, for he had spoken very little with his royal Mearan cousin.

"I—cannot say, my lady," he whispered. "But Kelson is my blood brother as well as my king, and I—believe he loved her, in his way. I know that on the night before the wedding, he talked about the marriage, and how he disliked having to marry for reasons of state. But I think he had convinced himself that he was falling in love with her." He paused a beat. "Is that what you wanted to hear?"

"If it is true—yes," she whispered. "And I sense by your face that you believe it is." She sighed. "Ah, me, if only I had been less stiff-necked, she might be alive now, and Queen of Gwynedd. But I've killed her, I've killed my sons,

I've killed my husband—Dhugal, I'm so tired of killing. . . ."

"Then, stop the killing, my lady," he said softly. "You're
the only one who can. Accept the king's terms. Give Meara
back to her rightful sovereign, and search for peace in the
years remaining to you."

"Do you really think he'll let me live?"

"He has given his word, madame. I have never known
him to break that."

She sighed and lifted her chin proudly, moving back into
the main room where the others instantly ceased their murmuring.

"Tell your master that we shall send him word of our final
decision at noon," she said. "I—must have time to consider
what I must do."

When Dhugal had gone, she sank slowly back into her
chair and laid her head against its back.

"Call my advisors, Judhael," she whispered. "And bring
me my crown."

# CHAPTER TWENTY-TWO

*But ye shall die like men, and fall like one of the
princes.*

—Psalms 82:7

At noon precisely, the gates of Laas parted to release a
lone herald carrying a white flag. Nor did the gates close
behind him.

"My Lord King," the herald said, bowing in the saddle
as he was brought before the mounted Kelson, "my lady
accepts your terms in principle, and will receive you in the
great hall as soon as pleases you."

"In principle?" Kelson replied. "What, precisely, does
that mean? I thought I made it clear that there would be no
further negotiation."

"I—believe she hopes for a softening of the terms, my
lord," the man whispered.

"I see. My lords?" He glanced at his chief advisors and
officers grouped around him. "Dhugal, what say you? You
spoke with the lady."

"I don't think there will be any treachery, if that's what
concerns you," Dhugal murmured. "She sounded very
weary of it all and almost contrite."

"They *all* sound contrite when they're pinned against the
wall," Morgan muttered.

"Hmmm, I daresay Loris and Gorony won't oblige us on
that count. I'll ask you and Jodrell to take charge of them
for the entry into Laas. Ewan, you're in command of the
main army until we return. If anything happens, you know

what to do. Archbishop Cardiel, I'll ask you to escort the bodies of Sicard and Ithel. Do you know Laas at all?"

"I'm afraid I don't, Sire."

"No matter. There will be at least a household chapel where the bodies can be taken. And we've discussed the other duties I'll need you to perform."

"Yes, of course, Sire."

"Duncan and Dhugal, you'll ride at my sides."

An hour later, King Kelson entered Laas in triumph, preceded by a column of Haldane lancers and archers and backed by a full two hundred men on foot. A crown glittered on his open-faced helm, and he bore his father's naked sword in the crook of his arm like a scepter.

He met no resistance as he rode through the streets of the city. His orderly progress elicited only silence and taut curiosity as his lancers drew up in the yard of the great hall and formed a cordon of honor, and he waited until foot soldiers and archers had entered and secured the hall before even dismounting from his great white battle charger.

Scarlet silk mantled his shoulders, softening the lion-charged brigandine hardly at all, and it floated on the warm summer air as he mounted the steps from the yard and the great double doors parted for him. Inside, hardly a score of Mearans waited to receive him: Caitrin herself, of course, lonely and vulnerable-looking on the throne at the far end of the hall, all in black, the crown of Meara on her veiled head; and half a dozen elderly gentlemen interspersed with her remaining bishops, the latter in episcopal purple, all of them clumped nervously to either side. Kelson's own guards lined the sides of the hall, and his archers commanded the upper galleries with quiet but deadly authority.

"All attend!" Caitrin's herald cried. "His Royal Majesty, the High and Mighty Prince Kelson Cinhil Rhys Anthony Haldane, by the Grace of God, King of Gwynedd, Lord of the Purple March—and Prince of Meara."

Suppressing a smile of relief at the last appellation, Kelson paused a moment in the doorway to let the full impact of his presence take effect upon those within, even allowing a ghost of his Deryni aura to play about his head—pale enough that no one could be sure whether the glow came of his power or merely the sparkle of sunlight on the jewels of his crown.

Then, slowly and with a dignity not usually associated with seventeen-year-olds, he gave his sword to Morgan, removed his helm and handed it off to Dhugal, then casually removed his white gauntlets and tossed them into the helm before starting down the hall to meet the Mearan pretender. He had not expected her to be so tiny or so frail-looking. Morgan and Dhugal flanked him, half a pace behind, Duncan and Cardiel following, Cardiel mitred, Duncan crowned with a ducal coronet, both wearing scarlet bishops' copes over their armor. Jodrell remained outside with the prisoners.

Caitrin rose as the king and his party approached, her courtiers and bishops making strained bows of deference as he passed. Kelson's escort split to either side as they reached the dais, but the king continued straight up the steps to stop, facing Caitrin. Her grief had ravaged a face that was never beautiful, even in youth, but a taut dignity kept her composed as she slowly sank to her knees before him, thin hands clasped on her breast. Her eyes burned with passion as she removed her crown and extended it to him; nor did she flinch as he took it from her.

Cardiel had moved to his side as the exchange was made, and Kelson passed the crown to him, only turning slightly so the archbishop could set it on his head. He offered Caitrin his hand then, to help her rise, but she caught up the hem of Cardiel's cope and touched it to her lips before rising on her own. Duncan was waiting to ease her to the side as the rest of Kelson's party mounted the steps to range themselves to either side of him, and Kelson took back his sword and laid the naked blade across his knees when he had seated himself on the throne of Meara.

At the rear of the hall, more of Kelson's barons and officers waited with the Mearan men who had already reaffirmed their allegiance to Kelson at Dorna; and these now filed into the hall to group themselves opposite the dissident bishops and nobles as Kelson surveyed them. When, as Kelson did not speak, uneasy silence had settled over all, Judhael of Meara detached himself from his fellow bishops and moved forward. His cope fell away as he left them, revealing him clad not in episcopal purple, but a rough, homespun monk's robe, his feet bare. He fell to both knees at the bottom of the dais steps, bowing low over his clasped hands, but his face, as he raised his eyes to meet Kelson's, was that of a man who knows what his fate must be.

"My Lord King," he said, his voice carrying to every corner of the hall, "I, Judhael Michael Richard Jolyon

MacDonald Quinnell, Bishop of Ratharkin and Prince of Meara, do renounce all future claim to the sovereignty of Meara and acknowledge you as my rightful liege. I do further submit me to Your Majesty's judgment, begging pardon for all offenses and vowing never again to say or do you any harm. If mercy can be found in your heart, I beg that I be allowed to live out my life in strict confinement with some religious house, for in truth, I never sought a crown; but if that cannot be, then I accept whatever fate Your Majesty may deem meet for my offenses. In the name of the Father, and of the Son, and of the Holy Spirit, Amen."

Sighing as Judhael crossed himself, Kelson allowed his gaze to shift briefly to the other bishops waiting to hear his decision; to Caitrin, standing taut and tortured before them, hands clasped in supplication. But though he had Truth-Read Judhael as he spoke and knew the man's future intentions to be honest, he knew he could not afford to be lenient in this matter. Judhael had been too much the tool in the hands of stronger men before. Best to be bluntly honest and implacable.

"Judhael Michael Richard Jolyon MacDonald Quinnell of Meara," he said steadily. "I freely give my pardon for any offenses you have committed against me and mine. However—" The word fell like a death knell between them. "However, in the interests of my people, both here and in Gwynedd, I cannot knowingly allow a threat of future rebellion to survive. I allowed your cousin Llewell to live, and he slew my bride. I spared Archbishop Loris, not wishing to take the life of a consecrated bishop, and he led a rebellion against me. Were I to allow you to live, even cloistered with some loyal religious house far from here, there would always be the chance that men of misguided loyalties would seek to use you again as a rallying point for yet another insurrection against my lawful rule, even against your will."

"But, you could keep him closely guarded with me!" Caitrin burst out, throwing herself to her knees in place and raising her arms in supplication. "Have mercy, my lord! He is all the family I have left!"

"And how many other families are bereft because of this senseless clinging to thoughts of Mearan independence?" Kelson countered. "Shall I spare Judhael, only to have him become a Mearan *cause célèbre* at some future date, to threaten me or my sons or my sons' sons? No, madame. I cannot and shall not lay that burden upon myself, my people, or my heirs. Judhael, I regret that I must reiterate your death sentence—though you shall be allowed time to prepare yourself. Despite the fact that you technically stand excommunicate, Archbishop Cardiel has offered to minister to you. Do you accept?"

Swaying a little on his knees, his eyes closed, Judhael bowed deeply, hands crossed on his breast.

"I submit me to Your Majesty's judgment and accept His Excellency's merciful offer. Will—will it be soon?"

"As soon as you are prepared," Kelson said quietly. "Archbishop Cardiel, will you go now with Prince Judhael, or do you wish to witness the judgment of the other two ecclesiastical prisoners?"

At Kelson's gesture toward the far end of the hall, where Jodrell and four guards were now walking Loris and Gorony through the great double doors, Cardiel drew himself to his full height.

"Your Majesty, I would not miss this for a remission of all my time in Purgatory. Guards, you may take Prince Judhael to the chapel to compose himself. Father Judhael, I shall join you in a few minutes. This will not take long."

Judhael did not look at the other two prisoners as guards led him past and out of the hall. Loris glared at him and, indeed, at everyone in the hall, but he and Gorony both had been gagged before being brought in. They stood defiantly before the king until the guards forced them to their knees. Kelson could read their hatred without recourse to his powers as he gestured to Morgan for the list of the men's crimes to be read.

"Edmund Alfred Loris, priest and sometime Archbishop of Valoret, and Lawrence Edward Gorony, also priest: you are jointly accused of high treason against the Crown and Kingdom of Gwynedd and inciting to rebellion. In addition, you brought about the judicial murder of Bishop Henry Istelyn and caused grievous hurt to be done to Bishop Duncan McLain. Your accusers are present in the hall. Lawrence Gorony, how do you plead?"

At Kelson's signal, the gag was removed from Gorony's mouth, but he only raised his chin defiantly and spat.

"I do not recognize the authority of this court to try me," he said, "or of a Deryni heretic to read out the list of accusations against me. I claim benefit of clergy and demand to be tried in an ecclesiastical court."

"Gorony, you and Loris were excommunicated more than six months ago, and your rights of clergy suspended," Cardiel said coldly, before Kelson could answer. "Nor has either of you made any attempt to gain reversal of that excommunication."

"I do not recognize your right to pronounce that excommunication!" Gorony objected.

"Guards, gag him again!" Cardiel barked, continuing as the guards obeyed. "Technically speaking, your excommunicate status affords you no rights whatever; but I *will* entreat the king to spare you the death that Henry Istelyn suffered: you will not be drawn and quartered. However, Bishop McLain and myself constitute all the ecclesiastical trial you are likely to get. Bishop McLain, is the prisoner innocent or guilty of the charges?"

"Guilty, Your Excellency," Duncan replied evenly.

"I concur," Cardiel said. "Your Majesty, we find the prisoner, Lawrence Gorony, guilty as charged and remand him to your sentencing. Edmund Loris, how do you plead?"

As Loris' gag was also removed, he seemed to explode into squirming, shouting action.

"How dare you presume to try *me*? And how *dare* you allow these heretics to sit in judgment upon me? A heretic king, with his heretic minions—and *Bishop* McLain, with his Deryni bastard standing at his side as if he merited the honor done him—"

"Gag him!" Kelson snapped.

"Dhugal MacArdry is McLain's bastard son!" Loris shouted, before the guards could control him. "Ask whether he dares deny it! And they are *both* Deryni—"

A guard cuffed him into silence long enough to get the gag in place, but the damage was done. The rumor had been rife among Kelson's men since the battle at Dorna a week before, but no one had dared to bring the allegation into the open. Now it could hardly be avoided. As Duncan cast a resigned glance at Kelson, the king gave him a faint nod. The hall grew very quiet as Duncan took a step forward and swept them with his eyes.

"It is not I or young Dhugal who are on trial here, but those two men, who have broken faith with their king and the sacred offices they held. Nonetheless, I will not deny that Dhugal MacArdry is my son. I *do* deny that he is base-born, and shall prove his legitimacy to the satisfaction of an ecclesiastical tribunal within the year. As to whether either of us is Deryni—that is the business of my king, my archbishop, and my God. If any man in this hall has quarrel with that, I suggest he take it up with one of them."

Awed reaction murmured through the hall, a few Mearans crossing themselves in protective signing, but no one dared any further outburst as Duncan gave first Kelson and then Cardiel a clipped but respectful bow. Further reaction was curtailed by Cardiel laying his hand on Duncan's shoulder in obvious approbation. Dhugal had not moved from his place at Kelson's left.

"Your Majesty," Cardiel said, turning his attention back to the king, "I find the accused, Lawrence Gorony and Edmund Loris, guilty as charged, and surrender them both to secular judgment. Bishop McLain, do you concur?"

"I do, Your Excellency."

"Thank you, my lords," Kelson murmured. "Lawrence Gorony and Edmund Loris, we likewise find you guilty as charged and sentence you to be hanged by the neck until dead. Archbishop Cardiel, is there any reason why sentence should not be carried out immediately?"

"There is none, Sire," Cardiel said evenly. "Inasmuch as the condemned approach execution obdurate and unrepentant, it is not meet that they be allowed to mock God's law by partaking of His final rites. And since, by similar reasoning, Edmund Loris justified the execution of Henry Istelyn without benefit of the Sacraments, I should think he will not mind if the same standards are applied to himself and his hound."

"So be it, then," Kelson said, lifting his eyes above the heads of the stunned Loris and Gorony to the men lining the upper galleries. "Guards?"

At his signal, two of the men tossed coiled ropes over one of the beams running the width of the hall, letting the ends fall to either side. The Mearans gasped as his intentions became clear, but no one made a move to interfere as the guards holding Loris and Gorony moved them beneath the ropes and secured nooses around their necks. Gorony looked stunned, finally afraid, but Loris' face was contorted with rage.

"Remove the gags and haul them up," Kelson said coldly, flinching a little as his orders were carried out. "And may God have mercy on their souls."

Kicking and squirming, their faces already beginning to turn blue, the two were hoisted up until their feet cleared the heads of those below; then the ropes were tied off. Caitrin reeled a little, catching herself against the arm of one of her supporters, and a few of the watching men went a little green as the kicking gradually subsided, but no one said a word. Kelson slowly counted to one hundred, only watching them all as he did so, before shifting his sword into the crook of his arm like a scepter. His movement gave him their undivided attention once more.

"Archbishop Cardiel, you have our leave to go to Prince Judhael now."

"Thank you, Sire. During my absence, I deputize Bishop McLain to act in my stead, in such action as may require the authority of my office."

When Cardiel had gone, Kelson surveyed them all again: Caitrin, her remaining nobles, and the dissident bishops. Many of his own nobles and officers were also present, and all hung on his every word.

"Men of Meara," he said quietly. "The time has now come for me to tell you what will be the fate of your land. Meara is and has long been an adjunct of the Crown of Gwynedd. The title of Prince of Meara was vested in me shortly after birth by my father, King Brion, and I intend eventually to vest it in my firstborn son. Had things been otherwise, that son might also have been the firstborn of your Princess Sidana. I devoutly wish that such were the case."

He swallowed before going on, one thumb rubbing the marriage ring on his little finger, and Morgan knew that Kelson truly had wanted that union. He saw tears well in Caitrin's eyes, and guessed that she, too, might eventually have come to accept that solution. But that option was now long removed from possibility. Another fate would have to be worked out for Meara.

"In opposition to the marital solution I had proposed," Kelson went on, "there was a Mearan plan for this land—and that was to reunite her with the ancient Mearan honors of Cassan and Kierney. That is now my intention as well, though I intend to accomplish that reunion in a different manner than your leaders had planned. Until I have a son and heir, it is my desire and intention that Duke Duncan McLain serve as my viceroy in Meara, with my foster brother Dhugal, the Earl of Transha, to be Lord Lieutenant of Meara, and Baron Jodrell and Generals Godwin and Gloddruth to assist them. To those who will swear me and them their unreserved allegiance, I shall grant full pardon and general amnesty, saving those offenses committed as individuals against the code of chivalry properly observed in times of war. For most of you, I believe that gives you a fresh start—but I warn you all: let no man come forward and swear me faith falsely, because I shall know. I shall require that your oaths be sworn with your hands between mine own, and ratified with your kiss on the Gospel book, administered by Bishop Duncan, and on my father's sword, which Duke Alaric shall present. I hope I need not remind you what that means.''

Again he let his aura flare to light the jewels of the Mearan crown, simultaneously signing for Morgan and Duncan to do the same. Like Kelson's, Duncan's aura might have been dismissed as the glint of sunlight on his coronet; but Morgan's, misting faintly greenish gold on his golden hair, could not be so rationalized. The three of them held the magic, casting the occasional meaningful look at the still twitching bodies of Loris and Gorony, until all the Mearan lords had sworn. Nor was Kelson surprised, as each came forward to set his hands between the king's, that all the oaths were earnest—at least in that moment.

When all was done, he took his sword in the crook of his arm once more and rose.

"But one sad task remains to be performed," he said quietly. "It is not one I relish, but it is one I must do. Lady Caitrin, may I escort you to the chapel to bid farewell to your nephew?"

She went with him, but she declined his offer of the support of his arm. Morgan, Duncan, and Dhugal accompanied him as he followed her along the silent way to the chapel opening on the yard outside. Mearan and Haldane men alike bowed them past—for whose sake, Kelson himself could not have said.

Inside the chapel, Cardiel and Judhael knelt together on the steps of the high altar; but it was the two plain coffins laid before the steps that arrested Caitrin's attention as she proceeded down the aisle. She gasped as she saw them, and sank to her knees between them, one fragile hand lightly touching each. Cardiel turned at their approach, and gestured for Kelson to come nearer.

"Prince Judhael has asked that you join him in a prayer, Sire," he said.

Swallowing, Kelson handed off his sword to Morgan and went ahead alone, aware that Morgan, Duncan, and Dhugal had sunk to their knees behind him. Passing the coffins, and Caitrin mourning between them, he made an obeisance at the foot of the steps, then rose to join Judhael at his right. When the three of them had recited the Lord's Prayer together, Cardiel rose and backed off a few paces to give them privacy.

"I—wish you to know that I bear you no animosity, Sire," the Mearan prince said, not raising his eyes to Kelson's. "I knew, when all of this began, that the burden of the crown was a heavy one, but I never knew *how* heavy until it began to be apparent that I myself might have to bear it. I never wanted that. All I ever wanted to be was a priest. Well, I *did* want to be a bishop," he conceded, with a tiny smile, "but only as the perfection of my priesthood. At least that was what I told myself. I know now that my sin was in letting myself be seduced by the wishes of others—my aunt, Archbishop Loris." He swallowed. "Is—Loris to be executed?"

"Sentence has already been carried out," Kelson said quietly.

Judhael nodded, briefly closing his eyes. "It was justly done," he whispered. "And mine shall be justly done as well. I—stood by and let him—do what he did to Henry Istelyn, that godly man."

"There is talk of making Istelyn a saint," Kelson offered uncomfortably.

"I hope it becomes more than talk. He died loyal to you and to God, Sire—and to the Church that Loris said had rejected him. I wish I had had the courage to go to him in his final hour, regardless of Loris' orders, and give him the last rites you have so graciously permitted me."

"Your own actions and contrition have permitted you this grace and solace—not I," Kelson murmured, almost wishing there were some way he could spare this surprisingly noble Mearan prince. "If Archbishop Cardiel had not vouched for you, no such concessions would have been granted."

"He, too, is a godly man, Sire," Judhael replied. "You are fortunate, indeed, to be served by such men."

"I know."

Judhael sighed, but it was not the heavy sigh Kelson would have expected of a man about to die.

"Well, then, I suppose I'm ready," he said softly. "Is the swordsman's blade sharp?"

"Aye, it is sharp," Kelson breathed, suddenly moved to compassion, and laying one hand on Judhael's to read as deeply as he dared without the other's awareness. "But perhaps there is another way than this. I said before that it would be too difficult to simply keep you locked away for the rest of your life—but if you're truly repentant for what you've done—and I see that you are—perhaps a way could be found—"

With a little catch of horror to his breath, Judhael pulled his hand away and stared at Kelson.

"You would offer me my life?"

"With your promise of future loyalty, yes, and against my better judgment. I'm tired of killing, Judhael! Your uncle and all your cousins have died because of me. Oh, all of them but Sidana brought it on themselves, but—God, there must be some other way!"

"No," Judhael replied, shaking his head dully. "There is no other way. You were right the first time. If you let me live, there would always be the chance that I might escape, that some ambitious Mearan lordling less honorable than ourselves might make me the focal point of yet another uprising—and you would rue this moment of mercy for the rest of your life. I think a king must have enough causes for regrets, without needlessly producing more of them. A king must be strong—and you are a king who can bring unity and peace to Meara at last, Kelson Haldane. If your Deryni touch can reveal men's hearts, then read my heart and know that I truly believe what I am telling you," he said, taking Kelson's hand and deliberately holding it to his breast. "Like you, I do not wish to be the cause of any more needless deaths. The only way to be certain of that is for me to die. You cannot afford to let me live."

Kelson shrank from the request, but he had no choice but to do as Judhael asked. And Judhael *was* resigned to his fate, believing it best for Meara and for Kelson.

"I still will spare you," Kelson said stubbornly, dropping his hand from Judhael's breast. "You have only to ask."

"But I shall not ask."

"Then I shall not press the point," Kelson said. "I shall permit you the dignity you have earned by your honor, and say that I wish we could have reached this understanding months ago, while there was still time to change things. Under better circumstances, I think I might have been proud to have you as my friend and counselor, Judhael of Meara."

"And I should have been proud to serve you—my Liege," Judhael whispered.

"Then serve me in one thing, at least, before you go," Kelson murmured. "Give me your blessing?"

"With all my heart, Sire." And his right hand lifted to trace the sign of blessing on Kelson's forehead. "May almighty God bless you and give you long to reign in wisdom and courage, Kelson Haldane. In the name of the Father, and of the Son, and of the Holy Spirit, Amen."

"Amen," Kelson whispered.

But he would not meet Judhael's eyes again. Tears springing unbidden to his eyes, he rose and turned away, striding briskly back up the aisle toward the yard where the swordsman waited, pausing only to take his own sword from the silent Morgan's hands.

He laid the sword in the crook of his arm like a scepter again just before he emerged into the sunlight, schooling his face to an expression of solemn resignation as he took a position at the head of his officers and beckoned for the swordsman to approach. The man was the same who had executed Llewell of Meara six months before, his great hand-and-a-half broadsword at rest between his gloved fingers as easily as a lesser man might lean upon a rapier. The man approached instantly at his signal, to kneel on one knee, great hands resting on the quillons.

"Sire?"

"He will be out in a moment," Kelson said in a low voice. "Do it as he wishes. He is unbound, and I do not think he will ask for a blindfold. Will that unnerve you?"

"No, Sire."

"Good. Grant him as much dignity as you may and remember that he is a prince. I would not have him suffer."

"I shall be quick, Sire."

"Thank you. Would that I never should need to call upon your services again."

"That is my wish as well, Sire."

"I know it is. Go now. He will be coming out soon."

The executioner did not answer; only nodded his agreement and rose to return to the execution area, which had been strewn with straw all across the cobblestones. Kelson started as Morgan eased into place at his left elbow, and was grateful that the Deryni lord said nothing.

Just then, Caitrin appeared in the doorway of the chapel, leaning on the arm of Dhugal, Duncan escorting her on the other side. And following them came Judhael and Cardiel, both of them with heads bowed in prayer, Judhael listening avidly to what Cardiel said.

The two paused there for a moment, Cardiel finally signing the condemned man with a cross. Then Judhael walked slowly into the center of the yard. The executioner knelt briefly for his blessing, which Judhael freely gave. Then it was Judhael's turn to kneel, letting the man position him with his back to the sword now lying partially concealed under the straw—and also to Kelson.

A moment more Judhael bowed in prayer, clasped hands pressed to his lips, as the swordsman drew the bright blade quietly from underneath the straw and took up his stance, waiting for Judhael's signal. Then Judhael raised his head, lips still moving in prayer, and dropped his hands to either side, palms upturned, and the blade flashed.

Even Morgan grimaced as the blade connected with a dull thud, but the blow was sure, as the executioner had promised, and severed Judhael's neck like a stalk of wheat. The body toppled slowly, blood fountaining from the severed neck and soaking into the straw like a sponge, and as Cardiel moved in to say a final prayer for the departed soul, Kelson handed Morgan his sword again and moved in as well, removing his silken mantle to lay over the body. There was blood on Kelson's hand as he came back to retrieve the sword, and at first Morgan thought it was Judhael's—until he saw more blood on the blade, and knew it was Kelson's.

"My prince, you've cut yourself," he murmured, keeping hold of the sword with one hand as he reached for Kelson's hand with the other.

"It doesn't matter," Kelson murmured, letting Morgan draw him aside to inspect it. "Alaric, I could have saved him, but he wouldn't let me. I offered him his life. He chose to die instead."

With the bonding of blood between them, it was easy for Morgan to slip gently into Kelson's mind to read just the barest ghost of what had passed between him and Judhael—and to know that this specter Kelson must exorcise for himself.

"Shall I heal your hand, my prince?" he whispered quietly. "Or would you rather let it stay?"

Kelson swallowed noisily and bowed his head.

"Let it stay, for now," he said in a low voice. "It's fitting that I have real blood on my hands. I've spilled a great deal in the nearly four years I've been king."

"And will spill more, in years to come," Morgan reminded him gently. "Pray God that it will always be in the cause of justice and honor, as it has been, hitherto. We do what we have to do, Kelson."

"Aye." Kelson sighed heavily. "We do what we have to do. But there are some things I shall *never* like."

"No. Nor should you."

Sighing again, Kelson wiped his blade on the side of his boot—the blood would not show against the crimson—then sheathed it. The blood on his hand he allowed to remain, though he cupped his fingers around it to hide the slight wound.

"What now?" he murmured. "I don't suppose there's any chance I can have some time to myself?"

"A few minutes only, I fear, my prince. Shall I clear the chapel for you?"

"No, I'll find a spot. Hold this for me, will you?" he asked, handing Morgan the crown of Meara. "It's given me a headache. And see if you can get a staff meeting going within the hour. In the great hall, I think. Ask all the newly sworn Mearan officers to attend as well. We have a lot of loose ends to tidy up before we can even think about going home."

"Aye, my prince."

Morgan was left holding the Mearan crown as he watched Kelson turn and make his way toward the horses, slipping between his own and Morgan's black to find at least a semblance of privacy even amid the bustle of the crowded yard. And he knew, as he watched Kelson bury his face in his horse's snowy mane, that it was not the physical crown in his hands that had given Kelson his headache. The burden of the crown was far more than the weight of the jeweled circlet that Kelson had entrusted so casually to his keeping. It was the blood, and the lives, and the loneliness.

The loneliness was one of the worst parts, Morgan knew. Some of the loneliness, at least, might have ended if Sidana had lived—but, as so many times before, Morgan made himself quit that dead-end reasoning of "if only." Sidana had *not* lived; and her death had necessitated this campaign to Meara—which permitted the attempted Torenthi coup that likely never would have reared its head except in Kelson's absence.

Now, once the Mearan royals were buried and the new regime set in place, must come the return to Rhemuth and dealing with the Torenthi question again and the remorse over the deaths of Judhael and countless others; and, eventually, choosing another bride. Perhaps that little novice, Rothana. Richenda had told him that the two seemed drawn to one another, even after so short an exposure as at Talacara. Regardless of what Kelson thought, a wife—the right wife—would be good for him.

But for now, Kelson needed his few minutes alone, to reconcile his conscience and his heart and find the inner strength to continue in his duty. He was only seventeen, after all—hardly more than a boy, despite the rigors life had already thrust upon him. No one had ever said it was easy to be king. It certainly was not easy to be a good king, much less the great king Morgan believed Kelson would become.

Even as Morgan watched, Kelson lifted his head and squared his shoulders, looking around the yard with new determination. And Morgan, as he hailed several of Kelson's junior officers and set about implementing the king's orders, knew that his king would persevere through this most recent trial of character as he had persevered through all the rest. As he had always been proud to serve Kelson's father, so would he also be proud and honored to serve King Kelson of Gwynedd.

Here ends Book II of *The Histories of King Kelson.*
Book III, *The Quest for Saint Camber*,
will chronicle Kelson's quest to fulfill his dream
of restoring Saint Camber to his rightful place
as patron saint of Deryni magic and Defender of Humankind.

# THE KING'S JUSTICE

## Index of Characters

AHMED—a grain merchant.

ALAN Sommerfield, Sir—a seasoned captain of the elite McLain lancers.

ALARIC—see MORGAN.

ALROY, King—late King of Torenth, eldest son of Duke Lionel of Arjenol and Princess Morag, sister of Wencit; killed in a fall from a horse while hunting, summer of 1123, shortly after his fourteenth birthday; succeeded by his younger brother Liam, age nine. Many in Torenth believe the "accident" was engineered by Kelson to eliminate a rival who had come of age.

ANNALIND, Princess—twin sister of Roisian of Meara. After Roisian's marriage to King Malcolm Haldane in 1025, Annalind's adherents maintained that she, not Roisian, was the firstborn of the two sisters and, therefore, rightful heiress to the Coronet of Meara. Her descendants are Pretenders of Meara. Caitrin Quinnell is the current claimant.

ARDRY MacArdry—eldest son and heir of Caulay; killed 1107, age twenty, in brawl with a McLain retainer.

ARILAN, Bishop Denis—formerly Auxiliary Bishop of Rhemuth, now Bishop of Dhassa; secretly Deryni and member of the Camberian Council.

AZIM, Lord—Rothana's uncle, and Richenda's former teacher; high-ranking Deryni adept and precentor of the

Knights of the Anvil, at Djellarda, successors of the Michaelines.

BARRETT de Laney—elderly Deryni; blind co-adjutor of the Camberian Council.

BELDEN of Erne, Bishop—Bishop of Cashien.

BRADENE, Bishop—former Bishop of Grecotha, now Archbishop of Valoret and Primate of Gwynedd.

BRAN Coris, Lord—traitor Earl of Marley and former husband of Richenda; killed by Kelson.

BRENDAN Coris, Lord—seven-year-old Earl of Marley, son of Bran and Richenda.

BRICE, Lord—Baron of Trurill.

BRION Donal Cinhil Urien Haldane, King—Kelson's late father; slain at Candor Rhea by the magic of Charissa, 1120.

BRIONY Bronwyn de Morgan, Lady—infant daughter of Morgan and Richenda, born January 1123.

CAITRIN Quinnell, Princess—the Pretender of Meara, age sixty-one.

CALDER of Sheele, Bishop—one of the twelve itinerant bishops of Gwynedd, with no fixed see; great-uncle of Dhugal.

CAMBER of Culdi, Saint—outlawed Deryni saint of two centuries previous; patron of magic.

CARDIEL, Archbishop Thomas—former Bishop of Dhassa, now Archbishop of Rhemuth, age forty-four.

CAULAY MacArdry—late Chief of the MacArdrys; Dhugal's maternal grandfather.

CIARD O Ruane—Dhugal's old gillie.

CONALL, Prince—eldest son of Prince Nigel, and Kelson's cousin, age sixteen.

CONSTANCE, Sister—nun at St. Brigid's, killed in attack by Ithel's men.

CORAM, Stefan—Deryni; deceased former co-adjutor of the Camberian Council.

CORMAC Hamberlyn—border chieftain and brigand who defected to Caitrin's service; all but outlawed in Brion's day.

CREODA, Bishop—Bishop of Culdi after dissolution of his former See of Carbury, and a conniver in Loris' return to power.

DELRAE, Sir—captain of Jehana's Bremagni honor guard.

DHUGAL MacArdry, Lord—foster brother to Kelson, age fifteen; Chief of Clan MacArdry and Earl of Transha; son of Duncan McLain by Maryse MacArdry.

DUNCAN Howard McLain, Bishop—Deryni priest-cousin of Morgan, age thirty-one; Duke of Cassan and Earl of Kierney, following the deaths of his father and elder brother; auxiliary bishop under Archbishop Cardiel; father of Dhugal MacArdry.

EWAN, Duke—Duke of Claibourne and hereditary Lord Marshal of the Gwynedd Royal Council.

GENDON—a sergeant in service to Brice of Trurill.

GILBERT Desmond, Bishop—one of the twelve itinerant bishops of Gwynedd.

GLODDRUTH, General—aide to Kelson, formerly in service of Duke Jared McLain.

GODWIN, General—one of Kelson's generals.

GORONY, Monsignor Lawrence Edward—aide to Archbishop Loris.

GRIGOR of Dunlea—a neighbor baron of Brice of Trurill, gone over to Caitrin.

HAKIM—Emir Nur Hallaj, Rothana's father.

HELOISE, Mother—Abbess of St. Brigid's Abbey.

HOAG—a Haldane lancer.

HUGH de Berry, Bishop—former secretary to Archbishop Corrigan and longtime colleague of Duncan, now one of the twelve itinerant bishops of Gwynedd.

ISTELYN, Bishop Henry—former itinerant bishop and assistant to Archbishop Bradene; briefly Bishop of Meara; hanged, drawn, and quartered at order of Archbishop Loris; sainthood is being discussed.

ITHEL, Prince—elder son and heir of the Pretender of Meara, age sixteen.

JANNIVER, Princess—daughter of a Connaiti prince, betrothed to the King of Llannedd.

JARED McLain, Duke—Duke of Cassan and father of Kevin and Duncan McLain; captured at Rengarth and executed by Wencit of Torenth at Llyndruth Meadows, 1121.

JASS MacArdry—a MacArdry retainer.

JATHAM—squire to Kelson.

JEHANA, Queen—Deryni mother of Kelson and widow of King Brion, age thirty-five.

JEMET—a Haldane scout.

JENAS, Earl of—see ROGER.

JODRELL, Lord—a young baron in Kelson's entourage, holding lands in Kierney.

JOLYON, Prince—last sovereign Prince of Meara, father of the twin princesses Roisian and Annalind and a younger daughter.

JOWAN—Conall's squire.

JUDHAEL Michael Richard Jolyon MacDonald Quinnell, Prince of Meara—priest-nephew of Caitrin of Meara, age thirty-eight; illegally made Bishop of Ratharkin by Loris.

KELSON Cinhil Rhys Anthony Haldane, King—son of King Brion and Jehana, now seventeen; Deryni.

KIRKON—a R'Kassan scout in Kelson's service.

KYRI, Lady—Deryni, around thirty, known as "Kyri of the Flame"; member of the Camberian Council.

LACHLAN de Quarles, Bishop—newly appointed Bishop of Ballymar, in Cassan.

LAEL, Father—Archbishop Cardiel's chaplain and battle-surgeon.

LAMBERT MacArdry—one of Dhugal's retainers.

LARAN ap Pardyce, Lord—Deryni physician, sixteenth Baron Pardyce, about fifty-eight; member of the Camberian Council.

LAUGHLIN, Father—a priest with Kelson's army.

LEWYS ap Norfal—an infamous Deryni who rejected the authority of the Camberian Council.

LIAM, King—middle son of Duke Lionel and Princess Morag, age nine; King of Torenth since the death of his elder brother, summer of 1123; Deryni.

LLEWELL, Prince—younger son of the Pretender of Meara, age fifteen; executed for the murder of his sister Sidana.

LIONEL, Duke—Duke of Arjenol and father of Wencit's nephews and heirs; killed by Kelson at Llyndruth Meadows, 1121; succeeded by his brother Mahael.

LORIS, Bishop Edmund Alfred—fanatically anti-Deryni former Archbishop of Valoret and Primate of Gwynedd; stripped of his offices and sent into forced seclusion at

Saint Iveagh's Abbey by his fellow bishops in 1121, but escaped; an ally of Caitrin of Meara.

LUDOLPHUS—Azim's peddler alias.

MACARDRY—see ARDRY, CAULAY, DHUGAL, MARYSE, SICARD.

MACARDRY, The Old—Caulay MacArdry, Chief of Clan MacArdry and Earl of Transha before Dhugal; believed to be Dhugal's father until Duncan proved otherwise.

MAHAEL, Duke—younger brother of the slain Lionel, and his ducal heir; regent, with Princess Morag, of the young King Liam.

MALCOLM Haldane, King—great-grandfather of Kelson who married Roisian, the eldest daughter of the last Mearan Prince, intending by that union to join the Mearan Coronet permanently and peacefully to Gwynedd; died 1074.

MARYSE MacArdry—eldest daughter of Caulay MacArdry; died 1108, age seventeen; wife of Duncan and mother of Dhugal.

MATTHIAS MacArdry—one of Dhugal's retainers.

MCLAIN—see DUNCAN.

MERAUDE, Duchess—Nigel's wife, and mother of Conall, Rory, and Payne.

MIR de Kierney, Bishop—one of the twelve itinerant bishops of Gwynedd.

MORAG, Princess—Deryni sister of Wencit of Torenth and widow of Lionel; mother of the current king, Liam, and Prince Ronal.

MORGAN, Alaric Anthony—Deryni Duke of Corwyn and King's Champion, age thirty-two; cousin of Duncan McLain and husband of Richenda.

NIGEL Cluim Gwydion Rhys Haldane, Prince—Duke of Carthmoor and Brion's younger brother, age thirty-six; Kelson's uncle and Heir Presumptive.

PAYNE, Prince—Nigel's youngest son, age eight; royal page.

QUINNELL—family name of Caitrin, the Pretender of Meara.

RAIF—a Forcinn scout in Kelson's service (and Sofiana's); Deryni.

RAMSAY of Cloome—a cadet branch of the Mearan royal line.

RANDOLPH of Fairhaven—one of Ithel's officers.

RAYMER de Valence, Bishop—one of the twelve itinerant bishops of Gwynedd.

RECHOL—a blade merchant.

REMIE, General—one of Kelson's generals.

RHYDON, Lord—Deryni; a former Baron of Eastmarch, member of the Camberian Council, and ally of Wencit; deceased.

RICHENDA, Duchess—widow of Bran Coris, Earl of Marley, and mother of the current earl, their son Brendan; now wife of Morgan and mother of his daughter Briony; Deryni; age twenty-four.

ROGER, Earl of Jenas—one of Kelson's retainers.

ROISIAN of Meara—eldest daughter of Jolyon, the last sovereign Prince of Meara, and queen to King Malcolm Haldane; died 1055; firstborn twin sister to Princess Annalind of Meara.

ROLF MacPherson—Deryni Lord of the tenth century who rebelled against the authority of the Camberian Council.

RONAL, Prince—Deryni younger brother of the current King of Torenth, age five.

RORY, Prince—middle son of Prince Nigel, age thirteen.

ROCAIL—Grand Master of the Knights of the Anvil at Djellarda.

ROTHANA, Lady—novice nun at St. Brigid's; Deryni; daughter of Emir Nur Hallaj and related to Richenda by marriage.

SAER de Traherne—see TRAHERNE.

SICARD MacArdry, Lord—younger brother of Caulay, Dhugal's uncle, and husband to Caitrin, the Pretender of Meara.

SIDANA, Princess—daughter of Caitrin and Sicard, age fourteen; briefly, wife of Kelson; killed on her wedding day by her brother Llewell.

SIWARD, Bishop—former itinerant bishop, now in charge of the new See of Cardosa.

SOFIANA—Deryni; sovereign Princess of Andelon, and Richenda's aunt; member of the Camberian Council.

SULIEN—a R'Kassan Adept.

TEGAN O Daire—a border chieftain and brigand won over to Caitrin's support; all but outlawed in Brion's day.

THORNE Hagen—Deryni, in his early fifties; former member of the Camberian Council.

TIBALD MacErskine—a border chieftain and brigand won over to Caitrin; all but outlawed in Brion's day.

TIERCEL de Claron—Deryni, in his mid-twenties; youngest member of the Camberian Council.

TOLLIVER, Bishop Ralf—Bishop of Coroth, age fifty-two.

TRAHERNE, Saer de—Earl of Rhenndall and brother of Meraude, Nigel's duchess.

VIVIENNE, Lady—Deryni; elderly co-adjutor of the Camberian Council.

WARIN de Grey—self-appointed messiah who formerly believed himself divinely designated to destroy all Deryni; has healing power that does not seem to come from Deryni sources.

WENCIT of Torenth, King—Deryni sorcerer-King of Torenth and scion of the Festillic claim to the Gwynedd throne; slain by Kelson at Llyndruth Meadows in 1121.

WILLIAM du Chantal—a neighbor baron of Brice of Trurill; gone over to Caitrin.

# *THE KING'S JUSTICE*

## Index to Place Names

DORNA—plain where Duncan finally found Sicard's army.

DROGHERA—marcher holding on the Meara-Gwynedd border, south of Culdi.

EASTMARCH—former earldom of Ian Howell; ceded to the Crown on his death and subsequently given to Burchard de Varian to reward his loyalty in the Torenth War.

ELEVEN KINGDOMS—ancient name for the entire area including and surrounding Gwynedd.

FIANNA—wine-growing county across the Southern Sea.

FORCINN BUFFER STATES—group of independent principalities south of Torenth.

GRECOTHA—university city, former site of the Varnarite School; seat of Bishop Wolfram de Blanet.

GWYNEDD—central and largest of the Eleven Kingdoms, held by the Haldanes of Gwynedd since 645.

HALDANE—crown duchy comprising the central portion of Gwynedd and traditionally held directly by the king.

JENAS—a Gwynedd earldom.

KHELDISH RIDING—northeastern portion of the old Kingdom of Kheldour, held directly by the King of Gwynedd; famous for its weavers.

KIERNEY—earldom and secondary holding of the Dukes of Cassan, now held by Duncan McLain.

LAAS—ancient capital of independent Meara and periodic center of separatist uprisings in Meara.

LLYNDRUTH MEADOWS—grasslands at the foot of the Cardosa Defile; site of the final confrontation between Kelson and Wencit of Torenth.

MARBURY—seat of Ifor, Bishop of Marbury, in Marley.

MARLEY—former earldom of Bran Coris, now held by his son Brendan, under the regency of Richenda and Morgan.

MEARA—formerly a sovereign principality, now a possession of the Crown of Gwynedd, west of Gwynedd.

PURPLE MARCH, The—meadowlands north of Rhemuth; one of the Lordships of the Crown of Gwynedd.

RAMOS—site of the infamous Council of 917, which ruled stringent measures forbidding Deryni to enter the priesthood, hold office, own property, etc.

RATHARKIN—new capital of Meara after the union of Meara and Gwynedd in 1025, and seat of the Bishop of Meara.

RHEMUTH—capital city of Gwynedd, called "the beautiful."

RHENNDALL—mountainous earldom in the southern portion of old Kheldour, famous for the blueness of its lakes; held by Saer de Traherne, brother of Duchess Meraude.

R'KASSI—desert kingdom south and east of the Hort of Orsal, famous for its blooded horses.

SAINT GEORGE'S CATHEDRAL—seat of the Archbishop of Rhemuth, now Thomas Cardiel.

SAINT GILES' ABBEY—convent in the lake region of Shannis Meer, near the Eastmarch border, where Jehana went into retreat before Kelson's birth and after his coronation.

SAINT HILARY'S BASILICA—ancient royal basilica within the walls of Rhemuth Castle, of which Duncan is rector.

SAINT URIEL AND ALL ANGELS' CATHEDRAL—seat of the Bishop of Meara, in Ratharkin.

SHANNIS MEER—lake region site of the Abbey of Saint Giles, where Jehana went into retreat before Kelson's birth and after his coronation.

TALACARA—town where Ithel of Meara was captured by Kelson.

TOLAN—duchy in Torenth, formerly held by Charissa.

TORENTH—major kingdom east of Gwynedd, now ruled by regents for the boy King Liam, nephew of the late King Wencit.

TRANSHA—seat of Dhugal MacArdry, Earl of Transha, in the border marches between Kierney and the Purple March.

TRURILL—ancient border barony between Gwynedd and Meara, west of Culdi; held by Brice of Trurill.

VALORET—old capital of Gwynedd during the Interregnum, and seat of the Archbishop of Valoret (and Primate of Gwynedd), Bradene.

# Appendix III

## *PARTIAL LINEAGE OF THE HALDANE KINGS*

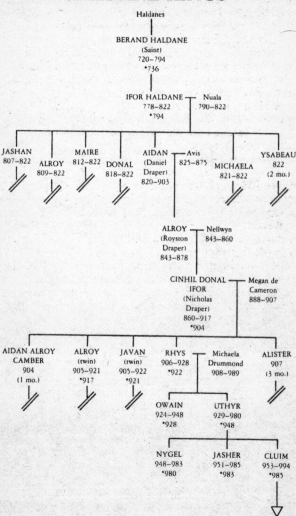

Haldanes

BERAND HALDANE
(Saint)
720–794
*736

IFOR HALDANE ── Nuala
778–822      790–822
*794

JASHAN          MAIRE          DONAL          AIDAN ── Avis          MICHAELA          YSABEAU
807–822   ALROY   812–822   818–822   (Daniel   825–875   821–822          822
          809–822                      Draper)                                (2 mo.)
                                       820–903

ALROY ── Nellwyn
(Royston   843–860
Draper)
843–878

CINHIL DONAL ── Megan de
IFOR          Cameron
(Nicholas     888–907
Draper)
860–917
*904

AIDAN ALROY          ALROY          JAVAN          RHYS          Michaela          ALISTER
CAMBER              (twin)         (twin)        906–928      Drummond          907
904                 905–921        905–922       *922         908–989          (3 mo.)
(1 mo.)             *917           *921

OWAIN          UTHYR
924–948       929–980
*928           *948

NYGEL          JASHER          CLUIM
948–983       951–985        953–994
*980           *983           *985

*An asterisk indicates the data of the beginning of each king's reign.

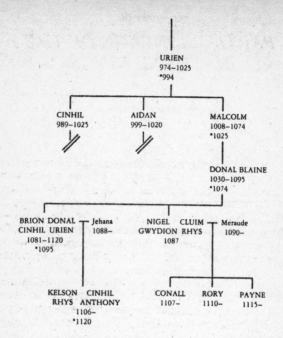

# About the Author

Katherine Kurtz was born in Coral Gables, Florida, during a hurricane and has led a whirlwind existence ever since. She holds a Bachelor of Science degree in chemistry from the University of Miami, Florida, and a Master of Arts degree in English history from UCLA. She studied medicine before deciding that she would rather write, and is an Ericksonian-trained hypnotist. Her scholarly background also includes extensive research in religious history, magical systems, and other esoteric subjects.

Katherine Kurtz' literary works include the well known Deryni and Camber Trilogies of fantasy fiction, an occult thriller set in WWII England, and a number of Deryni-related short stories. The first two books of her third Deryni trilogy were published in 1984 and 1985, with the third book due in 1986. At least three more trilogies are planned in the Deryni universe, and several additional mainstream thrillers are also currently in development.

Miss Kurtz lives in southern California with her husband and son, an orange cat called The Marmalade Bear, and a Bentley motorcar named Basil—British, of course. They hope soon to move to a castle in Ireland.

# By the year 2000, 2 out of 3 Americans could be illiterate.

It's true.

Today, 75 million adults...about one American in three, can't read adequately. And by the year 2000, U.S. News & World Report envisions an America with a literacy rate of only 30%.

Before that America comes to be, you can stop it...by joining the fight against illiteracy today.

Call the Coalition for Literacy at toll-free **1-800-228-8813** and volunteer.

**Volunteer Against Illiteracy. The only degree you need is a degree of caring.**

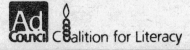

Ad Council   Coalition for Literacy          LV-2